THE FLIGHT FROM WINTER'S SHADOW

THE FLIGHT FROM WINTER'S SHADOW

A NOVEL BY

ROBIN A. WHITE

CROWN PUBLISHERS, INC., NEW YORK

Published by Crown Publishers, Inc., 201 East 50th Street, New York, New York
10022. Member of the Crown Publishing Group.

CROWN is a trademark of Crown Publishers, Inc.

Manufactured in the United States of America

Library of Congress Cataloging-in-Publication Data

White, Robin A.
    Flight from Winter's Shadow, The / Robin A. White.—1st ed.
        p.   cm.
    I. Title
    PS3573.H47476A69   1991
    813'.54—dc20   90-2385
                                                                                  CIP
ISBN 0517-57808-5

Book design by Rosaria Ieraci

10 9 8 7 6 5 4 3 2 1

First Edition

This book is dedicated to Lt. Col. Robert Mittelman.
His dreams of flight were strong enough to jump a generation.

FOREWORD

HE Pentagon accidentally released a budget document in February 1985 that revealed the existence of an ultrasecret "black" program, code-named Aurora. This $2.3 billion project was connected with neither the F117A stealth fighter nor the B-2 stealth bomber. When pressed for an explanation, Defense Department officials refused to discuss Project Aurora, citing national security concerns. Nothing more was heard for three years.

Then, in January 1988, *The New York Times* reported that work had begun on a replacement for the SR-71 reconnaissance aircraft. The Blackbird, designed in the late fifties, relied on its astonishing speed and operating altitude to elude enemy interception. But by the late eighties, its 100,000-foot, Mach 3+ performance was no longer enough to protect it against an array of increasingly capable threats. More important, gathering aerial intelligence was useful only as long as the watched was unaware of the watcher.

A revolution in low observables technology, stealth, had taken place in the eighties. The Blackbird's replacement could be—would have to be—both fast *and* invisible.

Then, in a surprise announcement, the SR-71 fleet was retired from operational assignment in March 1990. The Mach 5 stealth design intended as its replacement is now thought to be the elusive Aurora.

Some locations and flight procedures in this book have been changed from those found in the real world in the interest of telling a good yarn. It's a work of fiction. Aurora, on the other hand, is real.

1

ON THE
POINT OF
THE LANCE

A SOFT chime sounded in Harry Hill's helmet. The pilot looked up in time to see an orange dot blossom on his head-up display (HUD). It looked like an oddly colored star against the night sky, except that it was growing brighter as he watched. Hill keyed the intercom. "What do you have, Frank?"

"Target on passive," said Franklin Thatcher, Hill's reconnaissance systems officer, or rizzo. Seated behind Hill in a cramped and windowless cubicle, Thatcher nevertheless had a God's-eye view of the world through his sensors and the data beamed down by Lacrosse, a radar-imaging satellite high overhead. "On the nose and level. Range eighty."

"Rog," Hill replied. He caressed the pressure-sensitive sidestick with his gloved right hand. A second touch leveled the wings once more. *Pure silk,* he thought. This was nothing like horsing the old Blackbird around the sky. He and Thatcher had perhaps a thousand hours in the SR-71. The Sled was pure Lockheed: gorgeous on the outside and a beast in every other way. But this one was even faster and better yet; its computer-driven controls made it a pleasure to fly.

"Range sixty."

Hill had to think far ahead of his aircraft's black nose. After all, at Mach 5, sixty miles dropped to zero at the rate of one mile every second.

"Going to be close," said Thatcher. "Range twenty."

Hill swung his head and watched as the target streaked by off his wingtip. "Weather balloon." It was, Hill knew, about the only thing that could threaten Norton Aerodyne's experimental jet. No other aircraft flew so high or so fast. The pilots called her Excalibur. To the men on the ground she was Project Aurora, a stealth program so black it made the B-2 people seem chatty. To the rest of the world she simply didn't exist.

"Nothing on it from the bird," said Thatcher as his own passive infrared sensors tracked the balloon. In a matter of seconds, it had disappeared far astern. The radar satellite was supposed to warn them of anything in their path. The exigencies of stealth demanded that Excalibur's own radar remain quiet.

What else is it going to miss? Hill wondered as he took a sip of cool water from the tube in his helmet. *Relax.* He patted the black glareshield. He knew what he would trust and what he would not. Above all else, Harry Hill trusted this airplane. He believed that if an airplane looked right, it would fly right. And Excalibur looked very right indeed.

She had the purposeful profile of an obsidian arrowhead; one long aerodynamic sculpture from needle nose to her four blast-furnace exhausts. The smooth contours were no accident. They served to "spike" the hypersonic airflow into the gaping inlets of her ramjet engines. But even more vital, her wing/body blending masked her radar signature. While Excalibur was over a hundred feet long and nearly as wide, she had the radar cross section of a medium-sized bird.

"Range to the tank-up is four ninety," said Thatcher.

They had a date with a tanker orbiting between Hawaii and California, and it was not one they could afford to miss. The special-mission KC-135Q tanker carried fifty thousand pounds of cryogenic hydrogen fuel, Excalibur's lifeblood. She burned it, she used it to mask her thermal presence, and she even manufactured liquid air from it to keep the fires lit twenty-five miles high.

Four powerful engines drove her at her blistering pace. Two General Electric turbines served to bring the stealth jet to the velocity where the supersonic ramjets could begin their magic. And magic it was, for the faster they drove her, the faster she wanted to run. Harry Hill had discovered that just this night, hadn't he?

But Excalibur was also designed to do more than run fast and hide. Two internal bays served to accommodate a wide mix of stores, from reconnaissance gear to air-launched cruise missiles to rotary cannons. Norton Aerodyne knew that in an age of shrinking budgets, a single-mission aircraft was too expensive. They also knew that Excalibur's $300-million price tag worked out to just under $400 an ounce. Indeed, there were many at the secret base at Tonopah who feared the symbol on her black tail, a golden upthrust sword, was all too apt.

Hill glanced at the altitude stick that ran up one side of the HUD and checked their heading once again. *Any second now* . . . Eastbound, twenty-five miles above the Pacific Ocean, the stars burned down with a hard brilliance more familiar to astronauts than mere pilots of aircraft. He turned down the brightness on the HUD and peered out over the needle nose. A single pure line of indigo flashed across the eastern horizon. Speeded up like a film running wild, the dark blue flared into the brilliant crimson of a high-altitude sunrise.

Thatcher keyed his intercom again. "Tanker is turning inbound on the racetrack, range three forty." The backseater sounded worried. Pilots always cut things too close. Thatcher knew that without refueling, they would never make it back to dry land, much less accomplish the final mission of today's test run.

"Okay, Frank. Time to throw out the anchor." Hill pulled back the throttles on the two ramjets with his left hand, thumbing the safety covers off the two similar controls that governed the two General Electric turbines. As their speed bled off, the roar of hypersonic air flowing through the ramjet's combustion chamber fell away to a whisper.

It was exactly like stepping on the brakes. Hill was thrown forward against his restraint harness as they slowed and began the long descent to the waiting tanker.

An annunciator flashed on Hill's engine-control CRT screen. Their airspeed fell through critical Mach. It was time to put the ramjets to sleep and wake up the turbines. He pushed the two GEs around a detent into autolight. Far behind, deep within the gaping air inlets, a flush-mounted scoop began to rise and bite into the slipstream.

Robbing air from the ramjets to spool up the turbines, the scoops sent a shiver of turbulence through the titanium-alumide airframe. "Duct rumble," said Hill. He knew Thatcher was on edge.

"Spooky."

They were still traveling at better than Mach 1 when they swept over the tanker at an altitude of 46,000 feet. Hill banked up on a wing, secured the ramjets, and pulled enough G to slow them even more. They passed through the Mach with a slight aerodynamic shiver and fell in behind the plodding cow of a tanker. The yellow fuel-caution light came on just as the strobe on the KC-135Q's refueling boom switched on.

The connection was made with a quick, almost sexual shudder. In a moment, liquid hydrogen was coursing through the fat umbilical and into Hill's hungry tanks. In under four minutes, the boom disconnected in a white puff of boiling cryogenic fuel. The tanker pulled up and banked left, catching the first glint of the coming sunrise. Hill dived away to the right. Not a single radio call had occurred during the entire procedure. *Perfect.*

They were fat with fuel once again. Hill advanced the throttles on the two GEs as they dropped lower and lower into the thickening atmosphere. Inside his pressure suit, Hill had no direct awareness of the air beyond the cockpit, but it seemed strangely dense and humid all the same. The very top of the sun's disk burst over the far horizon.

"Ready?" he asked Thatcher.

"It's your quarter," Thatcher replied. "Got some low weather out ahead."

"I see it." A dark gray line of cloud shadowed the distant earth ahead. Hill liked it up here, away from those clouds and the ground they hid. But this test flight demanded otherwise.

As they dropped toward the altitudes frequented by commercial jets, Hill looked out through the triangular panes of his windshield, segmenting the sky to either side of the nose in a deliberate search pattern. That radar satellite had missed a balloon once this morning. There was no telling what else it might overlook.

"Keep your eyeballs out, Hill," Thatcher said as though reading his mind. "I got a funny feeling about this run."

Hill twisted his nerves another octave tighter. Enough hours cramped together in high-performance aircraft and Hill took the subliminals as seriously as he took his instrument panel.

Still, he knew why Thatcher was on edge this morning. "Come on, Frank," said Hill as he thumped his glareshield with a gloved hand, "this buggy doesn't care how low we fly."

"I do. And mark: one hundred miles to coast-in," he said as his inertial system flashed. "Feet dry in eight minutes."

"Roger." The California coastline was invisible under the dense clouds of the late-season storm. But beyond them, across the coastal mountains, Hill saw the sudden ramparts of the high Sierra Nevada blocking them like a saw-toothed dam. He checked his altitude. They were already through 18,000 feet. A hint of the low-level turbulence reached up to their altitude, rocking the knife-thin wings, making the stability-augmentation system (stab-aug) work hard. *What's it like down low in HUMMER?* he wondered. HUMMER 6 was a low-altitude-restricted airspace surrounded on all sides by sheer mountains. It was their destination. A mock-up of a Soviet mobile missile had been erected. All they had to do was find it and destroy it. And survive.

A faint vibration began out in the right wing. The long, black forebody amplified the shudder like a diving board. Hill pulled the two GEs out of afterburner and swept the CRTs for a sign of trouble.

"Everything copacetic?" Thatcher asked.

"Peachy." Hill was used to flying on the very edge of the envelope. At 150,000 feet you had time to react, to fix things, or if nothing worked, to punch out. But Hill would fly the HUMMER test course at fifty feet. Worse, he would be flying it blindfolded.

A stealth aircraft must remain silent to survive. No active terrain-following radar can be used to provide clearance to the hard and unforgiving rocks. The designers back at Norton Aerodyne knew this and so had provided a high-density optical memory of the terrain Excalibur would cover in its low-altitude run. Updating its position on the stored discs by signals from the radar-imaging satellite, it could remain utterly silent as it streaked through the mountains. It was, Hill knew, a very nice theory.

Stay loose, he thought. *Stay loose and smooth.* He pressed the intercom button again. "Come on, Thatch, you know you're god-damned lucky. You could still be riding standby on the Shuttle."

"Remind me after HUMMER." Thatcher's low, gravelly voice was untouched by the up-hollow drawl affected by many of the other pilots in the program. He didn't press the distinction of being the only black man at Tonopah riding experimental jets for a living. A gust sent them up on a wingtip as they dropped lower. Thatcher snugged his shoulder straps tighter. "Over the coast," he said. "We're feet dry."

"You know this deal's a lot sweeter than NASA."

"Keep talking."

A lot better, thought the pilot. He and Thatcher and the seventy other members of the secret flight-evaluations effort lived the jet jock's dream, yet their masters wore the uniform of the Ivy League, not the Air Force. Flying missions from an out-of-the-way corner of the vast Nellis complex in the Nevada outback, Norton Aerodyne's Flight Test Group was created around a nucleus of highly qualified pilots, so-called "sheep-dipped" Air Force, Navy, and Marine Corps men tempo-rarily removed from all military records. Their base at Tonopah, known as the Ranch, had been carved out of an unused Department of Energy nuclear-waste storage cavern.

The underground facility was, in almost every way that mattered, a buried, landlocked aircraft carrier. Only a tiny cluster of metal shacks appeared next to the new 14,000-foot runway, and these were simple window dressing, serving to hide the massive elevator shafts from the curious.

Hill watched the inertial navigation system roll down as they drew nearer to HUMMER at the rate of one nautical mile every six and a quarter seconds.

"Twenty seconds to the turn."

Hill nodded. "Got it." As they dropped lower, nearer to the heavy billows of storm clouds, Hill swept the skies to be sure that no other aircraft had popped up unannounced. They were invisible to air traffic control radars. That was both good and bad. No one would know of the test mission, but neither would ATC avoid sending a 747 in his direction. The high-flying radar satellite, Hill's passive sensors, and his Mark 1 eyeball would have to serve. A faint whine announced the computer's decision to extend Excalibur's low-speed canard wings. The stub controls slipped out from their pockets beneath the cockpit like two switchblades.

Thatcher exhaled and cinched his harness tighter as they dropped through seven thousand feet. "Coming up on the IP in five, four, three, two, one, and mark!"

Hill swung Excalibur onto the new heading. He could hear the backseater's breath beginning to come faster now as they neared the test range. The right wing suddenly lurched, then dropped as a heavy gust struck the airframe.

"Stand by for mode shift." Thatcher watched his distance display plummet. "Stand by. Mode shift in four, three, two, one, and mark! Stepping into attack." The word *attack* came up on Hill's HUD display as Thatcher selected one of the three master modes from Excalibur's flight computer.

Hill banked farther east. The high Sierra Nevada slid into view directly off the nose. For the first time since departing Tonopah that morning, Hill keyed his transmit button on the ARC-199, a frequency-hopping burst radio that compressed and scrambled data while jumping from one frequency to another. "Searchlight, Searchlight, Shadow Three is IP and in the turn."

"Shadow Three, Searchlight, copy IP and you are cleared in hot," said the clear, flat voice from faraway Tonopah.

Hill laid his hands back on the controls for one last feel, one final check. "Okay, Frank. Flight checks are complete. Perform your final nav systems check."

"Bit checks complete," said Thatcher. "I just hope they knew what they were doing when they put this thing together."

Hill slid the throttle levers forward. The GE turbofans gave a more throaty moan as they spooled up. Hill's nerves, despite his surface calm, were spring tight. On his HUD, a snaking flight path pointed straight at the mountains, necking down to the vanishing point at the target. "Nav data looks good," said Hill. He breathed in one more deep suck of pure oxygen. "Okay, Frank. Let's engage."

"You got it," said Thatcher.

A three-dimensional projection of the rolling ground far below flashed onto Hill's HUD, a blinking command box superimposed in the center. That box was HUMMER 6 Military Operations Area. Hill toggled the intercom record switch back to life and keyed the stick button. "ITB four four. Run Charlie," he said, his voice low and calm for effect. ITB stood for Integrated Test Block. The Charlie denomination meant that the attack run was the third discrete leg of the morning. "Run checks complete, handoff merge to AUTO at ten twenty Zulu." Then he pressed the transmit button. "Searchlight, Searchlight, Shadow Three has terrain autolock, HUMMER inbound."

"Roger, Three. You are go for Charlie." As the word from Tonopah came through the headset, Hill watched the autothrottles sweep full forward as Excalibur steered itself into a powered dive. Two nearly simultaneous booms echoed forward as the twin GEs stabilized at 104 percent. Ahead, the command box brackets on the HUD framed the entry to HUMMER 6. Hill pulled his own shoulder straps tighter and pressed the intercom button. "All set?" he asked,

"It's your quarter," Thatcher replied.

Hill chuckled. "Hang on," he said as they nosed straight for the Sierra Nevada. "It's time for Mr. Toad's Wild Ride."

* * *

The old physicist puffed on his pipe. "Well?" asked Dr. Aaron Templeman. His suit was baggy, his skin pale. But Templeman's eyes were keen and suspicious as a headmaster's as he regarded Arthur Dean Bridger, the current chairman of the Solarium Committee.

Bridger checked his watch. "Be patient, Aaron. They should be just about there," he said. In his rumpled tweed jacket and polished oxfords, Arthur Dean Bridger looked like the chairman of the English department at a second-rank college, and not at all like the head of a nuclear-strike planning committee. Bridger glanced over at Radway, the Norton Aerodyne representative. He couldn't help thinking *salesman* even as he smiled. "Well, Matthew. The last knot left to tie. Excited?"

Radway nodded. "Everyone on the team's holding their breath and crossing their fingers and toes."

"I imagine that's true," Bridger agreed. He knew that Norton Aerodyne needed this contract. William Enstrom, Norton's reclusive CEO, had bet the company on it.

"The world is full of risks," said Templeman, "we need to go find new ones?" He exhaled a derisive puff of smoke. At seventy-three, he was the last Manhattan Project survivor on the Committee. He had once been an ardent defender of strategic nuclear weapons. More than that, a creator: he had been responsible for a small part of the original Fat Man design. But now he mistrusted such weapons. And the men who built and sold them.

"Please. Not again, Dr. Templeman," said Bridger. He had unwillingly inherited the old fossil just as other Solarium chairmen had for decades. "This is a necessary project milestone for Aurora. Let's see what develops."

"Why?" asked Templeman. He pointed the worn stem of his pipe at Bridger. "What are the issues in question this morning? What possible gains outweigh the clear risks? *Why are we risking anything at all?* We identified a need for a reconnaissance platform. Not some sort of bomber. Intelligence is stabilizing. A first-strike weapon is something very different." He relit the pipe with his old Zippo. A cloud of blue smoke rose around him. "Very different indeed."

"Sir," said the man from Norton Aerodyne, "our company has given you Project Aurora, the finest recon bird ever built. But if we can multitask it, why not?"

Bridger nodded. "Besides, nobody on the Committee is speaking in terms of first strike. It's simply a matter of efficient use of dollars."

"Indeed," said Templeman. "I've been here a great deal longer than either of you two gentlemen, and you'd be astonished how many times I have heard those very words."

"Please don't lecture." Arthur Dean Bridger was a historian by training. It gave him perspective. He knew that Russia had experienced seven centuries under the czars and seven decades under the equally despotic rule of the commissars. He trusted history, not personalities. History marched over mere men.

When the world returned to its normal combative state, Bridger knew that the United States was going to need Excalibur. In an age of mobile ICBMs, a hypersonic bomber, flying unseen, could find its targets and take them out before the opposition knew a war had begun. Couldn't Templeman see how vital it was to keep the third leg of the nuclear triad whole?

"But Dr. Templeman is right," Matthew Radway said to them both. "The world's a risky place. We don't need to manufacture threats. Our aircraft will do just fine. Tonopah has done its homework," he said. "Besides, this HUMMER site is in the middle of nowhere." He bent back one finger, then another. "Plus we have a recovery crew standing by just in case. Norton is taking a belts-plus-suspenders approach on this one. We have to."

"When people tell me not to worry," said Templeman, "I worry."

The single-engine Cessna blasted skyward, riding a powerful updraft like a cork in a hurricane sea. The young man was in trouble; his hands gripped the controls tighter and tighter as raw fear took command. He fought the controls, pointing the nose down until the airspeed indicator rose far into the yellow caution zone. It didn't help. The rising column of air was far more powerful than all the efforts of the Cessna's 150-horsepower engine. Even in a steep dive, it was climbing. It wasn't fair. He had been trained in all of aviation's routines. Getting trapped by weather in the mountains wasn't part of the program. *What am I supposed to do?*

He had been tricked. First the clouds had solidified under him. Then they began to rise. He tried to keep pace with them, but soon there was no choice but to pick his way through the towering cumuli. The way ahead closed like a dank, gray curtain drawn across the landscape. And then there was no turning back. His circle of clear air grew smaller, closing in like a noose as the updraft drove him skyward.

The outside view was suddenly blotted out as he was sucked up into solid cloud, no up, no down, only strange, sick lurches that dissolved the last shreds of his skill, leaving only vertigo and panic behind. He wanted to scream but his throat would not let him. Air ripping by his wing struts moaned as the propeller wound up into a tight, ominous buzz. "Oh, Jesus!" Only the calm voice in his headset was anything like normal; it was his last, tenuous connection with the world, with life itself, and he held on to it like a lifeline.

"Okay, Cessna eight eight Papa," came the reassuring voice of Oakland Center, "say heading and altitude, and what is the nature of the problem, sir?"

The pilot's headset was torn from his head as the Cessna struck a downdraft. He yanked back on the yoke, more, more, desperately trying to regain lost altitude. The mountains were near, dark and jagged as a reef.

"Cessna eight eight Pop, if you read Oakland Center ident—"

The airspeed needle sagged as the stall horn blared. Suddenly, with a last violent lurch, the Cessna dropped a wing and began to spin, throwing him against the side of the cockpit. This time, his scream made it out from his throat and into the microphone, now wrapped around his throat.

At Oakland Center, a hundred miles away, the controller heard it and tagged the Cessna's data block with 7700, the emergency code. An alarm bell sounded in the dark, hushed radar room. His neck crawled in sudden chill fear when he saw the altitude readout from the Cessna's transponder. "Turn *immediately,* eight eight Pop! Turn west immediately and climb! Climb!"

The Cessna tumbled out of control in a fully developed spin. He took his hands from the controls and his feet from the rudder pedals. He wanted someone else to fly. The controller, anybody. Someone else. He had given up.

"Eight eight Pop! Climb! If you read . . ."

The wind spit him out into a mountain canyon, hemmed in on all sides by sheer walls. The Cessna spun down, down, the world a gray-streaked pinwheel rushing up at him. Here was the last chance of all last chances. But this was oddly familiar. He had done this, practiced this before. The pilot stomped the rudder pedal and the Cessna popped out of its spin. He willed his shaking hands to take the wheel again. As he touched the sweat-slick metal, the shakes ran right up his arms and into his body like an electric shock. His sweat turned icy as he gingerly brought the nose back up, up and away from the rocks.

". . . Cessna eight eight Pop, Oakland Center. If you hear, *climb immediately!* You're way below the minimum en route altitude!"

The canyon was all around him. The only break in the wall of stone lay dead ahead. The clouds at the mouth of the canyon were lighter than the rest. Beyond them he saw the flatlands of the Central Valley. He shoved the headset back into place. "I see it!" he said, his voice an octave too high. "I can . . . I can see it! I'm out of the clouds. I have it now!" *O God in heaven,* he thought, *I am saved.*

The black jet skidded and dropped as the air became rougher. "Through three thousand," Hill remarked as casually as he could. Their altitude was their bank account, and they were rapidly going broke as they dived.

"Easy, Hill. This isn't some kind of mountain-climbing tank we're flying."

"Through two thousand." Hill swept his eyes across the panel, lingering on the double green row of annunciator lights. A single red flash and he and Thatch would be out of there in a hurry. "Through one thousand."

"Picture's coming in," said Thatcher. Line by line, the view of the target area up ahead was filling his screen. An SS-25 mobile missile, or at least a very good replica of one, was centered on his display. The radar bird in orbit scanned the target area and beamed down the raw data to Excalibur's own image-recognition system. "Target lock."

The turbulence increased in proportion to altitude lost. The sharp ridges heaped the wind and threw it at them. "Five hundred." The narrow slot canyon that was their entry to HUMMER lay beneath a layer of wind-torn clouds, dead ahead. "Two hundred."

"Christ," Thatcher said, but Hill didn't answer.

"One hundred . . . fifty!" The nose suddenly came level as the stab-aug computers fought to arrest the dive and follow the sharp undulations of the mountainous terrain.

The low, broken cloud layer swallowed them whole and painted the faceted windshield with a gray, milky blankness. Only the green display projected on Hill's HUD showed the ridge and valley country clearly.

"Shadow . . . Three is going . . . autoarm," Hill transmitted between gust impacts. Hill pressed the intercom nib. "Ready . . . Thatch?"

"Your . . . quarter." It felt like a square-wheeled truck running a hairpin-infested mountain road at over six hundred knots. Venturi winds slammed into them as the computer drove them along at fifty feet. The clouds grew dark, not with rain but with the very rocks that surrounded them, as the aircraft, a small black dart in a great hallway of granite, raced up the narrow canyon, trailing thunder in its wake. Treetops suddenly exploded through the mist and flashed by in a dark green blur.

"You . . . get . . . tone yet?" Hill asked, his hand thrown away from the intercom button by the rough air.

"Coming . . . uh!" The jet lunged and dropped. "Okay, okay. Coming on now. Steering commands . . . Shit!" Thatch's helmet slammed against the brittle skin.

Hill was having difficulty keeping his hand on the sidestick. *Got to rig up some kind of strap.* It never occurred to Hill that the best solution to the problem was to avoid flying jet airplanes at high speed near the ground.

"Hang in . . . there . . . baby," Thatcher squeezed out. "Turn . . . turning . . . *NOW!*" Thatch watched as the INS rolled down to zero on the intermediate waypoint. Excalibur executed a high-G turn, nearly pivoting on its wingtip as it entered a narrow side-canyon. *I hope to hell it knows where it's heading.*

The clouds broke open, the roaring winds tearing them into flat, ragged strands as they neared the summit. Out of habit, the pilot looked out into a frightening vista of crumbling granite and lenticular clouds.

"Release . . . release in fifteen . . . green panel." Thatcher punched in the backup arming sequence. "Good light."

"Almost . . . over." Hill sensed the edge of the cloud approaching as the view darkened again. They punched into its side, but just as quickly they shot through. A tree-studded ridge flashed below. Hill looked up. A flicker of orange light blossomed on the passive threat display. *Shit!* Hill's eyes had only an instant to travel from the threatboard to the windshield. Suddenly, horribly, they were no longer alone: a small aircraft appeared out of the wall of cloud ahead and to the right and slashed across the pilot's side vision.

What the . . . Hill was stunned into silence as a sharp, snapping report filled the cockpit. Red annunciators flashed on the Master Caution panel as Excalibur's airframe shook. The jet began to tumble, the horizon tilting crazily across the windshield as the collision destroyed the delicate balance of forces it depended upon for its survival. The impact flung Hill's arms away from the autopilot disengage. Missing that switch saved his life.

The stability-augmentation system fought to regain control of the skidding jet, faster than any human eye or hand. It quickly added trim here, power there, aileron deflections. The sidestick controller buzzed in a hundred tiny deflections as it blindly executed its last instructions to maintain the ground-hugging flight path. Hill thumbed the manual altitude preselect wheel. He felt the sudden weight of a solid climb mash him into his seat as they climbed at a steep deck angle that was getting steeper by the second, up forty degrees, up sixty; eighty degrees, vertical and beyond.

Hill tried to push the nose over and felt the stab-aug resist him. He savagely disengaged it and rolled level.

"What the fuck did we hit?" Thatcher's pulse raced, his ears boomed with pounding blood. All his instruments had suffered a nervous breakdown. Instead of his row of friendly greens, his systems panel was dotted with warning reds and yellows.

"That was a midair! Son of a bitch took out some wing. Christ!" Hill craned his helmeted head toward the right wing. A good two feet of the outboard wing panel was gone. Strands of carbon fiber streamed aft in the 500-knot breeze. A sudden trembling vibrated through the aircraft like a fever chill. "Thatch! Arm your seat! If this sucker goes, it's going fast!"

"Okay. Okay, we're armed and ready to blow," said Thatcher, the phrase *in-flight breakup* glowing in his mind brighter than any of the red lights before him. He glanced at the ejection-seat trigger as though it were a gun pointed at his head.

Hill felt the nibble of instability shudder through the airframe as the broken wing flew in ways the computer had not been programmed to consider. "Shit." With computers unreliable, the only thing that would get Excalibur home was Harry Hill. *Power!* He moved both turbine throttles around their safety detents right into afterburner. Harry Hill pressed the transmit button and sent his voice out into the sky.

"Searchlight! Searchlight! Shadow Three! Fox Four! Shadow Three is hit!"

2

EVIDENCE

RADWAY hung up the STU-3 encrypted phone and slowly exhaled. He composed himself and applied a look of concern before turning to face Bridger and Templeman. "Good news," he said. "Shadow Three has landed back at the facility."

"Is there any word yet on what happened?" asked Bridger. A thin glistening of sweat reflected the bright lights of the conference room. Aurora might be Norton Aerodyne's, but Excalibur was his.

"Some," Radway replied. He was picking his way through a mine field. Norton needed this program. There weren't many opportunities these days for builders of $300 million jets. "As far as we now know, there was some kind of airframe failure," he said carefully. "The right wing sustained some damage. Our site manager at Tonopah doesn't know all the details yet." Every word was true as far as it went. "Adcock's just about to debrief the pilots. We'll know more by this evening."

"Adcock," Bridger repeated, "I hope your man knows how delicate this situation is."

"Not to worry," Radway said.

This elicited a response from Templeman. A thick blue cloud of pipe smoke ballooned angrily around him like a locomotive gaining speed. "Not to worry? You only have six of these things, Mr. Radway. At what they cost, a sixth of your fleet is hardly expendable."

"Sir," said Radway, "there's absolutely no reason for second-guessing our man until he's had a chance to speak with the pilots. He's done a fine job for us so far." He looked at Bridger, who nodded appreciatively.

"Mr. Radway is correct," he said. "We had some sort of technical failure. Let's leave it with the technical people to solve."

Dr. Templeman cleared his throat and set his pipe down on the highly polished table. "May I ask an obvious question?" Radway cringed. Templeman was famous for beginning fights with just those words. "Once again, we know that Aurora works in the reconnaissance role for which it was intended. Why are we trying to make a bomber out of it?" he asked. "Isn't that really the source of our problem here?"

"Aaron, you know the answer," said Bridger. "You know what's happening in the world. Every pipsqueak power is going nuclear. Look at them. India. Pakistan. Half the Middle East. It's become a status symbol. God help us when the last World War Two generation dies out in Japan. We need Project Aurora. A missile just isn't smart enough, and it's too damned provocative. We need Excalibur's capability to get in, identify potential threats, and remove them should the need arise. And don't forget the Soviets."

"An old war we've already won," Templeman replied. "The Soviet Union has problems to solve, whether we like the man who happens to be running the show or not. Whatever happens, nothing will change. No," he said. "It's intelligence we need now more than ever. Not another unusable weapon."

"Dr. Templeman," said the Solarium chairman, "I came on board to deliver a real nuclear option and I mean to do just that. Midgetman is dead. Rail-mobile MX is dead. The B-2 is dead. With the economy the way it is, there may never be another opportunity to build a weapon, a platform, like Excalibur. Not in our lifetime."

"Then fortune has not abandoned us after all," Templeman said.

"No, sir," Bridger replied with a shake of his head. "You're dead wrong. Excalibur gives us a way back to strategic dominance."

"Dominance," Templeman snorted. "What a quaint old phrase."

"But a damned good one," Bridger replied. "If you're not on top of the heap, Aaron, you're getting squeezed. Period."

"It's a foolish investment. Every dollar we spend is one less we have to play in the *real* race. The one for technical dominance. Meanwhile, we pile up bomb upon bomb, and none of them can ever be used. Ever."

"That's conjecture. We don't know they can't be used," said Bridger. *Damn*, he thought as he turned and stared out the window. He knew he should not have brought *that* up again.

"Ah. There you are correct," said Templeman. "But we'd know if you'd listened to me five years ago." He and another group of outside scientists had discovered the nuclear winter effect; the destruction of the earth's climate in the shadow of nuclear mushroom clouds. "Let's be plain with each other," he said to Bridger. "You want Excalibur because it re-creates the fantasy of a perfect first strike. Don't say it isn't so. But it's still a fantasy," said Templeman. "I ask you, Arthur, how many bombs have *you* seen detonate? I've seen quite a few. Including the very first. Do you know," he said with a shake of his head, "we had a pool at Alamogordo. A betting pool. There were those who thought the first device would set the earth's atmosphere on fire. Imagine! Now we know it will do both. Death by fire, then ice."

"Gentlemen, please," said Radway. "I propose we wait for hard data from Tonopah. Let's be sure of ourselves, and then take the appropriate steps."

"Exactly," said Bridger with a note of exasperation. "We've covered this ground before." He turned to Templeman. "Your concerns are not being ignored. You know we're looking into the climate aspect."

Templeman picked up his pipe and waved it like a sorcerer's wand as he leveled his clear, brown eyes at Bridger. "Too little," he said, "too late."

"You picked the investigator," Bridger reminded him. "It's a little late to question the process, isn't it?"

"Your security requirements strangled that process," Templeman said bitterly. "I didn't pick an investigator for their merits. I picked the one I could fool."

Dr. Julia Hines sat back on her bunk and listened as the wind whipped over the exposed peak of Bald Mountain. *This* had been a good storm. A strange storm. Now it was dying as its clouds struck the stone wall of the Sierra Nevada. The mountains would strip it of its energy, its moisture, leaving nothing but a few high wisps to taunt the worried ranchers and farmers to the east. The blustery wind sweeping around her small trailer was its death rattle. She puffed up the pillow and put her arms behind her head, listening. For a climatologist specializing in cloud physics, it was a grand place to be.

The trailer was home, office, and laboratory combined. Its interior was stuffed to the ceiling with electronics racks and data recorders. A PC sat on a small metal desk. A printer whirred softly nearby. The trailer was remote and austere, but what it lacked in amenities was made up for in coziness. And the amenities weren't that bad, either. She had, thanks to a weekly resupply by the Air Force, all the electricity she could use, and equally important, the only flushing toilet for miles.

Julia could just make out the dull drone of the diesel generator outside, but the swishing of the tall pines around the command site was louder. It sounded like a small boat caught in dangerous surf. She pulled her arm out from beneath the down quilt and checked her watch. It was an old, mechanical Hamilton. *Time,* she thought, and swung her legs out of bed to start the day. She tugged her Princeton sleepshirt over her head, tossed it atop the growing pile of clothes needing washing, and padded naked to the single window. Remote field assignments had their advantages, and privacy was one of them.

She opened the curtains and peeked out. The ground was soaked. Steam was rising from the generator case. At least, she hoped that's what it was. She would tell Kansky, the Air Force sergeant assigned to be her helper up here in HUMMER. Her eye caught movement from the edge of the clearing. *Kansky.*

She stepped away from the window and let the curtain fall back into place, pausing at the small mirror hung next to the calendar. *Not bad for July.* Julia's colleagues back in Washington would still be fish-belly white. Most research climatologists at NOAA, the National Oceanic and Atmospheric Administration, spent more time watching the weather on their CRTs than in it. Her month in the Sierra Nevada had left her deeply tanned. There was a lot of UV in high country sunlight, and her brown hair had become streaked with gold. Her body seemed to radiate, to glow with the high country sun. She took a marker and crossed off another day on the calendar. There were a great many black crosses behind her; the field portion of her cloud study was nearing its end.

The trailer shook as a fitful gust struck and fell away to a whisper. She glanced up at the barometer. It was definitely on the rise. *At last,* she thought as she quickly brushed out her hair. Julia Hines looked more like a model in an outdoors magazine than a climatologist. She stood nearly six feet tall; it was, she knew, a positive adaptation for a woman seeking to enter the male-dominated profession of research meteorology. Julia had learned that much at Princeton. It was just too difficult for some of the old dinosaurs—or the young ones—to take her seriously. A climatologist was supposed to be competent, not beautiful. Julia was both.

She quickly donned her standard outfit of cutoff jeans, T-shirt, and light canvas boots. She settled into her chair and called up the hourly summary from her network of AWOS units. She'd been lucky to get another storm under her belt before the dust and the heat of a California summer set in. The more cloud data she could assemble on the ground to compare with NOAA's satellite information, the better grip she had on the confusing debate raging over the so-called greenhouse effect: the warming of the earth's atmosphere due to industrial pollution.

Warming climates generated more clouds, but more clouds shaded the earth's surface, resulting in a net cooling effect. Could the greenhouse turn out to be an icehouse after all? It was one of the pieces of her puzzle.

She glanced at the wind speeds and pressures beamed from her network of weather stations. It had been an exceedingly strange storm. Not only was it very late in the year, but oddly violent. This morning, for example, there had been one long detonation of thunder. Just one: a wild, ripping sound that had gone on and on before it finally faded. *Strange*.

But strange weather was why she was here.

The world's climate had become even more unpredictable than usual. All the old patterns, carefully assembled over the years, seemed to be falling apart. Rain fell in torrents over the high deserts while normally temperate areas dried up in blistering drought. Bitter winters were followed by record-breaking heat waves. *Fire and ice,* she thought. *But which?*

Some researchers pointed to the increase in CO_2, others to the breakdown of the ozone shield. On one thing, everyone agreed: industrial pollutants were changing the makeup of the atmosphere. But how? The sheer perversity of the changing weather guaranteed that experts could be found to back up nearly any assertion. The task of unraveling the mystery of a changing climate was too complex for even NOAA's banks of Cray supercomputers. That was where Julia had made a modest proposal.

If the problem of large-scale weather was too difficult to unravel, why not look at smaller events? Suppose a satellite was maneuvered to watch one tiny square of the earth's surface, while the same square was intensively instrumented on the ground? That had brought her, and her thirty AWOS (automated weather observation station) units to HUMMER, a suitably remote and controllable area for study, unaffected by industrial pollutants. Wind straight off the Pacific Ocean was swept up into the atmosphere by the mountains, making it an ideal cloud hatchery for both the satellite and her AWOS units to observe.

If the scope of her microclimate study was small, the rewards were enormous: she was after the key to weather prediction, a mathematical

Holy Grail that would permit the larger forces of climate to be accurately predicted from the smaller. And perhaps answer the question of fire or ice.

A knock came from the trailer's door. It cracked open an inch. "Morning," said Kansky. "Working already?"

"Come on in and dry out," said Julia as she folded the night's accumulated printout.

"One hell of a storm," he said as he pulled off an olive-drab rain poncho and dropped it by the door. Kansky was as muscular and compact as Julia was long and lithe. His hair was a mass of dark ringlets that the rain had caused to tighten into a dense mat. Sgt. William Kansky had the look of a man who took pride in his condition but had to work at it.

"And a strange one, too," Julia said as she read through the data sheets. "It's late in the season for this much rain."

"Tell me about it," said Kansky, picking up his drenched poncho. He hung it on the back of the door and listened as a gust of wind shook the trailer. "Still blowing up a storm."

"Frontal passage. Did you hear that thunder this morning?"

"You bet," said Kansky. "I don't remember seeing any lightning. But it sounded close, you know?"

"I know." She held up this morning's satellite image of the eastern Pacific. "Well, it's all over for the year. No more rain until the fall."

"Wanna bet?"

"No bet," she said with a smile. Her finger traced the whorls of cloud on the fax. Who really knew? The way the climate seemed to be changing, it might snow. Still, the Pacific jet stream was beginning to lock itself into the typical summer pattern that made for hot, dry weather throughout California, and especially the Sierra Nevada. She looked up at Kansky and caught him eyeing her. Julia crossed her legs and cleared her throat. "I saw some smoke coming out of the generator," she said.

"Probably steam. But I guess I better check it out," he replied. "I'll try to get the fire going if you want some coffee."

"Maybe later." A shaft of sun swept the summit of Bald Mountain.

Kansky put a hand on the doorknob and stopped, cocking his head first one way, then the other. "Damn," he said.

"What?" asked Julia. Then she could feel it, too. A low rumble came vibrating up through the floor of the trailer. A glass jittered in a sympathetic shiver beside the sink. "What is it?" she asked. "A helicopter?" HUMMER was an Air Force practice area, and they were used to hearing jets screaming overhead. But few helicopters other than the weekly resupply bird.

"Roger that," said Kansky as he opened the door. "But we aren't due for a visit so soon." They could both hear it now, a low, heavy beating of the air, distorted by the wind, rising and falling, growing louder and nearer. Another shaft of sun came and went. "Big one, too. It's got to be a heavy to fly up here in this wind. Jolly Green or a Skycrane from the sound of it." Kansky listened to it as the sound of its rotors slowly diminished. *Pilots,* he thought. They were all crazy. Who would be up flying in all this wind and cloud? In a moment, he couldn't hear it at all.

It was plain luck that the wreckage of the small Cessna had come to rest on the rocky spine of a ridge above the middle fork of the Stanislaus River. The wreck was more visible from the air, and its weak crash-locator beacon signal was not masked by the bulk of the mountains. It made MacHenry's job easier. "He almost made it," he said to the FAA helicopter pilot.

"Not almost enough."

"True." Brian J. MacHenry had seen a great many crash sites in his time as an accident investigator with the FAA, and even more during his long flying career. Most looked pretty much like this one. He watched the smoke rise from the burned fuselage as the small FAA helicopter circled the site. He shook his head. "I just don't know what he was thinking about, flying in that storm," he said over the intercom. It seemed simple enough to him. He made an effort to suppress the obvious answer. In his thirty-odd years in aviation, MacHenry had discovered that the simple answers occasionally lied.

The sun beamed in through the glass cockpit. MacHenry unzipped his light-khaki jacket and neatly folded it on the seat behind him. He had learned long ago that it paid to be meticulous in aviation. Now, long after his airline flying days had ended, it was still a habit that infused every part of him. MacHenry managed to make a pair of chinos and a button-down madras shirt look like a uniform. He glanced down at the smoking ruin. That was how inattention was rewarded.

"You want me to take it down?"

MacHenry looked up and saw his own face reflected in the chopper pilot's sunglasses. He thought: *I look like an old man.* "Yes. Take us down." The turbine whine dropped an octave as the Bell descended toward a small clearing tightly walled in on all sides by tall pines. The pilot pulled in the collective and the rotor blades bit deep into the thin mountain air, bringing the machine to a hover above Sourgrass Meadow. The Stanislaus National Forest surrounded them like a green ocean.

"Hang on, sir."

MacHenry gripped the armrest tighter. He loved airplanes. He could spend hours talking to a fellow pilot about the right way to brake an airliner to a smooth stop. But he hated helicopters. There was the whiff of magic about the ungainly machines, and they kindled a residual fear of falling that he had never felt in his years commanding an airliner. He heard the turbine revs fall away and saw the pine trees climb the crystal bubble of his windshield.

The pilot flattened the pitch a final increment, and they dropped straight down into the tiny clearing like an ill-mannered elevator, landing first on one skid, bouncing, then settling heavily on both. The Bell pilot took the power from the blades and the commotion overhead subsided.

MacHenry cracked open his door and stepped out, his ears still ringing from the sound of the engine, and into a hurricane of rotor wind that dried his sweat as fast as he made it. He grabbed his accident kit, making sure the can of fluorescent-yellow spray paint was still inside. Wrecks had to be marked so that they wouldn't get reported over and over again. He was glad to be out. The pilot cut the engine and the hissing fire in its guts was quenched.

MacHenry breathed a bit too heavily in the thin air. It was nonsense, but it made him feel old. *Too much desk duty.* Most people would have thought him far younger and plenty fit for his age; solid but not athletic, MacHenry was the very image of the Old Hand. His was the face found in the cockpits of airliners almost from their beginning. Tall and trim, but not wiry; sandy hair that silvered but never thinned, gray eyes set wide, eyes that transmitted competence and ease.

At fifty-three he was still seven years from mandatory airline retirement age, he reminded himself. Feeling better, he took the heavy canvas bag that held the tools of his trade and began to walk uphill.

The deep-woods clearing reasserted its silence as the mechanical noises died away from the windmilling helicopter blades. MacHenry looked up toward the crash site. He found the red ribbons indicating the blazed trail cut to the crash site by the Air Force. They had been the first on the scene, and given that they all but owned the HUMMER 6 airspace above, their cooperation was to be expected. The trail disappeared up the steep slope into the dense woods.

MacHenry approached the edge of the small clearing and passed into shadow beneath the tall pines. The trail was tough going. It made MacHenry feel out of fighting trim. He grabbed at roots and struggled up, concentrating on individual steps. Soon his hands were bloodred from the iron-rich soil.

He almost made it, he thought again. How many other accidents ended with just those words? In good weather you could get away with a lot. But the Cessna pilot had not found good weather. He received his last weather briefing at the hands of the winds and the mountains. He wondered about the pilot. All MacHenry had been able to find out was that he had been relatively inexperienced. But school was out, the final test called; the young man had failed.

The harsh metallic grating of a chain saw sounded up ahead. It was cool in the shade of the high pines, but without the fanning of the chopper blades MacHenry broke out into a dripping sweat as he scrambled uphill. *One step, one breath. Again.* Pine trees filtered the hot, clear sun. *One step, one breath. Again.* He stopped and rested by a chunk of andesitic granite, all red and shiny with mica. The air was rich with warm pine scent.

He was close to the top of Starr Ridge. Looking up through the branches, MacHenry watched the innocent cumulus sail by. Why had the Cessna been flown in such bad weather? What could have motivated the pilot? Couldn't he *see* out the windshield what he was about to fly into?

MacHenry continued the climb, his boots kicking deep into the needles and roots for grip as he went. He recalled the aerial view of the crumpled fuselage. Except for one of the wings, the aircraft was all there. Charred black, but there. Where was that wing? MacHenry filed away the niggling inconsistency. There was a lot of rugged country to comb if he wanted to find it. *Probably not worth the effort.*

He could smell the crash before he could see it. He looked up the steep trail and saw blue sky. *Almost there.* He pulled at the tree trunks, using them as handholds. Despite the dry wind, he began to sweat in earnest.

As he pulled himself up, a high insect whine buzzed overhead, ending in a sharp slap. MacHenry ducked instinctively, dropping his accident kit as he hit the dirt.

"Look out!" someone shouted. MacHenry looked up. An arrow was buried in the trunk of tree, its shaft still quivering from the strike. "Damn it!" A young man in a sage-green flightsuit put down a long bow and ran toward him. His polished black combat boots sent puffs of red earth up as he came. "Where the hell did you come from? Don't you watch where you're walking?"

MacHenry was speechless, then furious. He slowly stood up straight, dusting the dirt from his pants. "My name is MacHenry," he said, each word deliberately icy. "I'm with the FAA." He noticed that this kid had somehow become a major. In spite of the aviator's sunglasses, he didn't look old enough to drive a car, much less an airplane.

"MacHenry?" The major pulled the arrow from the trunk and tossed it away like damning evidence. He looked down at his feet and cleared his throat, then up at MacHenry, a small grin on his mouth. His eyes were invisible behind his aviator sunglasses. "Oh. We were kind of expecting you later in the day. Sorry for the excitement. I was just keeping in practice."

"So I see."

The major nodded at the neat hole in the trunk of the tree. "It's just a hobby." He extended his hand. "My name is Barnes. Major Pete Barnes."

MacHenry took it despite the way his heart still pounded.

Barnes chuckled and took off his sunglasses. "I'm glad you decided to join us." He looked at his elaborate watch. "I was told to coordinate the search with our ops in the area. I'm not sure why I was the lucky gent today, MacHenry, and there's a lot to do back at squadron, so let's try and clear this up as quickly as possible. Deal?"

Deal? It was a foreign word in MacHenry's lexicon. "I don't know why you're here, Major Barnes, but I'm here to do it like it matters, and we'll start by using some common sense. There will be no more bows and arrows at my site, understood?"

Barnes nodded, still smiling. "Hey, no problem."

MacHenry thought he saw a faint amused look hidden in the deep blue of the major's eyes. "Right." MacHenry bristled as he appraised the young Air Force officer. *Typical fighter jock.* As much as MacHenry belonged in the nose of a Boeing, Barnes would look out of place anywhere but in the pointy end of a fast mover. MacHenry scrutinized Barnes's sharp, strong features. *Do they issue them those blue eyes?* he wondered, noting that this one differed from the norm only in that his hair was dark brown, almost black, instead of the regulation blond.

"So," said Barnes with a note of impatience, "if you're ready, let's get this evolution started. What do you want to see?"

"There's a lot of work to be done." MacHenry looked down the slope once more.

Barnes saw what he was eyeing. "Okay. I'll get it," he said. "We don't want a medical emergency or anything." He trotted down and collected MacHenry's canvas satchel and just as easily trotted up the steep slope. It made MacHenry angrier.

"Thanks," he said.

Barnes shrugged. "No problem. Now," he said, his voice getting back to business, "I presume you've taken note of conditions at the time of the crash?" Barnes assumed this *civilian* was competent enough to recognize the clear fact that weather played the leading role in the accident. If he knew which end of an airplane was which. What more was there to know?

"I've seen the weather data," MacHenry relented. "I understand it was wild up here."

Barnes put his sunglasses back on and nodded, looking away into the billowing fair-weather clouds. "Bet your ass it was wild," he said. "It was still blowing when we got here this morning."

MacHenry glanced up as several enlisted men in Air Force uniform stood around the wreck. "I'm surprised the Air Force is making such a big show," said MacHenry as he opened his bag and removed a small clipboard. On it, FAA form 8020 was neatly clipped. Accident Investigation Record, it was called. "Did you have something flying in HUMMER at the time of the accident?"

"No, sir. Not a damned thing," Barnes said. "It may be a national forest down here, but up there"—he nodded up at the sky—"we own the airspace. It was stone cold."

"You're absolutely certain?"

"Mr. MacHenry," Barnes said, "in my business, I deal in certainties and unknowns. There is nothing in between. I am certain that HUMMER was cold. I am equally certain that we are looking at a plain and simple weather accident. If you were a pilot, you'd know."

"I am a pilot," said MacHenry.

"Fine. Then you should know," Barnes said again. He reexamined MacHenry. "Private or military?"

"Airline flying mostly," said MacHenry.

"Figures."

"Thank you for your confidence." MacHenry swallowed his real reply. With three calming breaths, he unclenched his jaw and turned to the wreck. Barnes was a minor irritation, but MacHenry would likely never see him again. The crash and its mysteries would last far longer. *Calm yourself. Observe. Everything is important.* He walked the last few yards to the crumpled Cessna.

The airplane had struck the ground at a shallow, glancing angle, coming to rest against a large boulder. It had burned eagerly. MacHenry's feet crunched the crusted ground as he approached the wreck. The earth was not so much charred as sterilized. No paint remained on the battered plane. Pools of molten metal had dripped from the left wing to recast themselves on the blackened earth. A sharp, metallic odor permeated the air, like machine oil and rust. MacHenry smelled the unmistakable odor of roasted flesh as well. It made him gag. He breathed with his mouth and looked at the signs of the fire. It had been a hot one. An oddly hot one, given the fact that it had been raining when the crash occurred.

Peering into the contorted shape of the cabin, MacHenry noted the charred seat frames burned clean of padding, the instrument panel bent in half, the instruments themselves lampblacked and shattered. The left wing was heavily dented but intact. The right wing and lift strut were simply gone, their fittings torn roughly from the skin of the little Cessna as though chewed rather than cut.

Odd kind of failure, he thought, looking around to see if the Air Force had removed the wing themselves to get at the pilot. *Where's that right wing?* Major Barnes appeared behind him like a missile homing in on MacHenry's thoughts. But Barnes surprised him.

"Sorry for that arrow business, MacHenry," he said. "I'm just a little on edge over this whole thing. The pilot? He was pretty well burned up, as bad as anything I've ever had to look at up close."

"Forget it."

"Yeah. That would be nice. But understand something. Fire is the one thing that spooks me," he continued. "In your line of work, people retire. They get transferred. Kicked upstairs. In the Air Force, fire is how you lose friends."

"I know. I commanded some contract flights for the military in and out of Southeast Asia." MacHenry stepped away from the wreck.

"Then you know what I mean." Barnes held out his hand. "Shall we try this again?"

It was a peace offering, and MacHenry accepted it as a way to get his job done. "Forget it, Barnes." He noticed the sprinkling of silver stars on the sleeve of the green flightsuit. MacHenry knew each one was worth a hundred hours of jet time. There were no golds among them, but that was to be expected; you earned gold stars by flying combat missions, and Barnes was clearly too young to have seen any of that. MacHenry walked farther away from the Cessna and its smell of death.

"So what do you want to know, Mr. MacHenry?"

"Okay. Once again: Did the Air Force have any flights in HUM-MER when the accident occurred? Anybody see anything?"

"Negative. We may not be too smart, but we aren't dumb enough to stick our noses into weather like that." Barnes opened his own file and reviewed the report filed by the last Air Force jet to run through HUMMER 6. "My sheet shows our aircraft out of HUMMER twenty-two minutes prior to the Cessna's last transmission. The pilot's weather report closed the range. You've got that transcript. I presume you have their conditions report on the ceiling and the winds coming down these mountains. You can check it."

"I will." MacHenry noticed the fuselage had left a deep scar on the ground, and the left wing had made a similar groove as it had jolted to a halt. He turned to find a third mark left by the missing wing, but there were only the hard backs of the rounded boulders to be seen. "What about the wing? Did your men shear it off to remove the pilot?"

"What you see is what you get, MacHenry. We arrived and the fire was still smoldering. The wing was nowhere. You want to know what I think?"

"All right."

"I think this son of a bitch got pulled apart in a rotor cloud and that wing is up there someplace." Barned nodded at the rough, pine-studded country to the east, back toward the high peaks. "There's a whole bunch of acres to scour, but it would be a waste of everybody's time. Planes go in on these mountains and some are never found. Besides, you and I both know what brought this poor bastard down."

MacHenry considered. "It explains the way the fittings are twisted. You're right about maybe never finding it." The image of the trembling arrow just feet above his head returned. "But I believe that we'll have to try just the same. This was a fatal accident. The National Transportation Safety Board will want the effort made."

"Why?" Barnes cocked his head. "It could be anywhere with the winds they were reporting. It won't make any difference to anybody. You know I'm right." He had his arms across his chest, an X over MacHenry's plans for him.

"Maybe. Let's decide that after we know it isn't sitting out in the open someplace," he said. "And the radio transcript still bothers me." MacHenry flipped to the doomed pilot's last words.

"Oh?"

"The pilot lost control, then entered clear air, and with no apparent damage began flying himself out of danger. Then he yells, 'We're hit, we're hit.' That's the last thing we know for certain."

"So? He didn't have the sense to stay out, and then he didn't have the sense to stay cool." Losing the inner ice was worse in any fighter jock's book than crashing.

"Don't you find it odd?" MacHenry was thinking aloud.

"Nothing surprises me anymore," Barnes said, looking up from the sheet, "nothing except why we are standing here wondering why some private pilot couldn't handle a situation I wouldn't try. No way. This guy flew into the ground because he either didn't see it or because nobody taught him to respect the wind in these mountains."

MacHenry looked away. Barnes was right.

Barnes saw his words strike pay dirt and pressed the advantage. "Lose your cool and you're liable to yell most anything, MacHenry. Men call for their mothers ten miles up in the sky. You think panic's rational?"

If *deal* was a foreign word, *rational* was not. "Maybe you're right, Major."

"Damned straight. That's how it looks from here. Open and shut."

"Okay," said MacHenry. "Find me that wing and I just might agree with you."

Barnes picked up a stone and sent it sailing. "You're a tough nut, Mr. MacHenry." Where was all the uncertainty coming from? Wasn't it clear? This was a case of aviation suicide. The man had killed himself through his own ignorance. And ignorance, Barnes knew, was a self-correcting problem.

As far as he was concerned, anybody venturing into the sky with less than thirty thousand pounds of thrust and several tons of government-issued fighter strapped to his back was a little on the unreliable side, anyway.

3

QUESTIONS

RADWAY waited for his secretary to leave before he dialed the Ranch. As the STU-3 secure phone warbled in his ear, he snapped on the tape recorder he had patched into the circuit for just such occasions.

"Adcock," came the voice from Nevada. Peter Adcock was Norton Aerodyne's site manager at Tonopah.

"Peter. Radway here." He flipped the handset to his other ear. "I'm calling to be sure we're adequately covered on this HUMMER incident. I wanted to speak to you in private." He glanced at the spinning tape cartridge.

"I guess we'll be all right, sir," said Adcock.

"There's no room for guesswork." Radway knew that they both could turn in their keys if this got away from them. Enstrom had said as much. "Then you're confident we're stabilized?"

"We were very lucky. We had the recovery crew up there before there was any official reaction. I . . . I had to take some fairly strong . . ." He stopped. "I just hope the company will back this up."

"One hundred and ten percent. You have my word." Radway had told the complete truth. With the company's sagging fortunes and a takeover bid under way, Radway knew Enstrom, Norton's CEO, would be following Aurora very closely indeed. "We need that funding decision behind us before we let too much out of the bag."

"Enstrom will support my decisions?"

"Absolutely." Almost as an afterthought. Radway asked, "What about the pilot?"

"It happened very fast. They haven't been briefed on the recovery operation. I didn't see the need."

"No. I meant"—Radway stopped, searching for the proper words— "the other one. The other pilot."

"Oh. Yes. The recovery crew found—I mean, they took care of that. But that's what I wanted to be certain of when I asked—"

"Okay," Radway broke in. "That sounds real fine. Stay right on top, Peter. Do whatever it takes." The words were right from Enstrom's mouth.

"Yes, sir. You know me," said Adcock. "I will."

Washington was enjoying a late spell of civilized weather. The streets below Henniker's fourth-floor window were crowded with tourists and federal workers streaming home. It was precisely 4:59.

Dr. James Henniker, chief of Mathematical Modeling and Forecasting at NOAA, picked up the handset to the fancy satellite radio Templeman's spooky friends had delivered. It was keyed to transmit to only one receiver, at least as far as he knew. And that receiver sat in a trailer set high in the California Sierras. He switched it on. *I hope Templeman appreciates all of this,* he thought. He pulled a thick blue binder, sealed and stamped with the logo of the Defense Nuclear Agency, from his safe. How did old Templeman poke his nose into *this?*

Henniker felt more than a little responsible. After all, when Julia Hines had given him the list of possible sites for her cloud study, it had fallen to him to reject each one until the carefully selected site at HUMMER was the only one left. The red *wait* light on the SatCom went out, replaced by the green *ready.* A warbling tone sounded, then abruptly went silent.

"Hines." It was remarkable. Her voice was as clear as a local telephone connection. Clearer.

"Dr. Hines? Henniker speaking. I thought I'd check up on you after that storm." Henniker put down the Defense Nuclear binder and held up the morning satellite shot. It had been a classic Pacific storm, typical in all ways except for its arrival so late in the season. But the weather had been growing very strange of late, hadn't it? "It looks especially well developed."

"It was, sir," said Julia. "We got almost three inches of rain up here at the site and the pressure dropped through the floor. We even got a single lightning strike out of it."

"Lightning? Your equipment is still safe and secure?"

"Wet but functional. I just scanned the hourly printout and it looked fine, but I had the computer request a diagnostic self-check for the next hour's data. We're coming up to the end of the field operation. I don't want to lose any data now. Did the satellite get some good shots of the cloud tops?"

"Beautiful," said Henniker, "just as you'd hoped." He flipped open the Defense Nuclear Agency binder. The title page read *The Effect of Nuclear War on Northern Hemisphere Macroclimate: The Nuclear Winter Hypothesis*.

"Was there something else, sir?" Julia asked.

"No. I just wanted to check. Wait, I think there is something," he said as casually as he could as he flipped through papers and found Templeman's note. "If you get a moment, I wonder if you could run some moisture-content samples."

"Moisture content?"

"You know. Trees, shrubs, the native vegetation. It might come in handy to the Forest Service. You know, they try and predict forest fires the way we try to predict the weather."

"There's a lot of shrubby growth up here," Julia replied. "It looks as though it hasn't burned in quite a while."

"No," said Henniker, "it hasn't." He couldn't very well tell her that apart from its sheer remoteness and security, HUMMER had been selected for just that reason. "Do you think you might be able to handle that?"

"Probably. I'll have Kansky do it."

"I'd appreciate it," said Henniker. "You know how they're always on us to come up with something practical."

"When I find the right climate algorithms," she replied, "they're going to have something very practical."

"Yes. Of course," he said. "Thank you, Dr. Hines. Call in if you need to." He switched the SatCom off and looked at the Nuclear Winter file before him. *Practical,* he thought. He flipped to an interior section that addressed the effect of moisture content on the upcoming test.

Henniker found the section marked *Implementation.* "Practical," he said to himself as he read.

A remote-piloted KC-135 tanker from the Strategic Air Command reserve fleet will be impacted at the site with full kerosene stores. The resultant fire and explosion shall fulfill the requirements established for minimum area fuel-loading when combined with indigenous growth of the Stanislaus National Forest. It should be noted that the moisture content of the site vegetation is a critical factor. For accurate scale-up purposes, a dry site is optimal for simulating the blast and fire effects of detonating nuclear weapons. . . .

Henniker closed the binder. Templeman had approached him when the first rumblings of the nuclear winter debate had stirred. Advocates for disarmament had come and gone, but the threat that the world's nuclear arsenals, the stabilizing force between the superpowers, could not be used at all without triggering a nuclear winter was far more troubling. Data was needed, the sort of data a big forest fire might provide. From its pall of smoke and ash, an accurate simulation of the effects of nuclear war could be obtained.

Unfortunately, forest fires were not easy to predict. Frustrated, they had even set a deliberate blaze, a small, one-acre test that yielded nothing persuasive.

And so, at last, they had decided to take the guesswork out of the equation. The weather observation instruments would be in place, albeit for another purpose. And the fire? They would take the guesswork out of that, too. Henniker stood up, slipped the DNA binder into his wall safe, and spun the dial. *Practical,* he thought again. *I hope not.*

The glow of MacHenry's desk lamp spilled out of the dark wall of Oakland Metro's old terminal, now the home of the Federal Aviation Administration Flight Safety office. The airport's rotating beacon swept the wall every few seconds, first green, then white, green, then white. MacHenry's car, a pale green government Ford, stood alone in the parking lot under the orange glare of the high-pressure sodium lights. He had not been home to change, and the dust from the crash site at HUMMER was still on his clothes. The red grit looked like dried blood on his khakis.

On the ramp in front of the old terminal, a twin Beech 18, loaded with car parts destined for southern California, was being run up by the night-shift maintenance crew. One of its big R-985 engines refused to run evenly, and the balky radial spat blue flame from its exhaust as it stumbled.

MacHenry looked up from a radio transcript sheet and listened to the roar from the tired old Beech. The engine caught with a bellow and steadied. He smiled.

The sound came from MacHenry's own past. His eyes were drawn to the retirement trophy his old airline had awarded him when he mustered out early, a bronze tiger with wings sprouting from its muscled flanks. The plate at its base read *Captain Brian J. MacHenry.*

His worklamp shed a pool of light over the tidy desk; pads of paper, a can of razor-sharpened pencils, and a manual Smith Corona typewriter. He tossed his pencil down and leaned back in his chair, arms behind his head. The accident niggled at him, refusing to settle in his mind. *Where's that lost wing?* He reached for another sip of coffee and placed the mug carefully back down on an old piston valve cover.

He picked up the weather data sent to him from NOAA. The Cessna had come down right in the middle of a thicket of automated weather stations, it seemed. The land below HUMMER was peppered with them. *What are they doing up there?* It didn't matter. Whatever the reason, they all agreed: the weather had been terrible.

It would be easy for him to write this up and file it with all the other weather-related accidents that had occurred this year. There had been plenty, and the flying season was not really in full swing yet. A corporate twin had gone in at Lake Tahoe, iced over beyond its ability to fly; a student pilot got caught above the fog and flew out to sea. There were plenty of good reasons to put the incident at HUMMER right in the same basket.

"All right." He sat up straight. "All right." MacHenry jotted down the facts on his yellow legal pad. There was no sense in denying the obvious. It was a waste of his time to puzzle out an accident whose cause was plain. MacHenry remembered the site, the transcript. Why, when the pilot was so close to making it, did that Cessna fall from the sky? MacHenry scribbled down the mysterious transmissions from the Cessna on a legal pad and circled them. *We're hit! We're hit!*

"Tornado?" he said aloud. A mountain rotor cloud? It could feel like a solid impact. It could tear off a wing and blow it a fair distance away. Just when the Cessna emerged from the moment of maximum danger, something had slapped it to the rocks. *He almost made it.* The words had the smell of an epitaph.

He tapped a pencil on the edge of his desk. *Is that what happened to the Cessna?* After battling mountain rotor clouds in instrument conditions, the pilot broke into clearing air. Once again, those reassuring voices of the calm men in the air traffic control center filled the headset. He was in radar contact. He could see the ground. Is that when the black gulf opened for the Cessna 88P, swallowing him whole? MacHenry was starting to believe that the obvious might also be correct. It happened that way sometimes. Why should he fight it?

Okay, he thought. Accidents always yielded more questions than answers. You had to stop someplace and go with what you had. He snapped off the desk lamp and stood. He could still hear the rumble of the old twin Beech as it taxied off into the night. His skin was itchy from the fine red soil of HUMMER. The room flashed with the light of the rotating beacon as he shuffled through the darkened room by feel. *Ninety percent,* he thought. *Sometimes it's as close as you get.*

4

ANSWERS

MAJOR Barnes drove down Airbase Boulevard toward the floodlights of Mather Air Force Base. The old Jaguar's engine was running well for a change, but the spate of wet weather had played havoc with its intricate and utterly unreliable electric circuits. His instrument lights blinked like a pinball machine as he rolled over the joints in the concrete road, but he ignored it. Life, after all, was never perfect. There were always compromises to be made. And as the owner of a beautiful green XK-140, he was used to it by now. He clutched and downshifted. The RPMs surged as he slowed, making something buzz on the panel like a trapped fly. Barnes slapped the panel and braked to a stop before the main gate.

The guard looked down. "Evening, Major. Or morning." It was early for the graveyard shift but late at night by normal reckoning. He didn't need to shine his flashlight to identify the pass the major was holding up. The old XK was Maj. Peter Barnes's trademark. "Kinda late, isn't it?" he asked, putting down a skin magazine. "What's up?"

"I left behind the tech manual on this sucker." He slapped the smooth green metal of the Jaguar's door, making the panel lights go dark. "Got some fixing to do," he said, "as usual."

"Get a Toyota next time," the guard replied. "They never stop running." The guard saluted him again and returned to his magazine.

That's why you're a sergeant, he thought. Barnes steered under the outstretched black wing of the gate building and crossed over onto Air Force land.

It had been a grueling day, and one he did not deserve. He was a pilot, not some groundpounder. He remembered the stiff prig Mac-Henry. *FAA,* he thought with a sour expression.

Barnes could take apart any problem in the air and come up with a solution. But ground work, paperwork in particular, left him impatient and irritated. Flying over the mountains was one thing; tramping across the incredibly wrinkled terrain that lay beneath HUMMER 6 after a missing wing was another. To do it under orders from MacHenry, a *civilian,* only made it worse. *Airline pilots,* he thought as he accelerated along the deserted road.

Barnes drove by the huge white water tank that served as Mather's aerial landmark, and on toward the squadron offices of the 104th Fighter Interceptor Squadron. *How I got to be the lucky bastard to ramrod the crash thing I'll never know.* Then, upon painful reflection, he remembered.

Jensen! Who else could it be? His gut told him the assignment originated with the squadron commander's secretary, a lovely but difficult staff sergeant named Cynthia Jensen. Despite himself, Barnes smiled. She would come around eventually. After all, was he the only man in history to make a date and forget about it until the next day? Didn't she understand that when a person troubleshoots a problem as deep as the electrical system on an XK-140, a certain trancelike concentration is demanded?

Barnes shifted the XK as he turned onto the loading-ramp access road. The squadron offices were dark and quiet under the security lamps. The tires crunched through loose gravel. "Paint chips," he grumbled as the stones were picked up by the wheels and flung against the wells. Then Barnes saw the source of the gravel ahead: a flatbed truck followed by two jeeps was proceeding slowly down the perimeter road toward the cargo ramp. Small rocks were tumbling from the bed of the truck as it drove over the speed bumps. He clutched the car down to a crawl rather than use brakes, making the engine rev and the panel buzz again. Swatting at the dash to find the loose piece, he wondered what would get the loading chief, his crew, and three vehicles out so late. He checked his watch. It was three minutes into the new day.

The Jaguar slowed to a stop behind the rearmost jeep as another rattle of gravel fell to the road. He could see an olive-drab canvas cover, the sort used to protect jet engines in transshipment, lashed to the bed of the trailer. It covered something longer than a turbine and more irregular in shape, with odd sharp points straining the fabric of the canvas. The small convoy stopped at the gate to the loading ramp. The airman inserted a security card and punched the control box. The fence began to move.

"Come on," Barnes said quietly. He had an early-morning test flight scheduled. "Let's do it."

Halfway open, the motor pulling the chain fence open sparked blue, then white, and then failed entirely. The gate froze. "Typical." What more could you expect from groundpounders?

He shut down the Jaguar's engine and flicked off the headlights. Perversely, they stayed lit. "Just fucking great." He knew the trail of mechanical mayhem that would follow: the lights would yellow, fade, then the starter would make a disinterested click when the key was turned. He got out and walked to the jeep ahead. "Say, Sarge, how long do you plan to be parked? I'd like to play through."

The loading-crew chief stood by the jeep, watching the maintenance tech attack the frozen gate motor. He turned and with a look of frustration saluted. "Not a good night, sir. I got a funny feeling we're going to be here for a while." He glanced back at the Jaguar's headlights. They were already yellow. "What's wrong, that frog car acting up again?"

"Ah, it's British."

"I'd stick with Chevies if I were you, sir. They never quit."

"Chevies," Barnes said. Curses erupted from the jet tech as he beat the motor with a big screwdriver. "I guess I'll walk. By the way, what's under wraps?"

"It's a scrap allotment going with Fat Al over there." The sergeant nodded at the old cargo plane standing in the ramp lights. "We're retiring the whole crapload to the boneyard at Davis-Monthan in the morning."

Barnes looked at the C-130 Hercules. It hardly deserved the name of *airplane*. It looked more like a dejected cow. Barnes shook his head. "You're shipping scrap out to Davis-Monthan Air Force Base in the middle of the night?" he asked, imagining the edict of some efficiency expert with too little to do.

"You got it, sir."

Barnes walked over to the scrap truck and tapped at the covered cargo. He expected to hear the rattle of loose metal, but instead, his fingers made a hollow booming noise. More bored than curious, Barnes pulled the rubber lash holding down one end of the tarp and unhooked it.

Raising the cover, he could just make out a dim rectangular form. Pieces of scrap metal had been piled next to it: old metal shipping containers, test racks for equipment no longer made, and drop tanks for aircraft that hadn't flown since Korea and never would again.

A cool breeze from the nearby hills picked up the tarp end and pinned it back. "What the fuck . . ." Barnes felt the hair on the back of his neck rise.

It was the battered blue-and-white wing of a Cessna 172, a black-streaked gash cut deep to its spar. "Christ!" Why hadn't they told him? He dropped the canvas as though it had scalded him and spun on the loading chief still standing by the jeep. "Sergeant! Where did this load come from?" He was angry. Nobody had told him the wing up in HUMMER had been located. It would mean reopening the investigation and changing all the paperwork. His tone became formal and icy.

"Sir? We got the whole load out of the base dump," the sergeant replied, sensing that the ground rules for the discussion had changed. "What's wrong with that?"

"By whose order?" Barnes demanded.

"Colonel Braden's, sir. The load was bundled when we got there. We just grunted it up on the truck, and if that brain at the fence gets off his ass, we'll load it onto the C-130 sometime this month."

"Braden." He shook his head, his jaw tight. Why hadn't Braden told him? "Not good enough," Barnes shot back. "Don't give me the pisswater version." MacHenry had ordered him back in search of the missing aircraft wing when it had not immediately been discovered. He still had blisters from the tough hiking of the high Sierra foothills. "We've been hunting for that goddamned wing all fucking day."

"Sir, I don't know nothing about wings. I just know scrap. The colonel says, 'Sergeant, you take your loading crew and move some metal into the 124 going to the mothballs tomorrow.' What am I supposed to say?"

Barnes eyed him coolly. "Okay, Sergeant, I'll get this settled right now." Barnes walked back to the Jag, its lights a dull orange.

He hopped into the cracked leather seat without bothering to use the door and turned the ignition. *Click.* "Oh, this is some fine shit." Carefully opening the door, he got out slowly, deliberately, and then, with feeling, slammed it hard enough to rock the car on its suspension. The weak headlights blinked off, but Barnes didn't notice. He was already gone, quick-marching toward the squadron office building. *Why didn't Al tell me?*

He was in the mood for either an explanation or a permanent discharge from this ground-pounding assignment. Colonel Braden, after he woke him, was going to do some talking.

Barnes pounded up the wooden stairs to the doorway of the World War II–vintage operations building and made immediately for the telephone on his desk. "Hope he's still awake," Barnes said as he punched in the base extension of his CO, Col. Albert Braden. No question: it was a risky maneuver calling him in the middle of the oh-dark, but Braden was supposed to be his friend.

They'd flown together a long time. Ever since Braden had come back from commanding a squadron of F-4s in Thailand and found a newly minted Barnes on his doorstep. As a combat veteran, Braden was a demigod, a member of an exclusive club that no amount of flying experience could unlock. Barnes had missed his war, and there was no way around it. But Braden, unlike the other Old Hands, made it a policy not to let that get in the way. They were friends. *And friends do not send friends in search of missing wings found and already on their way to the boneyard.*

The telephone's first ring made him hesitate. *Braden's not going to be too happy.* He checked the glowing green numerals on his watch. The hands had inched to 12:35. *Maybe it can wait,* he thought at the second ring. The third ring convinced him to hang up, but not in time.

Braden's drowsy, gravelly voiced leaked slowly from the telephone. "This had better be damned good," he said, each syllable dredged up like old boots from the bottom murk.

"Ah, sorry, Colonel, Barnes here. Look, Al, I've got a problem. . . ."

"Barnes?" he said, as though trying to translate the name from a foreign language. "Barnes? You sure as hell do, son. Do you know what time it is?" Barnes heard a loud clatter, just the sort of sound a slapped-at clock makes in a high-g impact with the floor.

"Okay, Al, it's late. I wouldn't call you unless I had to, right?"

"Go," Braden spat.

Barnes breathed in deeply and began. "You know this search I've been fortunate enough to draw duty on? The Cessna out by HUMMER? The little job that kept me off the flight schedule? Well, I've made a little, you know, discovery out here."

"Don't tell me," said Braden, his voice coming awake. "You've discovered the pilot had his head up his ass and crashed due to reduced visibility."

"Hey, I'm serious. One wing was off and it was nowhere around. It was kind of unusual, you know? It's not like it was going to be very far from the site. It was just gone. Well, I just found it."

A long silence was punctuated by a sigh. "You want to take this nice and slow, Barnes, 'cause when I wake up, I am going to get some kind of pissed. You don't want me to wake up that quick. Nice and slow and for the record. Where?" Braden was, in fact, completely alert as he sat up on his bed. His eyes snapped into focus, wondering what was coming.

"In a scrap pile. Believe it, Al? You should, because the sergeant on the groundpounder detail said you told him to put it in an old MAC 130 heading for the heap. Starting to sound, you know, a little familiar?" Barnes felt the anger rise in him. "You will recall the hours I spent trudging through the boonies, and worse, the reports? You know how miserable that FAA guy made life for a while? The sergeant must be screwed up, I figure. I mean, my good buddy Al wouldn't send me out to the woods if he already had the wing, right?"

Braden didn't answer the question. "Barnes, I'm going to do you a favor," he said. "When you hang up, you're going to realize what a kindly, understanding CO you've got. We are not going to delve into why your talents were singled out for this work. I trust staff sergeant Jensen has made that clear. If not, I am sure she will. Just ask."

Barnes shook his head. *Women.* He had been right, after all. "Okay, Al, we read you loud and clear. Maybe I had it coming. But why the hush-hush on a miserable wing? I didn't need the exercise."

"No hush-hush. If you'll extend your search to our own base scrap pile, I am willing to guarantee you will find at least one, and perhaps two, old airplanes. These airplanes were turned from perfectly good machines to scrap courtesy of the base flying club . . ."

Oh, shit, thought Barnes, jumping ahead to what he knew was coming. *I stirred up the Old Man with a busted stick.* Barnes knew the fledglings learning at the base club regularly rolled up their airplanes into balls of aluminum foil. The corpses of the poor, abused craft were stacked at the base scrap depot, just as Braden said.

". . . and that, Major, is that. Now, unless you would like to continue this little chat, I would suggest you drop this like a hot rock. You're scheduled tomorrow on a couple of maintenance hops. You'll need your sleep. And," he said, "unlike my merry band of pirates, so do I."

"Right, Al. I forgot about those little pudknockers over at the club. Sorry to have bothered you." *Shit shit shit SHIT!*

"No sweat. I consider it a trademark of my enlightened administration that my pilots can call me at *any goddamn time of the night!"*

Barnes held the phone away from his ear and winced. A full-colonel shout is not inconsiderable.

"Now sweet dreams, Barnsey, and next time check six, okay?" Braden hung up with force, leaving a wavering tone echoing in Barnes's ears.

"Great." Barnes left the squadron office, forgetting once again to take the service manual to the Jaguar. The night air had turned damp. He was already considering how he would get the XK running when he heard a banging clatter coming from the loading ramp. The sergeant's crew was busy tossing the metal pieces from the flatbed into the cavernous bay of the old transport. He watched as four of them picked up the wing and threw it into the Hercules's yawning after hatch. The lift strut, still attached to the underside of the busted-up airfoil, caught on the edge of the cargo door.

He began to walk, but then stopped short. "Huh?" He turned and zeroed in on the battered wing getting swallowed by the C-130. Something wasn't right. *Lift strut!* he thought as he watched the operation. If the wing they were tossing in had a piece of lift strut still attached, didn't that make it part of a high-winged aircraft? But the club flew low-winged Pipers. He whistled softly. *Nice try, Al.* He didn't know why, but Braden was lying.

"Everything all right?" Braden's wife turned over. His shout had woken her out of a dream.

"Yeah," Braden replied. "Just fine. Go back to sleep." Dammit! What had Barnes been doing nosing around at midnight? He picked up the phone again and tapped in a number with a Nevada area code. "I'm not even supposed to be aware of this crap," he swore as the connection was made.

"Nellis Operations," the voice said.

Braden hesitated. Barnes was a good man; an exceptional pilot and a real stick-and-rudder natural. Braden did not like having to lie to him. He hoped that Barnes would get the message quick. "Colonel Al Braden out at Mather," he began. "I've . . ." He stopped and corrected himself. *"You've* got a situation."

5

DANGERS
AND
OPPORTUNITIES

THE smell of woodsmoke was more intense inside the hunting lodge than out. It was a warm day for a fire. But Viktor Chebrikov, the former chairman of the Committee for State Security, the KGB, was a man who appreciated atmosphere and nuance. Fat birch logs popped in the conference room's fireplace, punctuating the low hiss issuing from the air-conditioning vents. A row of boar heads shot on previous hunts gazed down from above the mantel like a silent jury.

Chebrikov sat at the head of a long, polished table. Before his administrative exile, this room had seen the comings and goings of the party elite. But those were the old days. Few of his old friends, and there were a few despite his reputation, dared to visit him. It was as if disfavor were a communicable disease, and this lodge a kind of leprosarium. That same quality made it the ideal place for desperate men to meet.

Chebrikov sat back in his chair, a bit stiffly. His six-foot-three frame was not made for retirement. Inaction had plainly aged him beyond his years. He glanced at the other three men seated at the polished table.

One wore a new but cheap suit plainly bursting at the seams. Oleg

Guryanov, the KGB's Havana *rezidant,* had always suffered from a weight problem. Or, as Chebrikov preferred, a discipline problem.

Another man wore the green suede hunting outfit that had provided his cover for being at Zavidovo in the first place. Lev Zaikov had been the Moscow Party chief until his recent ouster by some newly unexiled Siberian poet. What was the world coming to?

The last sweated in the uniform of a marshal of the Red Army, his red collar blazes like two heat lamps beneath his flushed face. Nikolai Ogarkov's head had rolled when a small boy flew a Cessna into Red Square. A somber military man more loyal to tradition and stability than to any particular political view, his presence was one of the crucial links in Chebrikov's plan. But not the final one. *Where is he?* he wondered. Chebrikov checked his watch and glanced up at Guryanov. "You are certain he is coming?"

Guryanov cleared his throat. "Yes, Chairman Chebrikov. I spoke with him this morning. He will be here."

Chebrikov looked at Lev Zaikov. "You have obtained the figures?"

"Right here," said Zaikov as he patted a leather briefcase. He had managed to smuggle out a copy of next year's aid package to Cuba, a document so incendiary Zaikov feared it would explode when exposed to the air.

"Excellent," said Chebrikov. "Your efforts will be remembered." He glanced at Marshal Ogarkov. "Comrade Marshal?"

"I have made my inquiries," said Ogarkov. "What you seek can be obtained. Friendship runs deep in the Army, Chairman Chebrikov." *Unlike your friends,* his expression said plainly.

"Very good, Nikolai. I . . ." Chebrikov stopped when he heard an engine roar up to the villa's entrance. "Very good."

The villa's front door opened, causing a slight breeze to pass over the conference room table. Marshal Ogarkov, nearest to the fireplace and dressed the heaviest in his wool uniform, swiped at his brow. The front door thumped shut. Chebrikov waited, still in his seat, his back to the door, as the last man arrived.

"Compañero," said Guryanov, standing and smiling as Ramón Guiterrez walked in.

The Cuban defense minister stood in the doorway, weighing the meaning behind each of the men before him. His bushy eyebrows rose when he identified Ogarkov. Zaikov he only knew from pictures. And the tall man with his back to him? Who else could it be? You could nearly see the political balance beam tilt as his dark brown eyes took in the scene. *The Army, the KGB, and a politician.* It was, he knew, a potent mix. He fixed on Guryanov. "So," he said, "this is quite a place. But I am confused. When you asked me here, I assumed it was for a hunt. But all I see are trophies." He nodded ambiguously at the boar heads. "Stuffed trophies."

"Not all of our heads have been claimed," said Chebrikov as he twisted in his seat.

"Ah," said Guiterrez, a twinkle in his dark eyes. "*Compañero* Chebrikov. It has been a very long time. I see you have retired well."

"So it would seem," Chebrikov replied, his pale gray eyes unblinking. "Why don't we begin?" He indicated an empty chair. "Please."

"Begin?" said Guiterrez. "You will understand, Comrade Chebrikov, that it is not wise to begin something you know nothing about. My visit here is risk enough, yes?"

"Not compared with the risks you now face," Chebrikov replied. "I think you will find this both quick and exceedingly interesting."

Guiterrez checked his watch. "I am due at the Foreign Ministry in an hour and a half." He walked over to the table, pulled out his chair, and sat. "Interest me."

"Ramón," Chebrikov began, "time is getting quite short for us all. This is not a social gathering. I won't waste your time. Or my own." He held his hand out to Lev Zaikov. The former Moscow Party chief handed over the briefcase quickly and with evident relief. His part was over. Chebrikov opened it and gave Guiterrez a thin black folder.

"So?" said Guiterrez as he broke the seal and slipped out a bound report. "What is it you would have me read?"

"Ramón," Chebrikov began, "these are difficult and contradictory times. You understand what I mean. Your meeting with Eduard is not a social visit." Eduard Shevardnadze was both the foreign minister and right-hand man to the president. "It is a matter of survival. Our collective survival. Both for us and for you."

Guiterrez chuckled. "So far your *presidente* has done a very good job of that. And my own, for that matter. Better than you."

Chebrikov smiled, but his jaw was tightly clamped. "So far," he said. "But is it likely to remain that way? Is the Old Man that much of a fool to think he can stand alone against the world?"

"The *Comandante* is not a fool," said Guiterrez with a look of warning to Chebrikov. "Nor will he have to stand alone. The Soviet Union cannot afford us, *señor,* but neither can it afford to be without us."

"Oh?" Chebrikov nodded at the report in his hands. "I think, Ramón, that your intelligence service may need a new briefing. Why don't you look for yourself?"

Guiterrez scanned the title page. "Ah," he said. "So I shall come from the hunt with a trophy of my own." Guiterrez opened the aid document and turned the pages quickly. He stopped when he came to a simple line chart. "What is this?" The line represented an overview of Soviet aid to Cuba. After a relatively level plateau these last several years, it plummeted down to the vanishing point. Zero. Guiterrez turned the binder to read the small labels. "This is not what we discussed," he said. "There have been promises made. . . ."

"And broken," said Chebrikov. "To us all. But what did you expect?"

Guiterrez glanced up. "Is this an authentic document?"

Chebrikov shrugged. "You needn't trust me one way or the other," he said. "Ask Shevardnadze over dinner. Or even better, read your own copy from our esteemed president tomorrow. I thought," the former KGB chief said with a smile, "you might appreciate a warning."

"*Compañero,*" said Guiterrez, his dark face noticeably gray, "do you know what will happen in my country if this is not some little game? If your country really cuts out all aid to mine?"

"Of course. Why do you think I had you come?" said Chebrikov. His bony fingers were splayed out across the polished table like gnarled roots gripping smooth stone. "Disorder. Anarchy. Dissolution. The end of everything we have attempted to do with our lives. Welcome to the new world, Ramón."

"I see," said Guiterrez. He sat back. "But there is something else, yes? You would not have asked me here unless you"—he stopped and looked at the other three men—"you have some purpose, some idea how to change this."

"Perhaps." Chebrikov nodded. "It is very dark today, but not black. Fate has not abandoned us, or you, entirely. But I get ahead of myself."

"Then begin at the beginning," said Guiterrez.

"Very well," said Chebrikov. "It is no great secret that our nation is fracturing at every frontier. To the west, our buffer states are falling. NATO has won without firing a shot, and the Germans?"

Marshal Ogarkov grimaced but remained silent.

Chebrikov continued. "Even closer, there is the Baltic question. To the south, Azerbaijan and the forces of resurgent Islam. To the east, Mongolia and the Chinese."

"The death of an empire," Guiterrez remarked. "Without a bang. Just a whimper, yes?"

"Exactly," said Chebrikov. "Of course we still possess the largest nuclear arsenal in the world, but what use is it?"

Ogarkov snorted. "A billion billion rubles," he said as he shook his head. "And what have they bought?"

"I will tell you," said Chebrikov. "They have bought us our own destruction. The Americans have spent us into the ground and we all know it. Now more than ever we need to move those resources and apply them to more practical ends."

"Like Poland, perhaps?" said Guiterrez. "Or is it the Ukraine this month?"

"You see my point," Chebrikov replied. "Our expensive nuclear forces represent the last untapped resource available to throw into the battle to reestablish internal order."

"Is that not exactly what your president seeks to do?" asked Guiterrez. "Geneva is not far away."

"Yes," said Chebrikov, "but our president will simply hand away everything and get nothing in return. You cannot bargain with an opponent who knows your weaknesses. Our empire is nearly dead. How can we force them to give anything up?"

"Ah," said Guiterrez. "You must, but you cannot do so as long as the *yanquis* remain powerful, is that it?"

"Essentially." Chebrikov nodded.

"But are they really so powerful as you say?" asked Guiterrez. "What makes you think they are in any better shape than you? Their economy is nearly as dead as your empire."

"That brings me to the second problem," said Chebrikov. He shuffled his notes for effect, then began again. "You wonder whether they are still dangerous," said Chebrikov. "There is evidence that says they are. Perhaps more dangerous now than ever before. Their technology has given them something that changes the world."

"And this is?" asked Guiterrez.

"The specific advance I refer to," he continued, "is their stealth strike aircraft."

Guiterrez shrugged. "Then, *compañero,*" he said, "you may go back to your retirement. The B-2 is dead and buried. Even they could not afford it."

"No," Ogarkov broke in. "This is not the B-2."

"Correct," said Chebrikov. "We have reason to believe that they now possess another, more dangerous aircraft. An invisible bomber capable of astonishing speed." He paused and opened a thick folder. "This you cannot have," he said to Guiterrez. "Nikolai?"

Ogarkov nodded, glad to be back on his own, familiar ground. "What Chairman Chebrikov says is true. Our fleet of surveillance satellites has come up with something very odd: a high-flying object putting out tremendous infrared energy, but with no radar image. None. And such speed!" he said, shaking his head. "Our fastest interceptors cannot catch it. Not even our fastest antiaircraft rockets. As a result, this aircraft is now capable of unopposed flights over the Soviet Union. Anywhere. It goes without saying that it could cross your entire island in the blink of an eye. Not for nothing is it called Excali—"

"Ramón," Chebrikov interrupted, "at the speeds this aircraft can fly, we are an hour's flight time from this bomber's home base. You are but a few minutes."

"Interesting." Cuba had lived close beneath the American shadow for a very long time. "But what is the connection?" asked the Cuban. "Because of this ghost plane, the fraternal aid package goes to zero?"

Chebrikov knew he had the hook in the Cuban's mouth. Now, one firm pull would set it. "Our nuclear forces cannot stand down while under the threat of this first-strike weapon. But we must if we are to reestablish internal security. What is left for Cuba? You see the dilemma?"

"What is new? The *yanquis* have been crazy for thirty years," said Guiterrez. "Somehow we all have survived."

"You have survived because of *this*," Chebrikov pointed at the aid package Zaikov had spirited out. "This brings me to my final point," he continued. "Ramón, the Americans are worried about the weather."

Guiterrez looked up, puzzled. "The weather?" It was as if someone had just brought up mention of a particularly interesting performance at the Bolshoi.

"Yes," said Chebrikov. "They plan to conduct a simulation, a test of what they call nuclear winter. Do you not find the confluence of an invisible bomber and a concern for the aftereffects of a nuclear war to be ominous? I do."

"How do you know all of this?" Guiterrez asked.

"How we know this is irrelevant. Consider the issue at hand. An attack, a small, surgical attack, can be carried out by this invisible new bomber. And with the results of this test, they can be sure it will cause no lasting harm to anyone but us. Or you. If they do not plan it today, then tomorrow. If not tomorrow, then next year. Peace comes from balance, not imbalance." Chebrikov stopped, then let the last bit of line out for Guiterrez. "But this test is also an opportunity. It can be our lever. With your help."

Finally, thought Guiterrez. Still, the man was not insane. Far from it. Who knew what the *norteamericanos* would do if they thought themselves invincible again? "What is it you wish?" he asked. "And how does Cuba benefit?"

"I need your help"—Chebrikov smiled—"to make their test more realistic. How Cuba benefits is even simpler." Chebrikov reached over and took the aid report and threw it to the floor. The slap of paper against the polished floor made Guryanov jump. "We can return to a time more favorable for us all." An awkward silence fell across the room, broken only by the snapping of the fire.

Guiterrez eyed the others. Zaikov was clearly just a courier, and Guryanov was scarcely the material successful coups were made from. But Ogarkov and Chebrikov, they were the real thing. *The Army joined with the KGB*. And Chebrikov was clearly a man who could still make things happen. "Tell me more."

"We know the date, the time, and the place," said Chebrikov. "The Americans will crash an airplane to create a very large fire. A simulation of a nuclear blast. But," he said, "suppose it happened to be carrying a bomb? Not just a simulation, but a *real* bomb?"

"You said they were curious about the weather. No one spoke of a bomb," said Guiterrez.

"That is so." Chebrikov pressed a concealed button set into the table's rim. A slide lit on one of the several projection screens at the room's perimeter. He walked over to the wall display, his tall frame black against the brightly lit screen. "But what if there *was* one on board? One of, say, ten kilotons yield?"

"But . . ."

"It happened in Spain. It happened in Greenland. It's happened a dozen times at sea. Why not here, and why not now?" Chebrikov said, pointing at a place in the Sierra Nevada marked HUMMER. "Once again, the clumsy *and expensive* United States Air Force has crashed one of their airplanes. The plane has exploded, and with it a nuclear weapon recklessly carried on board. Not in Spain. Not in Greenland. Not at sea. But here." He slapped the screen, making the image waver. "The result? The American public, and their press, would ravage the military. In their haste to find the guilty party, no one would believe the explosion was anything other than an American weapon set off by accident in the crash."

"And what happens to you?" asked Guiterrez.

"The bomb can be made to any specification," said Chebrikov. "It would never be a Soviet weapon. But a client state?"

"Tajura," Guiterrez said quietly. It was the Libyan nuclear complex set up and run by the Soviets.

"For example," Chebrikov agreed, "the Americans look at our dear president through dark glasses. They see what they wish to see. This will allow them to see what *we* wish them to see."

"You have told me how you will pull the rug from under your president's feet," Guiterrez noted. "But not how any of this helps Cuba."

"Do you not see? The Americans can be forced *by their own citizens* into a complete denuclearization. They can be made to throw away their strategic forces and so permit us the breathing time to re-create internal order. And," said Chebrikov, "make good on our alliances."

Guiterrez chuckled. *This* was the Chebrikov he remembered. Life had been much better back then, hadn't it? "And what will happen to your president? Surely he is not completely unloved at home."

"Someone once said that a politician can promise a bridge, even where there is no river," Chebrikov replied. "But you cannot walk across a promise. Nor can you eat one. You see," said Chebrikov, "our president is like a man on a very high wire. He only looks good if he makes us think he is about to fall. But what if he *does* fall?"

"You will push him?" asked Guiterrez.

"I won't have to," Chebrikov replied. "When the moment comes, all his empty promises will weigh him down, heavier and heavier, until his wire snaps. It is a time for risk. And for reward. For you, Comrade Guiterrez, it is a time for survival. Perhaps for us all. The Americans say they need to reallocate resources away from defense. I say, let us help them do precisely that."

Guiterrez laughed. "Viktor," he said, "whatever else can be said, you have always been a man of surprising resources." He looked at Marshal Ogarkov. "I take it that this little bomb is available?"

Ogarkov didn't answer. A nervous tick below his eye was answer enough.

"As I thought," said Guiterrez. "But tell me, *compañero,* why should a man of such resources need the help of my small country?" He glanced at Ogarkov. "The Red Army will give you your bomb. What can Cuba offer, especially now?"

"A bomb is not enough," said Chebrikov. "Of course, the American government will know there was no weapon on board their own plane. We must construct a very careful legend, Ramón. One that makes perfect sense to them, even when the pressures are enormous. We need a man," Chebrikov replied. "A man who can be trusted not to fail. There are very few of them left."

Guiterrez smiled warily. "True. The Committee and the Agency are like an old married couple. They begin to look more and more alike the less they are called upon to do, yes?" His eyes suddenly sharpened. "Which man did you have in mind?"

"Petroushka," said Chebrikov, using the Cuban agent's code name. "He has the right skills. The right experience. Plus," said Chebrikov with a wry smile, "if things do not happen as planned, he can be made into anybody."

"Of course," Guiterrez agreed. Petroushka was dark skinned, even for a Cuban. "It will not go well for your president. Life will get very dangerous for him, I fear."

"Danger for him," said Chebrikov, "and opportunities for us all."

"Ah," said Guiterrez. He reached into the pocket of his shirt and pulled out a cigar. A match flared and a cloud of fragrant tobacco smoke rose to the ceiling. "I will meet with Shevardnadze tonight. And your president tomorrow morning. You know," he said as the end of the cigar flared red, "if conditions are not as you have described, I could mention this little hunting trip. It would be worth a few tankers of oil docked in Havana to do so. At very little risk."

"You could," Chebrikov agreed, "but I don't think you'll find it in your own interest. It was not by avoiding all risk that Cuba was taken from the *yanquis,* was it?"

"No, *compañero,*" said Guiterrez as he reached down and scooped up the damning report. The end of all food and oil shipments would mean the end of Cuba. But the risks! He stood and nodded. "We shall see. How can I . . ."

"Guryanov will be your contact," Chebrikov said. "I will wait to hear from you."

"Tonight," Guiterrez said, and left.

6

ARRIVALS
AND
DEPARTURES

PETER Adcock looked over the terse note from Nellis. Why had it taken this long to get here? He sat back in his chair and listened to the cold air spill from the overhead diffusers. *What's the probability?* he wondered. He almost pulled out his calculator, then stopped. It had happened, and chance or not, it had been a mistake to trust the Air Force to help him out with the Cessna's wing.

It was getting very late in the game for mistakes. It was just such a mistake, an incorrect "law" in the B-2's flight software, that had brought its entire program crashing to earth. Excalibur would not suffer a similar fate while he had any say about it. Not with the congressional procurement decision in the wings.

Peter Adcock was at a curious and professionally dangerous stage in his career. He was young enough to have succeeded at all the projects handed to him by others, but was without a track record for one that he, and he alone, was responsible. That the flight-test program for Excalibur was given to him to manage was as much a compliment as a statement about the fortunes of Norton Aerodyne; most of the Old Hands had seen the writing on the wall for several years now. As their defense projects dried up and blew away, they had all made quiet arrangements, and when the moment and the job arrived, they had leaped. Still, managing a piece of Project Aurora was an extraordinary plum, and Adcock knew it. He was not about to see it founder because some idiot Air Force officer, a *pilot,* had insomnia.

A sharp knock on his door made Adcock sit up straight. He composed his face, ordered his papers into two neat piles, and slid the troubling note from Nellis into his top drawer. "Come," he said.

Harry Hill loped into Adcock's office. About as tall as a pilot could be and still fit into the tight cockpit of a fighter, Hill kicked the door shut with his boot. Despite his leave from Tonopah's flight schedule following the accident, he looked neither rested nor happy.

"Good morning, Hill," said Adcock. "How was Las Vegas?"

"I didn't get that far," said Hill. "I stayed in town." *Town* meant only one thing, for there was only one hotel worthy of the name in all of Tonopah.

"The Mizpah?" asked Adcock.

The lanky pilot pulled out a chair and sat down. "Yep." It was a local bar destined to assume much the same glory achieved by Pancho Barnes's Fly-Inn Ranch out at Edwards. Hill's eyes swept the blank wall for a window, but of course that was not possible a hundred feet below the desert floor. He sniffed the air and screwed up his eyes. "Something stinks in here."

Adcock looked into his trash basket. The remains of a hamburger and fries, his favorite meal, lay dead at the bottom. "I've got to get the cleaning crew up to speed," he said. "What's on your mind?"

Hill squinted at him, examining Adcock as though he were a strange and not altogether agreeable creature. *Mouthbreather,* he thought. "I did a little checking with some old friends," he said. "It seems they had a radar track on an aircraft in HUMMER while we were inbound on the Charlie run. An emergency squawk at that."

"That's very interesting," Adcock replied evenly.

"Yeah. That's just what I said. Now this chunk of data got me wondering." Hill leaned forward. "If *they* knew, how come we didn't abort the run and wait until the range was clear?"

Adcock nodded. "We needed to verify the simulation. You know that. It was an accident. A communications foul-up."

"Right," said Hill. "It may have been an accident to you, but we smoked some bastard at HUMMER and it damned near killed us, too. *And* your pretty little airplane."

"Smoked?" asked Adcock nervously. He didn't know how to handle physical violence, and menace was written all over Hill's face.

"Killed," Hill explained. "As in, you know, murder?"

Adcock shook his head vehemently. "No. It wasn't that at all. Things were happening fast. We didn't know about the transient until it was too late. Who did you say you checked this with?" After the note from Nellis, Adcock didn't need another hole to plug.

"I didn't," said Hill. "Things were happening fast, huh? You should try it from *my* seat." *Twerp.* "That brings up another minor matter. You told us the pilot walked. Wrong. He burned. Did that little fact go by too quick for you, too?"

"No." Adcock picked up a pencil as though an equation needed immediate solving. "We found out. Our initial reports were not reliable. I didn't think it mattered to the program one way or the other."

"It didn't matter," Hill repeated. He pointed his finger at Adcock like a pistol. "Well, boy, it matters to me."

Adcock dodged his intense gaze. "I see that. Nobody's misleading you, Hill. Our information was in error. How many flight crews have we lost right here wringing the aircraft out? It's not like we're all sitting in a laboratory. This is dangerous work. Things can happen."

"Oh, indeed. You bet your sweet pink ass things can happen. But I *volunteered* for this project. So did Thatch. I don't know what *your* excuse was, but I know one damned thing. That guy who burned in HUMMER didn't volunteer. He wasn't on the payroll. Look," he said, "we hang it over the edge to make your little buggy fly right. I don't like fuck-ups, Adcock. They get people hurt. But this was *your* fuck-up, and it got someone more than hurt. It got them dead." Hill's pale blue eyes seemed to bore into Adcock like twin 20-mm cannon.

"It's a little late—"

"Quiet. Listen well. I'll be damned if I'll point that sucker into the mountains again unless I know the range is clear. Understood?"

Adcock laughed nervously and shook his head. "You're asking us to open the program? That's what it would amount to if we had to make those kinds of arrangements. We might as well advertise the aircraft in *Aviation Week*. Besides," Adcock said with a wave of dismissal, "that idiot was a dead man before you and Thatcher got there. The mountains and the weather—"

"Fuck the mountains and the weather. *I* killed him. You and me both. And I do not like the way that hangs. I like it a whole lot less that you don't think it's big enough to mention. It leaves me, you know, with this cold feeling. Like maybe next time it's me that won't be worth mentioning. That's bad for the lab rat's morale." Hill stood up. "Get this straight: No more fuck-ups, *Mister* Adcock. Or you can find another jet jockey to play games with."

Pilots. Adcock breathed deeply and shook his head. "I'm sorry you feel that way, Hill. But if you don't like the job, perhaps you should find something else you like better."

Hill looked at the engineer's pasty face, untouched by the high-altitude sun. He wanted to reach out and throttle him. "Don't tempt me," he said, and left.

MacHenry heard the outer door of the FAA's Oakland office open. He checked his watch. As usual, he had been the first in, and his secretary was the second. She would come in and with a mock surprise, shake her head and say the words she said nearly every day. How many years had they gone through this small ceremony? He reached up and straightened his dark woven tie. It was a touch formal, he knew, and it looked like hell with his short-sleeved shirt, but some habits die hard.

"You beat me again, Mr. MacHenry," said Dorothy as she poked her head into his office. Like MacHenry, she was within a few years of retirement. "Coffee?"

"Black, thank you," he replied, keeping tight to the script. He glanced outside as the fog rolled in off the cold waters of San Francisco

Bay. *Done,* he thought. The HUMMER accident was wrapped up as tidily as he could. He turned back to his desk to finish the accident report.

The final page of FAA form 8020 was still in the typewriter. HUMMER had been a fatal accident, and so more than the usual paperwork was involved. The National Transportation Safety Board, the NTSB, was gearing up already to take over from the FAA. MacHenry pecked in his two-finger style, filling in all the blanks. He stopped when he reached the bottom. Item number 24 read *Corrective Actions Planned or Initiated.* MacHenry tapped a string of *X*'s along the line. The pilot of that Cessna had flown in the face of a great many warning flags. He had chosen his path, and the results had been as plain as they were predictable. *Except,* thought MacHenry, *for the wing.*

"Black," said Dorothy as she slid a fresh cup onto MacHenry's desk. She watched as he ignored it. "Are you feeling all right this morning?"

"Raring to go," he replied, his eyes still clouded in thought about the missing wing. Maybe some hiker would find it someday, and then again, maybe not. Like MacHenry, the pilot had been unmarried, no dependents. Either way, it was over for them both.

He rolled the last sheet from the typewriter and signed the report. Next he folded it into the interoffice envelope and posted it back to FAA Oklahoma City. There it would be reviewed, sent to the NTSB, and transferred to magnetic tape storage to be filed away and forgotten.

He heard the distinctive jangle of the public line ringing in the outer office. "Mr. MacHenry?" said Dorothy. "Phone. Are you here?"

"Find out who it is, please. And no more lawyers." *They must listen to police scanners now,* he thought. He'd already had calls from several looking to make a case against someone over the HUMMER accident.

She peeked around the corner, holding the phone covered with one hand. "It's a Major Barnes. He said you'd know what it's about."

MacHenry had almost been able to forget that arrow, its head buried in a tree trunk over his head. "All right. Put him through." By habit, he reached for a newly sharpened pencil and a clean notepad. He picked up the phone. "This is MacHenry. What can I do for you?"

"Good morning, Mr. MacHenry," said Barnes. "How's life at the FAA today?"

"What is it, Major? Make it brief. I'm due at a flight-safety seminar this morning."

"I think you might want to make room for a slight, you know, change." Barnes chuckled. He let the silence ripen and then spoke again. "I think I found the wing, MacHenry. Your wing."

MacHenry sat straight up in his chair. "Where?" He started scribbling on his pad and opened the just-filed folder containing his notes on the accident. The wing! "Come on. Speak! I don't have time for games. This is serious business. Can it be helicoptered out?" MacHenry remembered the incredibly rough terrain the Cessna had come down in.

"Games? I'm not sure you're taking this the right way, Mr. MacHenry. The voice you hear is the sound of a blowing whistle. I presume you know how popular that would make me around here."

Whistle? MacHenry let the phrase ride. "I'm not concerned with your popularity, Major. Just let me know how I can arrange to bring that wing to Oakland. Can I send a truck?"

"Oh, it's *much* better than that, MacHenry. It's already loaded up inside an Air Force transport as we speak. How's that for the efficiency of the boys in blue? Only one little problem. Somebody here seems to think it belongs on a scrap heap."

"What? Explain yourself."

"Last night I found, by complete accident you realize, a busted-up wing getting loaded onto a bird headed for the boneyard. I figured some paper pusher had—"

"Where? What boneyard?"

"Sorry. Davis-Monthan Air Force Base near Tucson. It's where we mothball obsolete airplanes. You know, the Ghost Squadron thing? Anyway, I think, damn, but this sure does look like the very wing I've been busting my hump to locate for the nice guys at the FAA. So I call up the CO, and Al comes down like napalm. On time, on target. I'm standing there with the stuff dripping off me, you know? Crispy critters. Hotel Sierra to the max."

"What makes you think this is the wing we were looking for, Barnes?"

"Jesus! That's what Braden said. You guys rehearse this or something? What is this, 'let's bust Barnesy's balls' week?"

"No. It's just that there are usually two or three good reasons for anything. I want the right reason."

"Sorry. It was funny though. Al, ah, Colonel Braden is the squadron commander. He told me a little bedtime story about it. Where it was supposed to have come from. Only, you know, it didn't. I checked."

"You've only said that he misidentified it, not that it's the one we've been looking for."

"MacHenry, don't you think *I* know what my own eyes are looking at? The wing was blue and white and the lift strut looked like it got gnawed off. The fittings were munched. Starting to sound better?"

MacHenry considered. There were plenty of blue-and-white wings in the Cessna fleet, to be sure. But how many with torn-up fittings? *And a bad alibi?* "Okay," he said. "Assuming for a moment that this is the wing, why would anybody want to hide evidence of a private-plane crash? And where did you say it is now?"

"The old MAC C-130 left about two hours ago. As far as I know, it's still on board. You figure the why." *Why didn't Braden play it straight with me?* "That's not what they pay me to do. I'm just a good citizen. I figure the poor bastard who crashed up there deserves that much."

MacHenry looked at the sealed envelope in his out basket. "You say it's en route to where? Davis-Monthan?"

"The very same, nestled in the scenic Saguaro desert region of downtown Tucson. If it doesn't fall out of the sky or something. Call sign Shakey one zero three. Appropriate, right?"

MacHenry scowled as he wrote down the identifier for the flight. He could remember when the C-130 was the newest marvel, a veritable flying mountain of aluminum. "All right," he said. "But one thing has me curious. After our meeting up at HUMMER, I wouldn't figure you for the whistle-blowing kind. Why did you call?"

"A man burned up there. Somebody should find out why."

"But . . ."

"No buts, MacHenry. You want my motives, hire a shrink. Maybe I'm just a nice guy. One thing's for sure: if you want that wing, I suggest you get a move on. Whoever is running this little operation is one jump ahead of you as it is."

Or two, thought MacHenry. "All right," he told Barnes. "I'll check on it. Where will you be the rest of the day?"

"Me?" Barnes laughed. "Where I belong. Good hunting, MacHenry, and better keep an eye on your six."

"Why?" asked MacHenry, but Barnes had already hung up.

Barnes hung up the phone with a sinking feeling in his gut. *Nice guy,* he thought. *Who am I to put this in some civilian's hands?* If Braden wanted it quiet, why not leave it quiet? Barnes picked up a pencil and tapped it on the scarred desk top. *On the other hand, why didn't he trust me enough to tell me the truth?*

He snapped the pencil and tossed it into the rubbish can. *Done.* He looked over at the small framed photo of his archery instructor. They were standing together, each of them flight-suited, in front of a T-38 Talon trainer. Barnes had met Prof. Anthony Tanai at a Red Flag session down at Nellis Air Force Base in Nevada. Tanai had been brought in by the Air Force to teach the young tigers about SA, or situational awareness. They had all dismissed it as a parlor game, what with its silent rituals, but Barnes quickly changed his mind.

SA was the ability to keep track of everything happening in the sky while you tried to fly and fight your aircraft. It relied on a cold, inner calm that was hard to achieve with a bandit in the saddle and a missile homing your six. Red Flag was mock combat, but in the real thing, those who had high SA were usually the ones who came back at the end of the day. The rest became statistics.

It was ironic that it took a trip to Red Flag for Barnes to meet Tanai; the middle-aged Japanese American taught psychology at UC Davis, not many miles down the road from Mather Air Force Base. It was there that Barnes discovered they had something more in common than optimizing the human mind for fighter combat: they both liked shooting at targets.

While psychology was his field, Zen archery was Tanai's real love. Or, as he had told Barnes, discipline. Situational awareness, the "clue bird," whatever it might have been to Barnes, to the archer it was the effortless discipline of the moonlit path, the Zone, the perfect teaming of mind, eye, and will with a bamboo arrow. *The target exists to catch your arrow,* Tanai had said.

It sounded pretty good to Barnes, who quickly discovered that the state of awareness that guided a bamboo bolt applied equally to a 30,000-pound F-15. And it had certainly helped his SA, even if some of the older pilots at the 104th Fighter Interceptor Squadron called him Major Ninja.

Barnes picked up the morning's engineering test-flight schedule. His aerial abilities had earned him the right to test-fly aircraft newly out of maintenance, a job that others hated but that he loved. It was always a puzzle, a challenge. He came to the first entry and stopped. It was a McDonnell Douglas F-4 just out of an overhaul of its byzantine hydraulics systems. He didn't know why anyone had bothered.

In a world where a pilot lived through speed and stealth, the Phantom was a big monster of an airplane impossible to hide. After decades of attempted fixes, it still put out billows of black exhaust unless its two thirsty engines were in afterburner, and its combat range in afterburner was next to nil. As for stealth, the men who flew them over North Vietnam called them Magnets for the way they seemed to beckon to the radar-beam-riding SA-2 SAMS. Still, none of that mattered to Barnes. It was just an engineering ride, and the Phantom was a lady with an interesting past.

He flipped to the front of the F-4's log and eagerly read the old entries. The pages were stained brown with the damp heat of Thailand. This Phantom had accumulated an enormous number of flying hours on its airframe, most of them out of the Royal Thai air base at Korat. This fact alone made the idea of test-flying it tolerable; it was a connection to the Last Real War, an authentic combat veteran, even if it was afflicted with jungle rot and ready to be let out to pasture.

He tossed the log down and picked up another, newer one. "Aha." *This* entry on the flight schedule was even more promising. Some bright Pentagon staffer had commissioned a private company to update and modify the lowly T-33 into a modern attack aircraft.

Long used as a trainer, the new T-Bird was reengined with an afterburning version of the venerable Allison, and equipped with the latest avionics and countermeasures. Some aerodynamic tweaking had been done, and the old, tired T-Bird had become a born-again minifighter available on a shoestring budget. It was just the thing for the aspiring air forces of the Third World. He reviewed the maintenance log on the T-Bird.

Three of these converted jets, on their way to service in Ecuador, had stopped off at Mather for a full run-in of their navigation systems. The civilian pilot flying number three had blown a tire on a hard landing and had busted up a lot of hardware in the process of getting stopped. Numbers one and two had finished their systems burn-in and disappeared over the southern horizon. Aircraft three sat on an isolated ramp, living in a sort of bureaucratic limbo; a civilian-owned fighter at an Air Force base on its way to South America.

Still, the T-Bird had a special place in his aviator's heart. Barnes had spent hundreds of hours in its cramped cockpit during his advanced flight training. He stood and tucked the F-4's paperwork under his arm.

"Hey, Barnes," said another pilot as he entered the squadron office. "Whither are you bound?"

Barnes headed for the locker room to suit up. "I'd say it's time to slip the surly bonds," he called back, all thoughts of Cessna wings, FAA officials, and the misrepresentations of colonels locked behind a series of mental watertight doors. That was their affair. Flying was his.

7

PETROUSHKA

THE ringdoves called to each other as they strutted along the balcony. Their sweet tones sounded like small bells rung in quick succession. Petroushka's eyes popped open as he listened. It took him a moment to identify this time, this place. Indeed, it took longer and longer with each passing year. He checked his watch. The green numerals glowed on the bedside table. *Mierda*. He was already late.

He reached for his cigarette and swung out of bed. His legs were stiff as he walked to the balcony door. He breathed in the sharp odor of sweat blended with the tobacco and stale-rum vapor rising from the bedside glass.

Angel Calixto Garcia swung into a series of jumping jacks to get his blood moving, his small but wiry body falling into the rhythm of the motions. He started slow, then gradually moved faster and faster, his brown arms sweeping in quick arcs beside him until he once again felt completely alive. This also took longer these days. Breathing more heavily than was appropriate for a soldier, Angel pulled the heavy drapes back to let the morning light flood into the small room. Hot sun scalded his eyes. They were deep brown, dark and wet as olives, their pupils narrowed to black points against the brilliant light. *Another bright and beautiful day for the People,* he thought, surveying the early-morning hustle of activity below.

It was Zanja, a city within the city of Havana where the transplanted flower of socialism had never taken, not in thirty years of careful effort. Angel's eyes swept the street scene below. *Zanja.* Angel smiled. He heard a drum beat split the early-morning air into syncopated fragments as a musician practiced his instrument for one of the still-thriving clubs hidden away in Zanja's back streets.

Out in the harbor, Angel could see a few gray E-Bloc freighters. They were loading up with the sugarcane, and, Angel noted, there were fewer of them with each passing month. "Fuckers," he said in English as he watched the ships ride at anchor. *They are all yanquis.*

Kneading his aching arm muscles, he watched as the stiff-legged cranes began loading the ships. *I am too old for this.* But the hard, stringy muscles of his arms and lean, whiplike body uttered no surrender to age. If the spirit had lost some of its edge, the body remained an impressive machine of war. But that was necessary; Angel knew that only machines survived.

Most of his friends were dead, a surprising condition for a man just over forty-six. Less surprising, though, considering the way fate had reached out and struck down each one. Valdes in the Sierra Maestra, Almeida at the Bay of Pigs; Roque, who thought the Russians were gods, in an East German Speznaz camp; Peralta and Gonzalez in Angola. Che. His own grave was there in his mind, a hole in the ground, still empty, a date unwritten. It had been far easier when good and evil occupied a clearly delineated landscape. Now what was left worth dying for?

He didn't even work for Cuba anymore. Not directly, although his pay still bore the stamp of the DGI. Now, Angel lived from special assignment to special assignment, and meanings had lost their importance. The glory was dead, as dead and buried as his *compañeros*.

The Mexican assassination; Namibia; the Saudi embassy explosion. His most recent trip was very nearly his last: the transfer of delicate intelligence gear across the borders of America itself. He finished the stub of his U.S.-made cigarette and tossed it to the doves. They rushed it, and when the crowd of birds spread out once more, Angel saw that it had been eaten. Times were hard for everyone, it seemed.

What had it all been for? What use? His friends dead, his dreams dying. He could just see the Marina Hemingway district down by the docks. There was the future, and it was not one Angel was willing to die for.

The entire area was what the government called a "special economic zone." That translated to an area where dollars, *yanqui* dollars, were the only medium of exchange. It effectively excluded all Cubans except those who had squirreled away old dollars the way some had kept their ancient Fords and Chevrolets. The Revolution had come full circle. Begun as a battering ram to break down the barriers of capitalism, it was ending up by rebuilding them. Cuba was becoming the land of the *bisnero*, the black marketeer, once more.

Fuck. He watched as the dew steamed from the roof across the alley. The ringdoves brazenly circled on the balcony in hopes of breakfast. He smelled the thick, black coffee being brewed in the tiny kitchen down below and felt the hollow rumblings coming from beneath the hard muscles of his abdomen. He patted his stomach, feeling its unyielding, taut surface with satisfaction. *Not bad for 46.*

A soldier's breakfast of a cigarette and coffee would quiet his belly. No milk to soften its acid etch. He needed the stimulant. He'd gotten the call from the embassy last night, and that usually meant that Guryanov would be waiting for him. *Let them wait.* Starting the day with that pink-faced pig was bad enough without rushing. What good were the Russians anyway? All they did was use Cuba, use it like an old man uses a young whore. And now they didn't even pay.

Dressing in street-standard dark pants, white cotton shirt, and khaki jacket, Angel slipped the Ceska CZX automatic under his arm. The 9-mm was his prized possession and very much the tool of his trade. The leather holster was stained with the heat of three continents. Its comforting weight called out to something deep inside him, like the sight of a lit window at night. The CZX was, in a world of chaos and revolution, Angel's zero meridian, his Greenwich.

Checking the fit of the silenced weapon under his arm, Angel left the room and emerged into the thick, humid air. He let his nose lead him toward a small café. The Zanja drummer pounded his beat into the gathering heat of the morning. Angel found his own footsteps falling into the insistent rhythm of the drums.

The KGB's *rezidant* sat down at his desk and lit a cigar, letting the wheezing fan blow the rich smoke away, taking with it some part of his sweat. He was not a calm man, and this morning was no exception. Like a swimmer venturing into deep water, he had stopped, turned, and discovered that the way back was more distant than the dangerous channel before him. Chebrikov, of course, had seen to that. *They should have shot him while they could,* he thought. He looked at his watch. *Where is he?*

Oleg Guryanov had hurried off the morning's Aeroflot flight to Havana to be here in time. But where was that black-assed monkey? He unhooked his watch and placed it on his desk top, dial faceup so that he could see. The black plastic band pinched his soft skin. *Why are they always late?*

The intercom buzzed. "He is here," his secretary announced. Before Guryanov could reply, the heavy door swung open. *At last.* "Well. *Buenos días,*" said Guryanov as Angel walked in.

"*Stradvuyste,*" Angel replied. "*Kak tu prozhivitye?*"

"Quite well, thank you. Your Russian is still very good, Angel," the *rezidant* said with a small nod. "Better than your sense of time."

"My English ain't too bad either," he said, switching suddenly. Three months of intensive language exposure, three of field training, and a final three with the good comrades at Sluzhba Aktivnykh Meropriatiyi, the Active Measures branch of the KGB's First Directorate: his English had better be good.

Guryanov's shirt was splotched with sweat stains as he moved in his creaky leather chair, dark half-moons under each armpit. "You're late," he said.

Angel saw his sweat. It was odd. It wasn't that hot, was it? "I am here. What is it you wish to discuss?"

Guryanov didn't answer. Instead, he opened up a dossier, the one labeled *Petroushka*. Guryanov extracted a thick envelope and tossed it at the Cuban.

Angel slipped the contents, a Geological Survey sectional chart, out of the envelope and noisily unfolded it. He whistled softly. "This is not the Sierra Maestra, comrade. It is the Sierra Nevada. Perhaps you have given me the wrong package?"

"There is no mistake. You are going to California," Guryanov began. "You are to bring some equipment over for us again. We attach great importance to success. Even more than usual."

"To be sure. What is it you wish brought in?"

"Observation gear." Guryanov produced an enlarged copy of the Survey chart and opened it. "One large case, an antenna, and cabling. You will assemble it at one of these features." His stubby finger obliterated the symbol for a ranger tower. "You may choose any one of these three. A satellite link will be provided once you activate the device. Simple, yes?"

Angel sat back, his arms crossed over his chest. "I bring it over, put it together, and leave?"

"Not exactly," said Guryanov. "We want you to stay with it until a very specific event takes place. There is to be a flight demonstration, a test if you will."

"But if the satellite link is there, why do I have to be?"

"What if something comes loose?" Guryanov replied with a smile. "Once the test takes place, you are free to return by way of your normal route."

"Mexico again. Tell me more," said Angel.

"You will be sent in by way of the Gulf. I presume you remember your lessons from Angola?"

Angel had been hired by Chevron Oil to guard one of their oil wells in Angola. He had learned enough of the day-to-day operation to permit him easy and clandestine access to the United States through the oil-rig-clogged Gulf of Mexico.

"A fishing boat will leave you at one of three possible meets. There, depending on which connection we can make, you will be picked up by crew boat and taken ashore. The device will be completely sealed against the water."

"What happens when I get to shore?"

"A car will be made available. You will drive yourself to the site. You can use it to drive back across the border to Mexico or not. It is your choice."

He looked up at Guryanov. "And if something unfortunate should happen?"

"You will have your usual legend," said Guryanov, knowing that Angel had no reason to fear capture after delivering the device to HUMMER. "But again, this is very unlikely. You are not here because of your poor record, after all."

The "usual legend" could only mean Libya. That was a bit disturbing. The Libyans had become reckless of late. A poison-gas plant churning out weapons by the ton; a suspected parallel nuclear effort. They were reckless and undisciplined and wholly unpredictable. Smuggling delicate equipment was not something they would have been called upon by Moscow to do, was it? Angel hid his thoughts, put his two palms together, and bowed. "Then let us pray Allah wills success," he said.

"Yes," said Guryanov. "Let us both hope he wills it."

8

THE
CIRCLE
GAME

NOTHING was going right. As much as he liked the challenge, Barnes was exhausted from fighting the Phantom through its engineering test flight. The cockpit smelled of sweat, hydraulic fluid, and frying tube-era electronics. He had started the flight with a certain residual respect for the old war-horse; it was a combat veteran and he was not. Now, Barnes had no room for nostalgia. This veteran was trying to kill him.

The PC-1 hydraulic boost pump buried in the guts of the left J-79 turbine was intermittent, cutting in and then dropping off-line. One of three such pumps, its absence should have been a minor concern. The Phantom's control surfaces could be powered by the backup pump in the opposite engine. That was why there was a backup.

A red light blinked on the master caution panel. *Shit!* Barnes kicked the misbehaving pump off-line and watched the needle sag to just over 1,500 pounds. The backup system was not putting out full pressure. "Damn." It was precisely the repair Maintenance was supposed to have done.

Barnes brought the traitorous pump back on with a stab at the reset. Within three seconds, the red hydraulic-boost warning was glowing again. A small problem here, a minor squawk there, was one thing; this was turning ugly. Two of his three pumps were ailing. Only the utility pressure system was functioning normally. Barnes was under no illusions that it could make the Phantom fly. The failure annunciator flickered again.

"Goddammit!" Barnes felt the stick go slack in his grip. He punched the manual reset button on the secondary and watched the red light craftily wink dark. *Enough.* Barnes rolled the Phantom up on a wingtip and pointed the nose back across the Central Valley toward Mather Air Force Base. It was obvious that Maintenance had overhauled the hydraulics with a pen.

He leveled the wings and dialed in the canopy defog system as he began the prelanding drill: the J-79's rumbled back to flight idle, and the trim was set up for the penetration into Mather.

Barnes felt the Phantom sag beneath him, no longer pushed along by twenty thousand pounds of smoking thrust. The high sun streamed in through the canopy. Despite the air-conditioning, Barnes broke out into a sweat as he pressed the transmit switch on the throttle. "Hawk two seven, two five east, one for the penetration. Requesting a straight-in."

"Ah, negative, Hawk," Approach replied. "Straight-in is not approved. Traffic in the pattern. Report twelve miles out, left overhead break, landing Runway Two-Two."

"Rog." Suddenly the red PC-1 warning light flashed, followed close by with the double flash of a total control-boost failure. Somewhere an alarm buzzer sounded. "Fuck." He shoved the control stick full left. Nothing happened. Barnes felt a sudden hot fear wash up his neck when the F-4's nose didn't respond. *Calm down. What we need here is a little ice.*

His brain raced into high speed as he reviewed the ejection drill. If that red light did not extinguish in a real hurry, he would wrestle the nose away from population, yank that beautiful yellow handle, and let the airplane find its own way down.

A billowing white cumulus reared up dead ahead. Projected upon it was a solid circle of color, a glory with a tiny black dot at its center: the aviator's rainbow. As he watched, the colors and the dot swelled to form the shadow of the descending Phantom. *Start with a circle,* he told himself. It was the initializing ceremony he had learned from Dr. Tanai. He concentrated on the rainbow. *Step inside the circle.* His dark shadow suddenly ballooned as the Phantom *poofed* into the cloudbank. The air inside the cockpit turned strange and humid, but his inner ice was back. He felt the calm fall over him like cool water, his body relaxed but his senses extraordinarily alert. Barnes jiggled the loose stick. *Wake up, baby,* he thought.

"Hawk two seven," said Approach, "Mather wind is three two zero at six." A flood of light exploded around him as he burst into the clear. Mather's runways were dead ahead.

Let's do it, he thought, and shook the stick again as much to say "my airplane" as to test the loss of hydraulic boost. The double light was still flashing.

"Hawk two seven, did you copy that wind?"

"Stand by, Mather. We've got a little situation up here." He looked at the warning lights and the useless utility system's green. The F-4 was not an airplane, it was an unguided missile. One wing began a slow but noticeable drop. The control stick flapped uselessly from stop to stop. The airplane flew leadenly, still trimmed for descent. A gust of wind unbalanced his lift, and the bank steepened. He reached up and touched the cool metal trigger for the ejection seat once more. *Now?*

"Hawk two seven, Mather. What is the nature of the, ah, situation?"

"I said *stand by!*" With as much thought as it took to loose a bamboo arrow, a solution came to him. His thumb leaped to the speed-brake button. The right wing's drag board extended with a turbulent rumble and stopped its uncommanded roll. The Phantom staggered level once more. *See?* He was grinning behind the sweat. By running differential throttles and deploying the two wing-mounted air brakes, Barnes managed to slew the crippled Phantom away from the town of Carmichael. *That cuts down the body count,* he thought.

"Hawk two seven, if you read, go to channel three." It was the senior controller at the tower. It was the voice of home.

Barnes punched up button three. "Okay, Mather, Hawk two seven has a problem up here." Despite the adrenaline racing through his head and the dampness forming behind the oxygen mask, Barnes made his voice sound collected, almost bored.

"Roger, Hawk. Say the nature of your problem." The tower also sounded cool.

Barnes swallowed hard and spoke. "Hawk two seven just lost the power steering, guys, and things are a little grim up here. You might want to clear traffic for that straight-in I asked for. She won't handle worth a damn."

"Hawk two seven, are you declaring an emergency?"

"Negative!" Barnes knew it had been coming. He'd be buried in paperwork all week if he said those magic words. Then he remembered: the canopy was also raised by the hydraulic system.

Suppose he landed a little hard and something unfortunate happened? Jets, especially old broken jets, were remarkably easy to set on fire. He'd have a time getting out quickly, wouldn't he? Barnes pressed the transmit button again. "Ah, Approach, that might not be such a bad idea. Hawk two seven is declaring an emergency."

"Roger, Hawk," said Tower. "In that case, any runway you want is fine."

"Thanks," he said, "but it's a tad late." He was too close now for a straight-in approach. He would have to overfly the field, slew the stricken ship around, and line up once again. The fighter was trimmed level with lots of extra speed. But speed was his friend. There was no way he would slow the Phantom without a plan for wrestling it in one piece to the ground. Directly over the field, he looked down and saw the tiny, toylike fire engines scrambling along the taxiway.

"You are cleared to land any runway," said the calm voice of the approach controller.

"Hawk two seven is overhead. We'll try this once. If it doesn't feel good, we'll get it pointed somewhere and I'll take a hike."

"Hawk two seven, roger, and Colonel Braden is here."

"A real party. How come I didn't get an invite?"

"Barnes, you've got the boost reset on?" It was Braden.

"Hawk two seven is on reset, negative function. Sorry, Al, this is a job for Superman. You guys have a cape around there someplace?"

"Ah, negative, but we've got the equipment standing by for you. You know, the canopy might not come up if . . ."

"Roger," Barnes said. "I know. *Muchas gracias* for the warning, Al." He thumbed out the brake on the right wing and the Phantom lurched into a bank. "Hawk two seven on the break for Two-Two."

"If it doesn't feel good, Barnesy, I want you out of there."

"Rog." The F-4 swung in a wide, ungraceful curve. He looked down and saw the streets of Carmichael, then the open fields of the approach path. He saw his own street pass under the wing's leading edge, and the cluster of red-roofed apartments with number 24C somewhere in their midst. *I wonder if I get to check the mail today?*

"Okay, Barnes," said Braden. "Landing cockpit checks and reduce to approach speed. Check gear down."

"Hawk two seven," Barnes replied as he rammed the gear selector down. They were hydraulic. They shouldn't have extended. Maliciously, both red warning lights winked out, and the roar of the two-hundred-knot wind rushing through the landing gear filled the cockpit. P1 and P2 were back in business.

"Oh, just great." He could imagine what Maintenance would say: *Checks out perfect, Major Barnes.* They would look at him as though whatever happened was *his* fault. Oh, yes, indeed, he could hear that loud and clear. Worse, he had declared an emergency. Maybe it wasn't too late. He stabbed the transmit button. "Hawk two seven, cancel the equipment. We've got our boost back."

"No sweat, Barnesy, just hang with it. They haven't laid the foam yet anyway."

"Rog." Barnes let out his breath and sucked pure dry oxygen. He made a high-speed final to the runway. The approach end sped beneath the nose as he pulled the power back, letting the big jet settle in from a few feet.

Twin clouds of blue tire smoke blew from the landing gear as the old fighter ran along the concrete. Barnes reached down to the left side of his seat bucket and yanked on the drag-chute lever. A small explosion, one that always made him jump, sounded over the roar of the J-79s; it was the drag chute popping wildly in the 140-knot wind. The trucks raced after the slowing jet, catching up to it midfield, and paced it from a safe distance as Barnes made the turnoff to the ramp.

Barnes hesitated over the canopy lever for a moment, wondering what would happen, then pulled. The glass rose with a hiss of escaping air, and the hot kerosene breeze that was funneled in dried his sweat. His hand trembled slightly as he pulled the power levers on the two engines back and braked to a stop with his nose pointing right at the half-opened Maintenance hangar. *Start with a circle,* the voice of the master archer said again. "Fuck the circle," he replied. "I'll start with the maintenance officer's neck."

"Welcome back to Krypton, Superman," said Braden as Barnes stormed in. Colonel Braden sat behind his clear, meticulously kept desk, his eyes shrouded by deep folds he claimed came from squinting into too much high-altitude sunlight. He waived military formality, swatting his hand to indicate Barnes was to be seated. "Nice to see you," he said. "Glad you could stop by."

Barnes tossed the F-4's logs down onto Braden's desk. "Al," he said even before sitting down, "we have just got to get on the ball with those monkeys in Maintenance." His sage-green flightsuit was dark with sweat. "You'll notice this little piece of fiction is sprinkled with releases. It says that those P1 and P2 boosters were overhauled and checked out at full power."

Braden puffed a thick blue cloud of cigarette smoke. "I take it you have reason to think otherwise."

"What? Fuck yes. Those lazy sonsabitches never looked at those pumps. I checked. The paint on the hold-down nuts was nice and old. Nobody's yanked those pumps since fucking Kilroy was there. Something stinks here and it nearly had my ass this morning. I want the guy who signed off on this crap here and I want to find out what the living fuck is going on."

"Steady, Barnesy," Braden replied, taking a final drag and putting his cigarette down on an old piston-head ashtray. "I'm officially pissed off." Braden's deeply lined face screwed up in a look of distaste that accentuated its rough texture. "It may come as a shock, but I don't like the idea of trading one of my pilots for a twenty-year-old dog of an airplane. You should have punched out."

"Oh?" Barnes sat down heavily in the chair. "Would you?"

"I . . ." Braden stopped and reshuffled his thought. "We're not here to learn what *I* might have done. You *do* remember that a boost failure might leave the canopy down and locked for the duration, don't you?"

"I thought I could handle it."

"Ah, yes." Braden nodded. "It makes such a nice epitaph." He sat up straight in his chair. "But I'm glad you decided to drop by for a little chat. I've got a good news/bad news situation here I think you might be interested in."

"I'm listening," Barnes said warily.

"The good news is from Wing. They liked the way you handled that accident work up at HUMMER. Their pleasure is, of course, my pleasure."

"I bet. You're a real comedian, sir. If that's the good news, I think I better just head over to Maintenance and stick that guy's head up a tail pipe myself. That whole HUMMER business was a Charlie Fox from the getgo."

"Still, you kept all the pieces of paper in their rightful place. The FAA was happy. The NTSB was happy. The Air Force was happy. That makes me happy."

"And what's the bad news?"

"The bad news is also from Wing. Kind of funny how it works out that way. They want you TDY." It meant temporary duty elsewhere.

"Why? I mean," said Barnes, "what for? I've paid my dues. You can't—"

"Uh-uh. Wrong word, Barnes," Braden interrupted. "The word 'can't' has no place in this office. So let's cut the horsehockey and hang it out straight: there's a temporary reassignment in your future. Scott Air Force Base. One month teaching all you have learned about accident investigations to those fresh young Civil Air Patrol faces.

TDY starts next week. I think on the basis of your little flight today I will arrange for the time to be counted as flight duty so you won't lose out on pay."

"Scott?" For a moment, Barnes could not frame a response. "Al," he said finally, "what kind of bullshit is this? You know I hated that whole clusterfuck at HUMMER. How come I get to be so lucky?"

Braden kept his voice level. "I'm so sorry this makes you unhappy, Major. We try to keep everybody happy around here. Nevertheless, you are to be temporarily reassigned as an RMCT. That stands for 'rescue mission coordination trainer.' " Braden looked up as if to say, What? Are you still here?

"Me? But that's a job for some groundpounder who can't tie his shoes right in the morning. It's plain crud and you know it."

"We all get to eat some now and then," Braden said with icy command in his tone. Then, more warmly: "You need the break, Barnes. Your career in the Air Force needs you at Scott and away from things for a while." Braden smiled and shook his head. "Barnesy, you've got to trust that this is a compromise solution I went to bat for you on. Do what I say, go away for a month, don't get anyone pregnant, and come back. You'll see. Everything will stay rosy."

"Am I hallucinating or are you sweeping my tail through some shit? Is this crap over the wing you had me searching for when you had the frigging thing under wraps right here? Is that it?"

Braden sighed. "You started by pissing me off officially. You're starting to piss me off unofficially. This is not a debate. You are to be reassigned."

"Look, you owe me some straight shooting. Reassignments like this don't just come down like rain from Wing, right? So I believe you have some small amount of explaining."

Nobody's explaining diddly to me. "Look, one more time and then I throw you out, got it? You *will* assume direction of the search-and-rescue training course at Scott for a period of one month. You come back, I pin a medal for your hot-sticking the F-4, and life goes on. You have problems with that, mister, and I assure your ass that the next assignment you get will be the one originally suggested by Wing."

There was no way Barnes could mistake the absolute resolve in his commanding officer's words. But Barnes had a unique ability to tune out what he had no interest in hearing. "I don't think it could be much worse."

"Wrong," Braden replied. "Very very wrong. I, for one," he said, "was nearly alone in suggesting that you might not appreciate indefinite reassignment to Shemya, Alaska." Braden opened his desk drawer and removed a thin stack of paper.

"Alaska?" Barnes took the top sheet and stopped cold. It was an already signed reassignment order to the Air Force station at Shemya, and it had Barnes's name sprinkled in all the right places.

"Now, as for *owing* you something, Major, I don't recall that being part of any order of battle I was taught. When we're up in the air, let there be no bullshit between us. Down here it can't always be that simple. So it's your choice. Play it my way and things damp down a bit. Ninja wins. You fight it and Ninja's going to lose. Stone guaranteed."

Braden stood up from behind his desk. His deep-set eyes pinned Barnes to the spot. "Straight shooting. You stepped in a real pile of shit when you poked around and found what you *thought* to be the wing from the accident up in HUMMER last week. I honestly don't know why. What I do know is that I arm-wrestled Wing to get you a TDY to Scott. You had better believe it when I say *you* owe *me* on this one. Now get out of here and let me blister that wrench-monkey from Maintenance for the screw-up with your flight. Dismissed."

Barnes stood up automatically. "Al, you're all heart. Problem is, it's pure black."

"Out!"

Barnes felt his ears flatten from Braden's blast. He rode the shock wave right out the door.

9

THE
PHANTOM FLIGHT
OF SHAKEY
103

T was turning into one hell of a Friday afternoon. "You're sure, Captain?" said MacHenry. He could scarcely believe what he had just been told.

"I'm sorry, sir," said the legal affairs officer out at Davis-Monthan Air Force Base. "But without the insurance documents, we can't permit you in to inspect anything."

"Documents," MacHenry seethed.

"Yes, sir."

Barnes had been on target. Shakey 103, an old C-130 from Mather Air Force Base, had departed for the desert boneyard in Tucson. It had even arrived there. But now they wouldn't permit MacHenry in to see it. "Captain," he said, "I don't need *insurance! I'm* the FAA!"

His secretary peeked around the door. "Mr. MacHenry? Is everything all right?"

"No!" MacHenry picked up a pencil and flexed it between his fingers. It snapped. He swept the remains of the pencil off his desk.

"Okay, Captain," he said, his jaw tight. "I will take this up with Washington. If any evidence is destroyed, if so much as a single bolt comes up missing, I will personally hold you responsible. Is that clear?"

"Yes, sir," the man replied.

MacHenry slammed down the receiver. "Dorothy!" he roared, not realizing she still stood at the door to his office. "Get me the administrator and tell him it's important." Invoking the administrator of the FAA, an ex-admiral with impressive connections, was the organizational equivalent of employing an air strike to snuff out a barroom brawl. He didn't care. It usually took a few hours to climb the impressive thicket the FAA put around its top personnel. But not this time. In less than five minutes, he had one of the admiral's top aides on the line.

"I can *see* your bind," she said. The aide seemed to speak in singsong italics. "I'm *so* sorry, Mr. MacHenry. We can't, we *don't* have the authority to pursue this on our own. It would *have* to come from the administrator." The administrator, of course, was not in his office. It was late on a Friday afternoon. Her voice seemed to say, What did you expect?

"That's not good enough," he said. "This flight, Shakey one zero three? It's got some evidence on board. They plan to start scrapping the aircraft over the weekend. Our evidence will go with it unless you can get me in."

"That is a problem, isn't it?" she said. "All I can say is that it *has* to get the okay from the admiral. He'll be back in the office Tuesday morning, first thing, and I'll make *sure* he—"

"We'll lose this one if we don't act quickly," MacHenry broke in. "Tuesday is too late. I can catch a flight out to Tucson this evening and see it first thing tomorrow morning, but I need your help."

"I *see*. This is the HUMMER incident, isn't it?" she said.

A subtle alarm seemed to ring inside MacHenry. "Yes. Why?"

"Well, I'm looking at a copy of your *initial* report to Oklahoma City. Your eighty twenty form?" The sound of pages flipping could be heard cross-continent. "It *says* that the primary cause was 'continued operations into adverse conditions.' Am I *misreading* something here?"

How had they gotten hold of it in Washington so quickly? And why?

"No. That report was made on the basis of incomplete information. Since I filed it the whereabouts of some additional evidence has come to light. Now"—he cleared his throat—"can we proceed with the emergency authorization? Or shy of that, some kind of phone call from the administrator's office on our liability coverage?"

"I'm sorry, Mr. MacHenry. We're still processing your *first* report and now you come in with something *completely* different. Honestly, suppose we do what you ask and ten minutes later something *else* pops into your head? I know the administrator would agree with me. Let it settle. Don't rush to rejudge. I *promise* I'll take this up with him first thing when he gets back. You have my word. You'll hear from us by Wednesday."

When my wing will be scrap metal. "Much obliged for your attempts." And with that he gently returned the receiver to its cradle. *How did they get a copy so soon?* he wondered. He sat back in his chair and pushed away from the desk. The metal wheels rolled off the plastic rug protector with a lurch. *And why did they get a copy at all?*

"What was that all about?" asked Dorothy.

"What?" MacHenry sat up. "Oh. You know, nobody gets anywhere unless all the *T*'s get crossed." He consulted his file notes and punched in the number of the squadron office at the 104th out at Mather Air Force Base.

"Sometimes it makes you wonder whether we're supposed to do anything at all," said Dorothy.

"I'm starting to wonder that myself." The phone was answered even before MacHenry heard the first ring.

"What?" said the angry, distracted voice on the other end.

"Major Barnes? This is Brian MacHenry from the—"

"I know where you work, MacHenry. Look," he said, "this is kind of a bad time, okay? I'm in no mood for the, you know, social graces. In fact, I'm spring-loaded to the pissed-off position. Let me get back to you."

"Hang on just a second, Major. I'll be quick. I traced your Shakey flight all the way to Arizona. You were right. It landed at Davis-Monthan earlier today. The problem is, nobody is willing to let me take a look at it. I'm hoping you might have some insights on your fellow blue suiters."

"Forget it. My name is mud around this place."

"I don't know if it's real or imagined, but I'm getting a sense that someone wants that wing kept under wraps."

"You're not too dumb for a fed after all. I say Tango Sierra. You know what they're threatening *me* with? Shemya! That's Alaska in case you didn't recognize the name."

"I know where it is." *Threatening?* "Are you in some kind of trouble for reporting that wing?"

"Trouble? I was booked for the icicle harvest until my good buddy Al decided to be a nice guy, cut me a break, and throw me off flight status for a month instead. I guess it would be fair to say there's a spot of trouble over that little bit of good citizenship. You, my friend, are on your own."

"Back up," said MacHenry. "I understand the Air Force is unhappy about your finding the wing. What I don't understand is why. They've always cooperated with us before. I'm from the feds, remember? That puts us on the same side."

Barnes laughed. "Hey, big news. There are feds and there are feds. They might not put you in the know on everything." He stopped speaking for an awkward moment, then began again. "I don't know, MacHenry. Maybe this Cessna pilot was a DEA deal. Maybe the wing was stuffed with coke. Or cash."

"I checked that through the computer," MacHenry replied. "We always do that now. He was just a guy flying an airplane. He made a mistake and it caught up with him."

"I'll say. He should have stayed home and I should have kept quiet," said Barnes. "My advice to you is to drop this one. Unless you happen to like icicles."

"Barnes, are you sure you don't have some in I could use to get a look at that wing? Davis-Monthan may be the boneyard, but it's an Air Force boneyard."

"Forget it," Barnes said flatly. "For your own good, forget it. I just know the facts. I found a wing off a Cessna 172 that somebody up at

Wing wants bye-bye. You ran into your own brick wall. Go with the flow, MacHenry. Drop it."

"No, sir," said MacHenry. "No way on that at all. A pilot died in that crash, and if someone in the Air Force wants to keep that quiet, I can tell you right now that it isn't going to keep. No way." He calmed himself, remembering his gut feeling up at the HUMMER site that the Air Force had been involved. Why would someone at the Air Force care? To protect themselves against the discovery that they were somehow involved?

"Look," said Barnes, "if I had a magic wand I'd make it happen for you. There sure as shit's nothing better going down for me here. Braden's sending me off to reform school. That's a whole month away from flying. Do you know what that means?"

"All I know," said MacHenry, "is that I've got to get the wing off-loaded before the C-130 gets cut up for beer cans."

"That's what I like about you, MacHenry. You keep your eyes on the ball."

"It's the only way I know how to operate."

"Then let me ask you a question. If you're so fired up, why don't you just go there? You know, the direct approach?"

"You can bet that I would if they would let me on the base. They'd never let me by the main gate."

"I hate to think a sergeant with a polished helmet was all that was keeping you from, you know, your mission."

"But it is."

"Groundpounders," said Barnes as he looked down at the maintenance logs for the Phantom he had flown. The paperwork for the T-33 peaked out from beneath them. He whistled. "Sheeit," he said, and laughed. He brushed the F-4's records aside. "Damn."

"What's the joke, Major?"

"No joke. There is a way, MacHenry." *Don't do it!* He shook his head. That inner voice sounded just like Al Braden. He gave the reproachful ghost the finger and continued, "I really think there is. But it might be just a little bit too sporting for you." If it was a risk for

MacHenry, Barnes himself had no fears. He was already off flight status for the next month. What could they do to him?

"Name it, Major. I don't have time for games."

"Right. No games. You want to see that wing? Why don't we sort of pay a personal visit to the mother? I've got the way if you've got a little slice of, you know, the right stuff."

"Barnes . . ."

"No. Really. How long would it take you to get from Oakland out here to Mather?"

"How long?" What was he getting at? "About an hour and a half. Maybe two if there's traffic on I-80. Why?"

"Because it just so happens that T-Bird Air is scheduled for an afternoon departure from the scenic California Central Valley for an evening arrival at the lovely but haunted Davis-Monthan Air Force Base. You want a ticket, Mr. MacHenry? They're cheap. For you, free."

"You're serious? You can legally do this?"

Barnes ran his finger down the flight schedule on his clipboard. "Says right here I'm supposed to check out a repaired aircraft this afternoon. Doesn't say how long or how far to go in the process. Think of it as my last fling before I spend a month with the groundpounders. I think we can go take a look at old Shakey for you. I mean, why not?"

"If you are absolutely certain that this is legal. I can't get caught up in anything that remotely smacks of being on the fringe."

"It's completely legit. Meet me at the main gate in an hour and a half. I'll sign you in for a follow-up conference on our mission up in HUMMER last week. Since I'm about to be an instructor in search-and-rescue coordination, I think it highly appropriate that we meet. As for the flight, I presume, as one of the early birds from the golden era of aviation, you are checked out for jets? Life-support certificate current? Altitude-chamber checkout? Ejection chit? Your papers, you know, in order?"

"They're in order, Barnes. They say I'm legal to instruct you."

Barnes chuckled. "Oh, well! That's even better! You just show up and we'll have a little training mission. Deal?"

"I'll see you in an hour and a half," MacHenry said, and hung up.

Dorothy looked up as MacHenry hurried through the outer office, his flight case in hand. It was very strange. She had never seen him put in less than the normal workday, and she had never seen him in any sort of a rush. He was always so well planned. But this? "Early day?" she asked.

He stopped as he grabbed his tan windbreaker. "Nothing more that can be done from here. I'll see you Monday. Have a nice weekend." He snatched his battle-scarred Polaroid from the hat shelf. Barnes was giving him one shot at the evidence. It might prove to be the only one.

"You have a nice weekend, too," she replied as she returned to her typewriter. Then, as he disappeared, she called after him. "And try and have a little fun for a change!"

10

TIME

AND

TIDE

T HE growl of a heavy marine diesel died into the night. Angel shivered uncontrollably despite the warm Gulf air. His coveralls were drenched, clinging to his skin like a thin sheet of ice. *Bastards,* he thought, his teeth chattering. *Incompetent bastards!* When had he begun to trust in others? Trust was for other men. Dead men. He had very nearly joined their ranks.

Global Marine Platform 49 stood eighty-five miles off Morgan City, Louisiana. It was little more than a steel hypodermic needle jabbed deep into the rich gas pockets underlying the Gulf of Mexico. Standing forty feet above the waves, the lower valve deck was topped by a helicopter pad and a small trailer used by maintenance technicians. Their visits were infrequent. It was why, after all, this place had been selected. The transfer of Angel and his bulky cargo to this isolated place should have been the easiest part of his journey. Amazingly enough, given the haste with which the operation had been laid on, the preliminary steps had all gone as planned.

The Cuban trawler arrived at Global Marine 49 the second day's sail from La Fe. Threading the hazardous gaps between the drill rigs and production platforms, the fishing boat went about its business with undisguised efficiency; the steel legs of the platforms were home to swarms of fish, and they took on hundreds of pounds at each spreading of the nets.

But the rubber-coated case in the number two fish hold distinguished the Cuban vessel from hundreds of other similar craft. No one on board, least of all Angel, knew exactly what it contained. The heavy backpack shape had enough gasketed ports in its skin to make Guryanov's claims for it believable.

They arrived at Platform 49 well after dark. The trawler's captain, a commander in the Cuban Self-defense Forces, swept the horizon with his starlight binoculars. American music beamed from FM stations in New Orleans played on the trawler's radio as they drifted under steerage power toward the platform's waterline.

The platform's boarding catwalk was dark with seaweed and encrusted with barnacles as it appeared, then disappeared beneath the rhythmic Gulf rollers. Angel watched it for a few moments, then realized what he was seeing. The metal grating was half-drowned. They had arrived on an incoming tide.

The trawler drifted a boat-hook's distance away from the platform's boarding level. "Crew boat!" hissed the watch up on the bridge. His light-intensifying binoculars revealed a low-slung vessel approaching from the direction of the shore.

The captain turned to Angel. "We cannot wait. You must go."

Angel watched the grate as the waves sloshed over it, then turned to the rubberized case sitting on deck. "Wait until I catch hold of the rail," Angel said quickly, "then toss the box over. Lightly, *compañero,* very lightly." He remembered Guryanov's warning against handling the "device" roughly. That could be true of electronics, couldn't it? The engines of the crew boat could now be heard. It was getting very close.

The trawler drifted against the platform with a sudden lurch and a grinding of steel on steel. *"Vaya!"* Angel vaulted over the spray rail and landed, nearly slipping on the weed-slickened grate. White water foamed at his feet as it drained through the open decking. The first wave rushed him from the darkness. He saw the trawler's hull rise up, a dark wall looming high over his head. The water rose around his legs. The wave struck and pinned him to the pipe rail before he could harden his grip. The water surged to his chest and then, as the wave passed, it hissed away at his feet.

"Now!" The black rubberized case came tumbling across the gun-wales, its hundred-pound mass making the metal walk shudder as it struck. The trawler reared up again, and Angel hugged the case as the waters rose over his head, the blackness of the device merging with the blackness of the Gulf waters. Under water, he heard the trawler's engine cough and the propeller begin to spin as he grimly clutched his cargo, holding his breath. He felt a moment of panic, losing all sense of up and down in the inky darkness of the heart of the wave.

Holding, holding, holding his breath, Angel felt for the shoulder straps. His chest started to burn as the oxygen in his lungs ran out. He heaved the box to his back as he held on to the drowned rail. His lungs shouted for air as he let out what breath he had left in short, measured bursts. Though his chest felt like exploding, he did not let go of the black case.

The deep, roiling turbulence within the wave shoved at him and his cargo until he lost all sense of the edge of the catwalk. It might be here. It might already be behind him, and instead of the wave's passing there would be the endless blind tumble to the bottom. *Pass, you whore!* he silently screamed into his clenched teeth, his fingers beginning to loosen as the brain cried for air. Tiny rivulets of water now crept by his clenched teeth, his body betraying him, demanding a breath. *Open your mouth and breathe!* His lips parted as though they belonged to another man's face. *Breathe!*

Angel's ears popped as the water began to fall away. His hair! He could feel the surface. His eyes! Popped open wide, above the waters now! Still crouched over, clutching the heavy box, his nostrils snor-kled and he gasped, drawing a breath so hard and deep and involuntary he had water down his throat before he could turn off the reflex.

Air! He spat out the water angrily and sucked in four lungs' worth as the big roller disappeared. Already he could hear the sound of breaking water rushing at him. He wrenched the heavy box up the ladder. He must escape the rising tide! Another heave, another step. The next wave struck, smaller than the last. Another heave, another step. Angel now kept his head above the waves as he slowly, painfully climbed up the wrack-covered ladder.

He spared a moment to look around and to rest his shoulder. The trawler was making for the southeast side of the platform, using the bulk of its steel to come between it and the unexpected crew boat. The two vessels performed a minuet of deception as Angel made his way higher, above the reach of the dark waves. The American crew boat passed so close by that Angel could see men moving about its upper decks, and see the water wash over her low stern plates. The exhaust from its twin stacks passed over him as the boat, occupied with some other matter, droned out toward the open Gulf.

Angel heaved his load onto the trailer deck. Below him, the rising tide had swallowed the catwalk completely. *Trust!* The thrum of the Cuban trawler's main engines erupted behind him, startling Angel into reaching for the silenced CZX automatic nestled in the waterproof tool case at his waist. *Nerves. Calma te, Angelito, calma te.* He crouched beside the trailer door, not wishing to offer a dark profile against its stark whiteness. He yanked on the salt-crusted handle and the door swung open. He pulled the heavy case inside and shouldered himself out of the wet coveralls. His legs were shaking as he stepped out of them and kicked them into a corner. *Bastards!*

He fell into the damp bunk and looked over at the heavy container he had just risked his life for. It was a rectangle of deeper black against the unlit walls of the trailer's interior. "I hope you are worth all of this." It also reminded him that even well-planned operations were fragile things, always at the mercy of the unexpected. He vowed not to be surprised again. *What could be inside?* he wondered. It felt solid, not the least like a collection of parts so much as one, big part. Of course it would have been well padded, but padding was light. Where did its weight come from?

He sat back on the damp bunk. As he listened, the trawler's engines faded into the warm Gulf night. His body began to relax, but his eyes remained wide open. Angel was alone, alone and on a mission. If he lived, it would be by his own hand. If he died, he would have no one else to blame. It was, he knew, an agreeable state of affairs. It was the nearest thing to freedom he had ever known.

Not Guryanov, not Fidel himself, could make Petroushka do something that violated the operational demands of the mission. He felt the umbilical of their authority snap. He was a weed, and a weed didn't need cultivation. A weed survived on its own.

11

SCHOOLROOM IN THE SKY

MAC HENRY arrived at the main gate of Mather Air Force Base and braked to a stop. The guard-booth door opened and Barnes emerged, his back to MacHenry while he spoke to the airman inside.

"Hey, you don't have to believe me," Barnes said to the MP in the booth, "you can ask her yourself." Barnes turned to MacHenry. "Well, well." He squatted down by MacHenry's open window, his sunglasses hanging from a bright red cord around his neck. He rested his hands on the sill, his blue eyes bluer from the bright summer sky. "Looks like teacher finally decided to show." Overhead, a flight of four F-15s thundered into the pattern, breaking sharply for an in-trail landing.

Barnes turned back to face MacHenry. "I thought you might have lost interest, Mr. MacHenry. I was just about to give up on you. I can hardly wait to start our little training session."

MacHenry noticed that Barnes was standing between him and the guard. The airman couldn't have seen him, or identified him, if he wanted to. "Shall we cut the training business?" he said to Barnes.

"I'm here for one thing. I suggest we get on with it if that's still the case."

"My, my, is that how you used to treat Wilbur and Orville when you taught them how to fly jets?" Barnes stood up and put his hands on his hips, watching the four fighters roll out. "Yeah, well, I'm not too damned pleased myself. A month off flight duty is a long time to crawl in the dirt. This little adventure is going to be the highlight of an otherwise drab thirty days." He looked back down at MacHenry. "I, for one, intend to savor the sucker."

Another car honked as it pulled in behind MacHenry's Ford. Barnes trotted over to the Ford's passenger door and opened it with a squeal of misaligned metal. "Hey, nice car, MacHenry," he said, and got in. "What do they give, you know, the low-ranking bastards? Skateboards?"

MacHenry put the car into drive and they moved away from the guard station. "I hope this is all on the up-and-up." He looked up into the sky. The afternoon sun was still a respectable distance from the western horizon. "I'd like to get there while there's still some light to see."

"Eyes on the ball, MacHenry. You're a real tiger." Barnes slammed the door shut. "I've got a spare flightsuit picked out back in the locker room. I'll show you where to park."

MacHenry swung out onto the base perimeter road.

"Next right." Barnes nodded at the squadron office building. "Next to that beautiful Jaguar over there."

"The old car over there?" MacHenry asked innocently.

"Wherever you'd like."

MacHenry pulled in close to the green XK. Before he could open his door, Barnes was out and standing between his beloved Jaguar and MacHenry's leprous Ford. "Watch the paint, okay?" he said.

Barnes led him inside to the lockers where a row of sage-green flightsuits hung on a metal rack. Fiberglass flight helmets sat above them in a row as in a headhunter's trophy room, each trailing wires, hoses, and straps.

"Okay." Barnes surveyed the sage-green Nomex flightsuits. "This one should be big enough. It better be. It's the biggest one we have."

Fighter pilots, MacHenry thought as he put one leg into the slippery fabric. *They were always the little guys. Not like transport men.* Zippered in, MacHenry surveyed the helmets next. "I imagine I won't have trouble finding one of these that's big enough."

"Much better." Barnes nodded at him appreciatively as he handed him a helmet. "Now you look like a pilot." MacHenry was fully dressed in the regalia of the 104th Fighter Interceptor Squadron.

"I'm not used to wearing these things." MacHenry pulled the chin strap tight and experimented with the tinted faceplate, running it up and down on its center track. He left it up and screwed down the friction lock to keep the perspex from dropping. The helmet made his head feel as though an unbalanced fishbowl had been planted on his shoulders.

Barnes looked him up and down and nodded, trying to look grave. "Yep. You look like a real pilot there, MacHenry," Barnes said to the transformed FAA official. "Who would have guessed the truth? Mild-mannered B. J. MacHenry, truth, justice, and all that, has become, you know, Captain Ace Migbane, crack death-dealing jock of the 104th. The uniform becomes you."

MacHenry raised a single eyebrow behind his faceplate. "You think there might be a future in this?"

"Nobody would mistake you for a bus driver. Now, since you're all dressed up, I believe we have someplace to go."

Barnes opened the door for him and they both walked out onto the blistering-hot ramp. The tarmac oozed underfoot as they went. A refueling truck was parked by the wing of the camouflaged T-33. A small ground crew stood by it. Heat waves shimmered across the surface of the black ramp.

MacHenry felt an immediate bead of sweat develop on his forehead on a spot made completely inaccessible by the heavy white helmet. His head bobbed with his stride as he followed Barnes out to the jet. "I remember these when they were new," he said as he approached the sheer green wall of the small jet's hull. "Are you sure it's got one more flight left in it?"

"She better have two," Barnes replied. "Don't jump to any conclusions just because she looks old, MacHenry. This one's a little different. She's got a tiger in her tank."

The AT-33 was a derivative of the Shooting Star, the Korean-vintage P-80. Used for years as a general liaison aircraft and advanced trainer, it proved to be too good a design to send out to pasture. Her J33 turbine had been overhauled and uprated, her old, heavy, tube-filled radios torn out and stacks of modern avionics and ECM packages installed. Aerodynamic modifications gave her more speed and maneuverability. In the right hands, the reborn T-Bird could be deadly.

"Whose air force are we flying for?" MacHenry looked at the unfamiliar paint scheme and flag painted on the remanufactured jet's tail.

"Ah, *señor,* we fly today for the glorious Aero Fuerzas de Ecuador."

"That will be different."

The T-Bird's canopy stood open, hinged by a massive gas strut. Should they need to eject, it would also blow it free. MacHenry looked at it and thought, *Never.*

Barnes waved him up the boarding ladder. "Up we go. Don't touch anything until I get up there. You take the back and just sit down. I'll be up right behind you to get you settled in. Watch out for the armrests."

MacHenry put one hand on the boarding ladder and pulled it back quickly. He could have sworn he heard a sizzle.

"Don't forget your gloves," Barnes said as he walked off to preflight the aircraft. "And watch out for those armrests."

MacHenry slipped on the fire-resistant gloves and climbed the ladder to the top. He looked down into the narrow aft cockpit. It looked awfully small. *I'm never going to fit inside this thing.* He looked back at Barnes. "Armrests? Why is that?" MacHenry asked, eyeing the padded rests. They looked innocent enough.

Barnes stopped and shook his head, his hands on his hips. "Man, are you sure you want to do this? They fire the ejection seat, that's why. Now, if you'll just get in and wait for the stewardess to give you your safety briefing, we can get this operation moving."

MacHenry put one foot over the canopy rails and stepped into the cramped rear cockpit. "Okay to step on the seat?"

Barnes gazed up at him with a look of disgust. "This is not one of your corporate barges, MacHenry. Kick the cushion up with your heel and sort of scrunch down. Strap in and watch out for the two red pins on each side of the seat. You pull those and you're going to solo real quick. Got the program?"

"Okay." MacHenry did as he was told, feeling as if he were settling into the jaws of a mousetrap ready to spring. His shoulders spanned from rail to rail, and his legs extended invisibly beneath the instrument panel in front of him. He wondered what would happen if he really needed to eject. The panel looked ideally positioned to slice off his legs at the knee. He pulled the straps down over his shoulder and clicked them into the lap belt. He and the parachute and the ejection seat were now one neat package, ready to fire. The image of a basket of laundry tumbling from the sky came to him. He looked at the red safing pins on the ejection seat. Maybe he'd just leave them in.

Barnes completed his walkaround check, stowing the red landing gear pins in one of the T-33's tiptank compartments. He scrambled up the ladder. "Now be careful," he said as he pulled the safing rods from MacHenry's ejection seat and checked the tightness of his harness straps. "Remember: if I say *eject* three times, you raise your armrest, pull that trigger, and blow. If you ask me why, you're going to be talking to yourself. Got it?"

MacHenry eyed the hanging ejection seat safeties. "I'd just as soon you put those pins back in, Barnes."

"Leave them? Not if we had to take a hike, you wouldn't." He sat down and snapped on the ground master switch, examining the fuel status. Theatrically shaking his head, he shut down the power and descended to the ground again. "Over here." He motioned for the ground-crew chief standing in the shade of the fuel truck. "Got a discrepancy here, Schmidt," Barnes said, reading the name tag on the airman's uniform.

"Sir?" the ground-crew chief replied, puzzled.

"This checkout flight calls for fifty-two hundred pounds of fuel. I'm showing just over two thousand. Not good, Schmidt, not good. You want to get your guys over with the truck or should I call tower and cancel?"

"Sir!" the poor airman ruffled through the many pink sheets attached to his clipboard. "Sir, my sheet calls for a one-hour load for an engineering test flight. We filled the wings and left the tips dry, Major. This fuel is coming out of the ferry company's account, so we were told to go easy."

"Schmidt, it's getting late. If you have problems with my order, we'll just scrub the test and take it up with Colonel Braden. I really don't much feel like flying today after your friends over at Maintenance nearly had my ass in that F-4. Now, what say there, Schmidt, old pal, are we in business or do we do it the hard way?"

The airman hesitated, shuffling his papers in the vain hope of discovering the correct column of figures next to the right tail number. He had already heard about the foul-up with Maintenance this morning. He was not about to twist the tiger's tail again. North Air Transport, the interim owners of the little vest-pocket fighter, would pick up all the fuel tabs for the trip to South America. Still, there was no authorization on any of his papers to tank up the AT-33 beyond . . .

"What's your problem, Schmidt? Are they taking fuel out of your pay?"

Who gives a fuck? Schmidt concluded. "No problem, sir. It must be a misprint on the pink sheet. We'll top you off in a minute." Schmidt ran back to the low-slung refueler and marshaled the plane guard with his fire extinguisher to stand by during the pumping of the JP-4.

Fifteen minutes later, Barnes snapped the ground master back on and read a full 5,285 pounds of fuel. *Should be enough,* he thought. "Very nice," he said. "Very nice." Barnes hopped into the front cockpit.

"MacHenry, how do you hear?" he transmitted over the internal system. He looked to his upper left, into the rearview mirror. Adjusting it to fall on MacHenry's fumblings with the intercom cord, he unplugged his own, raised it above his head, and executed a graceful dive with it into its appointed socket.

Oh. There it is. MacHenry discovered the two small holes in the bottom right of the instrument panel, nearly hidden by the stack of modern avionics.

"And now, MacHenry? How do you hear?"

"Five by five, Barnes."

"Five by five? Is that what I heard?" A chuckle rumbled through the intercom. "Just say, you know, 'okay' or 'peachy' or something. I wasn't born when 'five by five' was invented, MacHenry. Now, I'm going to start this old engine, so I'd like you to watch for limits on the tail. We want to stay under seven hundred degrees or we become crispy critters. Going down?" The canopy slowly dropped down with a hiss of escaping gas and a high electric whine.

MacHenry scrunched his broad shoulders together as Barnes locked the canopy into place. *A mousetrap with a view,* he thought, trying to find the exhaust-gas temperature needle in the forest of dials in front of him.

"Okay," Barnes said to himself. *Fuselage tank OFF*. He began the startup drill, a litany as prescribed and definitive as any church ceremony. *Starter switch is ON, one, two, three seconds and ignition to normal*. A faint whine built behind them as the Allison came up through 9 percent. *Starting fuel AUTO*. A muffled *whumpf!* shook the T-33 as the turbine revs leaped up through 27 percent.

MacHenry searched the gaggle of instruments. They all looked like familiar faces popping out of the crowd on some foreign street. He finally found the tiny temperature gauge on the far right of his panel; it was already moving. Barnes had started the little turbojet before he had even found the right instrument to watch. He saw the throttle move, and noticed a new slot had been cut for an afterburner. "Barnes," he asked, "does this thing really have an afterburner?"

"A-firm," Barnes replied. "Okay. We have a good start, BJ. I'm going to call you that. It's easier than MacHenry, and I don't think you're the kind of guy who likes to be called Brian," Barnes said as he saw the EGT drop back to the green.

BJ! MacHenry made a rapid mental search and could not, not ever, remember being called BJ, not even when he himself was a rank, wet-eared copilot keeping out of the captain's hair in the nose of a drafty DC-3.

Throttle IDLE, starting fuel is OFF, and we are good for a disconnect. Barnes looked out to the ground crew and put his two fists in plain sight and pulled them apart in an unplugging motion. *Battery switch ON, generator ON, loadmeter looks good, and speed brakes are UP.* Barnes went through the drill and dialed up the Mather clearance frequency on his number one comm. The red transmit light winked on as he made his initial call-up. "Hawk flight, ready with the numbers, checkout cross-country."

"Ah, Mather Ground, roger. And Hawk, how are you filed? We show you as a local engineering test hop."

"Negative. Don't sweat it, Ground. We'll get our routing from Center on climbout," he replied a little too easily.

Ground didn't seem to care. "Roger, Hawk, advise ready to taxi."

MacHenry heard and arched his eyebrow. Something was not right; that was clear by Barnes's little exchange. He was about to say something when Barnes broke in.

"Ground, Hawk two three's ready to roll."

"Roger, Hawk. Taxi via the parallel Alpha, Runway Two-Two."

"Over to Alpha. Runway Two-Two, Hawk two three."

They fast-taxied by the row of light-gray, low-slung fighters of the 104th. The F-15s looked mean and purposeful, like a gun cabinet filled with exquisite rifles. Beyond them sat the F-4 that had nearly killed him. Two techs had their heads buried in an access panel. It looked like a circus lion act, where the trainer put his head inside the big cat's mouth. Barnes wasn't sure whom he would root for. He realized he had heard nothing over the intercom for some time. "Hey, BJ, you still with me? Kind of quiet back there."

"Still here," MacHenry replied, feeling very much the passenger. "What was that all about? The filing business? I thought you said—"

"No sweat," he said quickly. "Hey, BJ, forget the paperwork for once and kind of watch for anything a little wacky on the takeoff, will you? This little hummer got pranged pretty good on landing, and two sets of eyes looking isn't going to hurt any. How's your oxygen?"

Wacky? "Good flow," MacHenry replied, seeing the small regulator diluter lever positioned to supply his mask. *Pranged?* He suddenly realized what Barnes had just said. *Pranged?*

Barnes jabbed the castering nosewheel over with the application of the brake, and the 11,000 feet of Runway 22 stretched ahead of them. *Lineup check.* He advanced the throttle and the Allison began to howl. A quick scan of his instruments later, he brought it back to idle. *Good.* He pressed the transmit switch on the stick. "Hawk two three at Two-Two and ready to roll," he called to Tower.

"Hawk two three is cleared for an immediate, traffic on short final. Can you hack it, Ninj?"

"Rog," Barnes replied. "Here we go," he warned MacHenry as he released the brakes and ran the throttle to full open. "Hawk's turning and burning." The power came up as the flaps dropped to takeoff position. The turbine spooled up into a high-pitched scream and the runway markers began to sweep by, faster, faster. Soon, they were a continuous white blur.

One by one the needles in front of MacHenry came alive, rising into green arcs as the noise of the Allison rose to thunder. The seams in the concrete runway transmitted a rapid-fire drumbeat as the jet burned down the runway. At 85 knots, Barnes tugged on the stick and the nosewheel left the ground. At 125, the pounding of the runway fell away as the T-33's mains lifted free. Barnes hit the gear switch and the *thump thump* of the wheels striking home in their uplocks shook the airframe. At 140 knots the flaps crept back up into the wing's trailing edge, and Barnes leveled the aircraft at the magnificent height of twenty feet over the blurring concrete. He kept the T-Bird low, all the while accelerating with every bit of the 4,500 pounds of thrust the Allison put out. By the end of the runway, the airspeed indicated 250 knots. "Hey, BJ. Do you get nosebleeds?"

"No. Why?" But there was something in Barnes's voice that made MacHenry grab on to his seat.

"Ready? Pull!" Barnes laughed as he hauled the rebuilt old warrior into a vertical climb. "How do you lahk dee view, *señor?*"

MacHenry, on his back now, looked up beyond Barnes's helmet and saw nothing but empty sky. He craned his neck and looked straight up through the canopy as the ground fell away.

Passing two thousand feet, Barnes rolled around the vertical, first left, then right, then pushed over into a more comfortable attitude. *Not bad!* he thought with some surprise. This T-33 was a real hummer.

MacHenry let go of the metal seat bucket. "Is that standard takeoff procedure, Major?"

Barnes shook his helmet. "Ah, negative. This is an engineering test flight. Got to keep it nice and easy, right? Otherwise I'd really wring it out." Barnes slapped the stick full right, corkscrewing the jet three times in a fast aileron roll before MacHenry could frame a cry of protest. "Like that."

MacHenry eyed the ejection trigger. Maybe it wouldn't be so bad after all.

"And Hawk two three, Mather. Contact Departure on three four eight point four. They'll have your clearance. Nice day, Hawk." The tower frequency died into silence as Barnes punched up the new radio setting. They were already through eight thousand feet. "Hey, BJ," Barnes said as he leaned his head over to the left. "Take a look down at our eight. Look familiar?"

Indeed it did. They were already over the Sierras east of Sacramento. Mono Lake was off the left wing, and below was HUMMER MOA. MacHenry tried to see the particular ridge that had snagged the Cessna. Could it be only last week? He felt a small touch of vertigo as the distance between the climbing T-33 and the crash site below suddenly telescoped.

"Best fishing in the state right down there, BJ. You and I ought to go sometime."

MacHenry smiled as he noted that Barnes had undergone a transformation: he was no longer a prankster. Instead, Barnes sounded crisp and professional. "Maybe after we get this mess straight," MacHenry replied. "If you still want to, that is."

"Sure thing, BJ. When all this gets settled we'll . . ." he said, but the radio crackled into life.

"Hawk two three, Oakland Center, contact Edwards now on three one eight point one, so long." Barnes entered the new frequency, but before he could speak, the radio boomed in his headset. A commanding bass voice left no doubt that its owner was in complete control.

"Hawk two three, this is Edwards, confirm your destination."

"Ah, Hawk two three is an engineering checkout, landing Davis-Monthan and return," Barnes replied.

"Radar contact for Hawk two three. And Hawk, we have the ATC ticket on you but nothing on this flight from Mather. Say type aircraft."

Damn! The controller at Edwards sounded suspicious. "Must have slipped through, Edwards. And Hawk is an Alpha Tango thirty-three on loan from Ecuador," Barnes replied, not realizing how impossibly odd the words he just spoke sounded to the controller.

"Ah, roger, Hawk, you say a T-33 headin' to Ecuador?"

"By way of Davis-Monthan. That's affirmative."

"Roger, Hawk. We'll check this out on our end. Maintain heading for now and remain clear of the Complex four Alpha MOA. It's hot to two eight thousand. Next time get the flight plan together, mister. We can't have anybody cruising on through here. And say the full call sign."

Barnes searched the panel in front of him for the FAA registration number. He found the small tag and pressed the transmit switch. "Hawk two three is flying November two triple one Quebec." *Shit!* Barnes thought, *those picayune little knob-twisters are going to stick their noses in.* That increased the chances that somebody, somebody like Col. Al Braden, was going to find a little report on his desk on Monday. *Screw it,* he thought. *I'll be on a C-141 to Indiana by then anyway.*

The Edwards controller looked at the data sheet from Air Traffic Control. It mentioned under "remarks" that the flight had been filed as a return-to-service test flight. *This is one hell of a round-robin checkout for some taco T-33,* he thought. He tapped in the "N2111Q" into the CRT. The computer accessed the civilian records at FAA Oklahoma City, and in a few seconds the registered owner of the Lockheed jet scrolled across the tube.

He whistled when the name North Air Transport came up on the green screen. He hadn't been at Edwards for three years without knowing that NAT was not exactly what it seemed. He blanked the screen and stood up. "Take it for a while, will you, Hank?" he asked the off-duty specialist. Walking down the spiral stairs of the tower cab to the offices below, he looked up the number for the CO out at Mather. "Braden," he said as he tapped the number into the phone and waited while it rang.

"Colonel Braden here."

"This is the watch chief down at Edwards," he began. "I wonder if you could help us out?" Maybe he could shed some light on why one of his squadron's pilots was out joyriding an Ecuadorian jet registered to North Air Transport, a firm whose sole customer, as far as he could tell, was the Central Intelligence Agency.

12

THE BONEYARD

T HEY were an hour and forty-five minutes into the flight to
Davis-Monthan when the sun dropped below the tallest mountains to the west. Long, saw-toothed shadows spread out
across the brown desert floor eighteen thousand feet below.
The air was lulling, smooth as the deep blue velvet it now
resembled.

MacHenry saw the low-fuel light wink on his tank-selector panel. It
seemed unnaturally bright against the pastels of the desert dusk. He
reached over, spun the instrument brightness control down, and tabbed
the intercom to life. "Barnes, are you happy with the fuel situation?"
MacHenry never liked to land with less than an hour's reserve in the
tanks.

Barnes's helmet swung away from the sky and back down into the
cockpit. "Huh," he said, somewhat surprised. "Really uses the stuff,"
he replied. The Allison was burning just under three hundred gallons
per hour at their present speed. He jotted down a few numbers on his
kneeboard, looked up to recheck both the fuel and the readings from
their DME (distance measuring equipment). "It looks okay on my
board," he said with a nod of his white helmet. "We'll start our descent
in another"—Barnes did a rapid mental calculation, balancing dis-

tance, speed, and fuel burn as easily as a practiced juggler—"three minutes."

MacHenry watched the numbers on the fuel totalizer fall. Arriving at Davis-Monthan AFB with just enough fuel to taxi to the ramp seemed not to disturb Barnes at all. "Well, I'm not happy with it," he muttered to himself, though the intercom sent it forward into Barnes's helmet as well.

"Just relax, BJ," said Barnes. "You want to fly it? I'll take another look at the numbers." Barnes wagged the stick to draw MacHenry's gloved hand to the button-studded grip.

"Okay. I've got it." The FAA man took the little fighter's stick, feeling its enormous sensitivity. Despite the dead-still air, the wings wobbled and the nose dipped slightly as he overcontrolled. MacHenry rested his arm on his knee, trying to *think* the control motions rather than move them.

"Two fingers, BJ, don't ham-fist it."

The T-Bird wobbled in all three directions under MacHenry's hand. Barnes looked up and into the rearview mirror. "Hey, BJ, whither are we bound?"

MacHenry saw he had wandered off heading. "It's real light on the controls, Barnes. I'm not used to it." The amount of pressure he was applying wouldn't have budged a transport from its path. But in the T-33, it was too much.

"Not like those elephants you're used to flying, is it? Just try and, you know, average it out. Be smooth."

"Roger." The control inputs smoothed out some as MacHenry began to catch on. "And how about that descent?"

"Just leave her trimmed like I had it," Barnes replied, pulling power back a touch to yield an 850-foot-per-minute descent. *Who's the teacher now?* He announced the descent over the radio. "Good evening, Tucson, Hawk two three is out of one niner zero, skosh fuel. We'd appreciate a nice, slow letdown to a straight-in at Delta Mike if you can work that for us."

"Roger, Hawk, approved. Descent to Davis-Monthan is at your discretion. Report cancellation of your Item Fox."

"Roger, Tucson. Expect cancellation through ten thousand. Hawk two three." Barnes tapped the intercom switch on the throttle. "You have any plan to get in and see that wing yet?" he asked.

MacHenry nudged the stick forward a fraction and saw the needle on the vertical speed indicator fall. "Well, I did bring along a federal seal to stop them from scrapping that C-130 Monday morning. I just don't know if that gets me to the wing today. I'll have to sic my paperwork on their paperwork and see what happens."

"Uh-huh." Paperwork was not a matter of concern to Major Peter Barnes. Flying was. He tugged the stick back and the nose came nearly level. "Eight fifty on the descent, okay? There's a lot of rocks between here and Davis-Monthan. Just takes a smooth touch."

"Smooth," MacHenry repeated.

As the altimeter unwound through ten thousand, Barnes made his final call up. "And Tucson, Hawk is canceling our IFR, frequency change."

"Hawk two three, Tucson. Contact Davis-Monthan Tower now on frequency two five three point five. Good evening."

Barnes dialed up the new setting, but first tapped the intercom button. "Just about showtime, BJ. You ready?"

"As much as I ever will be. Your airplane," he said, relinquishing the controls to Barnes. The jet immediately became rock steady. *Be smooth is right,* MacHenry thought with a growing respect. Whatever his other, less generous thoughts might be about Barnes, the man could fly.

Barnes banked the T-Bird back on course. He did it not with the slow, measured precision an airline pilot might employ to fool the fares into not noticing; instead, he banked quick and hard and leveled the wings just as brutally. For all the abruptness of the maneuver, the directional gyro was frozen right on course at the end. "Davis-Monthan," he transmitted, "Hawk two three, forty out with the numbers, and we're a little thirsty up here. Appreciate an expedite."

"Hawk two three is radar contact. Straight-in Runway Zero Nine approved. Where you guys coming from?" The tower man at Davis-Monthan was lonely; as the lord of an airbase filled with nonflying relics, not too much business came his way.

"Hawk two three is on a cross-country checkout from Mather," Barnes replied congenially.

"You say Mather Air Force Base? What's going on up there anyway?"

The alarm rang good and hard inside Barnes's head. "Say again?" he asked, suddenly serious. The man down on the ground had no business being so curious.

"I've had several calls on the landline asking to confirm your arrival. I just wondered what's up."

Oh, shit. "Couldn't say, Tower," Barnes replied, his mouth going dry as he wondered who was so interested in their flight. None of the answers were very promising.

"Why don't you drop by the tower after landing?"

"Rog."

The brilliant double row of diamonds that marked the main runway at Davis-Monthan lay straight off the nose, surrounded by acres and acres of inky darkness. The island of light that was Tucson rose from the sea of desert. But the desert wasn't as empty as it seemed; all around them, invisible and unlit, was the boneyard. It was the place where generations of warbirds came to rest, and eventually to die under the cutter's torch. SNJ trainers from the Second World War sat nose to nose with the sealed husks of B-58 supersonic bombers. The secret weapons of one age slept with those of the next. Rows of shark-finned tails caught the last gleam of sunset, looking fast and purposeful even as they dozed under the wind and the stars.

For a pilot, it was a strange combination of graveyard and candy shop. Barnes glanced down at the ghostly fleet, permitting himself one moment of contemplation before returning to the task at hand. He flipped the T-Bird's landing lights on and sent two spears of light out ahead. He kept the throttle in, tugged the stick to slow to 190 knots as he dropped the gear on a short, high final, his thumb on the drag board. With the Allison spooled up nice and tight, all it would take to execute a go-around was releasing the speed-brake button. Not that there was any fuel for a go-around.

"And Hawk, Davis-Monthan Tower. Call your final and check gear down."

"Hawk two three is on final with the gear," Barnes said as he briefly closed the speed brakes to fine-tune his approach. The red fuel-warning light was now on. He had no intention of not making the runway because he was too low in the pattern.

Barnes held the jet in its landing flare and was rewarded with a shrill *chirp! chirp!* as the tires spun up on dry desert concrete. Stabbing the brakes to keep the T-Bird running straight ahead, he looked over the small, active ramp area of the mothballing facility. One airplane looked familiar, although its engine nacelles had been stripped from the wings and scaffolding partially obscured the tail. "Tallyho!" he told MacHenry over the intercom, pointing with his gloved hand at the tired, picked-at Hercules. Shakey 103 had made its final flight.

"Will you be needing anything, Hawk?" asked the tower controller.

"A-firm, Tower. Hawk two three would like to park it next to that old C-130. And we will be needing some go-juice. We're on a quick turnaround back to Mather." Barnes keyed the intercom: "MacHenry, you better be damned quick 'cause I smell some manure hitting the turbine."

"You mean the flight-clearance business?"

"I mean everything," he replied as he nosed into a parking slot next to the old C-130. The sun was completely down behind the distant desert mountains. Barnes ran through the shutdown list, snapping off the radios and intercom along with the flight instruments and inverter controls. He pulled the canopy lever and turned to MacHenry. "I'll go chat with the guy working tower, but hear this: sure as shit, somebody's on to us." Barnes cut the engine, letting the thin scream of the Allison die away into the gathering evening.

Why did bad news always arrive after hours? Radway checked his watch. It was ten o'clock, Washington time. "You're sure of it?" he asked. Radway watched the blinking ENCRYPT light on the STU-3 phone as he waited for an answer.

"Yes, sir," said Adcock. The line to Tonopah was clearer than normal. Radway could hear Norton's site manager breathe. "I got the word through the contractor a few minutes ago."

"North Air?"

"Yes. I presume it's gone both ways." It wasn't really a question in Adcock's mind. North Air Transport was a wholly owned subsidiary of the CIA. Langley was sure to know.

"Very well," Radway said. "Is there an option?"

"There is," Adcock said, his voice falling to a whisper despite the absolute security afforded by the STU-3. "But I want a go-ahead. I want to know how far to prosecute it, to take it. Something official from the company. From somebody."

Just what we don't need, thought Radway. "Look," he said, "we've been over this before. You have the authority to protect the project. You've certainly exercised that once already, haven't you?"

"That was an extraordinary . . ." Adcock stopped. "Time was critical. I had no idea that the recovery crew was going to burn . . ."

"No," Radway said. "Let's leave that buried where it belongs. It was extraordinary, as you said." Radway could hear Adcock's breathing accelerate. "Look, Peter, what you're doing out there has immense value. Not just to us, but to the country. You know that, and we know it here, too. But nothing this important comes for free. There are always casualties."

"But there must be some limit, something you—"

"Handle it, Peter," Radway interrupted. "That's the limit. When it's done, you're done."

The transcontinental line squealed and popped. Then Adcock spoke. "All right. I just want to be sure about the commitment."

Radway sighed. "You're just spooked over that HUMMER business. Calm yourself. It's the fruition of . . . the entire concept." Encrypted or not, Radway would not use the word *Aurora.* The words, like the stealth project itself, were blacker than black. "The company is depending on this procurement decision. There may never be another project like this one. If you can't handle it by yourself, for God's sake fess up now."

"No, that's not it," Adcock said quickly. "It's the ambiguity."

This made Radway chuckle. "Welcome to the real world, Peter. Let me be unambiguous: do whatever is required to keep the program on an even keel. Address the problem right at the source and do it right away. Right now. Tonight. I'll take a shot at calling in some chits over at the FAA. Clear?"

"Clear," Adcock replied. "We go all the way."

MacHenry watched as Barnes disappeared into the tower building. He heard a fuel truck's diesel engine start up somewhere off in the darkness and turned his attention to the old C-130 that held his evidence. *Maybe*. He walked up to what had only this morning been a flying airplane, a thundering transport with the radio call sign of Shakey 103.

Now it was a derelict. All four of her engines had been stripped and hauled away. MacHenry looked at the amputated stubs dangling from the wing high over his head. Control cables, wires, and fuel hoses streamed from each fire wall like nerves, arteries, and veins. They had all been crudely chopped, not unfastened. There was no mistaking the fact that this was no overhaul. Old Shakey was in her deathbed.

MacHenry could remember all too well the year the Hercules had first flown, the newest and the biggest thing in all the skies. But he had other business.

He walked up to the battered nose. Shakey 103's hide rose up in the dusk light like an aluminum cliff. *Problem number one*, he thought as he found the controls for the forward cargo hatch locked. Nothing shy of a cutting torch would open it up. He ran his hand along her tough old hide.

Still warm from the sun, it felt almost alive. "Been through plenty," he said quietly. He walked beneath the fuselage and after checking that her nosewheel was chocked and secure, he poked his head up into the nosewheel well. MacHenry tried the crew hatch. The T-handle pulled free, moved a small part of its arc, and stopped, frozen against the inside lock. *Strike two*.

He jogged back to the rear of the Hercules. He remembered from long experience that an outside hydraulic dump handle was usually installed to open the doors in an emergency. He ran his hand over the dented metal of the aft cargo door. *Somewhere back here,* he recalled, his hand racing his memory for the answer.

A torn edge of an access plate scratched his finger. He flipped the panel open. *Pay dirt!* Behind the hinged plate he found the handle of the dump valve and swiftly, expertly activated it.

The squeal of unlubricated metal was alarmingly loud as one of the two great clamshell doors fell open. MacHenry looked around. He could hear the sounds of the jet refueler and the voices of the truck's crew on the other side of the C-130. He looked up at the hanging clamshell door, the black interior of the cargo deck beckoning, and before he could convince himself otherwise, he chinned himself up and inside.

It was hot inside, as hot and still as a desert crypt. He stood up and brushed his slacks clean. *Let's see what you've got,* he thought as he reached into a pocket and pulled out a small flashlight. The pencil beam swept over piles of rope strewn on the metal deck; old olive-drab sling chairs marched off into the darkness ahead on the two side walls. He wrinkled his nose at the smell of mildew blended with equal parts of engine oil and spilled hydraulic fluid.

MacHenry stepped over the ropes, his footsteps booming in the belly of the metal whale. He patted the pocket of the borrowed flightsuit where he had put his federal identification. The small lump of papers somehow made him feel better, less like a cat burglar.

The jumble of shapes slowly resolved into distinct objects as MacHenry cautiously approached: two silvery cylinders, their fins bent askew, were identifiable as old drop tanks; steel racks, many with their tube-filled radios still installed, lay prone, strapped to the deck like fallen soldiers. Beyond these MacHenry could see two large bins lashed to the tie-down eyes. *So where's my wing?*

He stepped around the bins. A dark cloth tarp was spread over a rectangular shape. MacHenry got down on his knees and unhooked the heavy rubber strap holding the tarp. Pulling it aside, he let the beam from his light fall on it.

"Bingo," he said aloud. MacHenry felt a sudden heaviness, almost a sadness, as he pulled the tarp off the wreckage. *There's the lift strut, with matching damage. Same twist.* He remembered the crumpled fuselage back at HUMMER. *But what's this?*

MacHenry played the light across the top of the wing. The metal skin was dished in and nearly cut through at the spar. He reached out and felt the jagged metal cleft, running his hand along the rip. *Something made a damn clean slice,* he thought. *Chain saw?* MacHenry knew that a wing separated from the fuselage and left to flutter down on its own usually got banged up in the process, but this wing looked more clipped than bludgeoned. A sharp instrument had made the gash. He reached down into the break, feeling for something that might tell him what could have done such damage. Halfway across, deep in a recess where the spar ribs joined, he found what he was looking for.

MacHenry worked a small fragment free and held it under the direct beam of the flashlight. It was a piece of black plastic, with long fibers trailing away in frays, about the size of a matchbook. *This sure wasn't made by Cessna.*

MacHenry stuffed the piece into one of his pockets. Then, a sudden realization made him stop. "Jesus," he said. He swept the white wing with his light, back and forth, not quite believing what he saw. "Jesus." There was no sign of fire. The Cessna had burned, but not this wing. He focused the light on the attach fittings, then back to the gash, then along the smooth white metal. Something was very, very wrong. If the Cessna had burned, why not this wing? Had someone removed it before the fire? How could that be?

He reached for the Polaroid but froze. The sound of slow, stealthy footsteps were coming from the blacked-out cargo deck behind him. MacHenry snapped off the beam of his flashlight. Then, feeling in his pockets for the FAA identification, he pulled out the card and turned the light back on. "Stop right there!" he said just a bit too loud. "I'm with the FAA and this aircraft is sealed."

A laugh echoed back out of the darkness. "Oh, yeah? There's a mighty big back door open that says otherwise, BJ."

"Barnes! I didn't know . . ."

Barnes stepped into the glow of MacHenry's light. "Forget it. You see the wing? I hope so, 'cause we are wheels-up in ten minutes. I've got a story to tell you."

"The wing's right here," MacHenry said as he flashed the beam over its surface. "It's got a story to tell you, too."

Barnes merely glanced at it. "Yeah, that's the one. Look," he said, "we've got to beat feet, okay? I still might be able to talk our way out of this."

Barnes and the man in the Davis-Monthan control tower had swapped stories. Two calls had come to the tower seeking information about the flight of Hawk 23. The one from Mather could be nobody other than Col. Al Braden. That was the bad news. The good news was the second call from the T-33's owners, North Air Transport. They had authorized a full refueling on their account. There would be no running low on the way home.

"So it looks a mite grim, BJ," Barnes said. "I kind of hoped to execute this little maneuver without Braden hearing about it. No such luck."

"Something isn't right with this wing, Barnes."

"So that's news? I told you that first thing."

"No," said MacHenry. "I mean something stinks to high heaven."

"Hold your nose and start walking. We're out of here." Barnes turned and began walking back to the half-open cargo door.

"Barnes! Listen to me. The wing back there is the right one. But it's relatively undamaged." *Except for that gash,* he thought. "But it didn't burn. Do you understand what that means?"

"So what?"

"It means that somehow, that wing came off *after* the crash, but *before* the Cessna caught on fire. Tell me, how's it going to do that?"

"Beats me," said Barnes as he pulled free of MacHenry's grip. "Let's move it, BJ, before the shitstorm hits."

"And there's more," he said, reaching in and feeling the plastic fragment he had retrieved from the slash. "This wing was struck by something before it ever hit the ground." He flipped the black plastic fragment in his hand. "Something high speed, glancing angle, and"—MacHenry tossed the piece over to Barnes—"something made of this."

Barnes glanced impatiently at the dark fragment. "Plastic? Some kind of reinforced plastic. Carbon fibers maybe."

"From a military aircraft?"

"Christ, what a bulldog you are, BJ. You've been trying to pin this on us from the getgo."

"Where else could that piece have come from? You tell me. I'd like to know."

Barnes sighed. "It could have been from a military aircraft," he replied. "Or maybe he flew into a model airplane. They're plastic, too. Look, I'd just love to stay and chat, but I've got a return ticket to punch, you know? So let's get moving. It's getting late and I seem to have a pressing engagement with my CO. So, this is like the last call, okay? T-Bird Air is about to depart."

MacHenry followed him back out the tail of Shakey 103 and over to the refueled T-Bird. The boarding ladder's metal was cool to the touch. He had less trouble getting himself installed in the small fighter's rear cockpit. He was about to strap in when Barnes reached over and stopped him.

"Hey, BJ, you want to try the front on the way back?" It would be harder for Barnes to fly the plane from the rear seat if MacHenry did not prove up to the challenge; not only was the visibility poor from the back but the instrument panel was filled with radio gear rather than a full set of flight instruments. But Barnes figured the old airline captain deserved a second chance.

"No. That's all right, Barnes," MacHenry replied, remembering how delicate the controls had been. "I'm still just a passenger." He pulled the helmet over his head and snugged the chin strap.

"Last chance?" said Barnes.

MacHenry shook his helmeted head.

"Okay. I guess it's all up to me then." Barnes settled into the front seat and strapped down. He pushed the canopy handle and the glass dome hissed down, sealing out the desert.

The Allison came to life in a smooth start. Barnes copied the weather, what little of it there was, and taxied the jet out to the runway they had landed on half an hour before. The T-33's landing lights shot out straight down the long, black runway. "Dark night," he said. "Wonder if dark air has any lift in it?"

"You ever hear of a commander's moon?" MacHenry asked. It was a full, bright moon that allowed the older pilots to fly with more confidence.

"That's swabbo slang," said Barnes. "We call it—"

The tower man cut in. "Hawk two three is cleared for takeoff. Contact Tucson passing through three thousand. Good night, guys, and thanks for the business." Then he remembered the two strange telephone calls he had received. "Hope it was worth it."

"Hawk is rolling," Barnes replied as he shoved the throttle forward. The engine rose to a shriek as it thundered behind them. "You and me both."

13

AMBUSH

HILL reached into the bowl of steaming popcorn with one hand and switched TV channels with a remote in the other. The ready room was normally busy this time of night. Excalibur flew most of her missions cloaked in darkness. But not tonight. Tonight, it was just Hill and Thatcher and a TV image piped down fifty feet below the Nevada desert.

Hill switched off the set. "Can you believe it?" he said to Thatcher. "The asshole puts a note in my box. He says he wants to buy me a beer. After that HUMMER crap. Believe it?"

Thatcher put down the thick book he was reading. "He's just trying to get by the only way he knows. Don't let it bug you. Besides, you've got to admit the little guy runs a tight program."

Hill grabbed the book Thatcher was reading and shook his head. *Temperature/Time Performance of Schiff-Base Salts as Electromagnetic Radiation Absorbers*. He tossed it back. "You would say that." Hill took some more popcorn. "All I know is, I'd rather hop a damned desert rat than drink brew with the likes of him."

Thatcher smiled. "That last one you found looked like more of a *professional* desert rat." What could you expect? It was Nevada, after all.

"I know," said Hill with a sad nod. "The Mizpah sure ain't what it used to be. Used to be, the word got out that the hottest, hairiest aviators this side of the angels were hanging out someplace, and the gals just got, you know, *drawn* in. Now it's all business."

"I'll take your expert opinion," Thatcher replied, and returned to his book.

"Hey," said Hill, "did you see my new cards? I got some printed up in town." Hill handed Thatcher a business card.

Thatcher put his bookmark in and read. "'Aviation Test Consultant'? 'Cold, Steely-Eyed Professional.' That's you all right."

"Read the bottom."

"'Live by chance, love by choice, kill by profession.' Yep. That's you all over," said Thatcher.

"You like it?"

Thatcher grimaced his reply and reopened the book.

"Bad for the eyes. You'll never make flight engineer."

"Oh, well."

"Never mind. But look here, Frank, I still have these two questions."

Thatcher closed the book. He knew Hill. After a thousand hours together in the SR-71, plus twice that many in other, less well-known projects, he knew it was useless to try. "Like what?"

"Like, where was everybody off to these last two days . . ." The C-5s had landed and swallowed up Norton's Strategic Flight Test Group whole. And not just the pilots and RSOs. Five of the six Aurora aircraft had been loaded aboard as well. The huge transports had roared off the desert strip for places, and missions, unknown. All except for Hill and Thatcher and the Excalibur damaged up at HUMMER. "I mean, what is going down that we aren't supposed to know about?"

"Come on, Hill, nobody knew their destination. You know that."

"But why are we the lucky ones to get left behind? I mean, we *destroyed* two goddamned altitude and speed records. We hung it out on that fucked-up Charlie run up in HUMMER just so we'd pull a good assignment. You mark my words: there's an ops going down and just because we cracked the wing a little bit, see, they figure that we can't be trusted to keep our noses clean."

"Hill, I can't even hear what you're saying," Thatcher said. "Pass the popcorn."

"You know what?" Hill continued. "I feel like there's a party going on and we weren't invited."

"I don't know where everybody went, but if they're going up against real radars, I guarantee you it's no party."

"Damn!" Hill slapped the chair beside him. "That's just what I mean!" Hill and Thatcher both knew that the ultimate test of Excalibur would come when actual overflights of Soviet territory began. A hypersonic spy plane could be intended for nothing less.

"Relax. The other side's going to stick around for a long, long time," said Thatcher. "We'll get a mission. Just be glad they aren't taking it out of our salaries." The aircraft damaged in HUMMER had been the center of a beehive of activity. It was only now fit for flight testing once again.

"Don't bet they won't try it, Frank. I mean, your buddy Adcock steers us into a hot range and it gets someone killed and *we* lose out on a real live mission. You mark my words, that squirrel is going to hand that whole HUMMER fiasco over to us. You wait and see." He picked up the remote control and clicked the TV back on, aimlessly cycling through programs. The ready room interphone buzzed. "I ain't here. I'm too pissed off to be here."

"Yassuh," Thatcher said with a mocking bow as he got up and took the phone off the wall cradle. "Thatcher." He listened for a moment, then a smile broke out on his face. "With pleasure. Okay. Fuel?" Thatcher nodded. "Live weapons?" Another nod. "Very good, sir. The repairs are complete, I know, but what about . . . All right. We can verify that."

Hill looked over at the words. He punched the TV off. "What we got?" Hill demanded in a loud whisper, but Thatcher waved him silent. "What is it, Thatch?"

Thatcher hushed him. "Okay, Mr. Adcock. Sounds like a winner.

We'll get the briefing up on the hangar level. Roger that," he said, and hung up.

"*Mister* Adcock is it? Well?" Hill asked.

"Well well well," Thatcher replied as he reached for his flightsuit. "Mr. Adcock says it's party time."

Barnes checked his watch, then scrutinized the fuel gauge one more time. Where had all that kerosene gone? He should have told the ground crew to stuff everything full. It wasn't as if the Air Force was paying for it. What did he care what North Air Transport shelled out?

He couldn't coax the indicator to show more than 1,860 pounds. The slim reserves they had eastbound to Davis-Monthan were gone in the face of the twenty-knot head wind on the westbound leg home. He fought the urge to pile on more throttle. It would only use up his remaining fuel that much faster.

The glowing numerals on the chronometer he wore outside his flying glove read 21:56. *Another hour, hour and fifteen back. Damn.* He brought the turbine RPM back to 90 percent, yielding a fuel burn of just under 290 gallons per hour. Barnes ran the numbers through his head again. "Hey, BJ," Barnes called out over the intercom, "looks like the peanut butter and jelly's a little on the thin side, you know? I think we better request a more direct routing."

"You're the pilot in command." MacHenry doubted they could make it nonstop, but somehow that was not important. There were plenty of airports with fuel once they crossed the desert and the mountains. Barnes would sort it all out. MacHenry had that jagged fragment of carbon fiber in his flightsuit pocket, and a theory about that crashed Cessna that was beginning to feel ugly.

"Good evening, Las Vegas, Hawk two three at two five oh with a request." Barnes's voice over the comm brought MacHenry back to the humming cockpit of the T-33.

"Radar contact, Hawk, and we have an amendment on your routing. Call when you're ready to copy."

"Hawk two three is ready, but it better not be a delay. We're running tight on go-juice." Barnes read back the new, more direct course and dialed up the Nellis Air Force Base center on the number two comm. He shook his head and tabbed the intercom. "How's that for service? I was working out a new route and the groundpounders come through before I finish it. What, you got mind readers now in air traffic control?"

"They're just trying to be helpful," MacHenry replied. "But it also means we're going to be overflying some rough terrain."

"Might as well be the moon," Barnes agreed. "Black as the dickens," he said, looking out at the uninhabited desert. "But it's a good ninety miles quicker. Pretty night out there for a little moonwalk, wouldn't you say?" Barnes looked down and saw the faint, shimmering runway lights of the Nellis complex at his two-o'clock position. The dazzle that was Las Vegas was already behind them as they streaked northwest. The darkness surrounding the little island of lights below was not as empty as it looked; he knew that plenty went on down in those skunk works that didn't get lit up at night. The F-117 stealth fighter had come howling out of some secret desert range to the north; who knew what else went bump in the night?

MacHenry twisted in the hard seat and watched the flashing lights snap into eclipse as an intervening mountain blocked the view. They were now headed into the unbroken black—the unlit terrain of the high Nevada desert. "You know, Barnes," MacHenry said, still in a reflective mood, "I was prepared to find that wing was just a piece of scrap off another aircraft. Just like your CO claimed. I guess I bought into the weather factor a little too hard."

"Don't sweat it," Barnes replied. "You're the hero of the day. I'm the one who's still headed for the boonies."

"Are you still worried about catching flak over this flight? If you are, I think that with this little chunk of evidence, we can fix—" The communications radio suddenly broke in.

"Hawk two three, contact Nellis . . . now . . . twenty-four point . . . five. Good evening." Las Vegas was oddly weak given how close they were to its transmitter, and the controller's voice held a strange echo.

"So long, Las Vegas, Hawk two three." Barnes punched Nellis into the active comm. "And good evening, Nellis, Hawk two three is . . . Damn!" A teeth-rattling screech came in over the Nellis frequency. He ran the squelch control up and down but it made not the slightest difference. He turned the volume way down and punched in the old Las Vegas setting. When he brought the frequency up on the active comm, it sounded like a cat fight in progress. He shook his head. "Radio trouble, BJ."

"You want me to try it on one of the sets back here?" MacHenry offered. He did not like to be out of voice contact with air traffic control. There was a lot of empty desert below and a low-fuel warning light burning on his panel once again.

"A-firm," Barnes replied. "Better power 'em up. We've lost, you know, the audio portion of the program up here. Three twenty-four forty-five, if you please."

MacHenry toggled the rear cockpit avionics master. A wall of lights and numbers sprang to life on his panel. Designed as an attack aircraft, the rear panel included the T-Bird's offensive and defensive avionics, radar and infrared warning sensors, as well as more mundane communication and navigation gear.

Barnes saw the lights from MacHenry's radios glowing in the canopy overhead. "Go ahead and give them a shout."

"I think I've got the comm radio up back here." In fact, by toggling the avionics master switch, MacHenry had turned on the entire stack of electronics. MacHenry stared at the sudden Christmas tree of lights he had summoned into existence, hoping that somewhere in that intricate display he had correctly powered up the right radio. "Barnes," he said, looking at the unfamiliar lights and displays, "I'm not sure I can make heads or tails of all this—" *What's that?* A strong, clear signal suddenly cut through the hiss. "I think I must've done something back here." MacHenry did not know it, but the threat-warning unit in the tail of the T-33 was demanding immediate attention. "I'll switch off the—"

"Shut up!" Barnes slashed the air with his gloved hand. "Don't you touch a goddamned thing!" He was listening to the tone. It was not an unfamiliar sound; he had heard it before. "Shit," he cursed as he swung in his seat and looked out into the black sky.

"What is it?"

The tone shifted from a warble to continuous.

"Shit!" Instinct took immediate command. MacHenry felt the control stick slam into his left knee as Barnes savagely spun the jet into a high-g turn. The throttle shot forward and the Allison kicked in behind them, sending the engine gauges spinning. MacHenry, helpless to control the jet or understand the meaning of the sudden maneuver, was thrown deep into his seat. His cheeks pulled down and a ring of darkness shrouded his vision. He was too stunned to speak.

Barnes was not stunned. He knew exactly the meaning of the tone in his ears. Its meaning was wholly unambiguous. Someone was trying to kill him.

The radar room at the Tonopah site was a hushed alcove off a high-domed cavern. A small personnel elevator ran up to the surface, along with a larger platform that had been designed for other things but lifted aircraft to the runway above just as well.

Serpentine branches went on for miles under the Nevada desert. The Department of Energy had purchased it from the Atomic Energy Commission as a nuclear storage facility. It was the ideal place to safeguard radiating waste for ages; those same qualities of isolation and absolute security made it an excellent site for safeguarding secrets.

Now, with all the pilots and their aircraft gone, the quiet was absolute. Only the busy whirring of the cooling fans and Adcock's nervous pacing on the metal decking could be heard.

The man seated at the flickering green radar display watched as the two dots quickly converged. He had a God's-eye view of the entire event. "Nimbus two, Searchlight," he said, "fly heading two niner three. Target will be twelve o'clock and level, range eighteen." The pacing stopped. He could hear Adcock breathing close behind him.

"Rog," said Hill from twenty thousand feet. "Target drone is coming up on passive. Opening bay one."

The controller turned and faced Adcock. "Not bad," he said, ignoring the sick, pasty look on the engineer's face. In the green of the radar scope, it made Adcock look dead.

"Okay. Good. Very good." *Handle it,* Radway had said. *Do whatever was necessary.* He thought back to the hours following the incident at HUMMER. The fault was his own. It had been his own error, trusting the recovery crew to bring the evidence out from HUMMER and keep it out of sight.

"Nimbus has a lock."

Adcock had trusted someone else. That had been the mistake. As he watched Excalibur close in on his problem, he vowed to never, *never* make that mistake again. This would end it. Tonight. Now.

"Searchlight copies lock." The radar controller looked up at Adcock. "Sir?"

"Yes?" Adcock's eyes were distant, unfocused.

"They're going to want a release." The radar display showed the two symbols, one for Excalibur, the other representing the target drone, coming together rapidly. The stealth aircraft had its radar beacon on, of course. Without it, it would not have shown up at all. "Someone's playing easy to get." The drone was boring straight ahead, fat, dumb, and happy. It would be easy meat.

"It should be," Adcock replied. "My . . ." He hesitated. "The airplane will fly itself to a kill. Hill's just along for the ride."

"You bet." The controller looked over to the remote pilot's station. Normally, it would be occupied by one of the "zoomies," the word the technicians reserved for the pilots.

It had a faithful duplicate of a jet's instrument panel, right down to the rudder pedals on the floor. A CRT substituted for the windshield, and live video from the doomed target drone was beamed there from a camera in the cockpit.

The final moments leading up to the destruction of the target drone made popular viewing. But it was dark. *Where are they controlling that drone from?* "Where did you whistle this intercept from?" he asked as casually as his intense curiosity permitted.

"Need to know," Adcock replied. His eyes were drawn to the two dots on the screen. They were close now.

"Searchlight, Nimbus," Hill's voice spilled from the speaker, "confirm the area is cold."

The controller checked the screen. There were only two returns. The coded beacon from Excalibur and the uncoded transponder signal from the drone. "Roger, Nimbus. Searchlight confirms. Range is all yours."

"Weapons free," said Adcock.

The controller nodded. "Nimbus, Nimbus, you are weapons free. Say again, you are weapons free. Go get 'em."

"Roger, weapons free."

The controller started the stopwatch. They had run this particular game before, of course. Excalibur had two mission bays, one for reconnaissance gear and the other free for other uses the designers might contemplate. A standard rotary rack could accommodate guided bombs, the new small cruise missile, or a brace of the upgraded Sparrows known as ASPs. The inevitable acronym stood for Autonomous Sparrow Prototype. An aircraft sent into harm's way, even a hypersonic aircraft, needed some protection.

In previous trials, no target had eluded the reaching sensors and defensive missiles of Excalibur. The fastest kill time, kept on a pad taped above the CRT, was six minutes twenty seconds from the moment the passive systems picked up the target. Not one had lasted longer than ten. The speaker mounted on the controller's panel barked into life.

"Okay, Searchlight," said Hill, "guidance is up. ASP is up and tracking." The old Sparrows had to be guided by the aircraft that fired them; the new one found its own way.

Adcock shuffled nervously from foot to foot behind the controller, bending over every few moments to examine the radar display. On the screen, it was the large fuzzy circle in relentless pursuit of the small, brilliant dot.

"And Searchlight, Nimbus has tone." It would not be long now.

"Searchlight okays. Do it," Adcock said quietly.

"Searchlight releases," the controller transmitted up. They waited only a moment for the anticipated response.

"Fox one, Fox one. Nimbus two." Hill sounded positively bored. The scope showed a third return now, much faster than the other two. ASP was on its way.

Barnes shoved the throttle to its stop and dived for the desert. The sprinkling of lights far out on the northern horizon were horribly out of place as Barnes reefed the T-33 into a hard bank to the left.

"Barnes!" MacHenry shouted as his restraint harness bit into him. "What's wrong? What are you doing?" But Barnes wasn't talking. The warbling tone from the tail warning unit had just gone continuous.

Barnes snapped the stick full right and swung his head around, looking for the exhaust plume he knew must be bearing down on him from astern. If he could just . . . There! *There it is!* A bright-sparking comet streaking across the background of stars.

"Jesus," he said, "that sucker is moving!" There was no way to outrun it. You might as well try to backstroke away from a bullet. He would have to outthink it, outfly it. MacHenry was shouting something, but Barnes didn't have time to listen. He would either explain everything in a minute or they would both be dead.

Okay okay okay, he said to himself. *Begin with a circle.* He measured the sky that separated them from the reaching ASP. He felt a cool shower douse the panic, even as the bright circle of his situational awareness went to full bright. *Now!* He ran the throttle around the detent into full afterburner. A sudden explosion booted him in the small of his back.

Barnes flipped the T-Bird onto its back and split-essed, diving with all the thrust the little Allison put out. He was running on pure adrenaline, no thoughts spared for piloting, no concern for the dizzily spinning instruments. It was his blood that coursed through the turbine, compressed and on fire.

Begin with a circle and step inside. Barnes mentally reached out and felt the plane as though its wings were attached to his own shoulders. The turbojet's thrust issued from his own gloved fist wrapped tight around the throttle. His mind raced ahead, skimming his first panicky motions with frost, turning his thoughts icy and deliberate. He saw the spark of light bend its trajectory to follow him.

"What in God's name are you doing!" MacHenry demanded as he was thrown against his harness in the dive. Suddenly, he lost his entire mental picture. Up and down were meaningless abstractions. G forces pulled at his face as another abrupt control input whipped the little jet into an unknown attitude.

They were already below the tallest mountains. The far-off lights were snuffed out one by one as they were eclipsed by the rising Sierras. *Black out.* He rejected the impossible view out through the canopy and tried to make sense of the instruments on the panel. The artificial horizon made no sense. Only the stone-simple altimeter told the unvarnished truth: its hands were spinning down like a clock thrown into high-speed reverse. *Through 12,500; 11,000. Through 9,500!* The indicator blurred and the airframe shook as they dove at a velocity already beyond that called *never exceed.* MacHenry thought, *This is how it feels to die.*

He braced himself against the metal cockpit wall and imagined what the wreckage would look like. Another glance at the airspeed indicator, pegged out at 505 knots, and he decided it wouldn't look like much. Out of the corner of his eye, above and behind the diving jet, a spark, a firefly, caught his attention.

It was on Barnes's mind as well. Unlike MacHenry, he had no idea what his actual altitude might be in numbers; instead, he registered the onrush of the ground in terms of texture, of depth in the black-on-black terrain, a bare, subliminal awareness of the hard earth's rising. *Now?* he asked himself. *No. Let the moment select itself.*

The glimmer of the ASP's exhaust shaved the corner of its arc and efficiently dove to intercept them. His hand twitched, his nerves screaming demands to *do something.* He fought the impulse to get away from the rising desert ground, to pull out. It came at him over the nose like a black tidal wave. The fiery spark grew to a fat, lurid globe of deadly light. *Wait just a little . . . just a little more.*

The image of an archer swam before his eyes, projected against the blackness outside the canopy like a new and unorthodox head-up display. Tanai. *Let the arrow fly when it is ready. Don't shoot the arrow. Let the arrow decide.* Time seemed to speed up and slow all at once, his brain racing far ahead of his body, reaching for the surface of the desert, touching it, racing back and forth as they drew nearer and nearer.

His right arm tensed at the stick. He waited an additional sliver of time. *Now.* He felt like an observer as he calmly watched his hand sweep the stick into his gut. Time exploded into fast-forward. Barnes yanked back the throttle, causing the turbine to flame out from the oceans of cold air cascading through its intakes. Alarms buzzing, he ignored the flashing red lights on the panel from the dead engine and pulled the control stick back, back, back, right to the first nibble of a high-g stall; too much and they would break a wing, and the missile would win. Too little and they would get caught at the bottom of the maneuver, maybe by the sagebrush below, and the missile would win.

Just right and that son of a bitch goes into the ground, and I win.

The jet shook and bucked under him as it tried to turn the corner. The nose wavered, yawed left, then right, then began to stagger upward, no longer pointed straight down. Barnes was shoved down hard into the seat with sudden weight, his helmet a hundred and ninety pounds of iron on his neck. He could hear the *tick tick tick* as the igniters tried to restart the Allison. Barnes deployed the flaps and thumbed out the speed brakes to shorten the turn radius and hoped that nothing would tear off. He had to do something. The T-33 shuddered as the slipstream tore at the control surfaces. There was no need to look at the altimeter to tell they were very, very low.

Here goes nothing, he thought as he brought the belly-drag board out full. The speed brake bit into the air and shoved the nose upward, just as Barnes had hoped. The roar of the slipstream filled the cockpit. The T-33's airframe shook like a thing alive caught in the jaws of an immense but invisible trap. *Come on!* he urged, knowing now that there was nothing more to do. With the flaps and brakes out, the stick hard against his flightsuit, the nose would either recover or it would not. The arc of their ballistic dive would bottom out in the air or it would extend, at least mathematically, below the desert floor.

The jet heaved itself level, the energy of its dive feeding the terrible g-monster that had its foot planted on Barnes's body. His left arm was pinned to his knee, but his right hand remained gripped on the stick like death itself. The blood drained from his head as though hot mercury pumped through his arteries. Barnes started to pant, forcing the blood back to his head, straining to stay conscious. As the nose continued to rise, the heavy weight began to subside. This was where the missile had its best chance.

Speed! he thought from behind g-tunneled vision. *Flaps up! Power!* Barnes's hands flew to the gangstart power box. *Gangstart switch ON!—throttle IDLE.* He pushed the throttle forward to light off the engine again. *Where's that fucker?* He craned his head around and looked for the missile. *Who cares? Nothing more to do.*

The gangstart cycle dumped raw fuel into the hot burner cans, starting the engine with a tremendous *BOOM!* The ASP flashed by the wingtip and rocketed into the sand with an even greater detonation. The flash lit a lunar landscape like a brilliant strobe as it blew a hole in the hard desert floor just fifty feet below.

"All right!" Hill exulted over the intercom. The flash of the warhead was gone but bright flames still illuminated the heart of the rising pall of smoke. Hill racked Excalibur up onto a wing for a better view down. "Searchlight, Nimbus. Bag one," Hill sent out over the burst transmitter.

"Searchlight copies. Six fourteen on the time."

The ramjets were deep asleep, but the two powerful turbofans buried in Excalibur's belly roared like a pride of lions at a kill. Hill pulled the engines off reheat and brought the nose of the stealth jet above the phosphor-green horizon line on the head-up display, feeding in a little stick at the same instant. Excalibur did a slow victory roll to the left.

He couldn't have explained it to Hill, but Thatcher still had an eye on his displays, watching the cloud of infrared settle as the hot gases from the exploding warhead cooled. A bright green dot remained. He punched the clear function. Now only a small remnant of the ASP's detonation remained.

But the green dot was back. And it was moving.

"Hey, Hill, I'm still showing something, some kind of IR return out there."

"ASPs get mighty hot when they blow, you know."

Thatcher watched as the infrared return grew stronger on his display. "Hard target, Hill."

"You're sure?" Then Hill got his own answer. Beyond the rising cloud of smoke from the ASP, three lights could be seen moving at high speed across the black landscape—red, green, and white. *Lights?* Since when did they light up a target drone? Hill watched as it streaked low over the desert, its own dull-orange exhaust showing as it moved directly away from them. *Fuck.* He pressed the transmit button. "Searchlight, Nimbus two, and ah, we still show a possible target."

The radio crackled back. "Negative on the target, Nimbus. We copied the intercept."

Hill watched as the lights on the drone moved against the black ground. "Well, boys," he drawled back to the controller, "nobody's told that damn drone."

"Verify the intercept, Nimbus. Searchlight directs." It was Adcock, now.

"Nimbus, rog." Hill looked out into the nighttime desert landscape. The three little lights on the drone were growing faint. He toggled the infrared display back on. It was clear as a bell. The bright green dot and the three little lights were one and the same. "Damn." He reached down to cycle the rotary launcher, to bring a second ASP to bear. The master CAUTION light came on. "Hey, Thatch, I think—"

"Watch it, Hill. We've got a hang-up," Thatcher said.

"No shit." Hill struck the instrument glareshield with a gloved fist. It was a problem that had plagued the old F-117A as well as the canceled B-2. Plastic airframes flexed a great deal. The tight clearances demanded by stealth sometimes became a bit too tight. Whatever the cause, the rotary launcher was out to lunch. His second ASP was not available. But Hill was not totally out of options.

Hill swept both turbines back into afterburner. The small, knifelike canards to either side of the cockpit were switchblading in and out as the computer drove them to accommodate Hill's desires. The two shrouded GE-102s spooled into a deep, surging moan as he dipped Excalibur's nose toward the fleeing light ahead. A small light blinked on Hill's engine subpanel. If he continued to accelerate, the two ramjets would be available for even more power. But Hill didn't need hypersonics to down a drone, did he?

"What's the plan, Hill?" asked Thatcher.

Excalibur couldn't fire a missile. But it was still far from unarmed. *"Go to guns!"*

"Rog." Thatcher toggled the retractable blast door open. Under Excalibur's needle-sharp nose, a single, 20-mm gun port was now exposed to the slipstream. It reduced the stealthiness of Excalibur by an amazingly large degree. But they didn't need invisibility against a drone. The repeater panel in front of Thatcher winked green. "You got 'em, Hill. Good light."

"Searchlight, Nimbus two," Hill transmitted, "we are target verified and tracking. Negative on the second bird. We're going in with the mike-mike."

"Just do it," said Adcock.

"Are you okay, MacHenry?" Barnes fought to calm his breath. *Fly the airplane. Fly the airplane.* He searched the black sky for the source of the missile, but there was nothing to see except for the brilliant stars of the Milky Way.

"What was it?"

Barnes pulled the throttle back to cruise. "Missile," he said. "It moved like a goddamned Sparrow missile." His heart started to slow. *No!* his mind interrupted with a shot of straight adrenaline. *Somebody fired that missile.* Barnes twisted his head in the other direction. *Where are you?*

"You think somebody shot an air-to-air missile at us?"

"I don't think squat," said Barnes. "Maybe it's some kind of live-fire exercise. Maybe not. Shit!" Barnes looked at his wing and saw the position light burning bright red. He jabbed a toggle and the lights went out. "Some fucking combat ace I would have made." He scanned the horizon. They were too low to see anything but the dark wall of the Sierras. "I'm pointing this sucker home. We'll stay low for a while." He pulled the nose around until they were once more headed north, straight up the Owens Valley. Barnes looked out into the inky dark. "If we're good and lucky, we'll live to run out of fuel." Barnes altered the heading more to the right and began to climb. "Whatever you do, don't fuck around with the tail unit." The radar warning receiver had saved them. Barnes kept his neck on a swivel, looking once more for the source of the missile. *Black as hell out there. Never get a visual.*

"Do you see anything?" asked MacHenry.

"No visual, no clue, no hope." Barnes ran his finger over the stick trigger, the one that would release a stream of 50-caliber bullets from the nose-mounted machine guns. But there were no rounds loaded for a cross-country checkout jaunt. Suddenly, the thought made an iceball congeal in his belly. He was making it easy for them. His neck crawled as he slammed the stick full right.

"Hey!" MacHenry shouted over the intercom, his voice shaking as the jet once more wrenched into a violent maneuver.

"Hang on, BJ. Just stay with me and look around. Look real good. I'm turning back to see if anybody's sniffing our six."

Turning through one hundred degrees, he shallowed the angle of bank, hunting the blackness ahead for anything that wasn't a star. The faint yellow light-haze thrown up from the sodium-vapor lamps of distant Las Vegas made the sky slightly less pure, providing a thin, milky aurora to the southeast.

Barnes saw it first. It was a darker hole in the night sky, one that blotted out the stars in a deep, delta eclipse. As quickly as the image registered, and before the brain could give it a name, the shadow thundered over, just missing them. The air vibrated with the passing of two huge turbofans, transmitting a low, sinister shudder into the T-Bird's airframe. "Christ."

MacHenry looked straight up through the canopy as it roared overhead. "What in God's name is that?" His helmet was hard against the ejection rail as he stared. It didn't look like anything he had ever seen. Scepter-thin wings sprouted from an arrowhead's body. Needle nose to small, stub tail, it was a nightmare vision that was part bat, part machine. It was a nightmare that had to be real because he could never have imagined it. "Is it . . ."

"Bad medicine, BJ. Very bad medicine," Barnes answered. He had seen the black beast, but he had seen something else, too: a single marking, a glittering gold sword on its tail.

His mental calculations shifted, and the new numbers were not to his liking. He had heard there was an airplane that looked like this, one that flew from a place not even the Air Force was allowed to visit. But rumors were harder to control than secrets, and he had heard its name.

They were the hunted, and Barnes knew the dark skies belonged to an airplane called Excalibur.

Hill watched the drone streak to the west, straight and level, an easy firing solution.

"Getting low, Hill. There's mountains out here."

"You track. I'll fly." Then, as Hill watched through the HUD combiner, the target suddenly jinked.

"Break right!" Thatcher shouted. "He's going inside us!"

"Keep your cool," Hill replied. "We're going to nail this fucker and go home." The drone had reversed on him, a fighter jock's move. It would streak right under them any second now. Hill swept Excalibur into a tight bank.

"Watch it! He's going to be close!"

"Okay, I hear you." Hill saw the target vanish under his nose. "We'll swing around and zap him on the deflection." Hill charged the 20-mm rotary cannon. "Live by chance, love by choice," he said. He wanted to *feel* this kill, and killing, as his business card proclaimed, was his profession.

14

REVELATION

ILL squeezed out a few rounds into the night. Every sixth one was a phosphor-green tracer. The M61 laced the darkness with a hundred high-velocity shells per second. *Good.* At least something was working right. He banked harder left to bring his guns level at the instant the drone would pass before them.

"Okay, okay," said Thatcher, his breath coming hard over the intercom. "It's running erratic, Hill." Thatcher watched as the little green dot shifted again. "He's boogying to the southwest again."

Damn, thought Hill. This wasn't going to work out. "Okay. We'll keep it coming around and fall in behind him for a zero-deflection shot. Then it's shake and bake for *señor* drone."

Hill craned his neck around to follow the flight of the drone. Hill's HUD combiner showed the bright green star of the drone's exhaust. The symbol edged toward the illuminated ring of the gunsight. He was going to catch this little hummer. The lights of Lone Pine, California, were clear, dead ahead and close.

"Gun range coming up!"

"Just a little bit more, just a little," Hill said to himself as he

watched the target climb to the middle of the HUD's sweet spot. The
IN RNG light flashed.

"He's slowing!" Thatcher warned.

As Hill watched, the green symbol began dropping back down his
HUD glass. They were overshooting! *Fun and games,* he thought, *with
the fucking Baron Von Richthofen of drones.* Hill pulled back on both
throttles and deployed his wing spoilers. He was thrown forward into
the restraint harness. But he smiled. The drone was centered once
more.

"Nail him!" Thatcher shouted as Hill closed in to knife-fight range.
"Nail him, Hill!"

"Okay, okay, I got him." The green dot ballooned as Excalibur
streaked in. Hill readjusted the engines to keep from passing the target.
More! Slow it up! He pulled off more power. Excalibur was built for
hypersonic flight; she flew indifferently at slower speeds, and the
drone was slowing down too fast for them to compensate.

Suddenly, the gunsight annunciator flashed. *Now!* Hill jammed his
thumb down on the firing button and felt the airframe shudder as the
rotary cannon zippered flaming shells into the night.

The 20-mm rounds lanced toward the drone. They seemed to be
falling short, but Hill knew better. They always looked short when
they were right on the money. He held the button down as they swept
over the target. *Sloppy. Wasted rounds on that pass.*

"Got a hit!" Thatcher yelled. He had seen something tear off the
drone on his high-resolution display.

"Just watch him!" Hill commanded. He was not going to be guilty of
overconfidence again. If a second pass was needed, he wanted to
know.

"Lost him. I don't see him anywhere. Where'd that sucker go this
time . . . ?"

"Keep looking. We got a piece for sure." Hill had looked the 20-mm
right into the drone's right wing. Why hadn't it just exploded? "Did he
auger in?"

"Still don't have him." Thatcher was getting that worried sound
again. "Wait . . ."

As Hill swung his head around to eyeball the kill, a flashbulb seemed to explode inside his helmet. Pain-bright glare filled the cockpit, doubly intense on Hill's night-adapted eyes. Only the backseater in his tight little cell of electronics retained the ability to see.

On his defensive display screen, the persistent little green dot of the target drone reappeared like an annoying gnat. Only now it was above, above and behind them. "Hill! Hard—"

"I can't see! Thatch! What have you got?"

But before the backseater replied, Hill swung his neck back toward the source of the light. Above and behind them, holding perfect station with the slowed-up Excalibur, two high-beam dazzles burned directly at him. "What the . . ."

Somebody had just switched on their landing lights and caught them square in their fire. And *somebody* meant that their quarry was no drone. Worse, they were no longer invisible.

Hill reflexed both engines into afterburner. The solid explosion of power blasted them from the focus of the twin spotlights. They pushed through the Mach in less than five seconds. The ramjet annunciator glowed and Hill jammed both their throttles into AUTOLITE. Liquid hydrogen coursed into the maws of the two huge engines and lit off with a tremendous detonation. Hill raised the nose and pointed Excalibur toward her true home. The glare of his enemy's landing lights dimmed as they blasted through thirty-seven thousand feet, still climbing like a skyrocket. "Searchlight! Nimbus two!" Hill's eyes still burned.

"Nimbus two, Searchlight. And we show you out of the box."

"You got that right, Searchlight," Hill shot back angrily. "And Nimbus is breaking off! Nimbus two is bingo. You copy that?" Hill swept Excalibur onto her back, rolled level, and pointed the needle nose for Tonopah. He glanced around, nervous for once in a very long time. This was a new game, and nobody was going to creep up on *him*. Adcock! *That little fuck did it again!* They had been sent to attack a drone, but somehow they had gotten vectored into a real airplane. With real people.

"Nimbus!" It was Adcock again. "Confirm the kill, Nimbus two. We want a confirmation on the drone."

Trailing thunder, Excalibur rocketed through Mach 3. Hill fired his response. "Come get it yourself, Searchlight." Hill turned the volume knob on the burst transmitter down to the stop and pointed the invisible black snout of the jet back toward the runways of Tonopah.

"Barnes!" MacHenry shouted as he saw Excalibur's afterburner fire explode. In a moment it was gone, leaving four bright orange circles of flame against the stars. "Can you hear me? Barnes!"

Barnes looked at the ripped skin of his right wing and felt his hard inner ice fracture. His whole body shook. He tried to reach over and punch the remaining wing tank off, but his hand refused to obey him.

After more than a decade of service, he had been given his taste of combat, his initiation. Barnes knew he had failed the test.

He had seen the sky streaked with tracers as Excalibur tested its guns, just as he had guessed. His SA was working overtime tonight. Dr. Tanai would have been proud.

He had seen the knife-thin wings flash overhead like the Angel of Death itself, then scissor down and burn in for the kill. Barnes knew what was coming. He had whipped the T-Bird for every last knot, even as he knew there was no outrunning the nightmare closing in from behind. His fear clamored for speed, to run with the wind, but that was a good way to die.

Excalibur was supposed to be the fastest thing with wings, that much he had heard. He had heard that it was a recon bird, but clearly some rumors were worth less than others. Whatever its mission, fast ships couldn't fly very slow, could they? They couldn't fly as slow as this old T-Bird. *No way.* It would be a finely judged matter; to slow up prematurely would give the enemy a chance to adapt. Too late and it would be all over except for the ballistics. And he and MacHenry would be dead.

But aerial combat was far more art than science, and artists made mistakes.

Barnes nearly lost his ice when he turned, thinking that his enemy would be just turning into the saddle. Instead, he saw Excalibur hurtling at him, riding a prow of afterburner fire. It was already close to optimum firing position. Barnes tensed for the maneuver that would save them or kill them in the next few seconds. *Now!*

An instant before it opened fire, he pulled back the throttle, slapped the flap handle down, and thumbed out the speed brake on the belly of the T-Bird. As Barnes was flung forward, the air suddenly buzzed with a thousand brilliant meteors. One look at how they fell told him his maneuver was not going to work. "BJ!" he shouted in the instant before the inevitable.

Then it was too late. *"No!"* he screamed as a series of heavy thuds shook the T-33. *"No!"* His back tensed as though it could stop the shells from penetrating, as if the power of his own aura could deflect them from the now too thin metal skin of the T-33. "Eject!"

Striking shells jackhammered his vision to a blur. *Hits! Do something!* It didn't matter that the contest was absurdly unfair. Barnes had not lost a simulated dogfight since the Academy. But this was no simulation; it would not end with a gentlemanly wagging of wings. The T-33 shook under a drumroll of cannon fire. At once the damaged right wing began to drop. Barnes had no way of knowing whether it would ever right itself again.

"EJECT!" he screamed over the intercom, hoping MacHenry would have the sense to take the last chance offered. As the wing kept rolling under, Barnes pulled the right armrest up, priming the Martin Baker ejection seat to blow. He twisted his head around to see if MacHenry was doing the same. All it would take was the slight pressure on the armrest trigger and the nightmare of exploding shells and lights and sounds would be away, away in the cool night sky, and Barnes would be under a billowing parachute. He looked up into the canopy mirror. MacHenry wasn't moving!

"MacHenry! *Out!*" He couldn't leave him! *"Eject!"*

A shriek filled his ears as the stricken T-Bird shed its right tip tank. If it had been full, they would have exploded then and there. The shredded metal fell away in the slipstream, and the right wing stopped its roll.

A black delta roared close overhead, whipping the T-33 in Excalibur's turbulent wake. Barnes ducked as the canopy filled with the belly of the marauding jet. His stick shivered uncontrollably, the canopy vibrating so heavily he was sure it would disintegrate.

Excalibur's engines glowed a dull red as its momentum carried it beyond him. A glint of gold came from the single insignia on its black tail, a simple and nameless upthrust sword. A rising fury made his hair stand on end. It was as if a powerful electric current had been switched on within his helmet. "God*damn* you!" he shouted at the apparition, all thoughts of punching out now swallowed whole by his rage. He shoved the throttle back to full military power. The *boom* of the faithful Allison rewarded him with a stiff kick.

Barnes pulled back on the stick as the T-33 burned in behind the slowing stealth jet, rising level, then above, the hot rings of the other plane's strangely shrouded exhausts. Pushing over at the top of the zoom, he punched on the gunsight illuminator on his own HUD and carefully centered Excalibur's canopy in the inner circle. Closer now. The crystal canopy stood out against pure black, filling the gunsight, the range perfect, the angle exact. He wanted to *rip* it apart and hear the *plink!* of fragments as they flew through the wreckage. He wanted to see that mother explode. He wanted them dead. Dead.

"Adios, motherfucker!" Barnes squeezed the stick trigger. The firing circuit triggered the machine guns in the nose onto empty chambers. "*Die!*" he shouted into his mask, and then, without knowing why, Barnes reached over to the right front console and turned on every landing light he had.

The black delta sat at the apex of a triangle of light, swallowing it greedily, an unmarred velvet darkness against the landing lights' brilliance. Its cockpit was bathed in the direct beams and stood out as though flying alone and unattached to anything in this world.

Barnes held it in the laser brilliance of his beams as the foe stumbled left, then right. Barnes matched every move with his own, never permitting the hard focus of his light to wander from the glass canopy out ahead. *Get the message sucker? You're fucking dead.*

Suddenly, twin jets of fire leaped back from the stealth jet's engines;

Barnes's lights began shifting on the fuselage as the black craft accelerated. Barnes brought the nose up to keep his only weapon trained where it mattered, but there was no real contest. Excalibur surged away from his lights.

He felt the rumble of its Mach passage in the T-33's own wounded airframe. Suddenly, the two blast furnaces ahead became four. Excalibur took off toward the stars like a moon shot. "God!" He heard a shout and looked up into the canopy mirror. How long had MacHenry been calling him? A piercing whistle of air permeated the cockpit from a hole punched in the fuselage.

"Barnes! Are you okay?"

Barnes clenched his fist around the stick and willed the fear away. "Christ, MacHenry," he said finally. Barnes dialed up the oxygen to 100 percent and sucked the pure air in. It sharpened his thinking another notch. "You're a goddamned typical airline captain. You don't know how to follow orders. I told you to eject!"

"I . . . I couldn't," MacHenry said, glancing at his right armrest. It was up, ready to fire at the slightest touch, but nothing, not even the black vampire they had just fought off, could make him use it. "What in God's name was that thing?"

"Forget God. That was the fucking devil at work," Barnes answered. "It was supposed to be just a rumor."

"That's one hell of a rumor."

Barnes shifted in his seat and felt a small jab of pain in his left arm, just like an injection. He twisted to see if a shard of glass from the canopy was jabbing him. Barnes suddenly worried after MacHenry. "Any damage back there?" he asked.

"Just that wing and the tip tank. Is it going to hold?"

"No problem," Barnes lied. He looked out at the clipped right wing where the tip tank used to be. The aileron was vibrating badly, as though one of the hinge points had taken a hit. He reached over to the left subpanel and flipped open the guard on the tank jettison and toggled the button marked SALVO.

The undamaged left tip tank, as empty as its mate, blew off in a sudden explosion that made MacHenry jump. "Jesus! Did you do that?"

"Yeah. She won't fly for shit with one tip on and one tip off," Barnes replied. "You sure there aren't any hits back there?"

MacHenry checked his instruments. There was not much to check. "Power's out. My lights are gone. What do we do now?"

"Well," Barnes began, "we're going to set a new altitude record for a clip-wing T-33." He had already pulled the stick aft; there were serious mountains between them and home. The Sierras rose to nearly fifteen thousand feet to the south and almost that high to the north.

"What if they come back?" said MacHenry. He could no longer see Excalibur's afterburner flame against the stars.

"Beats me," Barnes said. It sounded like a joke, but he was dead serious. "Ram the mother, maybe. We sure can't do much else." His fist gripped the stick hard. If those damned 50s had been loaded . . .

The T-Bird struggled up the eastern slopes of the mountains. He checked his fuel totalizer again and just shook his head. "Anyway, we're going to go for an endurance record by flying this buggy back the last hundred miles on the sweet aroma of kerosene. I don't know about you, MacHenry, but all in all, I think we should, you know, get a medal or something."

The black hull of the Sierras fell away beneath their nose as they climbed, each hundred feet a small victory for the T-Bird's stoutness.

Barnes found he had to slew the jet slightly to keep it in its climb. The controls felt all wrong as they mushed upward. He pushed the throttle right up to the afterburner. He'd throw away the last of his gas if he used it, but he might be eating rock if he didn't. His brain felt mired in tar. Something was wrong there, too. The dark shapes of the mountains filled his windshield.

His left hand reached to shove the Allison into reheat when they whistled between two high towers of granite and over the crest. Beyond them, the lights of the Central Valley slowly reappeared, beckoning. Barnes smiled grimly. Just like the good doctor Tanai said, the best decisions make themselves.

Setting course toward the lights, Barnes pointed the nose of the

T-Bird northwest. Somewhere in that galaxy was Mather Air Force Base. *Home.* He picked up the E6-B slide rule computer to figure the time and the fuel burn, but put it down without entering the first number. He didn't really need it; the yellow fuel-warning lights and the ragged metal of the shell-pocked wing were evidence enough. He wouldn't bet even money on their making it.

15

THE DEAL

WHAT in God's name were you thinking about, Adcock?" Radway demanded as he rubbed his eyes. A small voice was already whispering, *And who gets to tell Enstrom?* Norton Aerodyne's CEO did his best to live in a world beyond all shock and surprise. To admit that an event had outpaced its own planning was exactly the same in his eyes as admitting failure. Enstrom didn't tolerate failure. Period.

"You said to handle it," Adcock replied. "I—"

"The vote on funding is coming up next week. We're talking a five-and-a-half-billion-dollar stream over three years, and you go kicking over the anthill. Jesus." He snapped on the bedside lamp and focused on the small clock: *3:15*.

"Sir, you told me the Agency was briefed," Adcock said. "You intimated that you had some pull with the FAA. But he was there, sir. *There*. They were going to blow the program wide open. You said—"

"I said that Aurora was more important than anything," Radway interrupted. "It's our lifeboat, Peter. It's our last chance."

"You said the company would back me up regardless, so long as the program stayed secure. I did just what—"

"Enough!" Radway shouted. "Don't give me the sordid details. I'm not stepping into this pile of shit with you." Radway slipped his glasses on. Somehow they made him able to think more clearly. "This could send the whole project down the toilet. Not even Langley would stay with us."

"No. That is *not* the case, sir," Adcock replied with the first hint of a stiffening spine. "It was Langley that gave me the information that permitted the intercept."

Radway stopped short. *"What?* Who?"

"Bridger. I assume it was through their North Air connection. I would never have known about the investigation flight in time without Bridger."

"Bridger ordered you to intercept them?" Radway had been very delicate in what he chose to reveal to the Solarium chairman. And what he chose not to reveal. Now Bridger knew. Knew everything. *Christ.* "You're sure it was Bridger who passed along the intel on this? He told you to try to . . ." Radway stopped. Secure or not, there were things that just could not be said into a telephone.

"No. Not exactly. He specifically mentioned the route and the time. He called it a window of opportunity. I assumed you had briefed him, Matthew. I didn't know that—"

"Peter," said Radway, "Arthur Bridger set you up. They don't let them play games over there anymore, so he got you to do it for him." *Window of opportunity!* The bastard. Radway shook his head.

"I thought I was doing what was best for the company."

"Yeah. Maybe Bridger's company. Not Norton Aero," Radway said bitterly. Adcock was not up to the occasion. Not one bit.

Adcock sighed, the cross-continental connection popping and squealing as two encrypted circuits danced in unison. "What do you want me to do? You tell me and . . ."

Radway laughed. "No way. That is most assuredly *not* how this game is played." Radway's inner balance had already shifted over to damage limitation. "Peter, Norton Aerodyne needs this project. At five point five bill it needs it a whole lot more than it needs you. If this gets out in an uncontrolled way, you might as well take up designing model airplanes. You realize what I'm saying? You've got to find these two—MacHenry and Bates?"

"Barnes."

"Get them off our backs," Radway continued. "Talk to them. Buy them. Say what you need to say. I'm talking a deal, Peter. No more of this Agency hugger-mugger. Is that clear?"

"Yes, sir."

"All right, then." Radway's brain was spinning up at 100 percent now. "Do your job or tomorrow we'll fly someone out who can." Before Adcock could protest, Radway hung up. *Bridger!* He pulled out a small notebook and punched a new number into the STU-3 secure phone. The ENCRYPT light blinked back on immediately.

"Bridger."

"Late night, Arthur?" said Radway. "I hope I'm not getting you up. Matthew Radway here."

"As a matter of fact—"

"Sorry," said Radway. "But I think you'd better listen. Your window of opportunity? It just got smashed."

Adcock hung up and pressed the base intercom button. Fifty feet over his head, the hangar level extension rang.

"Flight," said the sleepy voice of the North Air contract pilot.

"Get the MU-2 fueled and ready for an immediate departure. I'll be right up." As Adcock put the phone down, two heavy knocks shook the calendar off his office door. Before he could reply, it flew open, and Harry Hill, still dressed in his sweat-darkened flightsuit, came in like a bull released from a tight pen.

"God *damn* it!" Hill kicked the door shut. "I told you not to screw with me. I told you no more *fucking* errors." He marched over to Adcock's desk. For an instant, Adcock was sure the pilot was going to hit him. Instead, Hill leaned over and jabbed him in the chest. "You nearly got somebody smoked." Hill didn't mention the fact that if his opponent had been armed, he might not be standing here. "Do you hear me, asshole? Smoked."

Adcock adjusted his glasses and moved away from Hill's accusing finger. "A mistake—"

"You bet your sweet pink ass there was a mistake." Each syllable earned another jab. "Now listen to me, and listen tight." Hill leaned over and placed his still-sweaty face inches from Adcock's. "I've kind of lost track of the rules of this little game, but I've fucking got one for you: we do not go after our own. Never." He balled his fist and saw the engineer's face go blank like a switched-off television. It would be so easy, so gratifying, to send this lying little fuck sprawling. Hill brought himself back from the edge.

"You . . . you're tired, Hill. Go take a shower. We'll debrief later."

"Who was in that other aircraft?"

Adcock fought to compose himself. "It was an accident. Come on, Hill, you've got to trust me on this one." Adcock's eyes pleaded.

Hill took a single, deep breath and stood up. "Trust you? Is that supposed to be funny? You sent us into a fucking hot range at HUMMER. You fucking did it again, friend, and in my business, two errors is too many. Errors get people killed."

"What do you want me to say? You know what I know." Adcock quickly analyzed the forces arrayed against him. Could he afford to lose Hill from the program? Adcock shook his head. Another disaffected pilot was the last thing he needed right now. "I told you there was a mistake. Nobody's—"

"Listen," said Hill. "I want a full explanation. I mean the nuts and bolts. I want it by tomorrow morning. In writing. Otherwise"—Hill slashed his finger across his throat—"I'm out. Sleep on it, Adcock." Turning on his heel, he marched to the office door and slammed it behind him.

Adcock heard Hill's footsteps fade down the corridor. When he could no longer hear the angry pilot's boots, he ventured into the hall, checked that it was empty, and took the stairs up to the hangar level. He saw the activity around Hill's Excalibur as the night crew defueled the last of the liquid hydrogen into the cavern's cryogenic tanks.

The North Air MU-2, a fast, twin-engine executive transport, was already on the elevator platform, the company logo written in faded script above its windows.

The duty pilot, dressed in an unmarked flightsuit, looked up. He was older than Hill, a relic from the time of North Air's glory days in Southeast Asia. He looked up at Adcock with faint interest and amusement. "And where are we headed, Mr. Adcock?"

"You'll fly where you're told." Adcock's hair was plastered to his forehead despite the cool air drifting down the big elevator shaft. He stepped onto the steel decking. With a whine of the hydraulics, they began to rise.

"Talk to me, Barnes," said MacHenry.

Barnes pulled back power to the Allison, trading airspeed for fuel as they descended toward the lights of the Central Valley. He tried to figure the time they had left. Oddly, he had trouble with the stone-simple fuel-burn calculation. His helmet felt like granite on his shoulders as he shook away a pounding headache. "Half an hour and we make like a glider, BJ."

"There's no point trying to get back to Mather. We've got plenty of other closer airports where we can put down."

"That's easy for you to say." Barnes knew he would be better off with Colonel Braden if he could get the T-33 back to base. "You get anything on your radios?" he asked, giving his head another shake. Barnes was feeling drowsy. *Fumes?*

"No power back here, remember?" What was wrong with Barnes? "How about Fresno? We could put in there. Part of the field is still Air Force." MacHenry was already thinking about security. Not only for the piece of black carbon in his pocket but also—and urgently—for the damaged T-33.

"Oh. Yeah." Barnes had flown against some of the F-16 jocks stationed at Fresno. The 144th wasn't a bad outfit, but it would take more than a brace of '16s to protect him from the CO after this little jaunt. But MacHenry was right. Barnes sat up, shook his head to clear it, and dialed up Fresno Approach. A wave of lethargy seemed to settle on him like a dank fog. *What the fuck?* "Hey, BJ, how're you feeling, sleepy or anything? I think I'm getting some kind of vapor through my mask."

"Sleepy? I've never been more awake in my life. I'm not exactly used to getting shot at. How about increasing the oxygen flow?"

"Huh? Oh. Right." Barnes tried to spin the diluter dial on the oxygen up to 100 percent, but it wouldn't budge. He tried again, and once more before realizing it was already at its maximum setting. "It's been kind of a long day." He pressed the transmit button on the stick. "Fresno Approach, Hawk two three, how do you hear?"

With the powerful jammers at Tonopah switched off, the screeching was gone, leaving an empty hollow in the headset. "Fresno Approach, Hawk two three," he repeated. Nothing. His eyes went wide as a sharp, electric shudder ran through the muscles of his left arm. *Shit!* he thought. *Just what I need is a cramp!* He stretched it out, brushing the throttle and making the Allison surge. "Easy old-timer." He pulled back the throttle and the engine settled into its old rumble. He felt stiff. "I'll try the radio again."

"Keep transmitting in the blind. They might be able to hear and we might not be able to listen. How about turning up the TACAN receiver?"

What? "Good idea." Barnes spun the volume up and hit the Nav 1 button on the audio panel. The steady beeping tone from the radio station was broken by a voice.

". . . read ident. Repeat, military flight Hawk two three, if you read this transmission, squawk ident."

Barnes moved his thumb to the remote ident switch mounted on the control stick, right next to the trigger for the useless, empty 50-calibers in the nose. Empty or not, that black mother had been meat at the table. He smiled as he jabbed the button. "Hawk is squawking ident."

"Okay! I got . . ." the voice faded, then returned. "Radar contact, Hawk two three, we've got . . . we can hear your transmissions. How do you read, Fresno?"

"Hawk two three, transmitting out on two seven three point six and listening over the TACAN. Nice to hear your voice, Fresno."

"Where have you been, Hawk? We've been calling you for the last half hour. We thought we were going to have to crank up search and rescue."

"Ah, roger." *You damn near did.*

"Let us know next time you go off on a side trip. Present position direct Mather Air Force Base is approved."

"No!" MacHenry broke in. "We aren't going to make it that far. Tell him."

Barnes felt too tired to fight. "Whatever," he said. But the T-Bird's nose didn't waver nor did they begin their descent.

"Barnes! Are we landing or what?" MacHenry demanded.

Barnes saw the distant lights of Fresno creep closer. He pressed the transmit button again. "Ah, Fresno, Hawk's back with you. How's it look for a straight-in to Runway Two Niner at FAT? We might need to check out a little problem here."

"Okay, now you want to land at Fresno?"

"Just to take a look at a, ah, caution light."

"Roger, Hawk," Approach replied with a testy sigh. "Report the beacon inbound, cleared for the Fresno ILS Two Niner left. Will you need any equipment?"

"Negative."

"Roger. Contact the tower. So long."

"Copy all and over to tower." Barnes slowed the T-33 by pulling back the throttle while trimming up the nose. He was flying by instinct, as usual. But tonight, his instincts were not enough. Almost immediately, the battered right wing began to drop, the airflow disturbed by the torn metal. At this low altitude, a differential stall would send them into an unrecoverable spin. Barnes seemed oblivious.

MacHenry knew they were right on the edge. He wagged the stick to get Barnes's attention as the damaged wing started to roll.

"What's up?" Barnes said over the intercom, then, "Shit!" Barnes slapped the stick to the left, trying to raise the wing by brute force, but it had exactly the opposite effect. The wing began to rock furiously, faster, faster, the sudden, plunging drop an instant away.

"Barnes!" MacHenry yelled. "Airspeed!" One second. Two. Barnes seemed to be in a trance, unable to act. "Barnes!" When he didn't answer, MacHenry shoved the throttle in the rear cockpit full forward, grabbed the controls, and lowered the nose toward the flashing approach lights of Fresno. The Allison kicked in and the plane staggered drunkenly upright.

MacHenry was furious. "Don't you even *think* about slowing this thing, mister! You shoot this approach fast and like it matters. Where's the checklist?"

"I can fly this buggy, friend. Don't go getting uppity on me," Barnes snapped as he recited the prelanding check from memory. He grabbed the controls back from MacHenry's shaking grip. "Fuel is where it's got to be, flaps are staying put. Gear . . ." He looked down at the handle over on the lower-right subpanel. *Uh-oh,* he thought as he pulled the control out of its detent and rammed the gear selector down. The hard thunk of the falling wheels transmitted through the frame. How had he forgotten the gear?

The T-Bird dropped with the extra drag of the extended wheels. Barnes noticed a frantic green blinking coming from Fresno tower out ahead; he had forgotten to call them up. *Fuck them. Fly the airplane,* he thought grimly as his eyes swept the panel in a practiced pattern even this strange lethargy could not break. He glanced up at the rising sea of airport lights ahead. Blue ones, white ones, flashing reds; they were trying to tell him something, but what? Where was the picture? The lights seemed to merge with the stars, and for a panicked instant, Barnes could not tell the sky from the light-spangled earth. He shook his head furiously, clenched his teeth, and fought the creeping vertigo. *Something ain't right.*

"Settle down, Barnes," MacHenry said. "Be smooth."

"We're fast," Barnes mumbled as they streaked down the glide slope a good fifty knots above normal final-approach speed. His skin felt cold and sweaty. He pulled off his right glove and found his flightsuit soaked through. *Fuck.* His initiation as a combat pilot, a death-dealing fighter jock, and Barnes had sweated buckets, scared as a frightened schoolboy.

"Easy, easy," said MacHenry. "Roll her on, jus' roll her on."

Barnes pulled more power off, increasing the sink but keeping the nose pointed down to maintain the safety margin of speed. The dark black rectangle of the runway, edge lit in white, loomed up directly ahead. Barnes reached over and flicked on the landing lights. They, at least, still worked, and a large block of white pavement streaked black by thousands of landings came into view.

MacHenry was watching over the top of Barnes's helmet as the runway rose to meet them. It was coming quick. "You got it?" The military portion of the airport flashed beneath them as they dropped. A row of parked gray fighters hurtled by under lurid orange security lights. "Barnes!"

"Real fast," Barnes said as he checked the gear once again and braced for the hard landing. Fifteen feet above the invisible runway, he pulled the engine back to idle. The T-33 had given more tonight than its original designers could have imagined possible. It could give no more. The tail settled heavily, pitching the nose high into the air.

MacHenry felt the bottom fall out, felt the wing give up and start rolling. He braced himself against the inevitable crash. *At least we won't burn,* he thought. There was no fuel left for that. The right gear hit first and hard, so hard that it doubled MacHenry's vision and bounced his crash helmet into the glass canopy. The jet ran crazily at an angle along the runway. They were headed for the weeds at 130 knots. Half rolling, half flying, out of control. Suddenly, MacHenry felt the stick come under firm command, felt the pedals dance alive beneath his own feet. The brakes shrieked as Barnes, mustering himself out of dreamland, took over and herded the jet back to the runway centerline. Runway markers flashed by, slower, slower. The last turnoff appeared as a cluster of blue lights.

Barnes stabbed the brakes and the T-33 skidded into a sharp turn off the runway. "Not my best," said Barnes. He dialed up the tower frequency at last.

"Hawk!" the angry tower man shot. "This is Fresno tower. If you read, remain on this frequency and say your destination on the airport."

Barnes looked up into the rearview mirror. "Where we headed, boss?"

"Someplace safe," MacHenry said, wondering whether it existed anymore. He checked his watch. It was almost midnight. "Someplace public maybe?" He was thinking out loud. The military portion of Fresno might not be a very smart choice, given what had happened this night.

"Ah, Tower, Hawk here. What's open?"

"You've got radio problems, mister," Tower said angrily. "We've been trying to raise you all the way in on your approach. If you want fuel there's only Beechcraft West. Other than the 144th. Do you want taxi instructions to the air base?"

Barnes saw MacHenry shake his head vigorously no. "Beechcraft West will be fine," he said.

"Roger. Taxi to the ramp. They're the only one still lit up. Better get those radios checked."

"First thing." Barnes ran the throttle forward and taxied toward the parking ramp. "Hey, maybe we can buy some fuel. We won't need much to get back to Mather."

"*Fuel?* Forget it, Barnes. This jet isn't airworthy. Let them come and haul it out with a flatbed tomorrow."

"Tomorrow," Barnes repeated. "Tomorrow's going to be complicated." The angry image of Col. Al Braden flickered across the gunsight projected onto the windshield. "Real complicated." The jet's landing lights now illuminated a long row of one-story metal buildings. A row of private aircraft sat in front of them. Barnes slipped in between a Seneca and a tall-legged King Air and braked the T-33 to a halt, the Beechcraft West sign right off the nose.

Barnes pulled back the throttle and the scream of the engine fell off to a whisper. It seemed to take a lot of force to move it around the detent into idle cutoff, but Barnes forced the lever and killed the Allison. "Damn," said Barnes, sitting back in his seat, his helmet resting heavily against the headrest. The orange ramp lights bathed the cockpit in light now. "Oh, damn."

"What's the problem?"

Barnes's helmet bobbed as he took several exaggerated breaths. The landing lights were still on and MacHenry admonished him. "Where's your checklist, Barnes? Power down those lights if you want any batteries left."

Barnes's helmet nodded. "Ah, sorry, BJ, but I've got a small problem up here." He hit the canopy switch and the electric motor began to whine. But he was staring numbly at the throttle grip.

"What's wrong?" MacHenry leaned as far forward as he could.

Then he saw it.

The throttle, and the entire side of Barnes's flightsuit, was dark and wet with fresh blood.

MacHenry stood on the tarmac and watched as the ambulance van roared off for Fresno Community with Barnes inside. The air was cool with a hint of dampness, but the ground still radiated the heat of a summer's day. What should his next move be? It was after midnight. MacHenry's jaw clamped tight as Barnes's last words played over and over again in his mind.

Let that guy know I had his black ass. Promise or I'll haunt the fuck out of you.

MacHenry had promised. Somehow, he was going to keep that promise. Whatever it took. Whatever. He stepped inside the suddenly busy office and found the pay phone. He pulled out a slip of paper with the number of Barnes's squadron CO on it and dialed. The phone trilled twice and clicked.

"Braden." The voice was impatient, raspy, and unadorned with formality.

"Colonel Braden? This is Brian MacHenry from the FAA. I need—"

"You!" Braden erupted, his voice now needle sharp. "Where in God's name are you? And where is Barnes? Goddamn it but I will have an answer!"

"You'll get one, Colonel," MacHenry said, his voice even and controlled. "We're at Fresno, Fresno Air Terminal, at a fixed-base operation called Beechcraft West. At least I'm here."

"MacHenry, this may come as a surprise," said Braden, "but I for one do not give a *fuck* where *you* are. I want Barnes, I want that airplane, and I want them both immediately. Now quit the mouth music and put him on the line."

"I can't do it, Colonel . . ." MacHenry began, feeling the words stick. "There's . . . there's been an accident."

"What accident? Barnes? Is he all right?" Braden shot back, his tone suddenly different, protective.

"No, he is not all right. They tried to shoot us down—"

"*What?*" Braden shouted into MacHenry's ear. "Who was shooting? Explain yourself, mister!"

"West of Las Vegas. Over the desert," MacHenry said. "All I can tell you is what I heard and saw. We lost communications and the next thing I know we're in a dogfight. Somebody fired a missile at us. Barnes said it was a Sparrow."

Braden, for once, was silent. "A Sparrow?" he finally said, the message in his hesitation clear: *Then why are you still alive?* "You evaded it?"

"Barnes did. We're here—I'm here—talking to you, because he outflew it, and he outflew the aircraft that was chasing us, too. We took some hits, but we made it."

"You got a visual? You actually saw something? What was it?" The questions came from the phone like three quick shots from a hair-triggered pistol.

"I'm not sure you want to know. For that matter, I'm not sure you don't know already. Barnes said it was a rumor. He thought it was something called Excalibur. It did have some kind of sword marking on its tail."

"Jesus." Once again a silence. The wall clock above MacHenry's head moved in a soft *thock*. The face read *12:24*. He could hear a long, drawn-out exhalation over the telephone.

"There's more," MacHenry continued. "The medics just took him away on transfusion. He's lost a lot of blood."

"How did he look?"

"Not good, Colonel. His face was about as white as his helmet. I didn't hear or see anything else." *Promise me you'll let that guy know I had him. . . .*

"And you say the aircraft is damaged?"

MacHenry looked out through the window to the jet. It was all but covered in foam. The airport crash truck was still nearby. "Yes, sir, it is. I'm not sure how it made it this far. They hit us with something."

"Okay, MacHenry, straight-shooting time." Braden's voice was now recomposed. "First, I want the name of the hospital—"

"Why?" MacHenry broke in. "So they can finish him off?"

"Cut the sarcasm. I'm not in the mood. You don't have a rat's ass of an idea what kind of flap this crusade of yours has raised. *I* don't even know how far it goes." Braden paused. "I want Barnes in one piece and that airplane back. In that order. You can go to hell in your own way."

"Colonel, tell me one thing. Who wanted it hushed? Who didn't want it to come out that it was one of your own jets that knocked that Cessna down up in HUMMER?"

"MacHenry, the Air Force is not involved, and I see no reason to divulge what little I do know to some FAA loose cannon who brings pure shit down on one of my pilots. Now, where is Barnes?"

MacHenry knew he would get nothing more. "Fresno Community. The T-33 is right here. It's not going anywhere and neither am I."

"Keep it that way," Braden fired. "I want you to secure that T-33 and wait until I get there. Don't you move your ass off that spot, MacHenry. I might still get generous with you in my report on all this."

"I have no—"

"You just stay put!" Braden repeated, and hung up.

"—place to go," MacHenry said to the dial tone. He hung up the phone, walked over to a row of chairs, and fell into one, feeling the lump of carbon composite in his hip pocket.

"Coffee, sir?" asked the lineboy. "I can put on a fresh pot. You look like you can use some."

MacHenry looked up. "No. No thanks."

He shut his eyes tightly, the adrenaline and the fear draining away his strength to resist what his body needed most. He heard the murmur of voices as the lineboy called his boss; the soft progress of the second hand around the wall clock. Then, the sounds dimmed and stopped altogether.

The dream was inevitable. In a slow motion made more terrible for the fact that MacHenry knew its outcome, he felt the T-Bird lurch inverted and begin its dive. Only this time a strange sun shone down, cool like the moon but brighter. He could see the hard ground rising, the controls frozen, the engine roaring, as they fell. A shout, but in a voice slowed like a record played too slow, said, *Eject! Eject! Eject!*

He pushed his arm through the strangely thick air and raised the armrest on his ejection seat. It took all his energy, all his focus, to pull the red trigger.

A blast of crystal shards shotgunned his face as he rocketed through the canopy. The T-33 fell away below him and began to spin.

As he neared the top of his ballistic arc, a black wing thundered overhead. It was no airplane. It was alive, alive with a shark's mouth filled with glinting teeth. The pale sun flashed from something gripped in that terrible jaw. He tried to see what it was, but he was already falling out of control. MacHenry began to tumble, a smoke trail billowing behind him; he was falling, falling, waiting for the chute to explode open, waiting for the shock. The seat fell away from him as he braced for it.

But it didn't come. He fell toward the desert floor. The ground rushed him like a tidal wave, faster, faster. He could feel the heat rising from the sand. He was a hundred feet; fifty. Ten. *"No!"* His eyes shot wide open, his heart thumping in his chest. Then he heard a new sound: the hoarse scream of approaching engines.

He looked up at the wall clock. It was 1:40. A Mitsubishi MU-2 was taxiing slowly down the parallel toward Beechcraft West. Its landing lights swept the row of parked aircraft, coming at last to rest full upon the T-33. The howling turboprop stopped for a moment, then nosed along in search of a vacant parking slot. MacHenry could see the faded markings on the MU-2: *North Air Transport*.

Adcock waited by the hatch for the North Air pilot to hit the release. He all but leaped down the airstairs. The night was cool and damp, but it barely registered as he ran up to the lineboy who had guided them into their parking slot. "I'm looking for someone—the pilot of that jet over there," he said, indicating the T-33.

"He's inside, sir. Will you be wanting some fuel?"

"No. Thank you very much." Adcock put a ten-dollar bill in the young man's hand and started to walk. He stopped when he came to the battered T-33. He walked carefully over the foam-slicked tarmac. A shiver ran up his neck as he ran his hands along the sharp, can-opener tears punched into the wing. A chain of craters the size of tennis balls was blasted into the dark green metal. *His* creation had done this. Adcock rocked the wings, listening for sounds of internal structure given way. He worked his way in toward the fuselage and felt smooth skin change to wrinkles, dents, and found one small hole in the underside of the cockpit.

He poked a finger into it and cried out in surprise. A jagged edge had cut him. When he pulled his hand away too quickly, it cut him again. "Damn it!" He sucked at the trickle of blood. His finger tasted sickly sweet from the jet's leaking hydraulic fluid. He did not hear MacHenry come up from behind.

"Sir, I'd appreciate it if you stayed back from that aircraft."

Adcock spun and confronted a flight-suited figure with a haggard, drawn face. *Barnes.* "Oh?" he said with a sneer. "I don't think so. I don't think you're getting the picture at all," Adcock said haughtily. "But I'm not surprised. Your judgment has been screwed up all day, as I see it. Do you know who I am?"

MacHenry sighed wearily. "No, and it doesn't make a damned bit of difference. You *will* stay clear." He stepped into Adcock's face and forced the smaller man to retreat.

Adcock nearly slipped on the foam. He caught himself and puffed himself back up. "You'd better start listening. I represent the owner.

This aircraft is ours, and I'll do what I please with it," Adcock said. "Get it now?" His eyes traveled beyond MacHenry. "Or don't they teach you about private property in the Air Force, Major?"

"Major? I'm no major. I'm from the FAA. My name is MacHenry." He pulled out his official identification. "Now," he said as Adcock eyed the plastic card, "maybe you've got a name, too."

Adcock looked down at the tarmac, the white foam covering his black loafers, then up again. "Williams," he said, not looking him in the eye but rather beyond. "Steven Williams of North Air, the owner of record on this T-33. So you're MacHenry. My mistake." Adcock smiled uneasily.

"Join the crowd."

"No. No. What I mean is, you weren't the responsible party," Adcock said as his smile flickered and died. "Just along for the ride."

"Mr. Williams," MacHenry replied wearily, "there will be plenty of time to sort through the paper track on who was permitted to do what. Frankly, I'm very tired, so if you'll remain clear of the aircraft until the Air Force arrives—"

"Air Force?" Adcock interrupted. "Air Force? What do you mean?" The more people brought in now, the harder it would be to clamp a lid on it.

"I spoke with Mather Air Force Base half an hour ago. Colonel Braden is on his way."

Adcock had a sudden vision of a bag of marbles dumped onto the floor, each heading off in a different direction. It was getting away from him, and Radway had been nothing if not clear: *contain it or we'll find someone who can.* "I see," he said.

"Good," MacHenry replied.

Adcock cleared his throat. "Mr. MacHenry, I think that you and I need to talk." He glanced up at the brightly lit offices of Beechcraft West. "What do you say?"

MacHenry examined the small man. He seemed a strange and suspicious mix of fear and assurance. What did he have to say worth hearing?

Adcock answered the doubt on MacHenry's face. "You see, I have this theory. You can tell me if it's right." His teeth shone through a thin smile. "I think that you probably have a lot of questions. I might have a couple of answers." He nodded at the glass door to the Beechcraft West office. "What do you say? Shall we see if my theory is correct?"

"Very well, Mr. Williams," said MacHenry. "You're on."

He followed Adcock back inside. There was a small pilots' lounge in the rear of the main lobby. MacHenry slapped at the conference room wall and struck the switch for the lights. They snapped on with a low buzz, revealing a scarred table with chairs, a collection of aviation magazines, and a huge wall map. He pulled out a chair and sat down. "I'm listening." His hand automatically reached for a pencil stub and a pad of jotting paper. "You were going to give me some answers."

Adcock sat. "Okay. Fair is fair, right?" He leaned forward over the table and folded his hands. "For your ears only. The key to the situation here is that North Air Transport is not just your everyday aircraft-ferrying company."

"Meaning?"

"Meaning we do quite a bit of sensitive work for the government. All branches." Adcock leaned back and smiled as though proud of North Air's corporate achievements. "The aircraft you and Barnes *appropriated* is one of a shipment of three."

"To Ecuador," MacHenry remembered aloud. "So far you haven't told me anything I didn't already know."

"I'll try harder. This is where I need your word, MacHenry, that none of this gets beyond the door." Adcock waited but MacHenry remained silent.

"What you and the Ecuadoreans do is of interest to me." MacHenry glanced out the window. A sparkling light was suspended in the dark sky as an aircraft maneuvered for landing. The high whine of its engines could just be heard through the closed window. *Braden.*

"The other two planes never landed in Ecuador, Mr. MacHenry," Adcock said in a low voice. "They were never meant to. They were diverted en route to an airbase in Honduras, where they were met by our pilots, mostly U.S. Air Force officers, who are flying them in support roles for the local military. Drug busting, counterinsurgency. Who knows? We don't ask."

MacHenry raised an eyebrow. "I can't say that it surprises me. What's the significance?"

"Simple. It is essential to our clients that none of this gets out. We'll go a long way to keep them happy. A very long way."

"You haven't told me anything I'd be interested in repeating. How does this tie in with what happened tonight?"

"Here's where I can help you out, MacHenry." Adcock reached into his jacket pocket and pulled out several papers. "It certainly wasn't anything to do with us. And it's vital that it stays that way. Can we deal?" Adcock glanced nervously out the window as a small jet taxied by.

MacHenry never liked the sound of that word. "Where I come from, a deal is an exchange. What do you know about what happened to us tonight?"

"The attack?" Adcock watched his words spread surprise across MacHenry's face. "You see? My sources are pretty good, aren't they?"

So it hadn't been an accident. "Go on."

"Naturally we're concerned. It's our property after all. Those conversions cost a bundle. Plus, we get paid when the jet lands in Tegucigalpa and not before. So you see," he said, "I jumped on it with both feet. This is what happened. Take it. Good faith." He slid one of the papers across the table. MacHenry picked it up.

"The complete radio transcript. They tried to warn you away from the exercise area," Adcock said with a satisfied smile as the color drained from MacHenry's cheeks. "Who knows what those guys were up to? All kinds of things fly out of Edwards. To that pilot, you and the target drone looked identical. When the first pass didn't knock you down, they got worried the drone was heading for someplace where it could hit a house, a hospital." Adcock listened as footsteps echoed from the hallway outside. "They thought they were going after a drone, MacHenry. Answer satisfactory?"

Was he tired, or was this man with a deal making sense? MacHenry couldn't tell. "How did you get this so fast?" Adcock motioned for him to return it and MacHenry pushed it back across the table.

"I told you. In my business, we make a lot of useful friends. Some very interesting people. But listen," he said with a chuckle, "they may be nice guys, but you never want to meet them at work. Never. So," he said with the look of a lawyer summing up a winning case, "do we have a deal?"

"Your information for what? My silence on the flight tonight?"

"That's a good place to start," Adcock agreed.

"And if I find it impossible to follow your advice?" MacHenry reached under the table and felt the lump of carbon graphite in his pocket.

Adcock sighed. "You'd be making a real mistake. We'd prosecute for theft. Grand larceny. You'd be finished at the FAA and Barnes's career in the service goes down the tubes. If you think that's an overstatement, remember who our clients are." Adcock shook his head. "I'm sorry if that seems harsh, but it's the way it is. We have to protect ourselves. All things considered, I think we're being very fair. So, do we have a deal or what?"

"MacHenry!"

MacHenry turned in his chair. He looked back at Adcock. "That will be Colonel Braden," he said. "Williams, if we keep quiet, you will, too—is that it? No repercussions—and I mean none—against Barnes?"

"Or you," Adcock said with relief. *It's going to work.* "Nothing. Just like it didn't happen at all. Whatever you were doing in that jet, you just weren't doing. Okay?"

"MacHenry!"

"I can handle my own fights, but Barnes doesn't need any more trouble." He looked up at the door to the hall. "In here, Colonel."

"Remember, MacHenry, we have a deal," Adcock warned.

"I'll remember it exactly as long as you do, Mr. Williams."

The door pushed wide and Colonel Braden, still in his flightsuit, marched in.

"Damn it, but I thought I ordered you to stand by that aircraft!" Braden shouted. "Who's this?" he demanded when he saw Adcock.

"This," MacHenry said, "is Mr. Williams. He's from North Air Transport. The owner of record on that jet outside."

Braden scowled. "You got here fast enough," he said to Adcock before turning back to MacHenry. "You and I are going to have a little talk."

"I think, Colonel," Adcock interrupted, "that as the owners we should be a part of any debriefing that—"

Braden spun. "*You* will join us *when* you are invited," he snapped. "In the meantime I suggest you maintain security around your property." The colonel nodded toward the door. "Out," he ordered.

Adcock stood. "I'm sure this will all work out," he said to MacHenry, a cold smile stuck to his face. "Remember our discussion," he said as he walked out.

"Go ahead, Colonel. I'm ready."

"First," he began, "the good news is that Barnes is going to be all right. We were in communication with the hospital as we shot the approach. They filled him back up with type O, glued a patch on, and it looks like it's holding. No secondary damage. He was lucky for a change."

"And the bad news?"

Braden listened as Adcock's footsteps receded down the stairs. "The bad news is I have reason to believe that the intercept was not an accident."

So much for his deal with the man from North Air. MacHenry shook his head wearily. "Well, I guess it's no surprise, is it? Someone wants to keep the FAA from laying the HUMMER accident on the Air Force's doorstep. That same someone thinks it's important enough to arrange a little accident for us on the way back home. Someone's reaching for all the easy answers tonight."

"Negative. We pull some boners, MacHenry"—Braden balled his fist—"but not this big. You're way out of line on that one."

"Then who wants to see the evidence of that crash kept quiet so badly that they are willing to risk murder?"

"I *can* tell you it wasn't us. And I can tell you that from here on in it's a new ball game. One," he fired, "you will not step foot back at Mather, not now, not ever. Two, I will see to it that Barnes is reassigned effective Monday and that he will not, repeat *not,* participate in this misguided crusade of yours again."

"I think you've overlooked something, Colonel," MacHenry said angrily. "A man burned to death in a midair collision with a military jet in your area. Yours, Colonel. And somebody went to one hell of an effort to make it look like a weather accident." He rubbed his blearing eyes. "A lot of effort, and maybe more that that. I don't know yet."

"Exactly what do you think you know?" Braden, suddenly icy, looked directly into MacHenry's accusing stare.

"The truth, God help us. And Monday morning I'll see to it that Washington knows, too. I'll wager that by Tuesday, you're going to get calls from about a dozen lawyers who have been hounding us to release something, *anything* remotely incriminating. If you think I've been a nuisance, you just wait until they smell green money. I've got a pry bar on a big, nasty rock and I plan to lift it and let the sun shine on all that crawls underneath."

Braden's eyes seemed to flare, then go dark. "I wouldn't," Braden said flatly. "I wouldn't if you value your career. Or Barnes's career for that matter."

"I'm too old for that, Colonel. Try again."

"Yeah, you may be, but what about Barnes? If you go ahead with this, it will be out of my control," said Braden. "If it isn't already."

"I can't believe that North Air Transport can pull those kinds of strings."

Braden shot a curious look at MacHenry. "North Air has nothing to do with this drill, MacHenry. They're just a complication."

"Then what are your recommendations?"

"Simple. My recommendation, Mr. MacHenry, is for you to let this thing cool off awhile. I am going to put through the reassignment for Barnes effective tonight. He'll be given two weeks' medical leave before he TDY's to Scott Air Force Base. Just like he was supposed to until you showed. By then, all this, I hope, will have blown over, and those responsible for the attack on you tonight punished. Somehow."

"Hang on, Colonel. You can't have it both ways. You're suggesting that you have a lead on who was responsible. Either it's the Air Force or it isn't. If it's not, then how are you going to keep Barnes safe? If you don't even know who ordered the attack, then what's to stop them from trying again?"

Braden suddenly looked, and felt, very old. He sighed. "Now you're asking smart questions." But his words sounded hollow, his anger spent. "That's why I'm reassigning Barnes tonight, but not requiring him to show for two weeks." Braden drew in a deep breath. "Barnes will be out in a day or so. He's good at disappearing when he doesn't want to be seen. I suggest you consider something of the same." Braden slowly walked to the door.

"Wait," said MacHenry as he stood. "If you're sending Barnes underground, it means you think whoever shot at us tonight might try again."

Braden shook his head. "Those are your words. Let me put it my way." He opened the door and nailed MacHenry with his glance. "You don't live long in the air unless you keep one eye on your 'six.' Remember that one," he said, "and live."

16

DRY RUN

NGEL drove the Blazer north along Highway 395, skirting the sheer eastern slopes of the Sierra Nevada. The sun burned over the eastern horizon just as he reached Mammoth Lakes. Almost at once, the black case in the back began to stink. It had spent two days in the bottom of a fish hold, after all. He cranked down the window, and a fine shower of grit blew in.

Soon, the divided highway died out into a twisting two-laner. He left the intense traffic behind that had been his constant companion ever since he first nosed the truck out onto Interstate 10. Beyond the turnoff to Yosemite he had the dusty highway all to himself. The road began to climb, invisibly at first, then more and more pronounced until the laboring engine demanded a lower gear. The morning was already becoming hot.

The sign for Sonora Pass appeared at last. With eleven-thousand-foot Eagle Peak to his left, he turned the Blazer up the road that followed the old Emigrant Trail into the mountains. Angel could hardly believe that a road could find its way through such country, despite the sign that read: *California 108, Sonora Pass, elev 9628 ft, 25 miles.*

The desert scrub of the eastern slopes gave way to more and more vegetation. The creosote bushes disappeared, to be replaced by deep stands of straight-backed pine. The air grew cooler and fragrant with pitch scent. Angel smiled. This was not like the desert, the endless miles of sere landscape he had driven across. This was good country.

The road narrowed as he climbed, the sheer walls closing in tighter and tighter. Third gear gave way to second and occasionally first on the wicked switchbacks the steep grade demanded. As he came to the pass itself, the road threaded its way through a massive boulder split by a deep crevasse.

Angel pulled over and stopped on the other side, letting the engine cool.

To the left, the roadbed fell off in a sheer cliff, ending far below in shadowed canyon. He could just see a ribbon of tumbling white water at its bottom. To the right, the mountain climbed up to its summit. He took a final look back at the Gap. It was an ideal ambush site, his professional eye told him. A man with a pistol could close the road forever. He checked his operational map, glanced up to the distinct peaks that crowded the roadbed, and back at his chart. There was only one way into HUMMER, and it would easily be missed. He clutched into first and began rolling downhill.

As the road crept around Strawberry Peak, a clearing opened in the forest to his right. It was a narrow slot where an old railbed had run up into the back country to bring out the timber needed to build, then rebuild, San Francisco. *Here,* Angel thought as he swung the Blazer onto the dirt track.

Nothing remained of the ties, and the iron rails had long since been reduced to flakes and dark, corroded strips. The trees overhung the roadbed in a dense canopy. Only a narrow slot of blue sky remained directly overhead.

A hundred meters in, Angel stopped the Blazer and looked back toward the highway. It was gone. More than gone; it seemed impossible for it to have ever existed. Why had the Russians picked such a place for him to come? What possible military worth was there? It was another sign of his age, he decided. Since when did he have to know?

He shrugged and shifted into first. Whatever the reason, Angel had arrived.

"Okay," said the Air Force captain. "Let's do it." Four throttles came forward under his hand and a shrill scream deepened to a roar.

"Power's up," said the copilot as he watched the engine indicators rise. "Okay, Cap, we have four engines, stabilized and on the bugs."

Capt. Alan Kinkaid pressed the transmit button on his yoke. "Beale tower, Whalebone Three is rolling."

"Roger, Whalebone," came the disinterested voice in their headsets.

The windshield was dark and the runway edge lights streamed ahead to a vanishing point. The distant muffled thump of the KC-135's nose gear's riding the uneven concrete came from beneath them. The howling turbojets shook the tanker's cockpit as they began their takeoff roll. The weight on those wheels was not inconsiderable. The kerosene load alone worked out at over 200,000 pounds; one hundred tons of joyously flammable JP-4 sloshing in tanks the size of railcars. Somehow, it was all supposed to fly.

"Vee-one." Rolling too fast to stop, the KC-135 was now committed. Looking out to the side, the copilot saw a blur of runway edge lights, taxiway blues, strobes all streaking aft as the big jet gathered speed. The airspeed indicator now was rock steady. "Okay, Cap. Vee-R."

"Rotate." The pilot gave the massive control yoke a tug and the nosewheel immediately lifted free. The rumbling from the wheels ceased as the heavy jet wallowed into the air.

"Positive rate. Gear up," the copilot said. The pilot shoved the gear selector up, filling the cockpit with the sound of whining motors and rushing air. "Vee-two," the copilot chanted. At this airspeed they could lose one engine and still maintain a climb.

But they could not lose two.

A double flash of red combined with an earsplitting jangle ruined the smooth ascent. Two engines, both on the right wing, had failed. Their indicators spooled down to zero.

"Both starboard engines out!" the copilot yelled. "Yaw boost!" But his call to activate the rudder boost system to counteract the effect of the two lost engines was never heard.

Kinkaid shoved the two remaining throttle levers to their stops. The nose was yawing under the effect of the asymmetric thrust. Involuntarily responding to the imbalanced condition, the captain pressed the rudder pedals to compensate. His left foot was flat to the floor and the jet was slewing sideways, broadside to the airstream.

"Watch the speed!" the copilot shouted. "Come on, Cap! Get it up! Get it up!" The tremendous mass of the jet was still throwing them skyward, but time was running out fast.

"Already got emergency thrust," the captain said as he dropped the nose. "Hold it, baby," he spoke soothingly to the half-powered tanker as he banked gingerly around to land. "Hold it, hold it. Now! Gear down!"

"You want it *now?*" The copilot was confused; letting the gear drop would increase the drag on the jet tremendously just when it needed every inch of spare altitude it could find, every mile per hour of speed. "I think we should—"

"Goddamn it! Gear!" The pilot reached over and pulled the gear handle from its detent and rammed it down himself. The approach lights to Runway 23 swung across the windshield from right to left, far too close. The copilot could see immediately that they would never make it.

"Oh, shit," said the copilot as the runway lights swerved dizzyingly in the blackness ahead. The KC-135 was no longer a flying machine. The stick shaker methodically announced the impending stall.

The cockpit tilted down and to the right when the stall came, throwing the pilots against their restraint harnesses. *Pull up!* the ground-proximity annunciator intoned as the runway lights showed the jet to be almost on its back. *Pull up!*

The lights swelled into fat globes that were strung at a deadly wrong angle running vertically up and down the windscreen. "So long, Ma," the copilot said. "I love ya."

Suddenly, the windshield filled with bright light and the cockpit tilted level. The copilot felt the heavy sweat drip beneath his flightsuit.

His hands gripped the wheel, knuckles blanched white with the pressure.

"And Whalebone Three, you are daid!" drawled the voice in their headsets. The cockpit lights came up full and the two men looked at each other. The humming of the Rediffusion KC-135 simulator was the only sound audible over the pounding of blood in their ears.

"Damn. I thought I could finesse it," the captain said quietly.

The back door to the simulator cracked open like a rifle shot, and the mission coordinator, the man who had failed the engines on them with a flick of a switch, came in with a stern look of reproach.

"Come on, Tink," said Kinkaid, "you don't lose two on a side in real life."

"Uh-huh," said Tinker. "You don't drop your gear until you have the field made in real life either. And there's the small matter of the rudder boost. You did hear your copilot call it out, didn't you?"

"I, ah, heard something, but the fire lights came on and . . ." the pilot stammered.

"No thinking on the bus, *Mister* Kinkaid," the simulator operator said. The copilot stood up and eased by him out the back door. The long, storklike legs of the simulator were shifting below them. The big hydraulic pistons stopped their motion. "You pull a screw-up like that on Thursday and you'll scatter your shit over half of Yuba City. And you will take out a lot of good folks on the ground. There's a procedure for everything, and you either hack it or you don't. I suggest we try this again."

"How about a break?" Kinkaid looked at his watch. "I could use a little breakfast."

"Breakfast is served." The copilot was now back, holding two cans of Pepsi. He popped both and handed one over to Kinkaid as the simulator operator disappeared aft. The cabin lights dimmed once again. The windshield's screen was already filled with the runway lights veeing off to the blackness.

The copilot put his can of soda down on the floor of the simulator's cockpit and sighed heavily. "One more time?" he asked wearily.

"Let's take it from the top. Prestart checklist," Kinkaid called as he tugged the plastic-covered sheet from its pocket. It seemed like a lot of work to keep from accidentally crashing an airplane they would, in fact, be steering to a crash.

"Power's up," the copilot said once again.

"Whalebone is ready to taxi," Kinkaid informed the simulator operator, but there was no answer. "Tower, Whalebone Three, do you copy?" he asked. "Tinker? Are you still on the—" The cockpit lights snapped on and the door to the rear opened. Kinkaid jumped.

"Okay, guys," their controller said, "we have a little change in plans. Go get some breakfast and come back fresh and ready in half an hour."

"Like what kind of change?" Kinkaid asked, relieved at any break. He started to unfasten his shoulder straps.

"You two lucked out. They moved up the mission."

"That's the good news?" Kinkaid asked. "How come?"

Tinker held up his hands and shrugged. "You think the spooks get chatty with me? All I know is it's not in two weeks. It's in four days," he replied. "Enjoy your breakfast, gentlemen."

Bridger hung up the phone and buzzed Templeman into his office. *Done,* he thought. Sometimes you just had to take a problem by the scruff and shake it good and hard. Adcock had been a failure; that was hardly unexpected, was it? Radway was the real surprise. Radway had made a serious error trying to play this one out himself. Now, regardless of what those two hatched, the wing from that damned Cessna was where it was supposed to be. In a matter of days, both it and the wreck it had come from would simply vanish, vaporized.

"So?" said Dr. Aaron Templeman as he entered Bridger's seventh-floor office. He had been summoned to Langley like an errant schoolboy. "What is it? You don't ask me up to your lair unless you have bad news."

Arthur Dean Bridger smiled at the old physicist. "I'm beginning to think that all those rumors are true. You've become a curmudgeon, Aaron. You must learn to relax."

"Piffle," said Templeman. "I've learned to be cautious around men like you."

"Well," said Bridger, "this time you're wrong. We're pushing up the nuclear winter test you're so concerned with. Happy?"

Templeman eyed the younger man warily. "Why? You've never taken a nuclear winter scenario seriously before. What has it been? Five years since I first raised the issue at the Committee? So why the change now?"

"Even I can learn from my mistakes," Bridger replied with an easy smile. "They'll fly the tanker into HUMMER in four days. The data will get massaged at NOAA, and you'll have your answers. Fair?"

That it seemed so made Templeman all the more suspicious. "What about the field team?"

"Don't worry, Aaron," said Bridger. "I'll keep them in the loop."

"And safe?"

"And safe." Bridger nodded. "What kind of operation do you think they let us run around here, anyway?"

Angel saw the tall, spindly ranger lookout from a long distance away. It sat atop the highest promontory in sight, rising head and shoulders above the tangled mesh of manzanita growing beside the dirt trail. He slowed the Blazer at a tight bend in the trail. The Crandall Peak Lookout dominated the wide valley of the Stanislaus, and it was here, in this valley, that the Russians wished to watch something very closely. He sniffed the rank odor of the sea rising from the black case in the back of the truck. The world was truly a very strange place. That he should risk his life, to nearly drown, delivering a box that reeked of dead fish to some secret site. He glanced at the superb scenery. At least the *yanquis* kept their secrets in nice places. What had Guryanov said? Some kind of military exercise would take place?

How do they know? Angel wondered as he watched the tower. It had to come from someone very close. Perhaps as they talked more with the Americans, they spied more, too. It would be like them to do so.

He swung the Blazer up a steep grade, rounded a corner in low gear, and saw the tower come back into view. *Dios! The whore sways!* He stopped and watched it, mesmerized by the metronomic swing of the tower in the wind.

Out ahead, the jeep track opened out onto a dome of naked granite. Angel started up the final climb, steered out onto the smooth rock, and crawled up to the bare summit in low gear. The safe path was marked only by a weathered, painted line. Too far to the left and he would find out the accuracy of the label *Ten-Second Drop*. The tires slipped on broken stone, caught, slipped again, and then he was there.

He stopped the small truck in the sparse shade of the tower and switched off the ignition, listening to the wind and the soft ticking as the engine cooled.

Angel rolled down his window and breathed in a deep lungful of high-country air. There was something in its purity, in its emptiness, its foreign clarity, that made him reach into the glove compartment for a cigarette. He pushed aside the silenced CZX and found a pack. A match flared; a cloud of blue tobacco smoke drifted around him. Angel slipped the stained leather holster on, inserted the weapon, and pushed open the door. He could feel the hours he had been forced to drive in the stiffness of his legs. The summit fell away in all directions, opening a vista of rugged foothills to the west and the high Sierra peaks to the east.

This was truly a good place. A parched breeze plucked at his jacket. *Good,* he thought wearily. *Now for that stinking box.* He turned and walked to the back of the Blazer and unlatched the cargo door. A strong whiff of the Gulf rose to greet him. He pulled the rubber-sheathed case onto the tailgate, making the car settle heavily on its rear wheels.

Angel gauged the tall ladder leading up to the lookout. It would be a job to haul the case all the way to the top. *The sooner begun, the sooner finished,* he thought. He would only have to carry it one way.

As he slipped one arm into a shoulder strap, a sharp snap came from high up on the tower. He froze for an instant, then dropped the strap and slipped his hand into his jacket. When it emerged, it held the 9-mm CZX, its gun blue glowing hotly in the bright sun. He slowly turned to face the tower.

From their sockets drilled deep into the bare rock, the legs rose to a high, enclosed lookout. There, hanging from the roof, he saw it. Angel almost laughed.

A coil of black wire extended over the edge of the lookout's wooden roof. The tower's sway made the loop slap the sides of the shuttered cab. A small whip antenna of the sort used in short-wave communications could just be seen on the roof proper. *"Bueno,"* he said aloud as he slipped the pistol back into its underarm holster. Fortune came in many shapes. The stinking equipment case was supposed to be mated with an antenna, too. One or two antennae on the roof of a remote lookout, who would notice?

But if fortune arrived in unexpected ways, so did warning; Angel's years in the field had given him a hard-won situational awareness just as good, if not as officially sanctioned, as any fighter pilot's. It was ringing a clear and unmistakable alarm. He had learned to listen to it. *Why is there an antenna up there?* he wondered. These old ranger stations were supposed to be abandoned. Had Guryanov made another mistake? Angel walked to the base of the ladder and began to climb.

The higher he went, the more pronounced the tower's sway felt to his stretched-tight nerves. Finally, he reached the open hole in the floor of the high cab.

The old lookout was hot and dark inside, lit with light welling up from the opening in the floor and seeping around the edges of the boarded-up windows. A thin rectangle of gold light filtered in around the edges of a roof hatch above. A wire trailed through the crack, keeping the hatch from seating perfectly.

Angel tugged the wire, feeling along its length as it went from the roof opening into one of the dark corners of the blacked-out fire tower. *What have we here?* He looked back at the source of the wire.

A wire-studded box sat in a corner of the lookout cab. A pair of cables led to what was surely a battery box, and another led up to the roof. As he watched, a tiny green lamp began to flash furiously on the face of the box, accompanied by a rapid-fire chattering of electronic tones. He knelt close to it and saw the light had a label: TRANSMIT. He swung the flashlight across the face of the device and saw two more: CALIBRATE and INTERROGATE. "And who are you speaking to?" he said quietly.

A researcher familiar with the technology of remote sensing could name the device immediately. Designed to gather temperature, pressure, wind speed, and cloud obscuration, it was the processor module belonging to Automated Weather Observation Station #12. Dr. Julia Hines had twenty-nine others just like it, strung across the mountains beneath the restricted skies of HUMMER 6.

As Angel stood up, his collar caught the wire leading up through the roof to the transmitter's antenna, pulling it partway out of the processor module's jack. The green light on AWOS 12 went dark, to be replaced by a red CALIBRATE.

Julia loaded a disc of AWOS data into the IBM and copied it for safekeeping. She wiped her brow with a blue bandanna as the computer's green light flashed. Temperature, wind, and solar values flew through the machine and onto the spare floppy disk. She looked at the streaks of red dust on the cloth. She had bathed in the small rock pool down from the summit only this morning, and already she was filthy. It was hot and dusty again, even though the unseasonable rain had been such a nuisance a few days before. Maybe she'd take another swim before bed.

She glanced over the screen, out the trailer's small window. The diesel generator was droning. Sergeant Kansky was working on it. She watched his powerful arm muscles bunch as he fought to free a pesky nut. She hadn't really been very kind to the sergeant, establishing from the very first the no-nonsense, technical nature of their relationship. It was a reflex developed by many young women seeking to enter a male-dominated profession. Still, Kansky had been okay about it. He kept his eyeballs where they belonged, mostly. At least, she thought with a smile, as much as she did. Julia decided to allow him to take her to dinner after they had been pulled off Bald Mountain. Then she could relax, celebrate even. Who knew? It would only be another few weeks.

Julia was going through the papers on the small desk when Sergeant Kansky opened the door and stuck his head in. "What's up, Doc?" he said with a grin that faded as he saw her disapproving expression. She was a real tough nut. Maybe she didn't like men. Who knew these days? "Everything copacetic in mission control?"

"Housekeeping," she said, holding up the black diskette. "You can't have too many copies around."

"Got all that weather stuff you need?"

"I have what I have," she replied. "But I won't know if it's enough until I start massaging it."

"Lucky little data," said Kansky. "I still don't know exactly what it's for. Nobody's ever going to figure out how to call the shots with the weather."

"For all our sakes, you'd better be wrong," Julia answered simply. "We're really closing in on something, but something's closing in on us, too."

"Like what?"

"Well, you remember that storm last week? The whole world's experiencing eccentric weather patterns. All the old norms seem to be breaking down. Some kind of new pattern is emerging. I hope that this"—she patted the IBM—"will figure it out in time to know where it's all leading."

"Like, whether I should buy a waterfront lot in Las Vegas?" said Kansky with a grin.

Julia nodded. "The level of the oceans is exactly the kind of thing to watch out for. But there's a lot more, too. Most of the world's population lives on coastlines. What will happen if sea levels rise? The same thing with agriculture. If rainfall is off a few percent, we call it a bad year. What happens when it's off forty, fifty percent? *Every* year?"

"Nature is nature."

"No. These aren't just natural cycles. We've done something, Sergeant. 'We' as in the human race. It's like we walked into a big control room, one that's been humming along for millions of years just fine, and started throwing switches at random. You might call it vandalism."

Kansky nodded. "Now that we beat the Russians, maybe we can figure out how to quit vandalizing the joint. You think?"

"I hope." Julia knocked on the wood-grain Formica. "It sure is a window of opportunity, isn't it?"

"I still don't trust them," said Kansky. "All the sweet talk is cheap talk. They wouldn't be trying to buddy up to us if they weren't on the ropes. What happens when they get back on their feet? You know," he said, shaking his head, "my father used to say, just when you think it's under control, things are fixin' to swarm you."

Julia formed a response, but before she could deliver it, the IBM chattered and printed a warning message:

Data disconnect AWOS 12: 13:30:22.

The signal from Crandall Lookout had stopped.
Kansky read the printout. "Sounds like my old man was right."

17

IN THE
LINE OF
FIRE

MacHENRY hung up the phone. *Done,* he thought. He'd managed to accomplish a great deal for so early on a Sunday morning.

First, he had nipped the incipient investigation of Friday night's affair at Fresno in the bud. The FAA's regional duty officer in Los Angeles was an old friend, and he really knew how to slow the gears. A missed call here, a lost form there, and it might take a week for the FAA to get its steamroller moving again.

Second, MacHenry had begun a little investigation of his own. First thing Saturday morning, still wearing the green flightsuit Barnes had loaned him, he was standing in front of the small Silicon Valley start-up firm known as Pacific Materials Analysis. They were smaller than the usual companies the FAA normally used, but their rates were lower and they were eager for work. By late that same day, PacMat had hit paydirt.

MacHenry rolled down the sleeves of his fisherman's knit. Just as Mark Twain had noted, summers were damned cold by the Bay, and the chill seeped into MacHenry's empty office. He needed the time and the space to think this one out, to think it out very closely. The fresh sheet of typewritten notes and the results of Pacific Materials' analysis of the chunk of plastic recovered from the Cessna's wing made a neat pile on his desk. He reviewed the radio transcript once again. It finally made sense.

Oh, God! . . . we're hit! We're hit!

The chemical analysis sealed any lingering uncertainty. *Carbon graphite/titanium alumide composite,* the report read, *with traces of Schiff Base salts.*

At the bottom of the form, in a space blocked out for "Remarks," the lab tech had added, *This is a typical, high-performance mix designed to yield strength and resistance to high temperatures at low weight. The trace salts are wild. I have no idea what they're supposed to do.* As further evidence of the exotic nature of the chunk of plastic retrieved from Davis-Monthan, he wrote, *WHAT IS THIS FROM?* and circled it in red.

"Good question," said MacHenry. A midair collision, a wing removed from the wreckage, and then, *then* a fire. *The fire,* he thought. He was sure the wing had come down with the Cessna. But it hadn't burned. Whoever cut it off had also set the fire to cover their tracks. There was no way around it. It was no longer just an accident in need of an alibi. It was murder.

The phone shattered the peace of the morning. He wasn't expecting any more calls. He let it ring. Three, four, five times. Then silence. *How will they try next time?* he wondered.

He might not have to wait long to find out. MacHenry was not the only one busy this weekend. He glanced at the executive summons on his desk faxed in from Washington. The administrator hadn't been around to get him legally onto Davis-Monthan Air Force Base, but somehow he had found the time to sign an order directing MacHenry off the investigation and onto an airliner headed for the FAA's Washington headquarters. The phone rang again. This time, he snatched it up. "All right! Who is this!"

"Your worst nightmare," the voice responded, dark and eerie.

"One more time and I hang up. Who is this?"

A deep sigh came over the phone. "Temper, temper, BJ. It's your chauffeur. Sorry about the car, it's a little bent up—"

"Barnes! Where are you?" MacHenry found it impossible to keep a broad grin from spreading across his face.

"Long distance from heaven. They said I could make one call, and guess what? You're it. You should see all the angels. Man, what pectorals! Listen, I have to run. Flying lessons start in a couple of—"

"Cut it out, Major." MacHenry laughed. "I tried all day yesterday to get through at the hospital. You're okay? Where are you?" Although Braden had told him the good news from the hospital, he knew what he had seen as they took Barnes away that night. He had been awash in his own blood.

"Home. What did you expect? It was just, you know, a flesh wound. I've been here since Saturday afternoon. Hey, I hear you and Braden met somewhere up the Richter scale."

"It was more like a collision than a meeting. But how'd they let you out so fast?"

"What? That scratch? I bet you lost more blood when Al chewed you out."

"It looked like more than a scratch from where I sat," MacHenry said seriously. "But you're right. Braden read me the riot act. He threatened to have me arrested if I placed a foot onto your base. I couldn't even pick up my car. It's still there on base."

"Al never was on the subtle side. He was awful nice to me though. He spent all afternoon explaining how it wasn't him who got us jumped. Can you imagine Al apologizing for anything? I told him to keep his explanations," said Barnes with a smile MacHenry could hear. "I had that sucker right in the middle of my gunsight. Can you imagine? A T-Bird smoking a plane that's not even supposed to exist? It would have been great. Great."

"You smoked it, Barnes. Not the T-33. Did he tell you who was flying the other aircraft?"

Barnes's voice changed at once. "I'd drop that line of inquiry, at least over the phone, you know? Besides, I have a small proposal for your consideration."

"Anything. Well, almost. I'm listening."

"In my position here as, you know, senior accident coordinator for USAF, I have discovered an item of some interest to the investigation. You're still interested, aren't you?"

"Barnes . . ." MacHenry growled unconvincingly. He was too glad to hear the other man's voice to be angry. "What do you have?"

"Oh, not much. Just the wreck of that Cessna," he continued. "The one without all its wings? It's still up at HUMMER." When MacHenry did not respond, he continued, "You there, BJ? I thought there might be some desire on your part to maybe go have another look at the sucker."

"It's really still up there?" MacHenry said softly. "Whoever took a poke at us seemed very concerned about the whole HUMMER thing's getting out. I can't believe they would overlook the wreckage itself."

"As of this A.M. it's still up there. I can't tell you why, except for the fact that we normally don't bring in wrecks out of the mountains. Maybe they wanted it to look like a normal thing, you know? No special attentions. By the way, the C-130 out at Davis-Monthan is history. I called out there first thing. Chop city. So what do you say? You want to go for a little trip to the mountains?"

MacHenry tapped his sharp pencil on the desk. "Listen. What I want is for you to forget this investigation. Just concentrate on staying out of the line of fire. It's my job now."

"Sure," Barnes replied. "I mean, why not? After all, why should I care who tried to kill me? Live and let live. That's my motto." Barnes went silent, then exploded. "Now you listen, ace. I'm fit for a little hike. If you think I'm handing this over to some gray eagle who doesn't even eject when the pilot in command says to eject, forget it. You think *I* have a loose grip on life? You may be ready to give up, but I, for one, am a little upset, you know?"

"I know. You have every right to be." MacHenry looked at the near-complete revision to the accident report on his desk. Another couple of hours would finish it. He remembered Braden's last words of warning that night in Fresno: *Check your six.* He looked at the edict from Washington taking him off the case. He had no authority to proceed. *But* . . .

"Well? We can drive fairly close, leave the car, and walk in. Couple of hours would do it. Piece of cake."

"I'll go myself. You can't con me, Barnes. I saw how you looked at Fresno."

"What, you think I walk on my hands or something? Besides, who's going to watch your tail? At least stop here on your way. I've got a bunch of trail maps thanks to you."

"Maybe. There's one more thing up there I need to nail down. About the way the wreck burned. But not you, my friend. It doesn't have to be your fight."

"Hey, big news, BJ," said Barnes. "It is."

The dark green UH-1N Twin Huey lifted off from a gravel ag strip in the California Central Valley and came to a hover. Almost impossible to read, small black letters announced its owners to be Skycrane Recovery. Two men ducked under the rotor blast to check the security of a cable connecting it to a large but light sling-load. With a thumbs-up signal, the helicopter climbed, dropped its nose toward the Sierras, and beat heavily to the northeast, its cargo swaying but under control. A small parachute had been rigged to keep the object pointed in the right direction.

An hour later, the sound of the helicopter's rotors thumped the announcement of its return, but this time the sling, and the cargo it had once held, were gone.

It was a gorgeous Sunday to fly. The Super Cub darted and rolled as the wind filled its broad yellow wings. Bone-dry northwesterlies were blowing in over the flat Central Valley, making for a rough ride in the high terrain, but Danny Yates didn't mind it a bit. He loved to fly, and best of all, they paid him to do it.

A pipeline-patrol pilot for years in addition to his job as part-time deputy sheriff down in Columbia, Yates had experienced far worse up in these mountains. There were days to fly and there were days to stay home, drink coffee, and think about how nice and stable the earth could be. *Bonecrushers* is what he called the bad ones. *Cake* is what he called days like this.

He banked against the wind and crabbed his way along a steep ridgeline, keeping Schoettgen—or Shotgun—Pass off his right wing. He then swung east, the tall peaks directly off the Cub's yellow nose. Out the open clamshell door on his right, the forests swept by at eighty miles an hour, close enough for him to smell the heavy resin scent liberated by a hot summer sun.

As he neared the pass, Yates added throttle, banked hard, and crossed the spine of the ridge at the proper forty-degree angle. Crossing the mountains at an angle was wise insurance; he could dive away from the rising terrain and into the deep valley on either side.

Schoettgen Pass stood in the low saddle of the mountain separating the two forks of the Stanislaus River. Behind him to the west, the gorges opened out into broad valleys; ahead, they cinched up ever tighter to the snow of the high peaks. Directly below, the river had been dammed to form Lyon's Reservoir.

He lifted his left wing and checked that no other aircraft was around. He saw Crandall Peak framed in the Cub's wing struts, its prominent ranger tower clinging precariously to the domed summit. In between, at Schoettgen, Pacific Gas and Electric operated a tiny maintenance station, abandoned except when there was a need to haul in heavy equipment for the hydro tunnels. *Or the farmers,* he thought. He knew the remote land below was a patchwork quilt of marijuana crops. While he was paid to look for pipeline breaks, he was, after all, a lawman. If PG&E subsidized a little drug intervention, so much the better. Someone had to.

Yates stood the Cub on its wing and circled the unoccupied barracks at the pass, catching a flashing sight of the narrow-gauge tramway beneath the trees. The rails descended steeply from the saddle down a thousand feet to Lyon's Reservoir. To Yates it looked more like a one-way roller coaster. He would never think of riding the contraption, although he knew plenty of utility guys who did. On the other hand, he took this little kite of an airplane into the Sierras as though it were a walk in the park. There was just no telling, was there?

Yates circled the gray metal shack at the pass and saw the twin flash of sun on steel from the rails. The farmers had been known to take up residence at Schoettgen illegally. By the time they were spotted and a ranger crew sent in to collar them, they could be gone up a hundred other trails to nowhere. But not today. The tram terminus was deserted.

After a final pass, he nosed over into a sharp dive down the flanks of the mountain. He felt the weight leave his body and his cowboy boots rise from the stirrups he had installed on the rudder pedals. He dived the Cub, following the tramway tracks to the floor of the valley. *This was the way to ride the rails.*

At the bottom, he hauled back the stick as he flashed over the bright waters, wheeling around to face the mountain once more, retracing his path as he climbed, keeping the lookout tower at Crandall Peak in the center of his windscreen. The altimeter swung through five thousand feet as he swept by, level with the cab. The heat of the sun off bare rock bounced the Cub with a sharp thermal jab.

What's this? A sudden flash of color pricked at his peripheral vision. In the stand of trees just below the gray summit, a swatch of color had been visible for just a moment. *Strange.* Nobody was supposed to be up here. All the trails in were closed off, although a determined person with the right vehicle might find a way. Who was up here today? It was a small truck, that much he could see, but it sure as shooting wasn't painted Forest Service green.

Yates racked the Cub over and circled the tower like a hawk. There it was again. *A goddamned farmer,* he thought. Someone, maybe a druggie, was down at Crandall Lookout. *Well,* he thought, *maybe this is my day after all.*

Angel shielded his eyes against the hot sun. *There!* The small airplane turned and dipped its wings toward the reservoir far below. *Bueno.* For the second time this morning, he had been roused by the alarming sound of flying engines drawing near. First a helicopter, now this. The thumping of that beast had gone away, and now, apparently, so was this little yellow bird.

But he was wrong. The buzzing of the engine grew more distinct as the airplane clawed back up the flank of Crandall Peak. Angel tensed, listening, wondering whether all this activity had meaning for him. Perhaps the very peace and isolation of this place had made him lazy. *Closer,* he thought as the engine note became a snarl.

A helicopter, and now this. Could there be a deliberate search for someone? *For me?* Why had Guryanov ordered him to wait with the equipment he had brought in? He had set up the antenna on the roof of the ranger tower, right next to the one that was already there. He should be halfway to Mexico by now. Why did he have to wait? A standing target is an easy target.

His eyes went to the spot his ears told him the small plane would reappear. His hand, almost of its own accord, slipped into the dusty brown jacket he wore and took hold of his CZX. It was warm from his body, a living extension of his nerves, his blood.

He drew the 9-mm from his underarm sling and thumbed off the safety. He could smell the rich leather scent mixed with the sharp tang of gun oil. It reminded him of his own smell. Or was it the other way around?

Suddenly, a brilliant flash of yellow exploded over the edge of the summit, dangerously close, as the small plane skimmed the tops of the trees and turned tight around the ranger tower. Its buzzing was like an angry insect trapped in his hair. Instinctively he drew back more into the shade, watching as it circled the tower again. *Stay stupid, compañero, do not be too interested.* Instead, it banked steeply onto its side and began circling; the center of its tether was a point that fell roughly at Angel's feet.

He watched as the circle drew tighter. A man was visible in the cockpit. He was looking for something. There was no doubt. A shiver ran through Angel's body as he raised the pistol, aiming first with a precise lead at the dark shape of the pilot. His finger tightened on the trigger. *No!* He flicked the safety back on and holstered it. To kill the man would be no great display of marksmanship; to damage the airplane would be even easier. Either one put Angel in more danger. The first would start a search; the latter would put an angry man on the ground nearby. This was not the African veldt, where an airplane might disappear forever without anyone to take notice. *Go away!* he thought as he watched the yellow airplane circle in the deep blue sky. *Go away!*

As though heeding Angel's wish, the plane suddenly rolled level and then banked steeply away, flashing across the summit clearing once more before diving below the cliff. Angel ran to the edge of Ten-Second Drop just in time to see the yellow tail disappear below the shoulder on the flank of Crandall Peak. He listened and watched for the small plane to reappear above the valley floor. "Come on," he said. "Come on!" But the yellow wings refused to show. *Mierda!* The small plane was not flying away. Somewhere down below, it was landing.

"Fuck," he said in perfect English. He picked up a heavy rock and threw it over the drop. Ten seconds later, a tiny *plink!* rose from below. He could see the glittering water of the reservoir at the foot of Crandall. He knew from his chart that it was fringed with land flat enough to land a small plane on. And how would a person get up the side of Crandall? That, too, he knew. There was only one quick way.

Angel turned and began to jog down the granite dome. *Bueno,* he thought. *If you are looking for me, you shall find me.* The Schoettgen tram was the only direct way up from the reservoir. There, complications aside, Angel would do what he had to do.

Yates lined up on the rocky beach that edged the reservoir, slipping off the last few feet, skimming the round rocks as the Super Cub gave up its last reserve of speed. He kicked the tail straight at the last moment, just as the fat tundra tires bounced onto the dry, baking rocks. He let the plane roll, the tail still in the air, taxiing away from the water's edge and toward the grassy margin of the shore. A wingspan away from the first stand of trees, he pulled the throttle back and let the tail settle. The mixture knob came back, and the 150-horse engine coughed and clattered to a stop.

Yates reached back into the aft cockpit and pulled out a red canvas bag. With an old-fashioned Colt six-shot and his badge, pipeline-patrol pilot Yates became Deputy Sheriff Yates. He grabbed his hand-held radio and stepped out. The bottom of the Schoettgen tramline was only a hundred-foot stroll from where the Cub stood.

He felt the sweat trickle down his neck as he unlocked the control box that stood next to the wooden flatcar. There were three big buttons within. A green one marked UP, a red one marked STOP, and a black one labeled RETURN. He punched the green one and stepped up onto the tram.

For a few seconds, nothing happened. Then, far up on the tramline, the fat steel cable drew taut with a sharp, echoing *twang!* The tram lurched once, stopped, and began its climb in earnest.

Angel stood beside the upper terminus of the tram and watched as the steel cable became tight, strained, and began to reel itself up the side of Crandall Peak. The big wire drum housed in the metal shack behind him creaked and squealed arthritically as it pulled. *Like a fish,* he thought. *But what have I caught?*

The tiny square of the flatcar showed far below as it was hauled over a relatively level shoulder. He could see there was a man on it, a dot of white against the dark green of the trees. One man. The odds were certainly favorable.

Angel stepped back from the rails and into a dense tangle of manzanita, working his way carefully into hiding until only a person staring directly at his eyes might know his presence. Through the tangle of red stems, he had a clear view down the rails.

Angel watched steel cable flow by him. It seemed to be taking forever! He tensed, then forced himself to relax. He felt the surge of energy that came with combat and forced it back into its cage. Control was what made the difference. The exuberant ones, the ones who cried out with fury as they fought, they were heroes to be sure, but of course they were all dead.

He pushed a bit farther out of hiding. *There!* Far below, the dot of white had become a man; a man with a baseball cap, a jacket, and . . . *What?* A brown object hung from his waist. Perhaps the odds were not as favorable as they seemed. The man, whoever he was, was coming armed.

Sometimes it was this way. He had no particular need to kill. He was a professional, not a thug, and a professional knew that killing was always a risk, a complication better avoided. But sometimes there was no other option. Angel opened the lid to that inner cage, just a crack, and felt the energy steam through him like hot vapor. His thigh muscles bunched, ready.

Yates looked uphill. At first, he headed pointed directly up the rails. Then he turned toward Angel. Somehow, despite the brush, the doomed man picked out the shape of a crouching man. Their eyes locked, and Angel's hair-trigger snapped.

He exploded from cover, his legs carrying him in one pounce from the heart of the manzanita to the clearing beside the tracks. He was wholly on automatic. He could no more stop what he had begun than he could command the tides. The CZX was level, dead, and sure.

Yates saw Angel leap into the tracks. *What?* His mouth shaped a shout of surprise, but before a sound could find its way out, the dark figure erupted into a hard-edged star of yellow light. The star exploded into a pattern of wildly zigzagging grids behind his eyes. The tram suddenly tilted beneath him. He tried to balance but his legs gave way, crumpling under him in a way he could not understand, and that for some reason was no longer important.

His head slapped the boards even as the terrible pressure in his head subsided, the brilliant light dimming to a dull red, then black.

The tram hit the top bumper and tripped the automatic stop switch. The take-up motor fell silent with a heavy *clunk*. The green button on the tram's control panel popped back out, ready for the return trip. A bird screeched in the trees as Angel cautiously approached the body. He held the 9-mm out in front of him like a black, accusing finger. The sharp stink of cordite rose in the pine-scented air. His footfalls on the needle-carpeted forest floor could not be heard at all.

18

R E U N I O N

MACHENRY lived a life of schedules and plans. But here it was Monday morning, he was not at work, and he felt like a fugitive. Barnes had found out that the wreck was still up in HUMMER. It would nail his theory down nice and tight if it was true. *Theory,* he thought with a snort. *It's a fancy word for murder.* But it still didn't salve the niggling sense of playing hooky he felt as he drove up to Barnes's apartment complex.

It was depressingly like his own. The same railed balconies overlooked a vista of blacktop and parked cars. The same brown fringe of grass was scattered with the same plastic toys. Women in tube tops, shorts, and sandals wandered the grounds pushing strollers, from which issued more plastic toys to decorate the sere grass.

MacHenry parked the car, a virtual twin to the one still at Mather Air Force Base, and found Barnes's apartment. He was fully prepared to chain him to a radiator to keep him from the trip to HUMMER. How strong could he be this soon after losing all that blood? MacHenry rang the buzzer and immediately heard the thump of booted feet. He should have guessed. Barnes was dressed for a hike.

"Well, well," said Barnes, "Look who's here. You guys make house calls now?"

"Not usually, but it's still good to see you, Major." MacHenry extended his hand. "You had me scared last Friday night."

Barnes's eyes twinkled as he shook his head. "I heal quick," he said as they shook. He was dressed in fatigue pants, a sleeveless shirt, and hiking boots. His dark hair was neatly combed and his pale blue eyes showed amusement. A thick bandage encased nearly the whole of his upper left arm. "Anyway, welcome to the Casa Ninja. Come on in. Beer?"

"Ah, no thanks," said MacHenry. Even if this wasn't the Oakland Flight Safety office, he was at work. MacHenry stepped inside. Barnes kept a very neat house, he noted. The pictures, mostly of airplanes, of course, all hung straight. The furniture, light yet comfortable looking, was the sort a man who planned to move with some regularity might find handy. It wasn't bad. It looked, MacHenry realized, a lot like his own place. Only the airplane shots on his wall were of older ships. But much the same.

He saw that Barnes was sorting through a pile of gear on the breakfast bar. "I came for those maps you were talking about," he said as Barnes opened the refrigerator and dumped some drinks into a large rucksack.

"Got 'em," Barnes replied, patting one of the outside pockets.

"Look, Barnes, I thought I made myself clear," said MacHenry. "You're in no shape to go tromping through the woods. I can't take responsibility for—"

"Can it, BJ. Let me be the judge of that one, okay?" Barnes hoisted the ruck to his good shoulder. "Oops," he said as he dropped it. He disappeared into another room. In a moment, he was back, this time with a bamboo bow and quiver, the same set MacHenry had last seen up at the crash site in HUMMER.

"No," MacHenry said as he eyed it nervously. "Never."

Barnes just looked up and grinned. "BJ," he said finally, "we're headed for Indian country, aren't we?" Barnes slipped on a pair of sunglasses. He had his mind made up, and nothing, not MacHenry, not the very real risks of returning to the crash site, could keep him back.

* * *

The trip across the baking Central Valley in the open roadster began as an adventure for MacHenry. He didn't remember the last time he had been in an XK-140, and it was a very different way to go. You were in the scenery, not just watching it scroll by behind a sheet of tinted glass.

But now, two hours after they had pulled away from Barnes's apartment, it was an ordeal. The road shimmered with heat as they began the long climb into the Sierras, and the air felt like the breath of a blast furnace on his face. Finally, beyond the small tourist town of Columbia, the altitude began to translate into lower temperatures. The dusty gray scrub became lost beneath ever denser stands of tall pine.

Barnes clutched the XK around a sharp bend in the road and gunned it up the grade. "You'll see," he said to MacHenry. "You'll be glad you convinced me to come."

"I convinced you?" MacHenry had to shout over the hot wind spilling through the convertible's cockpit. He held on to the windshield bar for his life as Barnes plunged into a series of uphill switchbacks. He closed his eyes as they came to an especially blind curve. It was well they had not seen a single car coming down. "Barnes, I'd appreciate it if you'd—"

"After all, someone's got to protect you, old man," Barnes said. "Something more than that." He nodded at the old pistol that sat at MacHenry's feet. He had shown it to Barnes when they were safely away from town and traffic. "What are you going to do with the popgun? I never knew antiques were your thing."

"Antiques?" MacHenry had hunted through his attic for the old weapon, finding it carefully wrapped in oil-soaked cotton and plastic. The .45 still gleamed, as good as the day he had retired it after his last Flying Tigers contract flight with MAC, the Military Airlift Command. The Air Force had insisted that civilian flight crews flying over a war zone carry them. Somehow he didn't think the Viet Cong would have been terribly impressed.

The back end of a big military truck appeared ahead, its camouflaged canvas top flapping and black diesel smoke streaming aft. Barnes shifted down and pulled in tight behind. A soldier waved.

Indeed, the back was filled with armed men. Barnes beeped at them and swerved out for a quick look uphill. "Hang on, BJ!" he said as he pulled out into the downhill lane and passed the truck in one fluid motion. *Marines?* he wondered as they passed the black lettering on truck's cab. He shifted up once more as the tach brushed redline. "What are they doing way up here?"

They found out soon enough. "Shit," said Barnes. A ROAD CLOSED AHEAD sign appeared and Barnes let the Jaguar slow. He shook his head and downshifted, winding the engine up through the tach.

MacHenry watched the performance. Barnes was surely good with machines, even if he didn't have the sense to let the nasty slice on his arm heal properly. MacHenry stole a glance. Barnes's green camo T-shirt contrasted sharply with the white bandage. *I just hope the stitches hold.*

Barnes caught him looking. "Don't worry, BJ. I'm not going to lose my stuffing." Barnes downshifted again and dove into the curve, the Jaguar's engine wound in a high, happy song. As the road straightened out, a STOP AHEAD sign came into view. "Crap." Beyond the sign a dark green jeep barred any further uphill progress. Another troop truck sat belching black smoke from its stacks as it idled. A platoon of soldiers sat in the shade of a tree as an officer spoke over a radio.

Barnes drifted up to the Marine sentry who held his white-gloved hand up for emphasis. "What gives, Sergeant?" Barnes asked, grabbing for a baseball cap. Without the wind through the open convertible, the afternoon sun was intolerably hot on his dark hair.

The Marine leaned over. "You'll have to turn around. The road is closed up the pass."

Barnes nodded gravely. "I can see that much. I asked a question. What gives?"

The Marine was clearly not used to having his words doubted. He seemed puzzled by Barnes's defiant tone. "Because it's closed," he repeated. "The road's shut down. No traffic is getting up to the pass."

"Sergeant, I don't think you're listening. I'm Major Barnes from Mather." Barnes reached into his wallet and pulled out the military ID.

"In case you've forgotten, that means you're supposed to answer my questions with a little more, you know, enthusiasm."

The MP took the ID and examined it warily. *Just what I need,* he thought. *A wingwiper.* He handed the ID back. "Sorry, Major, but I have my orders. We're conducting mountain-warfare training today up here against the boys at Devil's Camp—"

"Who?" asked MacHenry.

The sergeant turned to MacHenry, wondering what rank *this* one might be. He looked neat enough and old enough to be something more serious than a mere major. "Sir, the Corps has a mountain-warfare school up over the pass, sir. They're holding one end. We've got the other." The Marine mopped his face as he sweated under the sun. The helmet he wore made his head steam. "Sir."

"Come on, Barnes," MacHenry said, shaking his head. "Let's head back down. We tried."

"Sure," Barnes replied. "You know something? You quit too damned easy." He turned to face the sweating sergeant. "Thanks for the info." Barnes slammed the gearshift into reverse and shot back.

MacHenry watched as the sergeant kept an eye on them. "I guess it's checkmate. We can't walk in from here."

"You're going to let a little roadblock stop us?" Barnes screeched to a stop, swung the long nose of the Jaguar downhill, and booted the accelerator. They swung around the same series of switchbacks before Barnes slowed down. He was hunting for something, examining each dirt trail that appeared along the blacktop. "You know, for a field exercise, I didn't see too many troops on the move. They were just sitting around. In the way, you know?"

"I think they were leveling with us. Our bad luck." The sun was glaring off the rock outcrops. MacHenry didn't relish the trip back across the valley. He watched as Barnes slowed down again. "What are you looking for?"

"Remember all that running you had me do to find that damned wing of yours?" Suddenly, Barnes jammed on the brakes and swung the Jaguar off the highway and onto a short, unmarked drive. The gravel trail twisted first uphill, then down, across a dry creekbed, and then began to climb in earnest.

"Where . . ." MacHenry began, but stopped as they roared up to the back of a private ski lodge, shuttered for the summer. Beyond, a chair lift ran up a slope of dead, brown grass. Barnes downshifted as they passed the chalet and headed for the slope. "Hey! What are you doing?" MacHenry asked when Barnes accelerated. "Barnes! Where are we—"

"Hang on!" The low-slung XK dropped off the gravel and onto the grass, nearly bottoming out against the earth. Barnes pointed the nose uphill, his face a solid grin. "Almost like flying!" he shouted as they climbed the ski run in low gear. "Boom and *zoom!*" The slope was steep but Barnes pressed on, climbing the whisper-dry grass. It flattened as they rounded the top. MacHenry waited for him to slow, but instead, Barnes stomped on the gas pedal and the Jaguar surged toward the crest.

Suddenly, there was nothing ahead but pure blue sky.

"Barnes!" MacHenry panicked at the sight: row after row of mountains marched up to the east with a steep drop right in front of them. Barnes gave a yell and spun the wheel of the XK. They came to a stop, their wheels less than ten feet from the edge. "Jesus! Are you trying to kill us?"

"It's been tried," Barnes observed with a grin. "How's that for living close to the edge?" Barnes pulled the car next to the ski-lift tower. It offered a little shade.

MacHenry felt his heart subside as the hot engine *tick-tick-ticked.* "For a second there, I thought we were going over."

"Over? No way. Control," said Barnes as he looked at MacHenry over his sunglasses, "is the name of the game." He hopped out and unhooked the luggage strap that kept his pack, and his bamboo bow, in place. "Damn. I feel better already."

"Next time give me some warning." MacHenry reached in the back for his knapsack. He was anxious to get his feet onto real ground again. "How do we get up to the site from here?"

"The old-fashioned way, BJ. The old-fashioned way."

* * *

The printer chattered as Julia finished up a late lunch with Kansky. She jumped up from her chair and read the error message as it scrolled across the screen. She shook her head.

"What, again?" said Kansky distractedly. He had been enjoying himself immensely. First, the trailer was air-conditioned—for the electronics, of course; but more, it was awfully nice to sit across from a research climatologist with legs like Julia's. They went on, he thought, forever. "Same thing?" he asked as she leaned over to read the printout.

"It's running erratic." AWOS 12 up on Crandall Lookout was acting up. It had never quite settled down after that first error message. "I think we'd better go and replace it with the spare."

"Damn," said Kansky. "I thought we were finished up on that tower." He had installed the AWOS, including the rooftop antenna, and he had hated every minute of it. "That thing sways in the wind. I nearly fell off the last time."

"We'll take a rope."

"Yeah. Great idea. Then I won't fall. I'll hang." Kansky looked out the window of the command trailer and checked his watch. "An hour or so to check out the spare, the drive up there, climbing that bast . . . tower," he corrected himself. "We'll lose our light before we finish."

"What we can't afford to lose is all the Crandall data. Come on," she said, grabbing her jacket. Her cutoffs and T-shirt were fine for the day, but it got chilly fast when the sun dropped behind the mountains. "It's probably a squirrel chewing on a coax cable."

"Yeah," said Kansky. He looked out the window of the trailer again. "Squirrels."

"Whose idea was this trip anyway?" Barnes said between breaths. "You put me off my pace. It's hard walking with a slowpoke." He staggered a little as he placed his boot another step higher on the steep trail. The trees were clinging to the slope, but just barely. The downhill stroll from the top of the ski run had only given them a steeper uphill slog. They were crossing the ridges at right angles, up and down, working their way to intercept the trail Barnes knew was there, the one that would lead them to the wrecked Cessna.

"This . . . is some rough . . . country," MacHenry gasped. He sensed a competitive edge creeping between them this last mile. Who would fall dead first?

"It's . . . justice," said Barnes, breathing heavily. "You made me . . . do this to find . . . that wing."

MacHenry was almost too out of breath to speak. His foot slipped in the loose scree and he nearly fell. Barnes stopped and shook his head as though to clear it. He took three enormous breaths. It seemed to bring him back at once, MacHenry noted enviously.

"Ready for . . . a stop . . . Barnes?"

Barnes nodded. "Okay, old-timer. We'll stop." He put his pack down and shouldered out of the bow and quiver. "Had you worried up that little ski run, didn't I?" he said with a mischievous grin. "Come on, BJ. Admit it. You thought it was all over."

MacHenry's breathing began to settle down as he sat with his back to a tree. He still felt his heart pound in his neck. That was the difference age made, wasn't it? Barnes had sounded just as tired a moment back, but now look at him. MacHenry felt like never getting back up. "I didn't know what you were doing. But what I do know is this," he said. "They may pay you to get right to the edge, as close as you can. They used to pay me to stay as far from it as I knew how."

"Ah, yes. The voice from the flight deck. I bet you had to beat the stews off with a stick." He checked the bandage around his upper arm and saw a small red stain.

"I never had that problem," MacHenry said. "Remember, you may like hanging it out over the edge, pushing the envelope, but if the situation becomes too bad, you can always punch out. Airliners don't come with ejection seats. Think about how you'd like to bring a crippled ship in with a couple of hundred souls in the back, and nowhere to go but down."

Barnes looked up and nodded. "No thanks," he said, pressing the bandage down over the seep. "Is that why you didn't eject when I told you to?"

The falling dream flickered across MacHenry's eyes. "No," he said. "I just couldn't make myself do it."

"Next time, do as you're told." Barnes released the bandage. "Damn." It was definitely leaking. He looked up at MacHenry. "Rest stop's over. Let's move." He walked over and held out his hand to help MacHenry up. MacHenry thought for a moment, and then he took it.

The afternoon light was draining away, the yellow-hot sky catching fire with the reds of sunset. The trail was flattening slightly, or else MacHenry had found his wind. "I still don't know why you brought all that gear with you," he said, eyeing Barnes's heavy rucksack. Strapped vertically to it, the long, curving bow with a quiver of arrows jolted side to side as he struggled up. "This isn't a hunting trip."

"The hell it isn't." Barnes stopped and reached out to lean against a tree. "I think I could use a quick stop." The red stain had grown. He dropped his pack and reached into the pocket where he kept the medical kit.

That was quick. "Fine with me," said MacHenry, pulling up behind him and leaning his backpack against another lodgepole pine. "You know," he said as Barnes rewrapped his arm, "I hoped I'd never see that bow again. Once was enough."

Barnes chuckled. "I bet. Just think of it as a little relaxation device, that's all."

"Relaxation?" MacHenry asked. "You were *relaxing* up at the crash site when you shot that arrow at me?"

"Let's forget that whole scene, shall we? It was an accident. Besides, I don't shoot arrows. I loose them." He pulled the bandage tight across his upper arm and winced.

"Are you sure you're all right? Nothing's let go, has it?"

"Of course not," Barnes replied, though MacHenry could see a worried look on his face. "Here"—he handed the bow to him as a diversion—"check it out. I can't concentrate on this under, you know, interrogation."

MacHenry hefted it. *Light!* The bow was laminated bamboo, nearly six feet of coiled, resilient power with wax-wood edging. The arrows were bamboo as well, and much longer than a conventional Western bolt. Although it was large and powerful, the complex construction and exotic materials made it extremely light. He handed it back.

"I'll tell you one thing. If the bad guys show, I'd put more faith in it than in that hunk of metal you're hauling with you. I'd toss that blunderbuss away if you want to stay safe."

"You're probably right." MacHenry pulled the heavy pistol out of his pack. "I haven't fired it in years."

"See? Practice. Repetition. Concentration," said Barnes as he hefted the bow. "The target exists to catch your arrow. Whether it's a target pillow or a MiG. Those are the keys to the kingdom. And the way to get you right to the edge but not over. Why don't you give it a try?"

"Zen?"

"The gun, BJ. The gun." Barnes looked around for a likely target. "My teacher called it the Zone, but it's all the same thing." Suddenly, Barnes smiled impishly. "See that tree with the carved-up trunk?" Someone had carved *LCB* into the rough bark of a pine. It was about thirty feet up the trail. "Go ahead. Better now than later, right?"

MacHenry squinted, saw the broken bark but not the letters. Maybe his prescription needed changing again. "I see it," he said. He operated the slide on the old .45 and checked for a round.

Barnes watched him closely. "Be smooth, BJ. Just be smooth."

Holding the weapon in a two-handed crouch, MacHenry slowly leveled it at the tree. The letters were just a lighter area against the dark bark. He exhaled, and pulled. The gun exploded in his hands, kicking back with a totally unexpected force. It nearly flew over MacHenry's head before he brought it back under control. The tree was intact.

Barnes waved away the cordite smoke. "You stink, BJ," he said. "Want to see how it's done?" MacHenry handed him the smoking pistol but Barnes wrinkled his nose and waved it away.

His energy was coming back now. Barnes plucked a slender bamboo arrow from the quiver. He held it up to the light as though admiring it. Then he strung it in a single fluid motion that was too fast for MacHenry to see. Barnes breathed deeply and turned to face the target. MacHenry saw his breaths fall into sync with the subtle motions of his hands and feet. It was almost a dance. Barnes looked happy with a serene smile of utmost unconcern. He drew back the arrow, the wood bending into a deep curve. String, arrow, bow; to MacHenry, it looked as though Barnes had stepped into the center of a big circle.

The arrow flew, loosed as though by its own will. MacHenry squinted to see where the bolt had flown. He walked closer. The arrow was embedded at the center of the carved letters. "You didn't even look!" MacHenry said with amazement.

"You got it. That's the whole trick." Barnes looked refreshed, his sweaty face calm and his breathing regular. He looked up at the sky. "We'd better get moving if we want to cross that river in light." They had one more ridge to climb before arriving at the canyon of the Stanislaus. There, at the base of Crandall Peak, they could ford the river where the track crossed the head of a reservoir. Beyond Schoettgen Pass lay another gorge and another rocky spine: Starr Ridge, the final resting place of a burned Cessna 172.

They walked by the arrow as they continued the climb. As he passed it, Barnes reached out and snapped the supple bamboo. "Bang," he said without turning.

MacHenry smiled, but the smile froze when he noticed fresh blood welling up from Barnes's bandage. "Barnes, you better check that arm."

Barnes looked at it. "Shit," he said, as though the wound was committing treason by not obeying his orders for it to heal. "Hang on," he said, stopping again and applying pressure to it. The leak slowed, but the new bandage was already soaked. "Damn." He dropped his sack again and pulled out the medical kit. "Looks like I'll have to give up the piano."

"Or shooting arrows."

The old brush-crowded path ran straight up the side of Bald Mountain toward the high saddle that broke the summit in two. Over the saddle a jeep track ran in easy loops down to the river. "Starting to lose our light," said MacHenry.

The terrain flattened as they neared the top of the slope. Barnes had stopped. "I told you!" he shouted as he trotted out onto a dusty jeep track. "Easy sailing from here." The trail snaked downhill into the gloom of the overarching canopy of pine.

They both looked up into the darkening sky. MacHenry saw the first stars poke through the indigo veil. "Is it far?" he asked.

"Not too," Barnes lied. From his hunt for the missing wing, he knew it was a good three-hour walk down to Rushing Meadow, the place where they could ford the Stanislaus safely. And another two to the crash site. "Just put one foot in front of the other. We'll get there." Barnes started to walk down the road.

MacHenry took two steps and stopped, listening. "I think I hear a car coming."

Barnes stopped at once and cocked his ears. There it was, louder now, coming from behind them and without doubt going their way; there was no other way for it to go. "You're right. They let somebody through that roadblock after all."

"Maybe the Marines. They might be out looking for us," said MacHenry, a prickle of worry crawling up his scalp. "It could be anybody."

Twin headlights popped around the corner, close set and high in the unmistakable configurations of a jeep. Just enough light filtered through from the dying sky for Barnes to identify the vehicle. "Not the Marines," he said. "Wrong color. Damn. It's the Air Force. Hey!" he shouted, waving his arms over his head as he stood in the center of the dirt track. "Watch this," he told MacHenry. "Officers do not walk when they can ride. *Hey!*" he shouted as the jeep drew near.

"If it's that MP, he might not be too happy to find us up here."

"Who? That grunt? Don't worry. Hey!" he shouted, waving his arms for the jeep to stop.

It did not slow. Rather, upon catching Barnes full in its headlights, the driver flicked the high beams into his eyes and stepped on the accelerator.

"Stop!" Barnes commanded. MacHenry heard the jeep clutch and the engine rev as the driver fed more power to the wheels. "Goddamn it! Stop!" Barnes shouted as the jeep flashed its headlights and, swerving slightly, roared by, leaving a rooster tail of raised red dust. Its taillights dimmed in the natural smoke screen, and then, as the jeep rounded the downhill curve, it disappeared altogether.

"Son of a *bitch!*" Barnes snarled, stomping his foot into the dirt. "I will see that miserable pudknocker thrown into goddamned oil for that! A goddamned Air Force jeep!" Barnes was circling, kicking at the tire tracks in sputtering fury. "Assholes try and scatter me with phony maintenance, and now they're into, you know, hit and run."

"He's coming back," MacHenry said as he heard the engine note shift and the whine of reverse from behind the curve. His hand had automatically gone rooting through his pack. His fist closed around the cool metal grip of the old .45. "I think we might have some explaining . . . "

The backup lights now appeared as the jeep reversed up the trail toward them. Barnes moved for the intercept, a thousand pounds of reheated thrust building behind a full verbal broadside. MacHenry wanted no part of what he knew was about to happen.

Barnes stormed up beside the canvas-topped jeep.

"Just who the living fuck do you think you are, mister?" he shouted into the covered jeep. "Didn't you see me waving at—" Barnes stopped suddenly as a pair of long, bare, and very un–Air Force legs swung out of the driver's side of the jeep, nearly kicking Barnes in the shin.

"My name is Dr. Hines," the woman said, pinning Barnes with her coldest, most clinical gaze. She wore a T-shirt, cutoff jeans, and hiking boots, but her face belonged on a Valkyrie. "And who the living fuck," she said, holding her words before her like soiled laundry, "are *you?*"

19

THE
ONE-STONE
SOLUTION

ADCOCK tapped a pencil on his desk, waiting, watching the telephone. With five of six Excaliburs away on an overseas operational test, an unnerving quiet filled the underground warren at Tonopah. Now more than at any other time, Radway would not have strayed far from Norton's global communications center in McLean, Virginia. Adcock pushed a pile of papers on his desk to create a clear area when the telephone finally rang. "Yes!" He controlled his voice. "Adcock here," he said more calmly.

"Returning your call, Peter," Radway said without introduction. He sounded distracted and annoyed.

Adcock ignored the tingle of warning. "We haven't spoken since Saturday morning," he began. "I just wanted you to know that everything out here is still holding. It's still stabilized. How goes it overseas?"

"Stabilized?" said Radway, remembering his terse exchange with Arthur Dean Bridger. "I'm afraid that view is not supportable by fact." It was precisely the phrase Bridger had uttered. "Look, Peter," Radway continued, "I've been thinking. It's time we brought you out of Tonopah."

What had Radway just said? Adcock sat straight up in his chair. "What do you mean?"

"Enstrom wants to do a thorough debrief. Can you make it to L.A. tonight?"

"What for?" Adcock's voice jumped an octave. "Enstrom? What kind of debrief . . ." He stopped. "Are you trying to tell me I'm off the project?"

"Off? No, of course not!" said Radway. "We're just bringing you in where you will be more valuable. Enstrom wants the complete update. He knows how important this all is. That's why he's CEO. He'll debrief you himself. Right from the source."

"But I . . . I don't understand. The verification trials were interrupted and the overseas—"

"L.A. will have plenty for you to do," Radway broke in. "Look. Don't worry. Enstrom and I agree that your strengths lie in the lab. Not in the field. I spoke with Bridger." Radway paused, wondering just how much of their arrangement to reveal. "He's agreed to handle the containment from here on. You're off the hook. You can go to L.A. with a clear conscience."

"I—I still don't quite follow you," Adcock stammered. He had spent years working his way into a position to escape the iron-bound desks of the L.A. corporate center. He'd been with Project Aurora right from the start. Radway was pulling it all away. "You've kept your eye on my career for years, Matthew. Why do I feel like you're throwing me to the wolves?"

"Don't dramatize. It's just a reassignment. Trust me that it's for your own good."

But it most certainly was not. Adcock knew he'd just been fired. Fired. His neck flushed. The first project whose success would be his and his alone. He felt the world begin to spin. "Is this over the HUMMER incident? If it is, I *really* don't follow this logic train. HUMMER *proves* I can handle a field operation," he protested. "This whole incident—"

"Proves just the opposite," Radway finished for him. "Peter, I'm very busy just now. We're cooperating here in Washington to clean up the mess for good. That's all you really need to know."

"Cooperating? Who with? What does Washington know about my project?" Adcock said with a laugh that sounded almost hysterical.

"Plenty," Radway replied. "They've already brought in their own team. They found a piece of your airplane in MacHenry's desk. He's left a note at his condominium for a neighbor to bring in his mail. It seems that he and the Air Force major have disappeared for the duration. Does it still sound stabilized to you?"

Adcock was stunned into silence. *Another team?* He wiped a bead of sweat from his brow. "Nobody could have done anything more." It was almost a whisper. Then, his voice gathered more strength. "You know what I did up at HUMMER. I went all the way. You can't throw me out after that. You backed me up. You can't just throw me away."

Radway paused, then spoke. "Is that a threat, Peter?"

"It's a statement of fact," Adcock replied. His whole career was a pile of dust in the palm of his hand. What would it take to put it back together? "We're both in on this one, Matthew. I won't be isolated. A person who's not fully on board could make things very difficult for Enstrom." *And you.*

"I'd be careful how you choose your words," Radway warned. "Bridger is going to call you and ask so I might as well. Do you have any notion where MacHenry and the Air Force pilot could have gone?"

The wreck. Adcock's mind raced and came to a rapid conclusion.

"Peter? Are you there?"

"Let me get back to you on it. I can't get to L.A. tonight anyway. The MU-2 is down for repairs." It was a lie, but Radway would never know.

"I want you in Los Angeles," Radway repeated. "I mean it. Bridger has . . ." He stopped. He was going to tell him of the change the Solarium chairman had made at the HUMMER site, a change Bridger claimed would clean up the whole mess once and for all. But Radway stopped. "Bridger is behind us," he said finally. Adcock was the last link connecting the incident at HUMMER with Excalibur, the last *physical* link. And he had all but threatened to reveal it, hadn't he? A glimmer of a plan materialized in Radway's mind. Bridger's stone might knock down several birds at once. *Yes.*

"I can still do it," Adcock said grimly. "Let me prove it to you. To you and Enstrom both."

"Perhaps you can," Radway replied, as much to himself as to Adcock. Serious money was on the table. Where was Adcock in the scheme of things? After all, out on the streets of Washington, people lost their lives over pocket change every day, didn't they?

"My my," said Barnes as he grinned and extended a grimy hand to Julia. A quick appraisal came up a solid positive. "Pete Barnes, as in Major Barnes." He flashed her a raffish grin that glowed in the dusky light. "Pretty far out in the boonies for a house call, aren't you, Doctor?"

"I'm a climatologist," she replied, ignoring his hand.

Barnes looked beyond her into the jeep. "Who's the ground-pounder?"

"Sergeant Kansky and I work together. You're lucky he recognized you." She scowled. "Perhaps you'll tell me what you and your friend"—she looked at MacHenry—"what you two are doing back here? You know this is a restricted area, don't you?"

"Yes, ma'am," said Barnes. "I sure do." He glanced into Julia's jeep. "Kansky, you say?"

"Yo!" Kansky called out. "Major Barnes? I thought it was you." Kansky got out of the jeep. "It's okay, Doc. I know the major."

Too bad, she thought as she turned to face MacHenry. "And you?"

"Brian MacHenry," he said, extending his hand. She took it. "Sorry if there was a misunderstanding," he said in his best airline captain's basso. Her handshake was firm, but delicate and warm at the same time. "We saw that the road was closed and walked in anyway."

At least this one didn't look like some kind of backwoods madman. "Where were you headed? Surely you two aren't hunting." Julia eyed the long bow Barnes had strapped to his pack.

"Well," said MacHenry, "we are in a way. I'm with the FAA. The Federal Aviation—"

"I know what FAA stands for," she interrupted. "What brings you here?"

MacHenry cleared his throat. "There was a crash up on Starr Ridge a week or so back. I . . . we're coming back for another look at it." He glanced at Kansky and wondered whether he should have told the truth so quickly, but then again, he never really could lie with a straight face.

Julia shook her head firmly. "I'm sorry, but that's just not going to happen. We've got a great deal of expensive equipment installed up here."

"So I see," said Barnes as his eyes lingered on Julia.

She crossed her arms over her chest and looked at him as though he had only recently emerged from the primordial ooze. *Why do all the good-looking ones . . .* She shook away the thought. How to get rid of these two? She looked at MacHenry. He seemed the more reasonable one to deal with.

"Doc?" said Kansky. "What about Crandall? You said it was important. It's getting kind of dark for it, isn't it?" AWOS 12 was still misbehaving.

"Crandall?" said Barnes. "As in Crandall Peak? That's not far from where we're headed. You could give us a lift."

"I don't . . ." She stopped when she noticed the bandage. "Do you know that you're bleeding, Major?"

"What? Oh." Barnes checked his arm. "Damn." It was nearly soaked through. Something wasn't holding. "I must have pulled something open on the hike up here." He dropped his pack and rummaged through the top for another bandage. "I better quit ruining these things. This looks to be the last one."

"And you plan to head over beyond Crandall?" she asked. "That crash site is pretty far away."

Barnes looked up. "Don't worry, we'll make it."

Julia felt caught. Reason told her that she had to get to Crandall to repair the errant AWOS. Data lost was data lost forever. She watched

Barnes's bandage glisten darkly. Compassion told her something different. "All right," she said to MacHenry. "We'll get this sorted out later. We've got a good medical kit up at our campsite."

"That's okay," said Barnes. "We don't need any—"

"Hop in," Julia ordered.

MacHenry stepped up. "Barnes, maybe it's a good idea. We can get an early start tomorrow and be there in full light."

Barnes started to object, then thought better of it. This doctor was a tough nut, but a good-looking one. And he had to admit, he was dog tired. MacHenry had kept up a solid pace, one that he had been forced to outperform at no small cost. He looked once again at his bandage. "Well," he said. "For your sake." He tossed his ruck in the back and hopped in. MacHenry joined him on the other side.

Julia started up the jeep and turned away from Crandall Lookout and the misbehaving AWOS. She leaned over to Kansky. "We'll fix it tomorrow," she said. "We've got a whole week before we're out of here anyway, right?"

"Right."

The jeep track twisted and dropped to a dry creekbed, then began to climb the flanks of Bald Mountain. The cutoff to the top was well-worn but very steep, so steep that she had to clutch into low to maintain headway. Even then, the tires spit loose gravel and slipped. The engine began to wind up as the grade became flatter near the summit. They crested the top and parked at the bottom of the small clearing next to a second jeep. The bright lights of Julia's trailer shone like an alien spacecraft just landed in the Sierra wilds.

"Wow," Barnes said after the engine died. "All the comforts of home."

"It's okay for our purposes," she replied as she swung her legs out. "I'll be back with that bandage, Major."

Kansky followed her toward the lights. "What about fixing the unit up on Crandall?" he asked her.

"We'll do it tomorrow morning. Early. I'll drive them back to the road, and you can take the other jeep to Crandall."

"What if they won't leave?"

"I'll think up something. I couldn't let them go in there bleeding to death, could I?"

"I guess not." Kansky had heard of Maj. Peter "Ninja" Barnes. He suspected that before too long, Julia might well have a different opinion.

MacHenry shook out his sleeping bag and dropped flat on his back with a groan. "I can't remember when I was this tired," he said. "You nearly ran me ragged."

"I tried to slow it up for you," Barnes replied as he poked through his ruck. "But I didn't think we'd make it if we lollygagged around."

MacHenry slowly sat up. "I appreciate your wanting to come back up here. You didn't have to."

"I don't abandon my wingman when the shit hits the turbine." Barnes slowly pulled the sodden bandage away from his stitches. He looked up, waiting until Julia was at the door to her trailer. "You see, fighter pilots are taught one thing: you don't score unless you put your nose on the target. Lose contact and you're out of the game." Barnes's eyes tracked Julia all the way inside.

"Look out, Barnes," MacHenry said, chuckling. "That target shoots back."

Julia sighed in relief at the sight of the familiar tools of her trade; her hands automatically went to the printout from the IBM. "Good," she said, eyeing the unbroken stream of data coming in from all the stations. There were no new error messages from Crandall. As she stripped the last hour's worth of printout off for storage, the peculiar warble of her Motorola SatCom sounded. She glanced at the digital time display over her IBM. The red numerals showed nearly nine o'clock. Who was up in Washington this late? She picked up. "Hines."

"Dr. Hines? Henniker here. I'm glad I got you." Henniker sounded immensely agitated and relieved, all at the same time. What could inspire her boss at NOAA to call?

"I'm sorry about those moisture tests you asked for," she began, assuming that was the reason. "We've had some equipment problems with one—"

210

"Forget them," Henniker said quickly. "I want you to listen very carefully. I've received word from . . ." He stopped. Julia knew nothing of Aaron Templeman, and that was in everyone's best interest. "There's been a change in plans. They're supposed to let you know, but I wanted to make absolutely certain—"

"What change?" Julia broke in. "What's happened?"

"So they haven't told you yet?"

"Told me what?"

"Then it's good I called," said Henniker. "I want you and your assistant to be ready to evacuate HUMMER tomorrow. Is that clear? They're sending a helicopter in around two o'clock. You have to be on it."

"Tomorrow?" There was another week to the field segment of her study. A week's worth of data was not to be abandoned lightly. "I'm not finished collecting—"

"Yes, you are," said Henniker. "Trust me, Julia. You're in a military area and the military wants it back. There may well be some physical danger to anyone left at the site after tomorrow. The equipment will stay. Take all your records, your data, leave everything running. It's important that everything be left running. We'll remote the AWOS information for the next week, but you and your helper must be on that helicopter tomorrow at two."

"Can you tell me what's going on? I planned this study out for quite a while, Doctor Henniker. Changing things at the last minute is a little unfair. We'll lose a lot of microclimate data for sure."

"Trust me. You're going to have more data than you ever dreamed of."

"But . . ."

"Two o'clock," he repeated, and the SatCom went silent in her ear.

MacHenry and Barnes drifted over as the sergeant built a fire in the stone ring. Barnes dropped down next to him. MacHenry sat a bit more stiffly. He took a pine twig and poked at the fire.

"Tell me something," Barnes asked the sergeant, "is she as tough as she sounds?"

Kansky looked up and grinned. He liked seeing cocky officers put in their place. "No, *sir*," he said. "She's a whole bunch tougher." He looked at MacHenry as a flicker in the fire ring grew to a flame. "You mentioned that crash, right?"

"Over at Starr Ridge," MacHenry agreed. "Why?"

"Well, we were up here when that little plane went down. I can tell you one thing. The wind was wild. Really howling. I couldn't believe anybody would have gone up in weather like that."

Barnes looked at MacHenry. It was an old conversation for them. "That's what I told him," Barnes said. "But BJ here is a hard guy to convince."

"Respectfully, sir," Kansky said to MacHenry, "if you were up here that day, you wouldn't need any convincing. It was *blowing*."

"That bad?" MacHenry asked, leaning back and letting his aching muscles relax. He knew that the weather did not bring that Cessna down.

Kansky put a pot of spring water on the fire to boil. "Those guys in the rescue chopper must have had brass balls to come in like they did. Just a shame it was too late for that pilot."

"It wasn't so bad later in the morning. The winds were almost calm when I showed up," said MacHenry.

Barnes leaned back on the cushion of his rucksack. "And I was on the first sortie after the SAR guys pinpointed the signal. Our helo-heads weren't too happy about poking around up here so soon after the storm. They don't like to rock the rotors."

"I don't know when you showed up, sir," said Kansky, "but when I heard the chopper up there, I guarantee you his rotors were *rocking*." Kansky added some instant soup to the warming pot.

MacHenry glanced quickly at Barnes, then sat up. "When did the first search-and-rescue party from Mather make it to the crash site?"

Barnes looked up, trying to remember. "I guess about noon."

Kansky shook his head. "No, sir. This was way before that. Right in the middle of the storm. They should get a medal for it. Or be grounded. I don't know which." He shrugged. All pilots were crazy.

MacHenry wished he had a pencil and a clean notepad. He already knew that the Cessna had burned after the crash. Now, perhaps, he knew how the men who set the fire had arrived. "Barnes, think carefully. Was there anybody at the site before the helicopter from Mather got there?"

"Negative. I mean, when I got there they were still getting the pilot pulled out of the wreck. The ground was still hot from the fire. Smoking."

"That's what I thought," said MacHenry. He knew that one way or the other, this mysterious helicopter had not been on a mission of mercy.

"What do you mean?" asked Barnes. "I don't get it. HUMMER was dead cold at the time. I told you that way back when. No lie. Even if . . . " He stopped.

"What's wrong?" asked Kansky.

"Shit," said Barnes. "They burned the bastard, didn't they?"

MacHenry tossed the stick he held into the fire. The resin caught and flared in a shower of bright embers.

"We'll launch at first light," Adcock told the MU-2 pilot. The man was working on one of the engines, arms deep inside its guts. The underground hangar at Tonopah was strangely empty without the usual bustle of Excalibur's flight crews. "Did you hear me?" Adcock said when the man kept fussing inside the engine.

"You're the boss," the pilot said as he pulled his arms out of the turbine shroud and picked up a rag to clean off the bloodred hydraulic fluid. "You want me to arrange ground transport on the other end?"

"Yes. We'll need a helicopter. Someone we can trust."

"Skycrane Repo?"

"Whatever. Just get it done." Adcock stepped up and looked into the guts of the engine. It was dirty and smelled of jet fuel; not at all like a clean sheet of design paper. "Will it be ready?"

"She'll be ready." The pilot lowered the access door and snapped it closed. "Do you want me to wait for you at Skycrane?"

"Yes, I won't be long. You just be sure this thing is ready to fly."

"You're the boss," he said again, but with an infuriating smile. "Oh six hundred soon enough for you?"

He knows, thought Adcock. *Somehow, he knows.* Adcock narrowed his eyes. What did he expect? The North Air contract pilot worked for Bridger. Of course he would know. Adcock's ears burned. "No," he replied. "We'll make it five."

"Damn," Barnes said softly as he watched Kansky leave the circle of light to get Julia. The stew was hot and bubbling in its iron pot. "Do you think he was still conscious when . . ." He stopped. It was too close. Too real. He had spent far too many hours imagining death by fire. It was, as he had said, the way you lost friends in the Air Force.

"We'll never know," said MacHenry. He paused, recalling the layout at Starr Ridge. "We were looking for the wrong thing last week. We were looking for all the usual accident clues. Not for signs of a murder."

"Yeah." Barnes leaned forward and poked a stick into the flames. "You can go figure it, but my guess is that's how that wing got disappeared."

"It all fits. But I still wonder about this other character. The man I met that night from North Air Transport. He sure seemed eager to keep a lid on our flight to Davis-Monthan. He wanted to make a deal."

"Did you?"

MacHenry hesitated. "I guess I tried to. Williams said he would drop the whole thing if I did. I figured you might not want the owners of that T-33 making waves."

"That's a deal with the devil, BJ. He probably knew the whole story from front to back." Barnes snapped the twig he held and threw it from the ring of firelight. "Screw it. Braden still cut my orders for TDY to the boonies, deal or no deal. And that little message you got from your boss in Washington wasn't exactly good news either."

MacHenry looked up at him. "I just don't know, Barnes. It feels like we're up against a whole lot of horsepower."

"Horseshit. They don't know what horsepower is all about, friend," said Barnes. "Those assholes tried to smoke me. Well, they didn't. Now they've got problems. Three problems."

"Such as?"

"That chunk of plastic you dug out of the wing at Davis-Monthan. And two more: you and me. And I don't know about you, BJ, but I for one am pissed off."

"We'll see what we can find up there in the morning," said MacHenry. "In the meantime, let's not talk shop with our hosts, okay?"

"Roger that," Barnes replied. Julia's door opened. He swiveled and saw Julia and the sergeant emerge. Barnes tracked her as she walked. "Wow," he said.

He stood up as Julia came up to the stone circle. Kansky was right behind her. She looked worried. Kansky, too. "Hi." Barnes said. "I was wondering where you had gotten off to." He noticed with disappointment that Julia now wore a sweatshirt that hid her figure entirely, but she still wore her cutoff shorts. It made her long legs look even longer. He could well imagine running his hand along their smooth length. *Maybe.*

She crouched down beside the fire, poking a branch at it in a distracted manner. "Gentlemen, I've been thinking," she began. "I'm going to help you out tomorrow morning. We've got to get a piece of equipment fixed at Crandall, and you want to get to that crash site. Correct?"

"There's no big rush—" Barnes began, but Julia cut him off.

"There's where you're mistaken, Major. So I'm going to help you get to that wreck. Sergeant Kansky can take you out there and he can stop by Crandall Lookout on the way back. Is that fair?"

"Yes, ma'am," said MacHenry. "That's going to be a real help. We'll be happy to walk back out."

"No," she said, remembering Henniker's words. *There will be some physical danger to anyone remaining in HUMMER.* "You'll come back out with Kansky. We'll take you out to the main road or wherever you left your car. That's the deal. It's not a take-it-or-leave-it either," she added. "It's take it or leave. Pure and simple. You're up here illegally. I can place a call and fix that before you've finished dinner."

"No need to get—" Barnes began, but MacHenry cut him off.

"That will be fine. I'd rather ride than walk. Just thinking about that hike up to Starr Ridge makes me tired."

"Then it's decided?" asked Julia. She held out her hand to MacHenry. He took it.

"I think it sounds just fine," MacHenry replied with a quick shake.

Barnes watched a bit jealously. "You know, that's your problem, BJ. You think too much. In my business, it can get you into trouble."

"Oh?" Julia said, turning to him. "What do you do that doesn't take thinking?"

"Fighters," he said with a smile that made his white teeth dazzle in the firelight. "I fly fighters. And I didn't say that it took no thinking. Only that it takes a whole lot more than *just* thinking."

"That sounds pretty dangerous, Major."

"It is dangerous if you don't have it put together. Things can happen very fast," Barnes said slowly, his eyes bright and locked tight onto Julia's.

Despite herself, she felt an electric tingle at their contact. She looked away first, pretending to stir the ashes of the campfire. "And I assume you have it put together. Is that right?"

Kansky chuckled, but an icy glare shut it off at the tap. Barnes let the moment deepen, ripen, then said, "Count on it."

"I see." She looked at MacHenry. "How about you, Mr. MacHenry? Do you have it put together, too?"

"No, ma'am," he said, chuckling. "I'm about done ruining my second career. I seem to start out dumb and end pretty much the same way. There's a few golden years in between where you kind of creep up on being smart, I guess."

She liked the fact that MacHenry called her ma'am. "That sounds familiar," she said. "Doing honest science is just the same. You start out dumb and try to creep up on the solution." *So why are they pulling me out tomorrow?*

"Is that what you do? Honest science?" asked MacHenry.

"I try my best," she said with a sad smile. "It doesn't seem to work out very often for me either. There's a lot of money to be made in keeping some things quiet, I guess."

"A-men," said Barnes. "I told BJ here that, too."

MacHenry nodded. "What things are you studying up here in the middle of God's creation?" he asked her.

"Well, in a nutshell, I'm looking into the effects of pollution on the world's weather. You know, ozone depletion, global warming. The greenhouse effect? It's a microstudy. One small, well-defined area that's intensively instrumented. If I'm lucky, I might find out a few things."

MacHenry nodded. "And there are some people out there who are happy enough to leave things as they are, right?"

"Right," she agreed. "We know we're doing damage, but until the actual cause-and-effect link is proven, someone can always call your warnings into question. *Prove* that our smokestack emissions are causing a four-degree rise in the Peruvian current. That sort of thing. We get closer and closer to the edge, but nobody seems to be listening."

"Got to stop somewhere," said MacHenry.

"Exactly," Julia agreed. "Something's going to give. I just hope I find out the weak spots before it does."

Barnes laughed. "It's the same in the air. You watch how they move, you figure the weak spot, close their six, and smoke 'em from close range. Visual range. Bang. Give the other guy a second and he's gone. Maybe he's in *your* six."

Julia turned to Barnes. He suddenly seemed terribly young. "And after you *smoke* them? What do you do then?"

Barnes shrugged. "After? Nothing. They're gone. Puff! You gun for the next one."

Julia stood up. "Yes"—she nodded knowingly—"I bet that's exactly what you do. Good night, gentlemen," she said to them both. Her stew was untouched. "See you in the morning."

Barnes watched as Julia retreated to her trailer. "Did I say something wrong or what?" he asked.

MacHenry smiled. "Don't worry. She's not your type anyway."

"And I suppose she's your type?"

"Mine?" MacHenry asked. The question seemed absurd.

"BJ," said Barnes, "for your information, there are only two types: fighters and targets." He turned to face Julia's trailer. "And the good Dr. Hines is, without a doubt, a very prime target."

"I guess you know about those things," said MacHenry as he stood up. "See you in the morning." Barnes was still looking toward Julia's trailer. "Sweet dreams," MacHenry added with a chuckle.

20

WHAT? MacHenry thought groggily at the sudden racket. He opened one eye and saw the source of his wake-up call. *Blue jays!* MacHenry rolled to his less stiff side and drew the sleeping bag's hood over his head to muffle their shrieks. Just as he neared sleep, the jays in the pines began their spirited debate anew. *It's too early for the world,* he thought, pulling the bag away and looking at the sky. A band of brilliant crimson arched across the eastern horizon.

A tinny metal clack was followed by a dull thud. He heard the scraping shuffle of feet over dry pine needles. Julia, a bright red towel wrapped around her, sari style, walked toward the trees at the edge of the summit.

"Target at twelve o'clock," Barnes whispered from behind him. "And tracking."

MacHenry sat up. "You wake up awful quick." A moment ago Barnes was sound asleep; now his eyes were bright and clear, reflecting in their blue the tint of the dawn sky. "How's the arm?"

Barnes checked the new bandage. It was only a little bloodstained.

"Looks good." He turned and saw Julia walk into the forest. "But that looks a whole bunch better."

MacHenry smiled. "You're still dreaming."

"I think," Barnes said, "that it's time for a little armed-reconnaissance mission." He was half out of his purple sleeping bag. MacHenry observed that he had not dressed for sleep. Barnes pulled off the old bandage and revealed the puckered stitching and the angry red skin.

"It looks like it's getting infected."

"It just needs a good washing." Barnes looked off in the direction Julia had walked. "She said there was a natural pool down that way. Indeed," he said, standing, "a little scrub is just what it needs."

"You better watch your step. She was nice enough to give us a lift, give us a flat spot to sleep, and lend us a jeep for the trip to the site this morning. Don't blow it."

"You'll notice that she's insisting we bring her pet groundpounder along for the ride. Besides," Barnes protested, "what makes you think I'd overstep our welcome? I just think it's time for a little stroll, you know?" He slipped into his heavy cargo hiking shorts and rummaged through the rucksack until he produced a pair of striped flip-flops. "You're not jealous, are you?"

"Barnes," said MacHenry as the young man watched the edge of the clearing where Julia had disappeared, "I think you're misreading the situation."

"I doubt it." He smiled, breathed in deeply, and walked toward the trees.

The very tops of the trees on the western edge of the summit now were tinged with bright gold as the sun edged above the broken horizon formed by the high peaks. The high clouds flamed brightly and then paled to white. The still air held the dust from Barnes's passage suspended, motionless. *Going to be a hot one,* he thought as he glanced at the sky.

Angel woke with a start. He threw off the blanket and jumped to his feet, forcing his eyes to focus, sweeping the gray granite rampart to

Crandall summit. There had been a scream. He reached under his balled-up jacket and pulled the CZX from its sling, rubbing the sleep from his eyes as he watched and listened.

Was it a dream? The sound of a woman shouting? He blinked and massaged his stiff arms, letting his grip on the silenced pistol relax. His muscles were sore, but not from a night on hard ground; they were sore from the effort of burying a man in the flinty soil of Schoettgen Pass. *Fool,* he thought. *Both of us.* It was not a good portent. The most successful of missions were those he came back from with all his bullets unfired. It was a matter of planning, of control; he had let the moment rule him. Now look what he had done. Who might come looking for that overcurious pilot?

It was a sign, Angel decided, a sign that he was too long in this business. When all the choices were bad ones, a man would be better off doing other things.

When the appointed day came, and after he was sure the mysterious box did its work, he would be on his way home. *Home.* Perhaps, when he returned to Havana, he would tell Guryanov. Enough was enough. The odds could be beaten for only so long. They could not be beaten forever.

Barnes followed the narrow trail as it plunged down and away from Julia's campsite. The steepness made his sandals worse than useless, so he took them off. But the ground was deep in pine needles. They were sharp as brads. Hadn't Julia been barefoot? *Maybe she's not my type,* he thought. *Dr. Hines indeed.* Women had always come to him before; they had always made the effort. But Julia seemed completely disinterested. That was new. He realized with a grin that it didn't make her less attractive to him. *Fighters and targets.* It made her a challenge.

The path widened where it joined the cut bank of a running stream. The water seemed clear and miraculous, an apparition in the dead dust of high summer. He stuck a toe into it and immediately pulled it out. *Cold!* He shook off the icy drops and continued along the bank. *No way I'm jumping into that.*

The stream shouldered its way through a cut in the rocks, tumbling white from ledge to ledge. At the bottom of the rock stairs, the stream emptied into a black and silent pool. A red towel lay beside it. Julia was swimming in the pool, oblivious to his presence. He watched as she ducked under water, letting her long brown hair billow out, her eyes closed. *On the other hand,* he thought as he stood there, the flash of her long limbs clear beneath the surface, *I could use a little washdown.*

Whistling tunelessly, he strolled down the final feet of the path and dropped his sandals beside Julia's towel. "Morning!" he called out cheerily.

She froze in midstroke. "*You!* What are you doing here? I mean"— Julia blew ballast and submerged to her chin—"I mean, *go away!*"

"Nice place." Barnes looked around, pretending to examine the scenery. There was only one view that held his interest. "Water must be cold." He stuck a toe in. Far from cold, the water was near bathtub temperature. "Hey! This is all right!"

The rocks held the heat of the previous day and slowly released it to the water. Barnes tossed his towel atop Julia's and stepped out of his shorts. He lingered naked at the rim of the rock pool to allow Julia to appreciate his fine, muscled physique. *You've got to show the goods,* he thought as he watched her watching him, *to make the sale.*

"Look, this is my last chance to . . . I'm trying to take a bath," she said firmly. Her arms were paddling strongly in the clear, deep water.

Barnes observed the shimmering flash of her body below and smiled. "Mind if I join you?" he asked as he splashed into the shallows and then, before she could warn him, dived into the black pool.

"Yes!" she said to the expanding circle of ripples.

The dive carried him deep. Far deeper than he would have planned if he had known that four feet below the surface, a permanent basin of water, cold as glacier melt, sat waiting.

He burst through the sudden and absolute division and thought, for one, frigid instant, that his head had struck stone. Lights flashing and warning bells hooting in his ears, Barnes felt his whole body constrict, double in upon itself, shrivel against the intense thermal shock. His temples pounded and an involuntary shout went unheard. *Yi!* His scream was an explosion of bubbles. Barnes pulled strongly for the surface, sputtering and spitting, drawing a stinging curtain of cold with him as he rose. "Goddamn!" he roared as he broke surface.

Julia was in the opposite corner of the rock pool. "I see you have discovered thermoclines, Major," she said, trying to keep from laughing. She turned away to keep him from seeing her amusement.

"Ah. Yah," he said, shivering. "You knew."

She turned, still submerged, a necklace of diamond-bright water around her throat. "Of course I knew. I've been using this pool for almost a month now. This was going to be the last time and you've ruined it. Congratulations."

"Last time?" He was still shivering. "Anyway, I asked if you minded."

"You didn't wait for an answer." She put her face under water and ran her fingers across her scalp. She shook the brown hair, streaked blond by the intense sun of the mountains. "It's just what you said last night. You don't think. You just do. Well, Major, just doing can get you into trouble."

Life was returning in electric tingles to his numbed limbs as he beat the water with his arms to send warmth to them. "Sorry. It usually works out a little better. Forget it." He breaststroked back toward his towel. "I'm finished anyway. I just wanted a quick dunk."

"Don't be a child." Julia paddled toward the opposite rim. "You're already wet, so you might as well stay."

"Child? You want to talk who's the . . ." Barnes stopped as she rose a tantalizing fraction above the water, a stream running down the cleft of her breasts. "Okay," he said. "We're all adults here, right?"

"If you say so." Julia suddenly dove and swam strongly over to the side of the rock pool fed by the cold stream. She turned away and stood up, the dark waters lapping at her slender waist. She picked up a plastic bottle of shampoo. "This is the mixing zone," she said, rubbing a peppermint-scented soap into her hair. "Where it's just right." She stopped and looked over her shoulder. He was all but mesmerized. Good.

Barnes watched her wash her hair, paying close attention to the play of muscles beneath the smooth skin of her back. His eyes carried the line of her hips into his imagination. His imagination carried the line of his thoughts well beyond that. "Ah, so I see," he said, distracted.

She dropped back down into the water and rinsed her hair before standing up again. She turned her head but not her body. "How'd you get that scar? It looks recent."

"What? Oh. It's not that bad," he replied as her words finally cut through a deepening fog. "Friday night. Saturday morning, actually." He carefully stepped into deeper water, felt the cold at his toes, and began to swim; the stitched-tight skin in his left arm made it more of a lopsided paddle. The sweet peppermint grew stronger as he came up from behind.

"What happened?" she asked, her back still turned.

"Just an accident," he said as he came up close behind her. "Want me to do your back?"

"My what? No!" It was her involuntary reaction.

"You're missing out on a treat." He was close enough to touch her now, close enough to see the tension in her muscles. This was more familiar terrain. *One finger,* he thought, *and she'd execute a four-g climbout.* "So why is this the last-chance bath?"

"My plans have changed," she replied uncertainly. "We're leaving sooner than I thought."

"Too bad. It's a real nice place up here," he said as he stood behind her. The rock bottom was warm to his still-cold feet. "You sure you don't want a scrub? You can trust me."

A slight tremor ran over her back even though Barnes had not touched it. Julia stopped rinsing and turned her head to face him. She thought of his face lit by last night's fire, his startling blue eyes and dark hair. *No.* She thought of the briefest flicker of his body as he had stood poised, ready for the icy dive. But she *had* tricked him, if only with his own bullheaded connivance. "You don't look especially trustworthy to me," she said.

"Me? Come on. I've got a commission signed by the President of the United States. He trusts me."

"To scrub his back?" She tossed the bottle of soap at Barnes. "Here."

Barnes grabbed it and squeezed soap onto his palms. He rubbed them together with undisguised glee. He moved closer to her, standing up behind her naked back, his hands reaching, closing the distance until they made cool contact with her smooth skin. He smiled when he saw the ripple cross her muscles at his touch. He worked the soap across her back with infinite care not to miss a square inch.

"I haven't had a good back rub in a while."

"You couldn't get the sergeant to wash your back?" asked Barnes as he risked his hand up her side, under her arm.

She stepped a few inches away. "I never asked him. He never offered."

"That," said Barnes, "is why he's still a sergeant." He began to knead her skin harder now, his thumbs in the two dimples at the small of her back.

She braced herself against the rocks as Barnes soaped her sides, from her elbows down to the flare of her hips. How he wished the water were just a bit lower. "Still nice?" he asked.

"Don't worry. I'll tell you when to stop."

"I bet you would, too." He let his hands work their own way around her waist. She suddenly tensed as he worked his way to her firm belly.

"Somehow I think you've done this before." Julia was shocked when she found herself enjoying his touch. What was she doing wasting time here? She and Kansky had to be ready when the helicopter came at two. She stiffened and pulled away from his hands. "I think it's getting late." Julia dunked and pulled herself out of the rock pool.

"Late? MacHenry was in deep-zee mode when I left him. There's . . . " But his voice failed him when she stood up, turning to face him fully while she reached for her red towel.

Barnes found his imagination and his vision coincided perfectly in Julia's firm, athletic body. Her small nipples were hard, like two red raspberries, and her face was flushed even darker than her tan.

"It's going to be a long day," she said as she dried off. *Even if it stops at two o'clock.* Julia noticed his frozen, glazed stare and found that she was enjoying it. "Are you feeling all right?" she asked as she wrapped herself with the towel. "You look a little pale, Major."

"I had this dream running right up to about ten seconds ago," he finally replied. Barnes tried to shake off the spell, but it clung to him like perfume on a humid summer night. "You wouldn't believe how real it was."

"You'd be surprised." Julia looked at the angry red stitchery of Barnes's wound. "Your arm looks better. Cleaner, anyway."

The moment broke and his thoughts cleared. "I heal fast."

"You see? That's exactly the problem," she said as she walked to the path. "I don't."

Adcock watched the dawn-lit landscape unroll beneath him at the rate of 260 nautical miles to the hour. First the desert, then the dry, shattered mountains of the Owens Valley passed below the MU-2 long nose. He saw the shadow of the fast turboprop flit across the harsh landscape. It was hypnotic and suggestive of the other aircraft whose presence was nearly as spectral. The sunrise had been spectacular, a blaze of reds and purples. Now, the day was settling into a glare of pure heat.

"Doing all right?" the pilot asked.

"What? Oh. Yes." Adcock was mentally tracing a dense maze of actions and reactions. It was his morning *option tree* exercise. Every day began with one. It was his discipline. It was the secret to his success. The whine of the twin turboprops buzzed in his head as he leaned against the cockpit window, bringing him upright in a start. The pilot looked over, concerned that Adcock's nodding was a prelude to airsickness.

"Need anything? The bar's stocked in the back."

"I don't drink and this isn't a pleasure trip," Adcock replied. "How soon before we land?"

The pilot checked the panel clock against his watch, then checked both against the distance-measuring display. "We're eighty miles out. Eighteen minutes. Should be on the ground about quarter past six. Everything's set on the other end." He had made the call to Skycrane

Recovery, another to Washington, and a third to the Los Angeles headquarters of Norton Aerodyne. *Busy busy busy,* he hummed to himself as he banked back on course.

Adcock unscrewed a thermos of bitter black coffee and resubmerged into his silent diagrams. He did not notice the engines throttled back, the descent to the private airstrip outside Sacramento, the smooth landing, the cloud of dust kicked up behind them as they rolled out.

The hoarse scream of the engines became a whisper of windmilling propellers as the pilot cut first the right, then the left turbine. The Garretts wound down, freewheeling, as Adcock snapped back into the present.

The pilot set the brakes, and then, as the gyros spun down, he walked aft and dropped the airstair. Adcock stood up, squinting out into the early-morning sun. A row of parked helicopters and a small building were the only objects on the isolated dirt landing strip. The birds were painted a dark, military green, but they bore the name SKYCRANE RECOVERY on their sides in faint, faded lettering. This was the company Adcock had used in HUMMER before. They could be trusted, he knew, because they had more to lose than he did if anything untoward surfaced. They were at the very bottom of the chain of plausible denial. Adcock could crucify them, and it made him feel good for the first time since his call from Radway. He was getting things back into shape.

There. He saw they were not alone. A man beckoned impatiently, from within the smallest of the fleet of helicopters. Adcock walked over, his footsteps kicking up small puffs of dust as he went. It was dead dry and hot for so early in the day.

"You the charter?" the pilot shouted through the open hatch of the small helicopter. He wore an olive-drab flightsuit, pure military issue, but his mirror sunglasses would never have passed an Army inspection. Despite its faded paint, the helicopter was a brand-new MD-500E, a jet-powered five-seater that could cruise at 150 knots, a smooth teardrop of metal and plastic from its chin bubble to its raked tail. The 500 was a real speedster, but to Adcock it looked small for the task at hand.

"I'm Williams," said Adcock. He looked over the tiny machine. "Have you been briefed on what's needed?"

"Get in, strap on, and then we talk," the pilot said, shoving open the door and motioning Adcock inside. He sat in the right seat.

Pilots. Adcock looked up into the clear morning sky, breathed in the last sweet air before the day became summer hot, and climbed in on the left. He snapped the buckle on his seat belt and noticed the weapon strapped in a rack by his feet. A canvas sack held six curving magazines of ammunition. It was an AK-47 assault rifle. "I asked you a question," Adcock said after settling into the olive-drab-covered seat. It seemed an odd fabric for a civilian machine.

"The company said you wanted a pilot and a chopper for a special SAR," the pilot replied.

"This will be a search, not a rescue."

"I understand. They said you wanted to go small and low and that you wanted equipment." He nodded at the canvas sack at Adcock's feet. "You do know how to use an AK?"

Adcock picked the rifle up and unfolded the metal stock. He was about to experiment with the metal safety bar on the Kalashnikov's right side when the pilot closed his hand over his.

"Okay," he said. "Just watch and keep your hands off the controls. And at no time will the weapon be off safety unless the muzzle is pointed out the door. Understood?"

"Let's go," said Adcock.

The pilot nodded at the rifle. "Weapons safe and in the rack." Adcock grudgingly secured the AK. "Good." The pilot turned the master ignition key, rolled off the collective throttle, and engaged the autostart.

A high whine came from the starter motor as a hiss permeated the cabin. The fuel controller brought on the *tick tick tick* of the jet igniters, and suddenly the hiss grew to a roar, then the roar itself submerged beneath the whine of the gearbox and the rapid blurring of the rotor blades. The pilot indicated the green headset hanging from a hook behind Adcock's head. He put it on. It felt like a vise clamped down on his temples. The intercom came on with a click.

"Normally this bird has a little bitty turbine," said the helo pilot. "This one's got a thousand-horsepower CTS-800. That plus the fact that we stripped out four hundred pounds of civilian crap makes us a real flying machine. With just you and me on board, it will do anything you want done." He checked the instrument panel and turned back to Adcock. "You ready?"

Adcock nodded, and the chopper pilot brought in takeoff power. The big turbine screamed with impatience. He briefly rolled the throttle off to split the torque and RPM needles, and when this was done to his satisfaction, he looked over at Adcock with a grin. Adcock saw two images of his own face in the man's eyes. "Hold on," he said. The rotor blades flew by in a gray disk, too fast to register. Then, with the jet roaring and the blades slashing the air at high RPM, he pulled the collective control. The 500 exploded straight up like a skyrocket. At a thousand feet, it nosed over to the east, the mountains framed in its wide Plexiglas windshield.

Cowboy, thought the MU-2 pilot who had flown Adcock in from Tonopah. He shielded his eyes against the rotor blast and dust as the helicopter beat swiftly to the east. When it became lost in the glare of the morning sun, he went inside the deserted operations shack and found a pay phone. The first number he dialed rang in Langley, Virginia. "Delivered," he said, and hung up. The second was the Los Angeles number.

The CEO of Norton Aerodyne answered it on the third ring. "Yes?" said Enstrom.

"Sacramento here. I've been instructed to tell you the package is ready," the pilot said, wondering who they would send out to Tonopah to replace Adcock. "Would you like me to wait?"

"No. That won't be necessary," Enstrom said. "Thank you so much for your help."

21

COUNTDOWN

JULIA'S hair was still wet when she reappeared in her usual cutoffs and T-shirt. "Good morning, Mr. MacHenry." She sat down on one of the sling camp chairs and took the hot cup from Kansky.

"Morning. You're, ah . . ." MacHenry wanted to tell her how nice it was to sit down to breakfast across from such a pretty woman, but his lips refused. "You're just in time for coffee," he said finally. "Did you see Major Barnes out there?"

"I saw quite a bit of Major Barnes. We ran into each other at the pool." Julia smiled as she took a sip of coffee. "Are you ready to go back to that wreck?"

"As soon as Barnes shows up."

"Breakfast," Kansky announced as the pot with the oatmeal boiled over, hissing against the hot metal of the stove. The sergeant's eye caught movement at the edge of the clearing. Barnes was shuffling up the track.

He ambled over to the campfire. "One hundred percent better," he said, though MacHenry didn't know what he was talking about.

"It always leaves me feeling better," said Julia. "Ready for the day."

MacHenry looked first at Barnes, then back at Julia. *Could they? Did they?* MacHenry cleared his throat. "Well, I guess we should eat some of this fine breakfast and get packed and going." He looked at his watch. "I had no idea it was this late." It was six-twenty.

"Remember," said Julia, "your time at the site is limited. Sergeant Kansky needs to spend some time up at Crandall Lookout, too. And you both need to be back here by noon." MacHenry and Barnes could have their look. With Kansky along, there would be no question about returning in time.

After breakfast, Barnes loaded his bow and rucksack into the jeep. MacHenry put his gear next to them. "Remember!" she shouted to them. "No later than noon!"

"Understood," said Kansky as he hopped in and started the jeep. He was used to plans changing at the last minute and for no obvious reason. It was the military way, wasn't it?

Barnes gave her a thumbs-up while MacHenry looked vaguely worried. Kansky clutched into low and moved off down the steep trail. As she watched them go, a gust of wind blew through the tops of the pine trees, raising a cloud of dust, obscuring the jeep as it dove into the trees that ringed the summit. Julia shielded her eyes against the sun and looked up into the sky. *That's strange.*

A line of horsetail cirrus drew a veil above the western horizon. Of course. That was why the sunrise had seemed so red. *Moisture aloft,* she thought. They were the shock troops of an advancing front: a storm warning. But in the middle of the Sierra dry season, how could that be? She'd check the latest satellite shot while she packed up.

Walking back to her trailer, she listened to the sound of the wind through the pine trees. It was beginning to get gusty, but that was normal. The clouds were not. *We're getting out of here just in time,* she thought.

The Visiting Officers' quarters at Beale Air Force Base was dead quiet, but the faint hum of the bedside clock was enough to keep Kinkaid from getting back to sleep. He turned over on the hard cot. *Six-thirty.* Kinkaid had stage jitters.

231

There was only one more day of training on the KC-135 simulator before he would be called upon to do the real thing; to fly a quarter of a million pounds of jet fuel into a controlled collision with the ground. A test of some new fire-retardant added to the fuel, he'd been told. How could jet fuel be jet fuel and not burn? It sounded crazy to him, but he wished them luck. Fire, next to weather, was the aviator's deadliest foe. As the old saying went, the only time you had too much fuel was when you saw flames.

Suddenly, the metal door lock clicked and the room lights snapped on. Kinkaid rolled back, his eyes squinting against the harsh fluorescent light.

"You up?" It was Tinker, the simulator operator, Kinkaid's appointed torturer. "Captain Kinkaid?"

It was the first time Tinker had called him by his rank. He surmised, correctly, that it was not a good sign. "I think so. You're early."

"Sorry to bust in, but there's been another little change in the test schedule."

"Like what?"

"Get dressed, and I'll brief you."

The pound of the rotor blades and the bright sun pouring unfiltered through the glass of the helicopter's clear roof turned Adcock's headache into agony. He pulled off the padded headphones and rubbed his temples. The sudden flood of engine noise made him wince. "How long before we get there?" he shouted. "Can't this thing go any faster?" The airspeed indicator registered 148 knots.

"Not if you want to keep flying." The pilot tapped his headset to remind Adcock to put his back on. "That's better. High-speed blade stall would ruin your day. Just relax. We'll cross into HUMMER in another thirty-five, forty minutes."

Adcock's fist balled in impatience. Time was a rapidly depleting resource. Radway would tolerate a bending of his orders just so long. He was supposed to be heading in to the home office, to Los Angeles. Debriefing with Enstrom would be his make or break; Norton's CEO tolerated no failure, least of all ones measured in the billions of dollars.

But he could still show them that he was capable of running a tight program. He could still do it. "You know where we're going?" he asked for the fourth time.

The pilot simply looked over and did not answer. The wavy line of mountains on the horizon became distinct; the hills and ranches below ramped up into desolate wooded country. Domes of granite poked through the stands of trees more frequently as they thundered east. The pilot added power and pulled in a little pitch, and the 500 climbed up the rising foothills of the Sierra Nevada.

"So"—Kansky turned around and grinned at MacHenry—"what do you think? Nice country, huh?" The trail was skinny and winding. There were no guardrails.

"I think I'd like you to watch the road." MacHenry looked down the steep dropoff and inched away from the jeep's open side, his toes curling up inside his boots for a better grip. Kansky was taking the turns way too fast for his liking.

"Gonna be a hot one, BJ," said Barnes. Their dust hung motionless behind them. The breeze they had felt up on the summit was gone down here, and the sky had turned from red to blue to a white-hot glare. As they negotiated a bare outcrop, the intense sun made MacHenry's face tighten in recoil.

Kansky clutched the jeep and slowed. A side trail angled off the main jeep track, up toward Crandall's summit and the balky AWOS 12. He briefly considered stopping and calling back to Julia to make sure the misbehaving unit had not gone on strike since they had left camp. *She would have called.* He glanced at the walkie-talkie by his feet. The steady red light, not blinking, meant no signals had been received for its scrambler circuits to decode. *Okay.* He pressed the accelerator and the jeep leaped forward, leaving the Crandall cutoff behind.

"Sure beats walking," Barnes said. "I don't think you would have made it last night. Pass the water."

MacHenry handed him the canteen. "I don't think we would have made it by the end of today. Not the way you were tiring."

"Me? Tiring? Are you kidding?"

MacHenry arched an eyebrow. "You look better this morning."

"Should have come for a swim," Barnes said with a slightly evil smile after a long gulp. "Freshen you right up." He passed the jug back. "On second thought, it's just as well you stayed in bed, old-timer."

The trees thinned as they drew closer to the edge of the canyon of the Stanislaus. They stopped and looked down into the still-shadowed depths of the gorge. The roar of white water rose from below, impressively loud for the distance. Huge boulders had tumbled down a side canyon to partially block the river's passage. Water that had been snow within the hour smashed and foamed wildly over them.

"How do we get across?" MacHenry asked the sergeant. The Starr Ridge crash site was beyond the opposite wall of the river canyon. They had to get across somehow.

Kansky pointed downstream, around the descending flank of Crandall Peak. The turbulent river widened into a broad, flat expanse of still water, edged in grassy marshes and rocky beaches. A narrow bridge jumped the water and climbed into the forest. "Rushing Meadow," he said, but then squinted at something not wholly congruent with the scene. A spot of unexpected color marred the view. "Hey," he said, pulling his binoculars out. He trained them on the flats and focused. "There's an airplane down there."

Barnes sat up straight at the word. "Where?" he asked, and then he saw the tiny yellow cross on one of the narrow beaches far below. "Looks like a beached kite."

"Piper Cub yellow," McHenry said. "Probably a fisherman. Goldens are up this way, I believe."

"Nobody's supposed to be up this way," said the sergeant. *Now there's someone else to kick out by two,* he thought. Kansky swept the small makeshift runway with the binoculars. "Nobody around. No campfire smoke." *Damn!* There was little enough time for driving Barnes and MacHenry around, much less hunting for some errant angler.

"It's still pretty early yet," said MacHenry. "Maybe they're still asleep. Do we drive by it on the way?"

"We can," Kansky replied. *We'd better,* he thought. Julia had told him of the sudden change in schedule. He assumed that if the military had anything to do with it, it was just more hurry up and wait. But orders were orders, even, or perhaps especially, when they came from the lovely doc. "He's over by where that old rail line comes down the side of Crandall. We'll stop and check on the way back. If we get done up at our crash site early enough."

"It won't take more than an hour," said MacHenry. "Now that I know what I'm looking for."

"Good," said Kansky.

Julia heard the wind pick up. She glanced automatically at the IBM for current data from the AWOS network. *Steep pressure gradient,* she thought as she read off the wind speeds from several of the remote stations. The early morning GEOS West shots had come over the printer. Now she knew why those thin cirrus had appeared so unexpectedly. "What are you up to?" she asked.

An unseasonal weather system was spiraling off the California coast. She looked at the small storm's tight-wrapped coil of clouds and marveled at the way certain shapes appeared again and again, even if the when of that appearance was impossible to predict. Here, in the middle of the high-Sierra dry season, was a storm that promised rain.

She tore off the printout. Rain would send the forest's moisture content up, and that was all to the good, even if it was completely out of season. There hadn't been a forest fire here in HUMMER for quite some time, and the brush was dense and resinous.

The distinctive warble of the Motorola SatCom broke her concentration. Julia assumed it was Henniker calling to be certain she had heeded his warning to be ready to pull out. She picked up the instrument, noting the red scrambler light was blinking. "Yes?"

"Dr. Hines, please," said the voice uncertainly. It was a voice unknown to Julia. "Put me through to Dr. Hines."

"This is she."

"Oh!" he said with a laugh. "I didn't expect . . .," Bridger began, then thought better of it. "I have an urgent message, Dr. Hines. You'll want to take some specific notes."

"Who is this?"

"I'm the military liaison on this project." He couldn't very well mention the word Solarium, could he? "There's been a change in plans."

"I'm already aware of them," she said.

"You are? How, if I may ask?"

"I received word last night from NOAA. We'll be ready for the helicopter at two. But just barely."

"That won't be quite good enough," Bridger replied. Who had given her the word last night? It had to be Templeman. He'd deal with him later. "You will need to be standing out in the clearing a bit earlier."

"How much earlier?"

"What time do you show on the master clock?"

Julia looked at the display atop the IBM. "It's just past nine thirty-five. Just exactly what kind of—"

"Very well," said Bridger. "You, your assistant, and all your data files will need to be ready for pickup in"—he paused—"three hours. Twelve-thirty your time. Is that clear?"

"Wait—"

"Three hours," Bridger repeated as though lecturing a slow child.

Julia looked at the glowing numbers. *Kansky!* "You can't make that kind of change!" As she watched, the number jumped to 9:37.

A short sigh was transmitted, encrypted, decoded, and then drifted from the speaker. "I already have. These are your new orders. A competing use has arisen for your area."

"Hey! You listen to me. I take orders from Dr. Henniker. Not you. I suggest you speak with him." As she looked at the impossibly small amount of time this man was giving her, she felt her anger turn to panic. *Kansky!* She glanced at the walkie-talkie.

"I'm sorry, Dr. Hines," said Bridger. "But there's no time for conferences. We're committed."

"Then find the time. I'm in charge out here, and if I say we can't do it, you'll just have to take my word for it."

"Excuse me, but I think there's a misconception. The helicopter will be there at twelve-thirty, whether that's convenient or not. I suggest you be on it."

Julia picked up the walkie-talkie and gripped it in her fist. "I think it's *you* who has a misconception. I've got staff out in the field!" *9:39.* "Don't you see?"

The CIA man nodded. He had one, too. But Adcock's running loose was not a problem anymore. It was a solution. "I see very well," he said. "And I suggest you get them out."

22

SEARCH

AND

DESTROY

COME right ten degrees," said Adcock as the helicopter rushed along the spine of a ridge. He looked up, trying to match the terrain out the window with the terrain on his chart.

The pilot seemed oblivious. This was a longer outing than he had planned for, and his eye was on his rapidly dropping fuel gauge. The big turbine in the MD-500 demanded its due. He wheeled the machine around and picked up speed. The sooner this job was over the better. Adcock was making him nervous. He was used to dealing with professionals, and Adcock didn't fit the bill.

"Right on the ridge. Can you see it?"

"Negative." All the pilot could see was a lot of bad country to land in. Then his own practiced eye caught sight of an unnatural shape. "Hold on. Okay. I think I got it," he said, slewing the 500 in a pedal turn ten degrees farther left. "Over there," he said, nodding.

Adcock looked and at first saw nothing but large red boulders. Then he saw the remains of the Cessna. Against a backdrop of mountains and canyons, the tiny sparkle of metal seemed incredibly small, incredibly insignificant. "Can you bring it down?"

The pilot shook his head. "Maybe." He twisted off some power and let the machine settle in the direction of the wreck.

As they dropped closer, Adcock felt a growing fury that something so small as this charred heap of aluminum might have risked Aurora and his career. Then another shape caught his eye off to the side. He had nearly missed it. *What?* He grabbed the helo pilot's arm. "Take us over that stand of trees," he said, tugging the fabric of the man's flightsuit.

The pilot pulled away from his touch and banked the MD-500. Adcock's mouth fell wide open when the shape became perfectly identifiable. "How . . ." he stammered. His option tree, so carefully made, so lovingly detailed, had just been chopped out at its roots. "How did that get back here?" he whispered to himself. Below them, half in the trees, was the wing of a Cessna 172.

"Looks like a wing off the wreckage," said the pilot.

"Find a spot," Adcock ordered the pilot. "We have to land!"

The pilot swung the nose in a circle and looked for another place more hospitable to the helicopter, the blades blasting the wreck with wind and dust.

Adcock just stared at the wing. *How did it reappear?* It had to be the same one. It had a gash running right across the top, a deep, black gash whose origin he, Adcock, knew all too well. His hand tightened to a fist. "Someone's playing games," he said, his voice an almost unrecognizable growl. Adcock looked back to where the main wreckage had come to rest. He saw no sign of life below. The Cessna looked as though it had always occupied the boulder field atop the ridge. "Okay. Forget landing," he said, "we aren't after aluminum anyway." He reached down and lifted the AK-47 out of its padded cradle.

"Hey!" the pilot shouted. "Make sure the damn safety is on!" He trusted the assault rifle in his passenger's hands about as much as he would give the strange, intense man the controls of the helicopter. His gut told him it would amount to the same thing. "You know which end to point, right?"

"I know." Adcock checked the safety as the MD-500 hovered uncertainly above the wreck. *Radway,* he thought. He had to be behind this. He was being set up somehow, set up to fail.

He reanalyzed his circumstances. The site was empty. There were no signs of intruders. There was only one path cut from the clearing far below. He smiled as the entire, logical notion spread before him in perfect, branching clarity. His gut told him that they were down there someplace. His hand tightened around the smooth wooden stock on the AK. He would find them. He would put an end to the threat to his project and his own future.

"Well?" asked the pilot. "We can't hang in the sky all day. Where do you want to head now?"

"Okay," said Adcock, not returning the assault rifle to its cradle. His eyes followed the bloodred dirt of the jeep trail below Starr Ridge. "Take us down over that dirt road." He checked his watch. Enstrom was expecting him in L.A. by afternoon. The pilot hesitated. "Move!"

Barnes listened as the helicopter's beat became indistinct. They had been damned lucky not to arrive at Starr Ridge a few minutes sooner. Halfway up to the wreck, they had heard the beat of its rotors approach. No one needed to tell him to drop. He got up from the dusty ground and beat the dirt from his hiking shorts. "Okay," he said. "They're gone."

"Excuse me," said Kansky, "but what the fuck is going on?" He, too, had taken cover when he saw both Barnes and MacHenry dive. The dense canopy of the forest had saved them.

MacHenry stood up and only then realized the big .45 had found its way from his pack and into his hand.

"Jesus! Point that thing away!" Kansky shouted as MacHenry turned to listen for the beat of the rotor blades and swept the pistol through a dangerous arc. "What, is somebody looking for you guys or something?"

"Maybe," said Barnes. He turned to MacHenry. "Hey, BJ, I know you want to look at that Cessna, but I have the feeling it might not be too smart right now. How do we know they didn't put somebody on the ground up there?"

"I don't." MacHenry thought, *Good question, Barnes. You keep asking them.* He looked up the steep trail. "Okay, how do you want to handle this?"

Barnes shrugged. "I'm not exactly an expert in, you know, infantry tactics." He looked at Kansky. "This is a job for the groundpounders."

"I'll take the lead," Kansky said, and shouldered by Barnes.

MacHenry checked to see that the safety was on and slipped the old revolver back into his pack. "Let's be fast. Maybe it was just a coincidence. Maybe whoever it was in that chopper just happened by and saw the wreck."

"Yeah," said Barnes. "I'm sure."

They stopped at the last line of trees before the boulder-strewn clearing, listening. A heavy curtain of dust still draped across the top from the chopper's wash. "Okay," said Kansky as he motioned for them to follow. "I don't know what you guys are about, but we're alone."

MacHenry stepped from the trees and out onto the hot stones. It was like walking onto recently poured blacktop. The field of boulders reflected back the white heat of the sun. MacHenry felt the moisture in his throat parch and his sweaty shirt dry the instant he left the shade. The wreckage was directly ahead.

He stopped and took in the site again, trying to see it with new, unprejudiced eyes. He walked directly to the large boulder the Cessna had struck. He could feel the granite's heat bake through his canvas boots.

"Talk about augering in," said a sudden voice behind him. MacHenry jumped. Kansky had joined him, leaving Barnes at the edge of the site. "Didn't mean to scare you, sir. What's it look like?" *And can we get the hell out of here?* Kansky felt as though he were pinned in the focus of a spotlight.

"It looks different," said MacHenry. "A second visit always yields some more answers."

"From the look on your face I'd say it's added a couple of questions, too. What's the story with that helicopter?"

"I'm about to find out." MacHenry walked around the bent fuselage, winding up just aft of where Kansky sat in the shade of the one attached wing. You could still smell the char in the ground. He traced back along the gash the doomed Cessna had cut in the hard ground.

Kansky sat, nervously watching the sky. He held his hands over his eyes and looked back at MacHenry. "Find something?"

"See these streaks?" He pointed to a series of parallel courses of char that went from the wing's underside to the top of the passenger compartment. "Running fuel," MacHenry said. "But there's another piece of evidence from this wreck that didn't burn at all. The right wing was taken away before the fire was set."

"Set?" asked Kansky. "As in . . ."

"Set," MacHenry repeated, and then walked to the side of the Cessna that had suffered that amputation of its wing.

The tires had melted into black pools, leaving the stump of the landing gear. A long gouge ran back from the burned metal, showing the path it had plowed as the Cessna crashed. He looked over the bent roof of the cabin. The left wing had also left marks on the flinty earth as it dragged to a stop. "They took that wing away because it pointed right back at them."

"They didn't take it too far, though," said Kansky.

"Far enough. It's a pile of scrap metal in Arizona by now."

"No, sir." Kansky pointed at the opposite edge of the clearing. Half of a wing poked out between two pine trees.

MacHenry saw it, but even his seeing it could not make his brain obedient. *What?* Leaving Kansky behind, he walked over to the wing as though in a dream. As he came closer to it, he half-expected it to evaporate, to vanish like ice under the merciless sun. But it didn't.

"How in the hell . . ." There was the gash, the same one he had fished the chunk of radar-absorbent carbon from at Davis-Monthan. There it was. The whole thing. Right in front of him. It made MacHenry's head spin. "How did it get back here?" They had taken it away, secure in the belief that it would never be traced to them, that the wreck of the Cessna would be attributed to bad weather, and not a midair collision. And the death of the pilot? An accident; not murder.

But MacHenry knew otherwise. It *had* been a midair collision. It *was* murder. They had even tried to kill him and nearly succeeded that night over the desert. They had come quite a bit closer in their attempts with Barnes. But this? Why would they put this out where it couldn't help but be found? He slowly dropped to his knees and felt along the gash in the wing. Something was very, very wrong. Whatever it was, it made MacHenry's hair stand straight on his neck.

As he touched the hot, torn metal, he felt what was still too faint to be heard. It was the sound of an engine. No, rotors. The distant pounding shook the battered Cessna in sympathetic trembling.

"Damn it!" Adcock cursed as the wrinkled carpet of forest rolled below them. "Where are they?"

The pilot eyed the fuel gauge again. They had, at most, another thirty minutes before they would be forced to return. He tapped the gauge to draw Adcock's attention to it. "Another fifteen minutes," he said, "and we turn around."

"We turn when I say so," Adcock said, seething. He looked at the gauge. The needle swung crazily from the yellow caution arc to nearly half full. "You've got plenty of gas."

The pilot banked hard right and pulled off power, settling the machine toward the treetops. "Tell you what. Since you know so damned much, we'll just set down and you fly it. Keep the fucking thing all day."

Adcock leaned over and checked the gauge again. "That fuel looks fine to me."

"Hey"—the pilot shrugged—"you've got the big picture for sure." One way or the other, they would turn back in fifteen minutes. He wasn't going to autorotate for real because this squirrel didn't know what was good for him.

Adcock swept the ground with his binoculars, lingering over the open meadows and roads below. "Swing back to the west. I want to check along the trail to the site again," Adcock directed.

"Now you're talking." West was the direction back home, and the turn would cut time off the return leg. It would also put the hot sun behind them. Even with the doors off and the wind of their passage blowing through, the MD-500's Plexiglas bubble was becoming an oven. He moved the cyclic an almost imperceptible amount and the

500 tilted over and banked. Adcock, face pressed tight to the glasses, saw it first.

I knew it. "Over there." He smudged the plastic canopy with his finger. The blue jeep looked like a toy down below. Parked far under a tree, they had missed it on their first pass.

At treetop height, they flashed up the side of the ridge, the MD's nose pointed at the crash site once more.

Barnes watched as MacHenry made his way around the wreck and over to the opposite edge of the clearing. What was he looking at over there? Barnes couldn't quite see. The charred fuselage was in his way. He wished he had decided to stay back with Julia rather than tag along. Who knew where that might have lead?

He pulled a red bandanna from his shorts and mopped his face. The memory of her body came back. He had been right, of course. There were fighters and there were targets. Despite her cool demeanor, she made a very desirable target.

Barnes checked the bandage wrapped tight around his upper arm. A pinprick of blood was all that showed through the gauze. He touched it and felt the sting return at once. *Not good.* He might just as well have left his bow at home; there was no way he could draw it without opening up these stitches. *Groundpounders,* he thought. Couldn't they even get stitches right?

He looked up and saw MacHenry drop to his knees. *What's he looking at?* Then MacHenry suddenly stood up. Barnes saw that Kansky was shading his eyes and looking to the east.

Then Barnes heard it, felt it; the air began to shudder with the sound of a helicopter's fast approach.

Oh, shit. "Hey! BJ!" The sound grew louder, the rotor thumping the air. "MacHenry!" he shouted. Barnes stepped partially out of the shade. The helicopter was coming from behind and from below where the high trees blocked his view.

The sound grew louder. He stepped into the full sun. "BJ!" The slap of the rotors changed to a tight whine. MacHenry was looking in the wrong direction! "Get down!"

Barnes turned to shout another warning, but the helicopter suddenly swept over him, blinkering the sun and drowning his yell. It reared to a sudden stop and wheeled in a near-aerobatic right turn. There was a figure leaning out now, pointing at the ground, not with his arm, but rather with a rifle.

"No!" Barnes yelled as billowing clouds of ocher rose from the blast of the rotors. *"No! BJ!"* He sprinted into the open as the man with the machine gun opened up with a long burst. "Get down!" Barnes yelled, his legs pumping like pistons as he ran into the open. The slugs chewed into the hard soil around the wrecked Cessna, raising a second cloud of dust and chipped rock. Something shot by his ear with an insect buzz and a snap as a ricochet buried itself into a tree.

The chopper suddenly twisted into another tight turn as the gunner saw Barnes run into the open. He caught sight of Kansky, already flat beneath the wing, and MacHenry scrambling for cover. Barnes dropped behind a boulder as the predatory craft maneuvered for a clear shot. The gunner had changed his mind. He was ignoring Kansky and MacHenry. The chopper was coming for him.

Barnes tried to merge with the rock as automatic fire erupted from above. A row of bullets fountained behind him. He clung tight, edging around the boulder, keeping its bulk between his body and the deadly fire from above. The helicopter maneuvered again to catch him in its sights.

"Barnes!" he heard MacHenry shout as he scuttled away from the marauding chopper. "Look out!" MacHenry held the ancient revolver at the chopper and fired. Three spouts of white smoke erupted from its black muzzle to be driven flat before the hurricane wind of the rotor blades.

Suddenly, there was no place to hide. Barnes looked straight up at the chopper's belly and saw it climbing straight up like an elevator. He shot a look at the wreck and saw MacHenry move out into the free-fire zone. "What are . . . ?" Barnes mouthed wordlessly.

"Barnes! Run! Back to the trees!" Dust swirled around MacHenry as he held the pistol in a two-handed grip. He stood tall, unmoving, deliberately making his body into a target. The helicopter obliged,

THE FLIGHT FROM WINTER'S SHADOW

spinning to face the easier prey. Once again the flat staccato of an assault rifle punctuated the heavy beat of the rotors. Once again, the old .45 snapped its reply. The dirt and dust boiled up at MacHenry's feet. "Run!" MacHenry shouted.

Barnes leaped from behind the rock and darted toward the safety of the tree line. He slipped, rolled, got to his feet without being aware of any of it, and tumbled in a swimmer's dive beneath the screening pines. His stitches tore apart like a cheap suit.

He looked back, breathing in dry, heaving gasps. "Shit." Bullets pawed the earth all around MacHenry as he ran zigzagging from boulder to boulder. The helicopter's engine screamed as its pilot swung into more violent maneuvers.

"Here!" Barnes shouted above the roar of the machine and the spit of the gun. MacHenry looked up at him, glanced back at the turning helicopter, and judging the instant with adrenaline-powered precision, made a desperate run for the trees. *"Run!"* Barnes yelled. *"Run run run run!"*

MacHenry's legs pounded up and down, a look of utter concentration on his sweat-streaked face. Barnes saw the helicopter straighten, then slewed to the left, approaching MacHenry like a giant, evil crab.

He wasn't going to make it. There was too much distance to cover and not enough time. Barnes closed his eyes as he heard the gun open up with a quick burst, sending metal whining over his head, and then silence. *No!* He forced his eyes to open.

MacHenry was still up! The man in the chopper was doing something in the cockpit. A spent clip fell out of the bubble. *"Run!"* he shouted again. MacHenry leaped into the air as though his shoulders had suddenly sprouted wings.

The helicopter spun to face them as MacHenry tumbled ten feet down the trail before coming up in a hard slap against a tree. Barnes, one quick look behind, rolled down the dirt trail to follow.

MacHenry was breathing hard, his face caked in a mask of red dirt. His eyes were still closed and his body heaved like a newly caught fish. "Did . . . I hit . . . him?" he asked. "Did I get a . . . piece . . . ?"

"Jesus, MacHenry. Are you intact?" When MacHenry didn't answer, Barnes grabbed his shoulder and shook it. "Hey! I asked a question!"

"—Okay," MacHenry answered between gulps of air. "Did I hit him?"

"Fuck if I know!" Barnes peered from cover. "I don't think so. You just got him riled up." Barnes looked behind and saw the helicopter circling in frustration at the top of the ridge. "Look! We've got to move. Come on," Barnes said quickly. He heard the chopper's blades change pitch as the engine growled a deeper note. "Those fuckers are landing. We have to move. I said *move it!*"

"Kansky was . . . you're . . . hit!" MacHenry propped himself up. Barnes's arm was no longer oozing. It bled with a vengence. "Kansky . . . "

"I'm not hit. That asshole couldn't hit anything. He was spraying it like a fucking garden hose." Barnes pressed the bandage against the strained stitches. Then he looked up. "Where's Kansky?"

MacHenry tried to speak between gulps of air. "That . . . first . . . he was trying . . . to see where it was, and then . . . it was on top of us."

Barnes looked back up the trail. "He's dead then." A mental door shut. "Okay. There's nothing we're in a position to do."

"We can't leave him. He might . . ."

"No fooling, BJ. We're out of here or we're in the same shitboat." Barnes half-pulled him upright, and MacHenry stumbled to his feet.

"Kansky," MacHenry repeated as he wobbled against the tree trunk. "Kansky . . . I saw it." He looked back up the tunnel of trees to the top of the ridge. The engine sound peaked as the machine began to descend from a hover. "Barnes," he gasped, "who are they?"

"I don't know. But we aren't waiting for an introduction. How many rounds do you have left?"

"I don't know." MacHenry handed the .45 to Barnes.

It was still hot, a thin curl of cordite rising from its barrel. He checked the clip. "Damn, MacHenry, you stink." Three bullets gleamed a bright gold in the sun. He shoved the magazine back into the handle. "Let's move."

23

THE
LAST FLIGHT
OF WHALEBONE
THREE

A HEAVY electric motor whined as a line of brilliant light burst into the darkness of the closed hangar. Inside, a battleship-gray KC-135 tanker gleamed like burnished silver. Its tail towered above the techs performing their last-minute checks, making ready to tow her onto the start-up pad.

Captain Al Kinkaid watched from the hangar catwalk as the tug clamped onto the nose gear and with a belch of black diesel smoke began pulling the fully fueled aircraft outside into the sun.

"Morning, Cap. You ready?" It was his copilot.

Kinkaid checked his watch. Ten-fifty. "I guess so," he said. Together, they watched the tanker move. "They tell you what the rush is all about? This was all supposed to happen tomorrow."

The younger man shrugged. "Base motto around here is *need to know*." Home to Dragon Lady and Blackbird, Beale had always been that kind of place. "Look at it this way," he continued, "it means we leave Tinker Bell and his damned simulator a whole day sooner." Tinker was their simulator controller, their master of disaster.

Kinkaid turned his back on the tanker. "Back to the world. Good-bye, old niner zero three." It was SAC's side number on the KC-135.

It sat out on the start-up ramp, baking, its wings creaking as they expanded in the heat. Kinkaid realized he would never see it again. Its next incarnation would be as a smear of fiery wreckage across a target zone. Unless, he told himself, the flash-retardant stuff they were supposed to be testing really worked. He had his doubts. What earthly concoction could keep 200,000 pounds of jet fuel from going up?

"Time," said the copilot. He nodded back to the broad floor where the storklike legs of the Rediffusion simulator stood. Power lines, air-conditioning ducts, and data cables seemed to anchor it to the floor, but it could move quite convincingly in pitch, roll, and yaw. Twenty feet above, the cab of the simulator was dark, waiting for the switch to be thrown and the curtain raised.

They settled into the cool confines of the simulator's familiar cockpit. The lights came up as though bringing on the first act of a play.

Kinkaid's hands went through their polished motions, checking the positions of the switches and calculating the takeoff roll, while his copilot went down the prestart checklist. The simulator's switches and controls were now linked with the actual KC-135 outside. A tug on its yoke would deflect a real elevator; a push of a throttle and a Pratt and Whitney J57 would roar. Kinkaid looked at the outside-air-temperature gauge. "Huh," he said, and tapped it. It remained fixed at ninety-two degrees. "I wonder if this thing is remoting right?"

"It's supposed to." Each and every display in the simulator had to be faithful to the real ones in the KC-135 outside. "All set. You ready to crank 'em?"

"Might as well." Kinkaid looked out his windshield, a multiple-screen CRT that showed the view from the actual KC-135. He saw the ground crew standing to one side, expectantly looking up at the blind eyes of the remotely piloted jet as though Kinkaid were really up in its cockpit looking back down at them. *Do they know?* he wondered. The senior flagman waved a hand in a quick, tight circle above his head, while holding up three fingers on his other hand. "All right. Let's crank three."

The simulator lights dimmed as the copilot shunted power to the port inboard engine. A muted roar came over the loudspeaker as the engine dials ran up into their green arcs. "Good start on three," the copilot said.

"Crank four."

He tickled the autostart on the outboard engine. "Okay, rev's comin' up through nine percent on four." The copilot watched as the engine instruments all rose in mechanical choreography as the fires took hold in the KC-135's turbines. A synthesized whine was broadcast through the simulator audio circuit, but when the copilot took off his headset, he could just hear the high scream of the real jet outside on the run-up pad. "I did find this." The copilot tossed a copy of a news release into Kinkaid's lap.

"What is it?" Kinkaid looked away from his start-up checklist.

"Read it. Engines are stabilized, power's up on all four."

"EPR's set." Kinkaid scowled as he began. "Jesus," he said. "These guys think of everything."

RELEASE 18-1: Tuesday
Beale Air Force Base Public Affairs Office

The Air Force acknowledges the loss of a KC-135 aerial refueling aircraft while on a training mission in the HUMMER 6 Military Operations Area east of Sacramento, CA. Search and rescue operations are under way at this time. Air Force personnel, already at the site for a previously scheduled ground exercise, are assisting in the search for survivors. . . .

Kinkaid looked up at the copilot. "Figures." He'd wondered just where the target zone was. Now he knew why it was hush-hush. Not even the Air Force could get permission to burn down a forest, could it? He tossed it back. "Did you notice? They got the day wrong."

The copilot took the sheet back and shook his head. "You're right, Cap. It still says Tuesday." He shrugged. "You think they asked old Smokey whether it was okay to light a little fire?"

"They got it squared away somehow," Kinkaid replied as he looked out through the simulator's windshield. A scene of men and moving support vehicles filled the screen. The picture was being transmitted from a camera mounted on the pilot's chair looking forward through the panes of the KC-135's windshield. "Looks like an antheap out there." Kinkaid watched as earmuffed men scurried about, removing ground safety pins from the jet. He pressed the transmit button on his yoke. "Ground, Whalebone Three is up, how do you hear?"

"And good morning, Whalebone, hard signals from both sides, datalink is up, Echo feature is up, and confirm the INS is initialized." The radios and gyros sitting in the empty cockpit of the Flying Dutchman out on the ramp were working in synch with the repeater presentations on the panel of the simulator.

"Whalebone's INS is sweet," Kinkaid replied.

"Roger, Whalebone, pushback in two minutes, range is clear and ready. Tower will have the winds for you."

"Roger." Kinkaid looked up at the temperature gauge. It had climbed to ninety-seven. "Scorcher. Gonna take a whole bunch of runway to lift."

The copilot looked up at it and nodded.

"Whalebone Three is cleared for taxi." It was all up to them now. The taxiway shimmered in the heat beyond the tanker's nose.

"Here we go." Kinkaid's right hand advanced the throttles and the view on the screen began to move. "Whalebone is rolling."

He herded the KC-135 down through the maze of paths leading to the departure end of the main runway. "She feels like she's asleep." The crisp, even responses of the simulator were gone, replaced by a heavy, almost drunken lurch. It felt as if his hands and feet were connected to the tanker by overstretched rubber bands. He stepped on the right rudder pedal as the run-up area slowly swung from view. The scene on his screen slowly shifted to include the distant foothills of the Sierras.

"Pretakeoff checklist is complete," the copilot replied, all business.

Kinkaid made the call. "Tower, Whalebone Three is ready to roll." The runway lay straight ahead, a black rectangle beneath the hot glare of the sun. He could see the heat in the air, distorting the view of the distant hills.

The cabin speaker crackled overhead. "Whalebone Three, you are cleared for takeoff."

"Here we go." Kinkaid grasped all four throttle handles and smoothly pushed them forward. A bead of sweat popped onto Kinkaid's brow as the engine needles rose. "Beale Tower, Whalebone Three is on the roll." The jet began to move sluggishly down the runway. "Okay, call my speeds."

The copilot glanced at the airspeed indicator. It was still dead. "I will when there's something to call." With a full load of kerosene and the hot, thin air, the acceleration was less than vigorous. The airspeed needle twitched. "Seventy knots," the copilot chanted. "Through ninety." Kinkaid could hear the strain, something new, in the copilot's voice. "Five-thousand-foot marker." Kinkaid didn't need to hear that. He had seen the big sign with the number 5 on it pass by. "Six thousand."

He ruddered the tanker back onto the runway centerline. "Come on, you pig." Kinkaid had to keep his hands from running the throttles full forward, beyond the maximum computed EPR settings. He glanced at the engine torque gauges. The four needles rested at 96 percent maximum thrust. The seven-thousand-foot marker glided by like a slow-motion dream.

"Coming up on V-R," the copilot whispered. It was sure taking a long time to get ready to fly. "Damn. I don't . . . Okay. V-R! Go! Now!"

Kinkaid tugged at the yoke, and slowly, heavily, the nose picked up off the runway. The simulator cockpit tilted back and the view ahead shifted to pure, cloudless blue.

"Eight thousand."

The heavy main gear on the real KC-135 thundered along the runway, seemingly stuck in hot tar.

"Through nine thousand." Only three thousand feet of runway left, and the overloaded jet was still not flying. "Through ten." The copilot looked over at Kinkaid. "Eleven," he said in enforced calm. "We ain't gonna make it, Cap."

"The hell we won't," Kinkaid said, setting his jaw in drum-tight tension. With a sharp, deliberate motion he pushed the engines beyond their safe maximums. All four needles rose to 110 percent and stopped, not by the sensors deep in the guts of the howling Pratt and Whitneys but rather by the action of the peg on the instrument itself. "Now or never." The turbojets were burning their guts out. "Just this once, old girl. Just this once," Kinkaid whispered as the VSI poked its head tentatively into the plus side of the arc.

"Gawd! Positive rate!" the copilot yelled.

"Just hold it, hold it, hold it . . . Okay. Gear up!"

"Coming!" The copilot pulled the heavy metal handle from its detent and rammed it home. He glanced at the altimeter. "Got five hundred!"

"Flaps and slats," Kinkaid said coolly, once more the captain of a flying machine. He pulled the throttles back slightly to normal climb thrust. "Whalebone Three is climbing through one point oh for eight," Kinkaid transmitted, his finger slipping on the yoke button's sweat.

"Whalebone Three is cleared to enter the hold at four minutes past the hour. Remain in the racetrack for systems checkout. Expect release at twenty."

"Roger, copy," Kinkaid replied. He looked at his copilot as the radio-controlled jet banked out over the valley and headed east. "I think we busted something," he said, tapping the number-three-engine indicator. Despite his throttling back, it still showed emergency thrust. It would not stay alive long if it were true.

"Got twenty minutes to get it worked out," said the copilot. "It's probably just the gauge, anyway."

"Yeah," said Kinkaid. The exhaust-temperature needle was rising as he watched. "No doubt."

24

PURSUIT

BARNES felt his knees start to buckle as he ran down the steep trail. The jeep was down there and the helicopter that had just killed Kansky was close by. He listened as the sound of its engine swelled and faded, then stopped altogether. *Shit!* There was no doubting it. That helicopter had just landed. Suddenly, his foot slipped on the loose needles carpeting his path.

"Barnes!" MacHenry shouted.

Barnes pitched forward, grabbing at a tree trunk to break the fall. He came up hard against the rough bark of a pine. He pulled his T-shirt sleeve up and checked. Sure enough, the shrapnel wound from his encounter last Friday was bleeding in earnest.

MacHenry reached toward Barnes's pack. "You need another bandage on it."

Barnes twisted away with a black look on his face. "I don't need a bandage. I need an air strike." He looked up the shadowed trail toward the crash site. There were men on the ground now. Men who had, once again, done their very best to kill him. *Fighters and targets,* he thought. *Which one am I now?* He looked over at MacHenry. "It's not far, old-timer. I can roll there from here."

The jeep sat where Kansky had parked it in the shade of one of the trees that ringed Sourgrass Meadow. Barnes got into the passenger's seat, one hand over the loose and bloody skin on his arm. He reached under the seat for the keys and found the radio. Its scrambler light was blinking. "One of my arms is on standby," he said. "Think you can drive this thing?"

MacHenry took the key and started the engine as Barnes looked nervously back up toward the ridge. MacHenry slammed the gearshift into first and moved off.

As the jeep shot across the open meadow, Barnes felt his neck crawl in an overwhelming sense of vulnerability. The cross hairs of a rifle sight burned on his back. He could imagine the scene all too well from the perspective of a flying machine. *Puny goddamned bug just asking to get squashed.* "Let's get under some cover, okay, BJ?"

"Agreed." MacHenry booted the accelerator and did not slow until the overhanging trees once again arched overhead. "Go ahead and use the radio. We've got to warn Julia."

"Chopper might be on the freq, too." said Barnes.

MacHenry slewed the jeep down an incline and around a tight corner. "Do it anyway!"

Barnes pressed the transmit switch. "Does anyone read this transmission?" He turned up the volume and listened.

"Try it again."

Barnes was about to speak when he stopped and turned. "Hey, BJ, I . . ."

"I know. I hear it." The helicopter's engine was roaring once more from the top of Starr Ridge.

The digital clock on top of Julia's desk rose with easy, insolent pace, the red numerals slicing into what little safety was left with uncaring precision. They were supposed to leave in less than an hour, and Julia had not been able to raise Kansky for the last thirty minutes. Where was he? Why hadn't Kansky called in? *Maybe I should go bring them in myself,* Julia thought.

Julia was about to do precisely that when a beep came from the secure walkie-talkie. "Thank God!" She snatched it from its charger. ". . . transmission? Over." Who was that? "Does anyone read this transmission?"

"Kansky!" she shouted into the microphone, her voice wavering and barely under control. "Bill! You've got to get back here for the pickup! They switched it on us."

"I've got . . ." The voice trailed away in a muffled roar of background noise. "Julia," the voice began again, "we . . ."

Who was speaking? "Where's Kansky?" Julia demanded. "Put him on right now!" Waiting for Kansky's familiar, reassuring voice, she glanced at the master clock again: *11:39*.

"I . . . I can't do that."

"Barnes? This is serious. No fun and games. Put Kansky on."

Barnes's frightened tone made Julia clench her jaw. She heard another voice. "Dr. Hines!" MacHenry shouted as though trying to make his voice heard unaided by the radio. "Get away from the trailer! If you can call the police, do it! But get away from that clearing and under cover!"

"What?" *Get away?* Of course she had to get away. They *all* had to get clear of HUMMER. Damn the military! "Where are you?" she asked. "I have to talk with Sergeant Kansky. You all have to get back up here right away. They've switched the timing on us and—"

"We're on our way back—" Barnes suddenly stopped talking. "Wait!"

His finger was still pressed on the transmit button, for she heard them consult with one another again, then the background noise swelled to a roar. The transmission snapped quiet and the red light on her set went dark. "Barnes!" She glanced at the clock: *11:41*. She recalled Henniker's agitation. *There will be the risk of physical danger to anyone left. . . .* The radio remained silent. "Damn."

She saw the neat pile of data disks, her clothes, a few odds and ends she had prepared for the rescheduled airlift out of HUMMER. Where were they? She looked once more at the clock and decided what had to be done. Julia grabbed the keys to the other jeep. She'd meet them halfway and bring them straight out. There wasn't much time. She stopped when she got to the door of her trailer and turned. What if it took too long to find them? They'd have to drive out, rather than risk missing the helicopter.

She grabbed the data disks, left the pile of clothes, and ran for the jeep. On the way, she gathered up the two small packs belonging to Barnes and MacHenry. On impulse, she took Barnes's strange bow and quiver as well.

There was barely room for the helicopter's skids.

Adcock jumped to the ground even before the MD-500 settled uncertainly between two massive boulders. He ran over to the wreck of the Cessna as the rotors wound down. He knew he had hit one of them. Adcock approached, the rifle out ahead of him as he came.

The dead man wore a uniform. Adcock had never seen death, but he knew the man lying next to the crashed Cessna could not possibly be alive. The body looked vacant, empty, an object sculpted from the red dust of Starr Ridge. The swinging rotors still kicked up clouds of it, plastering the strangely relaxed figure with a thick paste of blood and ocher. The last arterial blood from his torn neck flowed into a blackened pool. Adcock used the muzzle of the AK-47 to expose the corpse's dog tags. He leaned close, close enough to smell the rusty odor rising in the heat.

Kansky. "Who the hell is this?" He stood up and turned to the tree line where the other two men had escaped. They could be anywhere, even looking at him! The sudden thought made him fearful, no matter the full clip in the AK. He looked up at the sun. It was getting late. His option tree was narrowing, limbing out branch by branch until there was no place else to go. He turned and jogged over to the opposite tree line.

There was the wing. The missing wing. The one that had started his career, and his life, swinging like a pendulum run amok. Radway must have brought it back here, but why? He'd find out, but once he had shown them his success, not his failures. What could they say then?

Adcock walked away from the damning wing and moved cautiously to the opposite side of the ridge clearing. He looked down the steep trail. *Think!* His mind reduced the situation to its component variables. He had mobility. They had the terrain. *Terrain!* He spun on his heel and saw the slowly settling billow of dust. He tried to smile at his own cleverness, but his facial muscles refused to cooperate. Instead, he jogged back to the waiting helicopter and clambered aboard. "Let's go."

"There's not much fuel left," the pilot replied, his hand deliberately off the throttle.

"We won't need much more," said Adcock, his face a hard-glazed mask. It was fear, of course. Fear for what he had done, and fear for what he still must do.

The helo pilot saw it and recognized that look at once. This, above all other things, made his client a very dangerous man. He was considering taking the AK away, kicking him out, and lifting off when Adcock lowered the snout of the assault rifle to his chest. "Shall we?" Adcock said.

The pilot looked down the eight-millimeter hole and shook his head. He had taken too long in his consideration. "Put that fucking thing away," he said as he punched up the autostart. The turbine began to whine. Whatever doubts the pilot had were now confirmed. Adcock was a losable asset. It would only take a flick of the stick, a release of his belt, and it would be assholes away. He pulled in collective and the MD-500 leaped into the air. *Next time he points it at me, he's going solo.*

As they cleared the tops of the trees, Adcock saw what he was hoping for: the ribbon of dust ahead kicked up by the fleeing jeep. Adcock pulled at the pilot's shoulder, an eager child showing a prize.

"I got it," said the pilot as he swung the nose in pursuit. "Just be quick."

Adcock saw the jeep just as he had anticipated it. Now, with the dust rising from the trail below, it filled him with a terrible exultation. A blood fever crowded out his elaborate logic, his carefully constructed decision trees, as the MD-500 pounded in pursuit. He could see it now. He knew how this would end. His finger tightened on the trigger in anticipation as the helicopter dove.

The jeep suddenly broke out from beneath the canopy of trees. The

AK seemed to leap into firing position by an act of its own will. Adcock centered the little blue toy in the iron sights and pulled the trigger. The jeep drove right into the stream of fire.

Julia skidded around in a sharp, steep switchback and dove deeper and deeper into the heavy forest. She checked her watch. Why hadn't she thought to synchronize it with the clock back at the trailer? She gunned the jeep as she drove hard and fast along the trail. The roar of its engine masked the heavy beat of the helicopter until it was almost upon her.

Rounding a bend in the road, she saw it hanging in the air, low enough to send its downwash spilling over the tops of the pines. "Thank God." They had been smart enough to come early. They had found the trailer site empty, and they were out looking for them. The helicopter tipped and rocked above the treetops. She slowed as she watched it move. It was an odd place to hover. There were no clearings nearby for it to land. She'd come up to it and point to the nearest clearing.

The trail climbed once again and broke out into a rocky switchback. She was closer, the view far better. The helicopter was still there, waspish and swishing its barbed tail in her direction. The sun beat down on her and then was blocked as she drove under the shelter of the trees once more. The turnoff that lead up to the old ranger tower at Crandall Lookout flashed by. *That's probably a good spot for a pickup,* she thought. Then she smelled it. *Fire?* She swung around the last bend.

Black smoke was driven flat by the helicopter's wind. Then she saw why the helicopter lingered. "No!" There was the second jeep. Kansky's jeep. *An accident?*

A cold numbness cascaded down her neck as she slowed to a stop. The smoke was too dense to see if anyone was still trapped in the burning wreck. The fire suddenly blossomed dirty orange as the flames took hold. "Kansky!"

The helicopter tipped its nose and drew nearer. "Bill!" Her voice was drowned by the chopper's roar. She swung her legs out. The

MD-500 stopped in midair, turned, and then its glinting canopy nodded as though acknowledging her presence. It swung to expose its door. There was a man! But it wasn't Kansky. *Are they all up there already?*

Her thoughts were blown from her when a tremendous impact knocked her from the jeep and down to the dust, driving all the air from her chest in a gasp. The helicopter's whining hiss grew to thunder. As she tried to prop herself up, another blow drove her face into the dirt.

"Stay low!" a voice shouted in her ear as Barnes pushed her flat to the ground. He looked up at the helicopter, slicing time and space with the precise scalpel of a fighter pilot's eye. "Okay! Quick!" Barnes said as he pulled her toward the sheltering trees. The Kalashnikov opened fire as they rolled behind a fallen tree. The bullets thumped into dead timber. She tried to raise her head but he jammed it back down as a spray of rounds stitched the ground.

"What . . . Where is Kansky?" she asked, the world no longer making sense. "You're hurt!" She saw the fresh blood well up from Barnes's arm.

He didn't stop to answer. Nor did he need to. Another full clip of AK fire smashed against the log in front of them, moving, seeking them, probing into the trees. Barnes felt the ground vibrate from their impact. It took little enough imagination to know what one such round would do to living flesh.

"What's happening?" she said weakly. "Where's Kansky?"

Barnes clenched his fist. "Fucking AK-47," he said to MacHenry. "The Big Sound of Victor Charles." He listened as the chopper maneuvered, seeking an opening.

"Barnes! Where's—" Julia began, but MacHenry silenced her with a hand on her arm.

"Kansky's down," said Barnes. "They came up too fucking fast."

Julia looked at MacHenry. He looked away. He had brought this on them all. MacHenry had not been satisfied with the easy answers. And for his curiosity, another man had died. He rubbed the grit from his eyes. And now? The helicopter thundered overhead, searching for the clear shot.

"I don't like this," said Barnes as the helicopter maneuvered.

"This isn't what . . ." Julia hesitated. "We're supposed to leave. Something is going to happen up here. I don't . . ." Her voice was swallowed by her throat. "They wanted us out early. Some kind of exercise. The helicopter's supposed to pick us up, not this!"

"What kind of exercise?" asked MacHenry.

"I don't know!" Julia flinched as the chopper swept directly overhead again. The heavy staccato of an assault rifle made them all go flat.

MacHenry looked up into the trees. "This is no place to wait. They can just keep firing blind until they hit something."

"Roger that." Barned nodded. The ground was a trap. "I'm no grunt and I'll be damned if I'm going to die like one." Barnes pushed aside a tangle of manzanita. "There's our way out." He nodded at Julia's jeep.

"Agreed," said MacHenry.

Barnes listened to the helicopter, judging its distance and heading. "Let's do it."

They worked their way through the brush until they were next to it. Its engine was still idling. Barnes saw the bow in the back. He turned and nodded at Julia. "You'll do," he said softly, "you'll do just fine."

"He's moving off," said MacHenry.

"Now or never," said Barnes, and then he jumped for the jeep. He threw the shifter into first. The flap of skin hanging from his arm was caked in blood and dirt. "Come on!" he shouted when MacHenry and Julia lingered at the edge of the trail.

The marauding chopper hovered uncertainly, swinging in close to the rock wall that hemmed the trail, then back out. They couldn't turn to expose the gunner; the tail would strike the rocks. It wavered, its rotors grinding and slashing the air, then it throttled up and climbed out of view.

"Time to aviate," Barnes said, wishing his words were true. How he would love to make one single firing run on that bastard! To roll in hot and dive on it, centering the bubble canopy in his sights and blasting it to smoke and ruin. His fist tightened around the gearshift, his finger seeking the trigger that wasn't there. "Get in," he directed the other two. "I'm flying this heap now."

The helo pilot did a quick pedal turn away from the rock wall. He couldn't give Adcock a clear shot, and his fuel was quickly going critical on him. "What now?" he asked, looking over at Adcock. *Fucker points a weapon at me again,* he thought, *and he's dead.*

Adcock reached into the canvas sack and pulled the next-to-last banana clip of AK rounds. He shoved the thirty fresh 7.62-mm bullets into the rifle. His hands tingled from the recoil of the AK. "They can't cross open trail ahead or behind. We orbit between and wait for them to show. Unless they're walking, we'll catch them one place or the other."

"Ten minutes and we're walking, too," the pilot said with a grimace. "You might want to think about that, ace."

"I'll handle it." Here was the last window of opportunity. Hill's stupidity had put him here. Radway was going to pin him to that wing down there. Somehow. He felt alone, alone and up against a host of invisible foes. He gripped the wooden stock of the AK-47. He would not let it happen. He would not. A flash of motion below caught his eye. "There they go!" The dust was rising again from a moving jeep. "Get us over that clearing!" he shouted, and leaned out the open door. The wind whipped at his hair. He saw something move below and shot wildly at it. The dust kept rising. He had missed again. "Quick!" he yelled at the pilot, holding the smoking snout of the Kalashnikov in his general direction.

That's it. "Get that fucking thing out of my face!" the pilot yelled, and pulled the cyclic hard left. The helicopter tilted and Adcock went with it, his seat belt cutting into his stomach as he hung out the open door, his legs beating, and kicking wildly. The pilot grabbed the release to Adcock's belt and saw his eyes go blank white. "Got the idea?" Adcock wormed back into his seat from halfway out the open door of the 500. "Point that fucking thing at me *once* more and you get a flying lesson. Fucking accidents can happen. Sir."

Adcock refused to show his panic. *Later,* he thought. His heart was throbbing in his neck. But he pointed the AK back out the open door all the same.

"Much better," the pilot growled. The chopper swung uphill and beat at the dry dust. It swirled wildly in the rotor wash, a blinding, choking blanket.

"There!" Adcock caught sight of the moving jeep as it raced out from under the forest canopy. It looked to him like a damaged insect fleeing the poison spray. His wrath. His hands shook half with fear, half in a killing fury he would never have thought himself capable of. The jeep was going up a trail that would take it to the top of the mountain. He looked at the pilot. "Once more. Just once more."

"We may not be able to recover back to base."

"I can make it worth the walk," said Adcock.

The pilot shrugged and twisted on more power. The turbine's rumble rose to a scream as the helicopter shot straight up the flank of Crandall Peak.

Julia was nearly thrown from the bucking jeep as it lunged up the uneven trail. She looked back at MacHenry. His knuckles were white as he gripped a big black .45. "Hang on!" Barnes yelled. The jeep leaped across a dry wash and struck the opposite rim with a head-snapping impact. Ahead, the trail lightened as it opened out onto a clearing. Barnes had his foot flat to the floor as he raced to cross the open ground with as little exposure as possible. But a little was still too much. The enemy was there, waiting.

A stream of fire erupted just ahead of them as they crossed over open ground. A single round spanged off the blue hood and a second shattered the windshield into a million crystal shards. Barnes whipped the wheel around, driving on instinct now. His brain had not registered the branching trail leading up to Crandall Lookout; but his situational awareness, his clue bird, had. It pointed them right at the break in the trees. In a moment, they were back under cover, heading straight up the side of the mountain.

The dense forest became isolated stands. Huge boulders studded the ground, crowding out the trees as they neared the top. Ahead, a thin band of blue sky announced the summit.

"A car!" Julia shouted, too late for Barnes to do anything about it. They flashed by the nearly hidden shape of a small truck. Suddenly, and without enough warning for Barnes to react, they burst through the gap. Ahead was the granite rampart of Crandall Peak's dome. At its very top, the wooden legs of a ranger tower stood guard.

Barnes booted the jeep up to the tower and slewed to a halt beneath its legs. He turned and saw the glistening bubble of the chopper rise malevolently into view. It was already turning to unmask the gunner in the left seat.

"Let's get under . . ." Barnes began, but MacHenry was gone. "BJ!"

"God damn you," MacHenry swore. Holding the .45 out before him, MacHenry stood straight and vulnerable, drawing a bead with his weapon on the swelling bubble of the helicopter. *"Goddamn you!"*

"Get your ass down!" Barnes shouted as the AK opened up.

"Goddamn you!" MacHenry bellowed as the helicopter closed to pistol range. He leveled the .45 at the cockpit and squeezed off one, two, and then his final round. The last shot shattered one of the chopper's chin windows. The helicopter drew up suddenly and turned, its pilot reevaluating the danger. The motion threw the gunner's aim off. The helicopter fired again, single rounds, the AK no longer spewing out on full automatic. Chips of granite flew and the jeep rocked in solid thumps as the gunner adjusted his fire. The helicopter banked around to catch them from an unprotected side. MacHenry was still exposed. Barnes knew what would be next if MacHenry did not gain shelter. "MacHenry!" he shouted, but his throat felt too choked to let the word by. He knew it, he could feel it. MacHenry was going to be hit.

Barnes tried to move but felt the will drain from his hands, his feet, felt his voice mired in sticky fear. He shut his eyes. The firing began again. *Hits!* he screamed silently, his heart pounding in sync with the AK's beat. *Eject!*

His eyes were tightly shut, but he could see it all the same. The sharp slap of metal against flesh, the explosion of blood and tissue, the slow tumble down to the dirt. It was like a nightmare; your legs won't move, your arms refuse to swim. *Eject!* The bullets were tracers, the T-Bird shuddering under cannon fire. *Eject!*

His eyes popped open and brilliant mountain light flooded in. "Not this time," he said between clenched teeth. His fingers clawed the dust as he let out the breath he had been holding. "Not this fucking time"

"Don't!" Julia screamed.

Barnes jumped to his feet and turned to face the firing. "No!" The AK-47 pointed his way. Barnes ran for the jeep. Cordite smoke streamed back from the helicopter as the AK's muzzle flashed its distinctive yellow. The earth boiled at his feet as the rounds ricocheted off rock.

"Barnes!" MacHenry shouted.

Something plucked at his side and spun him like a carelessly set windup toy. He slammed against the jeep, leaving a smear of bright blood on the metal.

The helicopter buzzed closer, the firing stopped. He could see the man inside with the Kalashnikov. A sudden, icy calm descended over him as he breathed deeply three times in the opening moments of an ancient and useful ritual. He reached into the jeep and picked up his bow. *Start with a circle.*

He flexed it, sensing the coiled, hidden power so well disguised within its ancient design. He reached for the quiver and selected an arrow. *Create the circle.*

The MD-500 bored in, its canopy a bright oval of light. A mere twenty feet from his eyes, it swung, whining to a hover, and turned. The man within was framed in the open door, the canopy a circle of light that surrounded him like a halo, a bull's-eye. *The target exists to catch my arrow.* A blanket of silence descended over him, cold and silent as deep snow. Barnes heard no noise, felt no wind slap at him, felt no dust swirl into his eye.

He projected a circle of his own on the man with a gun, then let the circle widen like a ring of ripples from a cast stone. When it was large enough, when its edge reached to his feet, he stepped inside and nocked an arrow. He drew the supple bow tight and felt the incredible force run through its length, the force of the wood pushing through the earth when it was a tree, the force of all the winds that had tried to break it and had failed. He did not feel the tearing in his arm as his muscles pulled the feathered bolt back to his ear. The helicopter sat like a bubble impaled on its steel tip. He no longer saw a helicopter, but rather a target, a target whose sole reason to be was to catch his arrow. Barnes smiled and waited, listening for the voice of the arrow to speak to his fingers.

Then, as the yellow flash of the AK-47 began again, the arrow came alive, thrumming with the vibrant force of its own, independent will. In an instant it was gone.

Wind whistled in through the cracked chin bubble. Adcock felt his gut congeal into an icy ball as he saw another man below stand up, exposed and unprotected. He snapped off three rounds. Two puffed the dry earth at the man's feet. He moved the barrel up and fired. The man spun against the side of the blue jeep. "I got him!"

"Shoot him again!"

The man below stood to his full height and looked straight up at Adcock from behind a bow and arrow. He felt the sharp shock as their eyes met and locked, an electric discharge leaping across space. He shook the feeling off as the AK leaped in his hands, its snub barrel pointed at the incredible sight. *Idiot!* he thought, laughing. *Primitive idiot!*

"Do it!" the pilot said over the roar of the engine. "Do it!" The gas gauge rested deep in the yellow caution range.

Time mired and slowed as Adcock framed the man below in the Kalashnikov's iron sights. *Handle it!* The sound of the engine seemed to drain into a vortex of absolute concentration. The very light blanched to overexposed white. It was silent now; all he could hear was the beating of his heart. A gust plucked the empty canvas ammo bag out of the helicopter's cockpit as his finger tightened on the trigger. *Now.* As the rifle bucked in his hands, he felt the air split. A feathery tickle ran across his arm like the passage of a stinging insect. He slapped it away as the helicopter tilted sharply to the left, spoiling his aim. Time and sound roared back into full motion on the back of the screaming turbine. "Hold it steady!" he shouted, but the chopper kept turning. "Goddamn it!" he roared, turning in his seat. "I said . . ."

The pilot stared back at him, soundless words gurgling unintelligibly from his jaw. His right hand still gripped the cyclic stick; his left remained clamped around the collective. An arrow was buried in his throat, its head passing clean through into the olive-drab fabric of the seatback.

Adcock screamed as a dark gout of blood fountained from the pilot's mouth, turning the windshield crimson. The pilot's hand released the stick and the helicopter slewed drunkenly off into an uncontrolled bank.

Adcock dropped the rifle and grabbed at the control stick. He knew how these things were supposed to work. Hadn't he studied aerodynamics and controls theory for years? He could *design* this thing from a clean piece of paper, couldn't he? "Idiot! Fool!" He swung the stick savagely against the bank and was temporarily rewarded as the craft righted itself. But it kept right on going, falling into a steep tilt to the opposite side.

The rotors began to buzz, overspeeding, slashing the air, the turbine racing beyond redline. Adcock froze as the trees rushed near. The rotors hit first, and then a dark green fist exploded into the cockpit and struck him hard, driving his breath from his body in a single blow. The fist opened and then closed around his chest. He heard his own ribs snap like the slender wood of a thin bough. Adcock opened his mouth at the pain boiling in his chest, but his scream had no place to go. He let go of consciousness like a man leaping from a burning ship into cool, dark waters.

The dead turbine hissed as it vented its last pressure into the air. The broken helicopter swayed fifty feet above the ground, caught on the spike of a pine, creaking like an ancient schooner before the gathering winds. Adcock surfaced from a dream, a dream of a safe place removed from heat and sound and pain and men. Then he heard it, and his eyes popped open. *Thank God.*

It was the high whine of flying jet engines. He listened as the sound grew louder. He tried to smile, but his face would not respond. *They've come for me.*

25

THE FIRE

ND Tanker Control," said Kinkaid, "Whalebone Three leaving the hold at twenty-two past the hour."

"Roger Whalebone. Systems check complete. Your range is clear. Descent on profile is approved."

"Whalebone Three." Kinkaid checked the engine gauges. He tapped the face of the one still showing emergency thrust. Number three engine had never throttled back at his radio-controlled command. In any other flight it would be an emergency of the first order. Not this time. He looked over to the second-in-command.

The copilot glanced at the errant dial and shrugged. "Forget it. Forty seconds to pitchover. Looking for a minus seven fifty on the VSI. That should leave us enough room to play, say fifty feet or so, at the other end." The copilot returned to his INS display screen. "Okay, Cap, steady, steady . . . Mark!"

"Here we go." Kinkaid left the power levers in and pushed the big yoke forward, trimming nose down with a blip of the thumb-mounted button. "Okay, keep an eye on it." Kinkaid looked up at the display screens in the simulator cockpit. The red target symbol on the simulator's head-up display was beginning to flash more rapidly within the command bars. It was nothing more than a video game. *I wonder what it really looks like?* On impulse, he punched up the cockpit camera controller.

"Jesus," said his copilot.

The projector screen was filled with mountains as the last ramparts of the Sierra foothills fell away. A deep-green area of dense forest lay right off the nose. "Jesus," the copilot repeated.

"I hope to hell they know what they're doing," Kinkaid said. *What I'm doing,* he added silently. They were already below the highest peaks and still descending.

"Twenty miles, profile is good." The copilot now concentrated on the INS displays. It was too disturbing looking at the real thing. "Nineteen miles and three minutes twenty to impact. Altitude is good, heading is good, cross track zero. Wind drift zero. Watch it! Below the profile." Kinkaid nodded and added power. The VSI twitched upward.

"Back on. Zero wind and zero cross track. You're gonna nail it, Kinkaid."

"Call my numbers." Kinkaid found the view almost hypnotizing. The ground was rising right at them, slowly at first, but visibly faster now that they were lower. The dense green texture down there was a million acres of trees. The white scar of a road swept below as they entered the empty heart of HUMMER 6.

"Five out and fifty seconds. Above the profile." The copilot knew what was next. "Stand by on the fuel dump."

Kinkaid pulled power back on the outboard engines. "Ready for the dump." His hand poised over the valve controller that would release thousands of gallons of jet fuel. *Some test,* he thought. He was about to engage in the biggest act of arson since Nero played his fiddle. "Call it!"

"Stand by." The copilot watched the INS. "Stand by on the dump. Okay . . . Three seconds, two. One!" The trees were becoming individuals. The spiked tops were rushing by at a dizzying pace. They were close now. Very close. *"Now!"*

"Fuel is away!" Kinkaid punched the dump release and nudged the rudder to center the red target on his HUD.

High up a remote valley between Starr and Grant ridges, it began to rain ice-cold kerosene from a clear, blue sky.

"Profile is good! On track. No wind. Just hold it! Hold what you got. Shit! Fire in three!" The big red button was flashing on the eyebrow annunciator panel. The copilot's hands went for the extinguisher release but Kinkaid pushed his hand aside. "Two hundred feet!"

Pull up! Pull up! the mechanical ground-proximity voice, reading the rising terrain beneath the real jet's silver belly, began to intone urgently.

"Ten seconds to impact! Hold what you got! Just hold it!"

Kinkaid pointed the nose right at a sheer rock wall. The wall blossomed to encompass the entire screen. An instant before impact, he shoved all four throttles full forward, making three rows of engine instruments instantly go crazy, needles rising beyond maximums, red-warning and master-caution annunciators flashing. Three more fire lights all came on at once.

Kinkaid saw all the engine indicators make a simultaneous dive toward zero in the instant before every display on the simulator's panel fell dark. He could hear the copilot's heavy breathing in the dark.

"Impact."

Before Kinkaid could answer, the back door cracked, admitting a waft of fresh air and the simulator operator. His sweat-beaded face reflected diamonds of light off the high, yellow sodium-vapor lights illuminating the cavernous hangar's interior. "Congratulations, Al," he said, wiping his face. "Right on the money."

"Piece of cake," said Kinkaid as he stood up. The leather seat was stained black with his sweat.

Barnes staggered back to the jeep, his bow bent double as a crutch. Something was wrong, something was burning and painful and very wrong. His entire side seemed to be caught in a convulsive shudder.

"Barnes!" Julia ran to him. MacHenry was frozen, his jaw still hanging open at what he had witnessed. He took a step, then stopped again when he heard the sound of jet engines thundering at full takeoff thrust. He spun in time to see a streak of white vapor cut the valley below in two.

An instant later, the cloud erupted like a volcano.

"My God," he whispered, his eyes unable to move from what he was seeing. It was his own, unspoken nightmare. A big jet was going in. MacHenry felt the heat on his face when a thunderous crack split the air like lightning. Below, the entire valley echoed as the flames flashed from orange to pure white.

A spiderweb tracery arced overhead as burning metal began to fall their way. "Get down!" MacHenry shouted. Julia pulled Barnes flat to the ground and covered him with her own body. A jagged piece of shrapnel, trailing white smoke, dropped onto her back, burning through the thin T-shirt in an instant. MacHenry ran and picked the metal off her back. It sizzled in his fingers.

Julia held Barnes's head, rocking him, her tears cutting paths through the red dust on her face. There was something wrong.

"Barnes?" When MacHenry pried Julia away, her shirt was covered with blood.

Barnes looked up and shook his head sheepishly. "Sorry, BJ," he said, a smile flashing into a grimace of pain as Barnes fought the cold fire burning in his belly. "I think . . . I took a hit."

MacHenry pulled at Barnes's camo T-shirt and saw the jagged rip in his side. "Oh, God," MacHenry said, forgetting at once the thunder from the valley. He could see the lump of metal through the strained-tight skin, a hard, gray lump. "Barnes," he said, shaking his head.

Barnes winced as the pain boiled up his side. "Asshole got lucky, but not lucky enough." He looked at the fire and smoke rising from the valley. "That helicopter sure blew."

"Help him." Julia saw the gash in Barnes's side. "We have to help him."

"We'll get you off this mountain," MacHenry said. He turned to face the jeep. The explosion had scattered hot metal like the seeds of a fiery flower. One such seed had landed on the jeep's plastic seat cover. It had begun to smolder, then, in a puff, it had burst into dense, oily smoke. MacHenry pulled Barnes away from the eager flames, but Barnes held up a hand for him to stop.

"It's okay," said Barnes with a sweaty smile. His face felt cold and his gut felt flash frozen and burning hot all at once. "I'm mobile." He got to his feet, swaying slightly until Julia stepped next to him, holding him. "I'm all right," he said groggily, the shock flooding his system with powerful sedatives. "I'm all right." He turned and saw the fire in the valley below. "That helicopter sure did blow." He turned and saw flames dancing from the jeep, a tiny reflection of the gathering fire storm in the valley.

Where do we go from here? MacHenry wondered.

"You know," Barnes said to MacHenry, "you looked pretty good back there. I think you got a piece of him. The helicopter."

"We'll figure this thing through." The words came easy. MacHenry had no idea how to carry them out.

Barnes seemed determined to follow his thoughts. "Last shot, I think. One out of . . . how many? But you got him."

"Take it easy, Barnes."

"I just want you to know. I think you're okay, BJ." Barnes gathered himself up, building a wall against the rising tide of cold. Barnes stopped, gritting his teeth against the pain. His face looked pale and stretched taut over his bones.

"We'll get you off the mountain," MacHenry said, though it was a vow he was making to himself. He looked up. The actual crash site was now buried beneath billows of flame and smoke. A thousand smaller fires had sprung up all around, set by the burning, explosive fragmentation. He watched as the small dots of flame grew brighter, joining and marching in a rising flood around the base of Crandall Peak.

"I didn't know about it," said Julia. "None of this. I was just getting weather . . ." She stopped and turned to face the burning jeep. Her data disks were still back there.

A sudden wind stirred through the pines below Crandall's summit. MacHenry turned and saw the wind flare the fire below like a bellows.

"Mr. MacHenry, you have to believe me that I didn't know . . ."

"About the helicopter? It doesn't matter now. We have to get him out. It doesn't matter how far it is. We'll carry him. I'll carry him if I have to."

Barnes was listening. "Why don't we stay put? It's all rocks up here. Nothing much to burn." The AK slug pushed at his skin as he twisted, and a small stream of blood ran down his side. A new voice came to him as he felt the trickle and seep. *Hurry,* it said.

"Barnes is right," said MacHenry. "There isn't much to burn right up at the top."

"No. He's wrong," said Julia. "Fires burn uphill."

It was instinct. Angel ducked down into the lookout cab when he heard the rending scream of metal tearing itself apart in the valley below. Then, an enormous concussion thundered in his ears. It no longer mattered that he had just seen a man shoot down a helicopter with a single arrow. What was important was timing. He had been given a date. That date, he could now see, was very wrong. Like the tides of the distant Gulf of Mexico, one played the game as one found it.

He pushed the roof hatch up, chinned himself on the planks, and peered outside just as a rain of smoking metal fell. The hot fragments rattled off the roof. One look convinced him that waiting any longer was wholly unnecessary. He let the hatch drop back into place and quickly made his way to the black equipment case. He took out a spool of antenna cable and plugged one end into its side. He wrapped the rest around his shoulder, made his way back up to the roof, and connected the other end to the antenna he himself had installed. *Done.* Whatever that fish-stinking box was supposed to listen to, it could now do so. He tugged once to be sure of the connection, then dropped back into the shuttered lookout cab. *Bueno,* he thought. It was time to leave this place.

Checking the CZX automatic, Angel stepped away from his creation and kicked open the floor hatch. A flood of black smoke poured up through. *Qué?* He held his jacket sleeve to his face and felt for the first rung. He looked over and saw the flames rising from the jeep. He scrambled down hand over hand, moving as near to it as the heat permitted.

He dropped to the ground and saw the three others standing at the edge of Ten-Second Drop, staring as though mesmerized by the fire storm breaking over the flanks of the mountain. He looked up again at the tower, at the old wooden legs beginning to smolder from the jeep's fire. He knew what was necessary. He was a professional, was he not?

Ignoring the searing heat, he reached into the jeep's flames and felt for the gearshift. The transmission fell into neutral, and the jeep started to roll down the bare granite toward the three people and the cliff's edge.

A struggle of conflicting ideas fought within his mind. He had killed a hundred men without remorse. He had killed once already on this assignment. What was three more? *It is the way!* he thought, but the words fell empty before the image, the picture of an archer standing straight and brave before the flat stutter of a Kalashnikov. Angel shook his head. A final sputter of protest sneered *fool* as he shouted, "Look out!"

The woman turned and saw the burning jeep rolling straight for them, her mouth opening wide in horror. The other man, the older one, turned.

MacHenry yanked Barnes out of the way as the jeep rolled by them, out into open space, trailing black smoke as it curved in a ballistic arc. Ten seconds later, a crash from below announced the end of its terminal dive.

MacHenry's sudden pull and the sight of the flaming jeep sailing out into space injected a fresh dose of adrenaline into Barnes. His voice was almost normal and his eyes flashed. "What are you trying to do, BJ? Kill me or something?" Then he saw Angel. "Who the fuck is that?" Barnes stared at the small man in the dark brown jacket. Julia's hands were still on his arm.

"The car." Julia remembered the car they had passed on their race to the top. "He must have driven up here in that car."

The man looked at them, then ran toward the trail leading down the mountain.

"Wait here," MacHenry said, stepping back from the edge and setting off in a run after the mysterious stranger and his truck.

Julia turned to face the conflagration. A flock of birds flashed by in panic flight, their wings buzzing in frantic beats to carry them away to safety.

"That's what we should be doing," said Barnes. *Hurry.* "I always knew I'd hate the infantry." The flames rose in a solid sheet now. Thousands of feet above Crandall Peak, the gray smoke condensed into sooty cumulus, punching upward into cooler air with a budding cauliflower shape. The uprushing air drew in the winds from all quarters, and following their Newtonian instincts, the hot gases began to swirl in cyclonic rotation as they blasted skyward. A shudder tossed the trees as a new wind began to take hold. The flaming wallcloud slowly spun in the valley below. Barnes felt the heat on his sweaty face. "I'm cold," he said.

Julia laced her fingers with his, feeling their iciness. "I warmed you up once, I can do it again."

Barnes smiled. "Promises," he said, "are cheap."

They both turned in the direction of the new sound. It was the truck they had seen parked at the edge of the summit. The engine roared and the blue Blazer shot from its shelter and headed straight for them. It veered away from the edge of the cliff and stopped in a spray of loose rock right beside them. MacHenry was in the passenger's seat.

"Get in," the man in the dark brown jacket said as the first reaching tendrils of smoke drifted by.

"What—" Julia began, but Angel cut her off.

"No. Just get in."

Adcock was dreaming again, dreaming of a place distant from the impossible weight pinning him to the broken helicopter. *Where are they?* he wondered. He had heard the roar of jet engines, the familiar sound of Tonopah, of safety. *Where are they?* Suddenly, the sound of a million crickets clicking in wild discord brought him back to the here and now. Brilliant fireflies flared across the jagged cracks in the helicopter's windshield. They settled, lighting on the Plexiglas, and melted through in an instant. *What . . . ?*

Then he heard the roar of engines again, but the note was different, deeper. It made him feel better. It grew stronger, like the breaking of storm waves against a seawall. Adcock twisted in his broken seat and saw a column of pure white fire gobble a stand of trees, uprooting and dissolving them into its flaming body. *No!* His mouth opened into a silent scream as he felt the tree that imprisoned him bend in the wind, bend toward the fire. *No!* The wind moaned in a wallcloud of flame. Adcock felt weightless, tiny before the unleashed elemental force of the firestorm.

The roar grew to a deafening howl. A searing wind smashed through the trees. The helicopter trembled and shook almost as though it had once again taken to flight. But the rotors were still. There was only one final flight left to make.

The tree bent over more, nearly horizontal, and then it broke in a thunderbolt snap. The wind picked up the helicopter and carried it into the greedy mouth of the fire. It never reached the ground.

Julia cradled Barnes as Angel roared down the jeep track. "Slow down!" she said. "You'll kill him!"

Angel didn't even bother to turn. They all could feel the fire's heat, even through the glass. *Angelito,* he said to himself, *this is a very dumb thing to do.*

He turned to MacHenry. "Your friend is very brave, but he is hurt. Inside." It was, Angel knew, a very bad way to be wounded. Who better than Angel to know what an AK-47 round, even a ricochet, could do? He rounded a sharp curve and nearly rammed half a dozen deer as they bounded across the trail. Their eyes glowed white in terror.

"Oh, yeah?" said Barnes. "I wasn't meant to die like a grunt." He coughed, and his own breath felt chill in his throat. *Hurry.* "Besides," he said to Julia, "you promised . . ."

"I'll be there," she said. Suddenly, a ruddy light erupted overhead, and the very tops of the trees turned bright gold in yellow flame. The trees on either side of the path swayed like dancing, hundred-foot torches as the winds drove the flames across their crowns. The fire raced through the dry needles. A shower of embers fell as the strong winds shook the trees.

Entire branches began to fall as the uprooting firestorm neared. Angel steered around one fallen trunk, then another. A third smashed down, catching the rear bumper and tearing it off with an almost human scream.

Angel grimly kept to the track, outracing the advancing edge of the firestorm. He jumped when the rear window cracked like a rifle shot in the intense heat.

MacHenry saw a narrow opening on one side of the road. Angel steered straight for it as three more deer, one with enormous spreading antlers, frantically wheeled away from the heat and dove under the burning canopy. "Do you know where we're headed?"

"I know where you are headed." The air was dense with smoke; an acid stench of burning pine resin and wood stung their eyes. Angel flipped on the lights, and the beams arrowed ahead in the sooty fog. They crossed a small wooden bridge, a tiny trickle of water wetting the rocks below it, and began climbing again. Angel braked to a stop. The beams of the headlights penetrated the unnatural darkness and framed a gray shack with a huge wheel of cable mounted beside it. He nodded at the shack and leaving the Blazer running, he pushed open MacHenry's door. "And you have arrived." He pulled at the back door and motioned them out. There were limits to charity.

"What?" said Julia. "What do you mean?"

Angel looked at them. Soot already crowded his dark eyes. "Listen well. There is a railroad that runs down to water." He pointed again at the shack. MacHenry saw the flatcar drawn tight to a steel rail. "Get to the water. Quickly. *Vaya!*" Angel drew the CZX for emphasis.

The sight of the weapon froze her rigid.

"Move!"

"All right!" said MacHenry. He jumped out and ran to the other side, Angel's pistol tracking him as he went. He helped Barnes out.

MacHenry slammed the door. The air was choking, stinging with ash and charred resin. He looked in at Angel. The gun was a black circle pointed at his chest. "Aren't you coming?"

"No," Angel said simply, and motioned them to move.

Hurry, repeated the voice inside Barnes.

Angel nodded. "Good luck," he said as he shifted into low and gunned the engine in a spray of rock and dust. Soon, it, too, was lost in the dense smoke.

Mierda! thought Angel as the road behind became engulfed. A howl of swirling vapors and burning gas set the very glass of the Blazer buzzing in demonic harmony. A dry manzanita bush suddenly lit off in rushing, reaching brilliance. Angel swerved away from it and the Blazer rocked in the sudden wind.

A tree dropped in a slow-motion arc ahead of him and he skidded to a stop just short, clutched down, and started to climb over it. He wasn't going to make it. Not this way. He backed up and with a running start only managed to come close to pinning the truck with all wheels spinning in air. The Blazer rocked back and the rear wheels bit. He backed off, feeling a sudden heat penetrate the glass. He had stopped sweating.

Angel turned and saw the hard brilliance of the fire behind him. The Blazer's paint began to blister. *And now?* he said to himself. *Fool!* his inner voice admonished. He backed partly off the trail and turned to face the wall of flames bearing down on him. "Perhaps the old priests were right," he said almost meditatively. It certainly looked like the gates of Hell. He pressed the accelerator to the floor, and the Blazer leaped into the fiery mouth.

26

ANGEL

OF

MERCY

OSMOS 2149, a fourth-generation Soviet imaging satellite, was nearing the end of its life as it swept over southern California. It had kept a constant watch for fifty-three days, a near-record, and was overdue for replacement. Like a soldier nearing the end of a combat posting, Cosmos 2149 had not been given very much to do as its orbit wound down like a cosmic watchspring. Fifty-three days was a long time, after all, and luck could be pressed only so far.

But it was luck that placed it above an intense flare of thermal energy rising from the heart of the Sierra Nevada range. Programmed to seek just such events, its on-board processor commanded the aging craft to swing its sensors for a better view. After all, the launch of an ICBM left just such a thermal trace, and they were not to be ignored, even with the Cold War over. Its cameras zoomed in on the suspicious event, even as its transmitters broadcast an alarm signal to Raduga 26, another Soviet satellite in high geosynchronous orbit. The link to an earth station outside Krasnoyarsk took less than eight seconds to complete. The link to Viktor Chebrikov took somewhat longer.

A second signal was sent up into the sky, stored by the high-flying

Raduga, and retransmitted to Cosmos 2149, by now over the Pacific Northwest. The aging Cosmos dutifully recorded the new message and waited for the next pass to execute the encoded instructions.

MacHenry stopped for a breath, crouching low for the marginally cleaner air that hugged the ground. Panic nibbled at the edges of his mind when a pall of acid smoke drifted between him and his two companions. "Julia!" he called, but she did not answer. He turned at a sudden flush of heat on his back. The fire storm raged with brilliant orange flares as the smoke and flame wheeled in majestic circulation. The heat turned up full and he felt the last of his sweat dry in its blast. He tottered, his knees growing liquid below him, the sizzle of the fire growing loud in his dimming sight. *Tired.* He fought the seductive whisper to sit, to rest.

"MacHenry!" Julia grabbed his shoulder. "Come on!"

"I'm okay," he said weakly. "Just hot." Her eyes gleamed red in reflection of the towering column of fire. "Where's Barnes?"

"Where you're headed," she said. They nearly stumbled onto the tram car before MacHenry saw what it was. Just a six-foot square of planks and pipe rails sitting on large iron wheels. "You've got to help," she said. "I can't figure out how to release it."

Barnes leaned back against the metal rail of the tram. He had said nothing since leaving Angel's truck. His face was white, drained of even the reflection the flames cast across them. "Glad you could join us," said Barnes as he gritted his teeth and shook his head. *Hurry.*

"Just hang on." MacHenry looked up into the gloomy sky. An eerie and unnatural dusk was starting to settle. A sheet of thin, almost transparent white flame drew across the sky above him, pale and delicate as the aurora borealis. The trees overhead immediately shook violently as a new wind blasted their tops. The firestorm paused as it extended a tentative awning of burning gas ahead of it, feeling its sightless way along the side of Crandall Peak. MacHenry looked down the shiny rails of the tram. It plummeted very close to the edge of the fire.

"MacHenry?" Julia said hoarsely as she looked at the alien sky. "I think we're running out of time."

"Get on." He opened a metal control box and saw three buttons within. The plastic was already hot to the touch. He punched all three in sequence, but nothing worked. He turned and traced the heavy steel cable to its source inside the metal shack just uphill. "Wait," he said. "I'll figure out the release." *Somehow.* He turned toward the metal shack, and Julia stepped onto the rail car. She noticed for the first time that the planks were black with dried blood.

MacHenry peered into the locked shack. *Clutch?* he wondered as he ran around to the door and tugged at the lock. It barely moved.

He felt the heat on his face and started to turn to face the fire. *Don't look up!* A shower of bright embers fell like flaming snow. *Don't look up!* He pulled at the locked door again. *Nothing.* He turned to find something to strike the hasp with when he heard the pound of running booted feet. He squinted into the acid haze. A man covered with soot appeared from out of the dense smoke. At first, MacHenry did not recognize him.

"Stand away!" Angel shouted. MacHenry stopped his struggle and looked at him. Angel's face was blistered and raw like half-cooked meat. He shoved MacHenry aside and reached inside the tatters of the once brown, now black, jacket. He brought out a gleaming automatic. The weapon glowed ultraviolet in the orange firelight.

Angel pointed the CZX at the hasp and sent three of the big slugs crashing into it. The shattered lock fell free. As the distilled gum of the fir needles boiled off into vapor around them, Angel shoved the door wide and jumped inside the shack. The purpose of the long iron bar connected to the take-up reel clutch was unmistakable. He reached up and pulled it down hard.

A loud *clank!* accompanied the release of the take-up reel. Angel sprinted outside, colliding with MacHenry at the doorway. "Come," he said to MacHenry. The railcar was already moving.

"MacHenry!" Julia had her boot jammed against a timber, but it wouldn't hold the mass of the railcar for long. "Hurry up!" Her boot slipped, scraping the dirt as the railcar began to roll. MacHenry ran and jumped on board. Angel was right behind. He grabbed the hot iron of the brake bar that might or might not slow them down enough to live.

With a sudden lurch, the railcar tipped over the edge of the slope and plunged downhill.

The wheels clattered over the steel joints, faster, faster, as they flew down the side of Crandall Peak. A sudden lurch nearly sent them into the woods. Angel bore down on the heavy brake bar and a shower of sparks fountained up from the rails, a rooster tail of fire lost beneath the flames that surrounded them.

Trees torched high on either side of the tracks. Wooden power poles licked flames skyward in eerie blue cylinders, leaving their creosoted surfaces black and alligator-skin charred. But it was the sight overhead that was the most unnatural, the most alien.

A thick tower of fire reached up from Crandall to the heavens, a ring of white-hot gases streaming out its top like a burning halo. The fire storm was pumping soot and debris into the high reaches of the atmosphere. Julia grabbed the side railing and looked up at it. It was the most extravagant display of thermal pumping she had ever seen. Wind was sucked in from all points of the compass as the fire blasted superheated air into the atmosphere. The wind stoked the flames like a furnace. It was a textbook firestorm. And she was right beside it.

Barnes opened his eyes and looked at Angel as they moved faster and faster down the rails. As the rails took off in an unbanked curve, Angel yanked the brake, throwing them all forward. But he was looking straight back at Barnes, his eyes reflecting the yellows and reds of the fire. His face was wild, exhilarated. "You did very well with the bow and arrow!" he shouted. "You must show me how you do this, yes?"

Barnes swallowed but his throat was dead dry. "Who are you?" he asked.

A sudden hot gust of wind made MacHenry look up. He saw the sheet of burning gas fall down toward them like a delicate, animated curtain. The new heat was unbearable. The tram banged around another bend and over a forested shoulder. The blackened boughs streaked by. "Don't breathe!" he shouted to them above the roar of wind and the sudden sheeting hiss of fire. It was going to be a close race to get through before that fire dropped to the ground. He looked at Angel. "Let go!" he shouted. "The brake! Let it go!" Angel looked up at the sky, then back down at the rails. He grinned crazily, his teeth white in the dusky gloom of the conflagration. With a shrug, he let go of the brake.

The tram seemed to drop from beneath them as it hurtled down the tracks. The veil of fire closed in, blocking the view of the towering smoke clouds. "Hang on!" MacHenry yelled. "Don't breathe!" The translucent wall rose high out of sight, a mile-high tidal wave of fire curling to break upon them.

MacHenry moved closer to Julia, shielding her and Barnes. Only Angel sat apart, clutching the brake, ready to use it again. A furnace-hot wind whipped his black hair.

Julia felt weightless as they were jolted clear of the tracks, the sound of squealing metal sounding as the wheels hammered down again. Ahead, a glowing curtain of fire was falling toward the ground, falling toward the tracks over which they would pass. Julia closed her eyes when MacHenry shouted his last warning. The curtain of burning gas dropped to the tracks. An instant later, they were inside.

The world flashed brilliant blue as a lightning bolt struck nearby, a titanic *CRACK* of thunder following a split second later. It became bright enough for MacHenry to see behind his closed eyes, then dark, then light again. His face felt a sudden wash of cold air, cold enough to make him shiver in the heat. For a moment, he didn't know if he was burning to death or was, in fact, saved.

"Hah!" Angel bore down on the brake bar, and the railcar began to slow, the clacking from the rails winding down like a broken clock. His face was black with soot, his eyes darting left and right.

MacHenry opened his own eyes. It was a vision from the end of the world: blackened slopes burned clear of all growth, leaving only foreshortened stumps of pine, miniature volcanic puffs of smoke rising from the still-burning roots. He wiped away the tearing and saw his left arm cooked red. They had rolled under the edge of the firestorm. Now it was behind them, working its way up the slope of Crandall Peak.

"Jesus," Barnes said as he breathed a lungful. "You look terrible, BJ." He moved out from under Julia's shielding arm. His own face was soot blackened but for his eyes, and a thin, foul smoke rose from his T-shirt. He stared at the devastated landscape. "Jesus," he repeated.

"No, my friend. Not Jesus," Angel corrected. "But the Devil himself."

The railcar rolled out along the flat approach to the reservoir, slowing, dragging a thousand feet of heavy steel cable behind. Then, with Angel still gripping the iron brake bar, it struck an old tire used as a bumper and stopped.

Angel leaped off before MacHenry's eyes or nerves told him they had survived.

Barnes looked down at his hand and commanded it to move, but it did not. Above all else, this brought him to the edge of panic. He gasped as though his lungs would be the next in line to forget their mission. "I can't . . ."

Julia heard him. "We're almost there. We're almost to the water." She looked across the rocky beach. *What?* It was a mirage. It had to be. Against the slate-gray waters of the reservoir, a soot-covered airplane stood, its yellow dulled to mustard by ashfall. She squinted at the apparition, trying to clear her eyes.

But Barnes saw it, too. "Hey." The sight of its jaunty wings was as impossible as the vision of a desert waterhole. He stared, daring it to dissolve. It didn't. "BJ," he whispered. *Hurry.* "There's an airplane out there."

MacHenry's eyes widened in disbelief at the sight of the yellow Cub. *How . . . ?* He shook his head. How did it survive?

"Do you believe in miracles?" said Barnes as they stared.

Angel turned his back on them and made straight for the water. Charity had its limits. He had saved these three because one of them had been foolishly brave. He could tell from the gray look on the archer's face that he did not have long. As for the others? Angel owed them nothing. He owed himself a return trip home, and the longer he remained here, the less likely that trip became. He splashed ankle deep, pausing to look back up at the smoke-wreathed summit. *Burn,* he cursed the foul-smelling box Guryanov had ordered him to bring here. *Burn.*

Barnes looked at the yellow Cub and tried to smile, but his face was frozen into place, his skin pulled like old parchment across his teeth. "I guess we don't have to swim," he said. A stiff wind, drawn from the cool lowlands up the burned slopes and into the spiraling heat engine of the firestorm, rocked the little wings as though to remind them of their duty. Barnes looked at the small plane and felt an enormous and urgent longing to fly away, anywhere, just so long as the dirt and the smoke and the pain could be left behind. *Hurry.* He mouthed the word. "Hurry."

"We will," Julia answered, hearing him. "We will." She and MacHenry gently took hold of his arms and brought him upright.

"I'm the pilot," Barnes said to himself as he tried to understand what was happening. He looked at Julia, who found herself frightened to her bones by the emptiness of his expression. "I'm the pilot, right?" he said. *Hurry.*

Angel was waist deep when he looked back again. The peak was totally obscured by the fire and the billowing drifts of smoke and ash. Angel laughed and dove into the cold water, stroking for the far side.

"BJ," said Barnes, "can we leave now?"

MacHenry looked at Julia. "Let's go." They helped Barnes to the side of the Cub. As they drew near, they saw its skin was not just covered by ash; it had burned through in a hundred different places. The fabric was a shambles. "I don't know . . ." said MacHenry.

Barnes leaned against the smooth skin and shook his head. "Come on, BJ. I know . . . where the edge is, right? I say let's fly the mother. Make like Superman and just fly away, okay?"

"What about him?" Julia asked as she watched Angel swim into deeper water.

MacHenry saw Angel's head bob, pause, and disappear as he began to swim again. "He seems to know where he's going."

A dry whisper came from Barnes's lips. "That's what has me worried, BJ."

"We couldn't have taken him with us anyway." There was barely room for three. One in front and two in the larger aft seat. MacHenry remembered the man's face at the locked shack at the top of the tram. He had saved all their lives. It was time to save their own. MacHenry watched as his head bobbed up far out in the gray water. He looked up at the soot, the clouds of smoke rising high into the sky, and back at Barnes. His deep blue eyes flashed from the cold clay of his face. Then he smiled.

"BJ?" he said almost too soft to hear. "It's time to aviate."

MacHenry settled into the front seat of the plane as Julia cradled Barnes in the back. Barnes opened his eyes as she strapped the webbed belt tight around him, cinching them both with the single belt. MacHenry looked out beyond the Cub's high wings and saw the firestorm eat its way up Schoettgen Pass. The dense wall of smoke hung like funeral bunting around Crandall Peak. Light pinpricked in through a thousand scorched holes burned in the airplane's fabric skin. MacHenry knew the wings would be no better, maybe worse. The steel inside them wouldn't fall apart. But the flight surfaces? Maybe they still had an airfoil. Maybe not. It was time to find out.

The infrared sensors aboard Cosmos 2149 caught sight of the firestorm first. The angle was oblique, for its orbits were designed to just overlap one another. This was done to ensure fresh territory with each pass, yet permit an item of interest to be reexamined.

Still, even from over a hundred miles south of its previous groundtrack, the fire was the brightest object, except for the sun, in its electronic universe. Identification was not a problem, even though Cosmos 2149 was a geriatric spy. It still knew where it was and what it had to do. At the closest approach, it slewed its directional transmit whip and beamed a triggering signal at the ground. The maneuvering cost it the last of its thruster fuel. Paralyzed, Cosmos 2149 swept along its Copernican trajectory, its mission, and its life, both fulfilled and ended.

* * *

The antenna on top of Crandall Lookout picked up the one signal it had been built to hear. It sent the tiny current down the cable, into the ranger cab, and into the receiver section of the weapon case. The identification circuitry filtered it through its coding gates; a small initiating signal was sent to the master timing controller.

Deep within the guts of the bomb, a series of safeguard switches fell from safe to armed. A metal wheel turned on top another, nearly identical wheel, until a hole in the upper half matched one in the lower. A short barrel was thus formed, ready for a cartridge to detonate a sphere of high explosive that, in turn, would compress the uranium into a fissioning mass.

MacHenry turned the brass stopcock and watched the fuel flow down from the Cub's wings toward the engine. He unlocked the primer knob and began to pump. The smell of raw avgas wafted dangerously through the cockpit. He turned to face Julia and Barnes. He saw that they were both strapped in together in the small rear seat. "Take it easy," MacHenry warned. "We're going to get you out. I'm going to bring you off this mountain."

He turned back and surveyed the simple controls: stick, rudder pedals, black-knobbed throttle on the left with the red mixture control right below it. They were like an old picture in an album come to life. He looked back at Barnes as he checked the stick. "Just stay with us. We're going to be out of here real quick."

MacHenry cracked the throttle an eighth of an inch, ran the mixture forward to full rich, and pressed the starter button.

The wooden prop began to whir in slow, groaning revolutions. Three blades; six. MacHenry pumped the throttle impatiently. Twelve blades through. The engine coughed once, blue smoke erupting from the stacks. It cleared itself of raw fuel and caught with an irregular beat.

Barnes smiled, his eyes still shut, at the old familiar beat of the pistons. Julia reached around his body and cinched the loop of the seat belt as tight as she dared. "It's going to be okay," she said.

"I . . . know." Barnes's eyes opened, their blue a shocking contrast to his white, drained face. "I know," he said, "but . . ." He hesitated, shifting under the tight belt. "I'm glad you're here." *Hurry*.

"Me, too," Julia said, rocking him. "Me, too." The engine clattered, surrounding them in a sheath of sound. When Barnes spoke again, Julia leaned close to hear him.

"Julia," said Barnes, "I want you to remind him of something. Remind him about Excalibur. That . . . black bastard. Make sure he tells him."

"Tells who?" Julia said as she stroked his cold brow.

"Other pilot," he whispered. "Tell him I had his . . . ass."

They taxied over the rounded stones and turned at the end of the gravel bar, pointing back along its length with the narrow Stanislaus canyon behind them and the opening flats of the reservoir directly ahead. MacHenry ran the unmuffled engine to full power and they started to roll. He pushed forward on the stick. The overweighted tail rose sluggishly as the fat tires bounced rapidly along the tops of the rocks. The thumping of the main gear suddenly vanished as the Super Cub lifted off. MacHenry looked out at the tattered wings. *Thanks*.

Barnes felt the weight leave the wheels, felt the wings fill with air. He could let go. *Home*. He smiled. Julia held him tight as she pressed against the small back window and looked at the flank of Crandall as they rose, almost levitating. He was saying something, but she couldn't hear it. Julia bent and put her ear next to Barnes's lips.

"I'm frightened . . ." He was no longer cold, the creeping chill replaced by a warm, soft midnight tide within him, snuffing out all the little lights, drowning the nerves as it came, heavy and numbing. *Hurry*. "I'm . . ."

"No. Don't be," she said. "Remember? No thinking on the bus. Just doing."

He smiled with his eyes. "You . . . believed that line?"

"Yes." She held him close as they rode the air beneath the Super Cub's wide wings.

The water was burning cold on Angel's raw skin as he swam. His intuition told him to keep swimming, but curiosity brought him to a stop. He turned and tread water, facing Crandall Peak. He reached under his arm and pulled the automatic from its holster, letting it fall into the black depths of the reservoir.

He splashed water on his face and allowed himself to sink slightly. His eyes were just above the water when a brilliant flash erupted. It seemed to come from everywhere at once, a scalding pressure so intense Angel thought he had been shot in the head.

The heat pulse arrived a microsecond later, driving him under water by primitive instinct alone. The heat seemed to penetrate his skull, to set his brain on fire. As he dove ever deeper, a million tiny bubbles percolated by his ears as the very water began to boil, and his blood pounded like the drums of Zanja. He had seen only a flash, felt the powerful heat, yet Angel knew just what he had witnessed.

Guryanov! he screamed silently as he dove, his anger at the Russian's betrayal pounded into a hard, immutable metal within him. He fashioned it into a blade he gripped tight in his fist. The water pressed into his burning skin, deeper, deeper as he dove, pursued by a wave of heat that dared his lungs to call for air; a dive so deep and so dark that even Petroushka might well lose his way, and never return.

The yellow Super Cub was like a butterfly caught in a tornado; MacHenry banked away from the towering wallcloud, but the in-rushing winds sucked them in with complete indifference. When they reached the edge, it slammed them skyward on an elevator of pure heat. They were inside it, riding it up, blind as the pilot in the crashed Cessna had been. There was a difference: MacHenry was at the controls.

The engine coughed, missed a beat, then smoothed out. "Too much crap in the air!" MacHenry yelled over the hiss of the soot as it blasted the windshield. It was clogging up the intake filter with ash. The smoke thinned out to their left. He tacked for it, banking away from the heart of the inferno. He checked the VSI. It was pegged at over two thousand feet per minute straight up.

The thick cloud deck became a lighter shade of gray, then dirty white. A patch of sky flashed bright blue. At just over eight thousand feet, they were spat out from the imprisoning smoke and into the clear. Julia put her hand out into the slipstream and cupped fresh air into the smoky cockpit and over Barnes's face. He smiled, his eyes shut, and shook his head.

"Okay," MacHenry said to himself over the roaring engine. He pulled the throttle back to keep it from tearing itself apart, then set up a ninety-knot cruise. There had to be a hospital in Columbia, the nearest settlement to the west. He banked until the compass settled on 270 and turned around in his seat. "I told you it was just an airplane," he said to them. "It's just . . ." He stopped as he searched Barnes's face. *No!* It was so empty. "Julia! Check . . ."

Barnes opened his eyes and locked onto MacHenry's. "BJ," he said, although MacHenry could barely hear his rasping whisper over the sound of the engine. "BJ . . ."

"Take it easy," MacHenry said as he tried to fly with his head facing backward. "We're out of it."

"Promised . . ." Barnes said, but stopped when he heard a different voice. *Here. Over here. It's very beautiful, isn't it?*

MacHenry grabbed the control stick with his left hand and turned in his seat. He offered his right to Barnes. He knew just what Barnes was trying to say. "I promise."

Barnes took his hand from his cold belly and commanded it to rise. "Right . . ." he said, his words squeezed out from his blue lips, ". . . to the edge." *Welcome,* came the old voice. It was Tanai, his archery instructor. *How did . . .?* Barnes felt a flicker of fear, but it subsided as a circle of light appeared, first a bright star against the clouds of soot and ash, then larger, larger, swelling into a full rainbow. An aviator's rainbow, perfectly round. It stopped at his feet and seemed to pulse, expectant, waiting. *Begin with the circle.*

Barnes moved at his mind's command. He stepped to the edge of the rainbow. He looked far below and saw MacHenry. He tottered on a sharp edge of pure color. *Let the arrow speak.* He hesitated, his head light enough to float, but his feet uncertain. *Let the arrow speak.* He smiled and was about to let go. He could see the air, warm and inviting. Barnes was ready, ready to fly. He stepped to the edge and put one foot over the clear drop. It didn't feel heavy, the air itself felt like a supporting solid. As he moved his other foot, something stopped him, something strange, yet familiar. Barring his way was a thin band of wood; the bow of a master Zen archer. *This is the edge,* the familiar voice said from within his surprise. *The true edge. Tell me. Are you still so very curious?*

MacHenry reached back and found Barnes's fingers were dead cold. MacHenry tried to squeeze life back into them, his own heat, his own blood, as though by will and hope alone he could stop the slow evacuation of the soul. "I promise you," MacHenry said again. Barnes didn't seem to register MacHenry's words. "Do you hear me? Barnes! Do you hear me?"

As MacHenry searched his friend's face, a high-voltage *SNAP* shot through the cockpit, followed an instant later by a flash of intense lightning. An electric charge surged through the cockpit. Crandall Peak was dead astern as the ten-kiloton charge detonated. The actinic dazzle enveloped the Cub's metal structure in lurid blue neon, flowing up Barnes's outstretched arm and into MacHenry. MacHenry forced his eyes to remain open as it burned into him. The light slowly faded, freezing the scene in fiery afterglow, Julia cradling Barnes, a pearly corona enveloping all of them.

Julia felt him loosen in her arms. "Barnes!"

MacHenry caught sight of a new, terrible shape rising from the heart of the fire storm. He knew what he was seeing even before the name came to his lips. He saw the advancing Mach wave from the explosion come like a strange bubble devouring the world before it.

"Barnes!" he shouted. He banked to face the shimmering overpressure wave. "Hold on!" He dived toward a rocky canyon below. He didn't care what the odds were, that a nuclear explosion had just gone off, that its blast was bearing down on them. He would ride that wave, crash the damned Cub into the hospital parking lot if need be. Anything. "Just hold on," said MacHenry. "Please. Just hold on."

The Cub dived in the lee of the canyon. The violence of the blast rolled overhead. MacHenry pulled out as a pale echo of its force smashed the Cub down toward the rocks. An instant later, the overpressure wave bounced off the canyon and spit the Cub back up into clear, strangely calm air. MacHenry shoved the black throttle forward until the engine screamed, the compass once again showing 270 degrees. Ahead, he could see the first buildings of Columbia. There was a hospital there. He pointed his nose at the small town and waited for the world to end.

27

THE MUSEUM

HE NORAD duty officer, an Air Force lieutenant colonel, was jolted by the buzzer and flashing light on the DSP South panel. *Not another drill,* he thought as he put aside his coffee mug. The Cold War was over. The good guys had won, or at least, it was convenient to think so. The world had been a dangerous place with the two superpowers toe-to-toe; it was unfortunately, no more secure with a dozen minor powers equally well armed with both hate and weaponry. Cheyenne Mountain had not lost its usefulness, even if nobody at NORAD thought about the Big One anymore.

DSP south was an early-warning satellite designed to respond to the brilliant infrared flares given off by boost-phase ICBMs. The lieutenant colonel silenced the annoying alarm as he tapped in an acknowledgment code.

"What is it?" the Royal Canadian Air Force liaison officer asked, drawn to the console by the light and sound in the otherwise hushed theater of the big room. "Blow another IC?"

"Don't know yet." The old computers dwelling in the guts of NORAD were getting more and more temperamental every year. Only one company was now willing, or able, to make replacement parts at who knew what cost. Most of the operators were computer buffs, and it was with no small irony they called this place The Museum.

He read the message the old Teletype printer had hammered out. *What was HUMMER 6?* he wondered as the coordinates were translated. "DSP South's picked up something hot. Could be a malfunction. Or maybe a snap readiness drill. We haven't had one in a while."

The RCAF liaison read the scrolling message. "High-energy event. Maybe it's another laser spoof. Our friends haven't played that game for a while, either. Still, I wonder."

The duty officer shook his head. "Nope. The new sensor is supposed to be immune to lasers. Besides, the coordinates aren't right for an intel trawler. Not unless the Russians are fishing in the Sierra Nevada."

"Right. Then what's your guess?"

The Air Force lieutenant colonel shrugged as his finger went down a list of California Military Operations Areas. "Bingo." He looked up. "HUMMER's an Air Force weapons range. So either it's a drill, or somebody hung a live nuke on a bomb rack by mistake and some poor bastard just dropped it."

The Canadian chuckled as the lieutenant colonel picked up the direct line to Washington. He stopped when he saw the USAF duty officer was not smiling. "But that's not possible, is it?"

The duty officer merely raised one eyebrow as the phone began to ring.

The President paced as he spoke on the phone, the cord connecting him to the Oval Office desk like a tangled jess. His hair was still wet. He had dripped water onto a thick stack of papers awaiting his signature. A towel was draped over his shoulders. Water and sweat had stained his green silk robe black. "No, no," he said into the phone. "Don't bother. Thank you, Henry. I'll give you the full brief later today. Yes. Good-bye." He carefully placed the phone back on its hook as Gen. Richard Wheeler, chairman of the Joint Chiefs, squirmed on his. "That was Senator Crawford again. The *Democratic* senator from California."

"Yes, sir," Wheeler said automatically.

"Damn it, General!" The President slammed the desk with his open hand, bouncing the new trade agreement and loan package with the Soviet Union nearer to the edge. "When will we know where it came from?"

"Sir, we're still gathering data," Wheeler said, knowing even as the words came out that the answer would be found wanting. "I can give you an opinion, but that's all so far. If that's acceptable to you then we can . . ."

"No," the President interrupted. "It is *not* acceptable. You aren't paid to waffle. You're paid to think." The President paused as the phone rang again. He pointed a finger at Wheeler. "I smell a cover-up. This HUMMER place is *your* territory. *You* had an airplane flying in there. Just how in hell do you think it looks?" He savagely yanked the phone from its cradle. "What is it!" He looked up at Wheeler. "It's for you."

Wheeler gingerly took hold of the phone as though it, too, were a bomb set to blow up in his face. He listened, nodded, and began to take notes on the fresh yellow pad he had brought over from the Pentagon but had not yet had the opportunity to use. "Very well," he said with a sigh, and hung up.

"Shoot." The President sat back down behind his desk. His eyes were glittering and cold, even as his skin flushed red.

"Sir," Wheeler began, "we have a Dragon Lady running back with the results of the upper-atmosphere sample. They match the flash spectrum our DSP bird picked up."

"Stop!" The President shot to his feet. "Who and how, General. That's it. Right now. No more, and by God, no less."

Wheeler swallowed. "It was very small, sir. No weapon in our inventory exactly matches the yield except for some very specialized man-portable devices. But even they don't fit."

The President drummed his fingers on the desk. "You've told me what it wasn't. Now tell me what it was."

Wheeler glanced at his notes. "The upper air sample brought back enough fallout to positively eliminate this as a U.S.-sourced explosive."

The President's eyes narrowed. "You mean somebody *else* set off a nuke in an Air Force test range? Somebody else? Who?"

"The explosion was small because the uranium was poorly processed. It had a lot of contaminant tags not found in our own mixes . . ."

"Stop. Where did it come from?" the President asked quietly. He had just realized that an accident, as politically damaging as it might be, was preferable to what Wheeler was suggesting.

"The information from the TR-2 is still preliminary, sir."

The President leveled his finger like a pistol. "You get one more chance to answer my question in a straightforward manner. Then I'm going to get angry, General. *Where did it come from?*"

Wheeler swallowed hard. "Tajura, sir. The Libyan nuclear site at Tajura. The fallout traces match the raw ore mix we believe is being processed at Tajura."

The President was silent for a moment, a complex political equation going on behind his eyes. Finally, he spoke. "Correct me if I'm wrong, General. The Soviets have a big presence there. Technicians and security types. Isn't that so?"

"Yes, sir," Wheeler replied. His blood was pounding in his ears. "About two hundred techs and twice that number of guard troops."

"I thought so. Christ." The President balled his fist and pounded the desktop again. The trade agreement and loan package inched closer to the edge. The open maw of a document shredder was right below. "General, are we in a position to take out that complex? I mean tomorrow. The *instant* you're convinced that was where this thing came from?"

"Sir, as you know we're down a carrier with the accident aboard *John F. Kennedy*. The Brits won't let us use our bases in England for staging." Wheeler stopped, a new thought shining clear and hot in his mind like the sun burning through a cloud deck. "However," he began again, "there's an operational test going on right now of Project Aurora. It just may be the way we can handle this."

"Aurora?" asked the President. He'd been kept too busy reassembling the interstate banking system to pay attention to the military's games. "What's Aurora?"

"Our new Blackbird, sir. Very fast, very high-flying. We have five Aurora aircraft overseas right now. The program people call them Excalibur."

"As in the sword. Cute. Go on." The President tapped his finger impatiently on the Soviet trade agreement. The sound was becoming more and more hollow in the hush of the office.

Wheeler nodded to himself as the plan came together in his head. "We could mate them to the appropriate weapons. At Mach 5, they could get in and out before anyone would know the difference. In fact, I believe that two were scheduled to fly against Libyan radars anyway." Wheeler made a mental note to call up Arthur Dean Bridger. Bridger and Norton Aerodyne were going to be very happy if this all worked out. So would the Air Force.

"I have one question, General," said the President. "Could the Libyans have cooked this up without Soviet technical assistance?"

Wheeler shook his head. "No, sir."

"No doubts?"

"None."

"Okay." The President gave the Soviet trade document a push. Three billion dollars in loans and twice that amount in food and farm machinery sales tumbled into the shredder. There would be hell to pay in Moscow, but someone had smuggled a goddamned nuke into California and set it off. What did they expect? A thank-you note?

He tapped the foot switch. The shredder noisily chewed up both paper and policy with crude indifference. When nothing was left but thin strips of paper spaghetti, he turned to Wheeler once again, a strange and dangerous-looking calm masking his face. "I want that complex leveled," he said so softly that Wheeler leaned forward in his chair.

"Sir?"

"You heard right, mister. Bounce the rubble good and hard." There was a quaver now in the President's voice, one he fought to control. "I'll be *goddamned* if I go down in history as the first President to pay three billion for the privilege of getting nuked."

28

MISSING MAN

COLONEL Braden stared through the blinds of his office window. The aircraft parking ramp at Mather Air Force Base was unusually busy for a Sunday morning. A line of four F-15s sat waiting, surrounded by idling start carts and groundcrew. "So," he said as he watched the small crowd out by the apron fence, "if you're permitted to talk about it, I'd like to know how it went."

Harry Hill stood, his arms crossed over his chest. He no longer wore the black flightsuit of Norton Aerodyne's Strategic Flight Test Group. He looked uncomfortable in his civilian slacks and windbreaker. Answering questions like this was a habit he had gotten out of at Tonopah. "Well," he began slowly, "I was brought in at the last minute. I'm not sure I can add much to what you've read in the papers."

It was not precisely true. Harry Hill had been sitting in the best seat in the house when the Libyan nuclear facility at Tajura was leveled by two Excaliburs, each coming at high Mach numbers from opposite directions. Four guided 2,000-pound bombs did their jobs, but Hill had come around for a low pass. The resulting shock wave leveled everything the bombs had left standing.

The raid against the reprocessing plant had taken place two days after the nuclear blast in HUMMER 6. But what was shocking news in July had nearly fallen off the public's scope by September. Now, in October, it was all but forgotten except within the professional community of military aviators.

Hill watched Braden stare out the window. Colonel Braden was part of the family. And Hill felt a niggling obligation. After all, he had once done his best to kill a pilot from Braden's squadron. He decided to open up. "They weren't expecting us, and then, when they finally caught on, we were gone. It was textbook."

"So it works," Braden said without turning. "Excalibur works. At least there's that."

"I'm not sure I know what you mean," said Hill.

Braden snorted. "I just hope it stays in the right hands."

"Yes, sir. I believe there were some changes along those lines, too." There had been wins and losses both. Norton Aerodyne, and its CEO, had been ousted in a vicious takeover battle. The new group at Tonopah promised results and accountability. Hill had his doubts.

One thing was beyond question: Hill had seen the Soviet-run Libyan nuclear facility at Tajura blow like a giant firecracker in the night. The explosion settled, at least in the eyes of the American public, a dangerously imbalanced score. The first case of international nuclear terrorism paid back by a devastating reprisal raid. Not a peep had come from Moscow, despite the heavy casualties among the Soviet technicians.

Silence was not the same as stasis. The man who had first started the Soviet Union toward a better future was now out looking for a job, shoved aside by the former head of the KGB, Viktor Chebrikov. There were wins, and there were losses.

"Hill," Braden said, "sometimes I think it's all smoke and mirrors. We move, they move. Like this flyby." He nodded out the window. "Pure theater."

Hill's eyebrows went up. "But he . . . Major Barnes was a pilot in this squadron. It's only . . ."

"I'm aware of that fact." Braden checked his watch and moved behind his scarred desk, fussing with a pile of accumulated paperwork, hunting for something. Braden found his cigarettes, but then thought better of it. He tossed the unopened pack in the trash. "I hope to hell someone thinks it was all worth it. From where I stand it was a miserable exchange. I don't like losing pilots."

"No, sir." Harry Hill shook his head. "About MacHenry . . ."

"Yeah. Him." Braden walked to the door to his office and nodded at the small cluster of people gathered at the ramp fence. "He's out there. The tall one in the long gray coat."

Hill saw MacHenry. He looked back at Braden. "Are you coming out to watch, sir?"

Braden shook his head, and his deep-set eyes seemed to glow from an inner fire. "Negative. I would just as soon not run into MacHenry ever again. He and I have absolutely nothing to discuss. Nothing. You go," he said. "I'm running late." Braden grabbed his flight jacket, but he did not follow Hill out the front door.

The day was cloudy and a cold wind hinted at an early winter. A gray shroud blocked the sun's heat, and a perfect, circular rainbow cast upon the high cloud deck gave it the look of a bull's-eye.

Hill had parked his Corvette next to a dirty-green Jaguar, leaving the engine running for the heat. The old XK was covered with dust. Franklin Thatcher got out of Hill's car. "You find out?" he asked.

"He's here." As the two men walked toward the chain-link fence, a single boom of a jet engine sounded from the row of F-15s on the ramp, followed in short intervals by two others. Hill watched as three canopies slid down in unison. "So that's where he's going," he said. Colonel Braden was running across the tarmac toward one of the gray fighters. He leaped up the ladder and stepped over into the cockpit. The gaping air intakes cycled down, and a few moments later, his F-15 was howling, joining the other three, shimmering waves of heat rising from their tail feathers. Neither Hill nor Thatcher said a word as the fighters taxied away in staggered trail to the run-up pad. The Eagles pivoted and pointed their sharp snouts down the runway, a thunder-storm of heat and sound waiting to break.

Then, as though commanded by one hand, all four F-15s roared into afterburner, eight brilliant cones of flame blasting to the rear. They burned down the runway and ramped up into the gray sky, their thunder echoing in Hill's chest. They circled Mather once, gaining altitude, then departed the pattern.

Hill followed the specks as they darted to the east. When even his superb eyes couldn't take them out, he turned to Thatcher. "Let's get it done."

MacHenry watched the jets roar away. The sudden silence they left behind made him feel acutely empty. He gripped the cool metal of the fence and watched as they disappeared, his eyes glazed, a breeze flapping his coat open, penetrating him with its unseasonal chill.

"Mr. MacHenry?" said Hill. MacHenry turned suddenly, brought up from his thoughts. "I'm looking for Brian MacHenry."

MacHenry's eyes narrowed. "You found him."

"I . . ." Hill looked down at the ground, suddenly uncomfortable and uncertain. "I just . . ."

"Go ahead," said Thatcher. "Talk to the man."

Hill looked up as the sound of the four F-15s returned. "I just wanted to offer my . . ." Thatcher nudged him hard. "To apologize. To both of you."

Both? MacHenry's jaw tightened and his knuckles went white as he gripped the fence. "Why?" he said as evenly as he could. "Do I know you?"

"In a way. We met by accident. My name is Hill." He reached into his jacket and pulled out a card: *H. Hill, Aviation Test Consultant.* "This is my rizzo . . ."

"Frank Thatcher. Rizzo as in 'recon-systems officer.' It was the Owens Valley, Mr. MacHenry. The night intercept. We were told you were a target drone. We both thought you'd want to know."

MacHenry numbly fingered the card. The PA system popped and sizzled into life as the four-plane diamond streaked a few miles away from Mather and then turned back onto a final approach.

"We, I mean, I just wanted to say I'm sorry," Hill finished, taking his sunglasses off. His blue-gray eyes matched the sky perfectly.

MacHenry nodded his head and smiled. "I understand. But don't be. It's all going to work out right. Forget it."

"Forget it?" Hill looked at MacHenry. Didn't he care that he had tried his best to kill him? Hill glanced at Thatcher. His backseater's expression said the same thing.

"That's my advice." MacHenry put his hand on Hill's shoulder. "But I'm glad to finally meet you. I promised a friend to make sure you got two messages." A solitary trumpet blared the first doleful notes of taps as the jets came in low and fast, four dark shadows against the pearly sky.

"I'm listening," said Hill.

"It's from Major Barnes." The turbines screamed nearer, their fire nearly drowning MacHenry's words until he had to shout.

"Look," said Hill, "we're out of that program. We quit for the same reason you . . ." The four F-15s swept overhead. Hill's eyes followed them as they burned in at a hundred feet, their roar cascading down like thunder, drowning music from the PA.

As MacHenry watched, the fighter flying right wing in the diamond suddenly pulled up sharply, so abruptly that condensation trails streamed aft over its wings, as the other three maintained their solemn stations.

It was the Missing Man formation. The lone fighter climbed to the west, into the overcast, and was gone. MacHenry looked back at Hill as the last call was sounded, the solitary trumpet echoing from the metal hangars, the final note hanging in the air until it, too, disappeared. Hill had slipped his sunglasses back on. It didn't matter how long you were in the business; no aviator could remain dry-eyed at a Missing Man flight. Hill cleared his throat. "You were going to say something, Mr. MacHenry?"

"Yes. Major Barnes was quite adamant about it. First, he wanted you to know he had your ass that night over the Owens Valley. Cold."

Hill stared at MacHenry, his mouth set tight. "He was right." He spun on his heel to leave, but MacHenry grabbed him by the shoulder.

"Wait."

"What for, Mr. MacHenry?" Hill said, but MacHenry kept his face pointing west, to the place the Missing Man had blasted up into the overcast. A new sound drifted down from the gray sky.

The sound grew louder. It wasn't the bellow of the F-15's, not at all. This was a strange hollow whine, the sound of jet engines heard through a seashell, distant, empty. A dog began to howl from the squadron offices, and the air itself seemed to tremble.

Hill saw it first as it burst through the clouds. "Jesus."

"We're late on the IP," said the instructor pilot. "About five seconds behind."

"I'll make it up." The pilot banked up hard on his right wing and dropped the black nose toward the solid undercast of clouds. A chime sounded on the engine annunciator. The ramjets were ready. He ran the two outboard throttles by their detents into AUTOLITE. The liquid hydrogen lit off behind them like a bomb. Almost at once, the speed stick on his HUD surged through the Mach. He pulled back on the side stick, tightening the turn and winding up the G meter through five, through six. The moaning from the ramjets filled the tight cockpit as he bored in toward Mather Air Force Base.

The shadow cast by the diving jet swelled as they neared the cloud deck, surrounded by a bright rainbow. *Start with a circle,* he thought with a chuckle as the nose of the black jet burrowed into the clouds, and for a brief moment there was nothing outside Excalibur's cockpit. Then they burst through. Dead ahead lay the familiar runways of Mather Air Force Base. Familiar, but they were part of the past. Excalibur was the future.

"Take it easy, will you?" the instructor grunted over the hiss of his G suit. "You almost put me out."

Barnes smiled as he relented and let the stick go forward a fraction. This guy was just no fun. He'd have to check around for another checkout pilot back at Tonopah. So far they were treating him like royalty.

Barnes had overturned a rock, and now a great deal of effort was going toward keeping him safe and happy while the bugs were rounded up. An Agency spook named Bridger had personally sheepdipped him.

With luck, the Air Force would forget about him. That was good. It meant more flying from Tonopah. Who would come looking for him there? He leveled the wings and dived for the Mather perimeter road.

"Rein her in," the backseater squalled as they pushed through Mach 2. "Rein her in, Barnes! We're Mach-limited down this low!"

"What's the problem?" asked Barnes as he pointed the black nose right at the office complex of the 104th. "You want to live forever?"

Excalibur swept in silent and blisteringly fast, a black dart rocketing ahead of its own thunder. It was coming straight at them.

"Who the . . . *shit!*" Thatcher dropped to the ground as a huge concussion crashed over the ramp. The black jet flashed overhead and pulled straight up in a bone-crushing maneuver, following the Missing Man back into the overcast in a long peal of man-made thunder. Then it, too, disappeared, leaving a swirling hole in the clouds to mark its passage.

"*Damn,*" said Thatcher, getting up, dusting his pants off. Sirens were howling all over the base. "God *damn.*"

"Who was that?" asked Hill as he stood there, mouth open, watching the hole quietly knit itself back together. He turned to Thatcher. "Who . . ." He swung back to MacHenry, who was still smiling the same furtive smile. "No," said Hill. "Uh-uh. It can't be."

MacHenry shook his head gravely. "I said that Barnes wanted you to get two messages. I've only told you the first one."

"Okay, okay," said Hill as he tried to pop his ears from the overpressure. "He had me. What more do you want?"

MacHenry smiled. How would Barnes do this? He reached over and tapped his finger on Hill's chest. "The major wants you to watch your six the next time you're up there," he said, nodding up at the healed cloud. "Or he'll do it again."

EPILOGUE

COFFEE, Dr. Hines?" asked Julia's secretary.

"Please." Julia looked up from a complex series of graphs and out the window of her office. A wet snow was falling on Washington. Down on the street, the afternoon rush was already in full swing. Washington rarely got snow the week of Thanksgiving, and the government had responded by letting people go home early. She watched as the sidewalks drifted deeper. *Do they know that it's fifteen degrees colder than it's supposed to be?* she wondered. *Probably not.*

Washington was, after all, a political capital. Its true seasons were also political and had little to do with the weather. She glanced down at the request for HUMMER data sent by Dr. Aaron Templeman. He was a friend of her own superior, Henniker. His nuclear winter work was, to Julia's mind, technically interesting but ultimately misguided. Nuclear winter was, despite her experience, purely a notion, a possible outcome of an impossibly stupid act. A theoretical gun may be interesting to study, but not if a real one is pointed at your head, cocked and ready to fire. And that weapon, the change afflicting the world's climate, was all too real.

Something quite extraordinary had happened after the HUMMER blast. A month after the last fires went out, the weather across North America had turned freakish; the Northeast was blasted by successive waves of cold while the Rockies basked in warmth. Idaho enjoyed Indian summer, while Kansas froze. It was, as Henniker had quipped, a regular anomaly. But how could something so small as the HUMMER incident trigger such a massive change? It was as if a match had set fire to a city. *Or O'Leary's cow,* she thought.

Julia sipped her coffee and returned to her computer screen. On it, in graphic form, were the thousands of lines of data salvaged from her vaporized AWOS stations. The lines all stopped with perfect uniformity, like the clock at Hiroshima etched forever at *8:05.* The cursor on her CRT blinked patiently. It could consider the problem forever. But outside her window, the weather was warning her, challenging her to explain why an incident that was small when measured against the world was nevertheless sufficient to summon a Thanksgiving snowstorm.

What is going on? She scowled and looked out the window. Scudding gray clouds hurried across the sky. She watched as the street became blanketed faster than the traffic could clear it, deeper, wetter, the cars slowing, the arteries of the city clogging before her eyes. What if it never stopped?

There was a name for that, at least. *The White Earth.* One of the first computer models of the earth's climate revealed an ominous fact: cool the world sufficiently and it might not recover. Indeed, the effect of snow blanketing the ground acted to intensify the chill, causing more snow, causing more cold. It had happened before, during the Ice Ages.

Could it really be more than just an interesting computer game? It wasn't the same thing as Templeman's nuclear winter. It was far worse, for a climate bent out of shape by bursting bombs recovered. The Ice Ages went on for thousands of years.

Julia tapped a pencil on her coffee mug, deep in thought. She stood up and left the blinking screen behind. Down in the subbasement, the Cray was already loaded and ready.

"Be back?" the secretary asked as Julia passed the desk.

"I'll be down in Computing." The secretary knew what *that* meant. "No calls please, unless it's life or death." The elevator chimed and the door slid closed behind her.

She punched her code into the lock barring access to the Cray. The buzz of approval was immediate. She walked inside the cold, ultraclean space with its rows of access terminals. *Home again.* She picked her old spot, sat down in her comfortable, familiar chair, and fired up the Cray.

A map of the United States blinked instantly onto the screen, with a small flashing square over that part of California she had come to know too well. HUMMER. She enlarged the square with a joystick to cover the whole continent, then pressed the key for temperature analysis, pressure, wind speed, and cloud obscuration. She had the Cray map the extent of the bizarre weather afflicting much of the United States in the wake of the fire and the nuclear blast. Record-breaking heat here, below-zero cold there. Rain over the Southwest and parched fields in New England. Something, somewhere, was very wrong.

She sat back in her chair as the Cray assembled the new data. *Okay. It's all here. We're all set. The key is missing. Just the key.* She leaned back, her arms behind her head, and found her thoughts wandering. She looked over at a picture hanging in the otherwise stark computer room. It was a *Voyager* photograph of the biggest piece of weather in the solar system: Jupiter's Great Red Spot.

There, surrounded by the perfect, linear simplicity of the vast streaking cloud bands was a wart on the geometer's nose: a cosmic hurricane with turbulent eddies big as a planet, howling winds bending inward upon themselves in sheer, unpredictable perversity. The only thing constant about the Red Spot was that it had never dissolved. It was another regular anomaly. A kind of order, though not the kind either Julia or the Cray had yet been taught to see. *Stability in chaos?* Wasn't that a contradiction?

I wonder. On a hunch, she sat up and punched in a new command to the Cray. If her weather data refused to make orderly sense, how about *disorderly* sense? She asked the Cray to hunt for patterns in its *dissimilarities.*

That was a tall order, even for the Cray. She sat back again, watching the cursor blink in what looked like surprise. "Come on," she said. "You can do it."

The door into the next room opened and a man, once her colleague and now one of her staff, looked in. "Dr. Hines?" he said, his voice clearly as unused to her position as she was. "There's a call from your office."

"Damn!" she said, slipping her feet back into her loafers. "Just when it's getting interesting." She walked into the next room and picked up the phone. "Yes?"

"There's a call for you," said her secretary. "I told him you only wanted life-or-death messages, and when I asked him whether this was one, he said he didn't know. Do you want it?"

"No," she said, looking back at the Cray. "Get the number and I'll call back later." She hung up and sat back down at the terminal.

Something had happened in her absence. The screen was empty of numbers and charts. In their stead, a strange spiraling shape had appeared. "Did you do this?" she asked the man who had summoned her.

He shook his head. "I didn't touch it."

"Something happened," she said, pointing at the screen. The Cray had tried to make the most sense out of Julia's odd request. Nothing in the data matched up in any normal fashion, so, instead, it tried the abnormal.

The Cray had drawn a *phase-space* diagram, a graph of how events changed over time; all the different measures of pressure, wind, light, and temperature, clamoring chaotically for individual attention, now occupied a line that spiraled gradually in upon itself into a double coil; a butterfly, a Siamese chambered nautilus, joined together by a single, mysterious umbilicus. She eyed her colleague. *I bet.*

She commanded the picture to disappear and ran the data through the Cray again. The double-spiral shape returned. This time, she sat up and pulled the data apart.

"Okay," she said softly. "What are you trying to tell me?" The two coils of data represented two equally strong tendencies in the weather. The first coil was familiar. It charted the sort of temperature, rain, and cloud conditions anyone might expect of June. The other was nothing at all like that. She felt a chill of recognition as she examined the weather represented by the second spiral.

It was the White Earth.

She looked at the beautiful shape born from the incoherent points of data. Suddenly, she knew what she was seeing. "God," she whispered, *"it's a fractal."*

The spiral was the constant in a sea of change. *Like the Red Spot!* A regular anomaly. She pushed away from the terminal and focused on the air before her face. *Two seashells. Two endless, infinite seashells of fractal dimension. Start here*—she pointed at the line—*and wind up here. But sometimes . . . ,* she thought as she regarded its cold twin, *you get shunted over there.* Her pulse quickened as she had the Cray pull apart the presentation again. What did it take to push the world from light to dark? *One small bomb?*

Julia added years of industrial pollution in the press of a key. She left the real data behind, extending out year by year, adding ozone depleters, soot, smoke, and ash into the mathematical model, daring the beautiful pattern of her screen to jump from the light to the dark, from the warm to the cold.

The cursor blinked, the pattern shifted, and the temperature values began to fall. She mashed her finger on the freeze function. *What did it take to push it over the edge?* She backtracked, compared the damage she had inflicted with the real year-by-year accumulation of environmental harm. It was simple, now that she had the key.

It had taken centuries of damage to alter the world's climate by a few degrees; as more and more harm was wrought, the climate even appeared to resist, to cling to the familiar patterns. Right up to the last.

There was a zone of uncertainty, a chaos zone where small perturbations had large effects. *One bomb!* Then, very soon thereafter, a breaking point was reached. The world's climate shifted suddenly and dramatically from the familiar to the utterly hostile. How long would it take? The answer was right there, too. The journey from the zone of shadows to utter collapse was a matter of a decade, perhaps as much as two.

Was that the meaning of HUMMER? A small push could shove an already imbalanced system quite far. One nudge, one bomb. Was that the true warning? Not the threat of nuclear winter, but of environmental collapse?

One bomb. A third chill rose up her neck when she realized what this meant. For one bomb, one forest fire to have such a profound effect, the climate was already in the shadow zone, ready to fall into the White Earth.

The White Earth. It wasn't a computer model. It was for real.

Ten years, she thought again. It sounded like a long time, but it wasn't. Every five weeks you lost one percent of the time remaining until, until what? She commanded the screen to clear and sat back, her breath coming faster as she neared a revealing and terrible truth. She picked up a pencil and began to write.

Carbon dioxide, ozone depletion, particulates . . . acid precip . . . If angels had begun singing through the PA speaker in the corner, Julia would not have been the least surprised. *Changes in the world's climate may not be gradual, may not occur in direct proportion to environmental assaults. Change, when' it comes, might well be sudden and irreversible,* she continued, the words flying from the pencil faster than she could think them. She remembered the story of the Ice Age mammoths killed by the cold so quickly they were found, frozen solid, with green grass still in their mouths. Was that the future?

She signed off, her head spinning with a thousand ideas, and walked out of the Cray room in a near trance. She had heard the individual notes of the universe come together. *I'm only the eavesdropper,* she thought as she punched the elevator button.

Her secretary was long gone, but a neat pile of notes was stacked on top of her office phone. She flipped them, making mental notes as she went to call this one, write the other. "What's this?" she said, a smile breaking involuntarily onto her face as she read the last one. *Should I?*

she wondered. She hesitated for one added moment, then let her hand decide the matter. *Don't think. Act.* "You're right," she whispered. It was what Barnes had once told her. "You're right." Julia picked up the phone and dialed the number written on the note. It trilled once, twice, and then clicked.

MacHenry looked out the window of his hotel room and watched the snow drift by the streetlights. He slid open the glass and listened as the cars pushed their way through the slush. The storm was ending. He looked up at the deep-bellied clouds, lit orange by the glow of the city lights, and saw stars sprinkled around their ragged edges. He slid the window closed and drew the curtain.

Tomorrow would be the big day. The machineries of state were slow, but they were inexorable. Five months after the incident at HUMMER, the administrator was giving him half an hour to plead his case before he was expected to fall gracefully on his sword and resign from the FAA. He looked at the package of retirement papers the courier had delivered. The administrator was nothing if not clear.

MacHenry was prepared as best he could be. Some names would never be known, lost to the char and irradiated ash of the burnout zone. It could hardly have been more convenient for those wishing to keep the story lost forever. And after the successful Libyan raid, the fortunes of the black jet that still made nightly passes in his dreams were certainly assured. Look at Barnes. Even *he* was flying one now. And the missing wing? Well, everyone had said it was up there in the woods, didn't they? He shook his head. Someone, some shadowy entity, was quite literally getting away with murder.

Now what? he wondered. The sandwich he had brought up from the corner store was still wrapped. The clock said he should be hungry. He reached for it just as the telephone rang. Who knew where to find him? "MacHenry speaking."

"This is Julia. I got the message that you called . . ."

"Yes! I wanted—"

"I'd love to have dinner with you, if it's not too late."

MacHenry smiled as he took the phone to the window and opened the curtains again. "No," he said. "It's not." The snow had stopped, the clouds were gone, and the stars burned down clear and cold. "In fact, I'd say that you're just in time." The world was a very strange place. Who knew what might happen next?